Arabella
of Mars

Arabella of Mars

THE ADVENTURES OF ARABELLA ASHBY

BOOK ONE

DAVID D. LEVINE

TOR

A TOM DOHERTY ASSOCIATES BOOK

NEW YORK

ARABELLA OF MARS

Copyright © 2016 by David D. Levine

All rights reserved.

A Tor Book
Published by Tom Doherty Associates, LLC
175 Fifth Avenue
New York, NY 10010

www.tor-forge.com

Tor® is a registered trademark of Tom Doherty Associates, LLC.

The Library of Congress Cataloging-in-Publication Data is available upon request.

ISBN 978-0-7653-8281-8 (hardcover)
ISBN 978-1-4668-8949-1 (e-book)

Our books may be purchased in bulk for promotional, educational, or business use. Please contact your local bookseller or the Macmillan Corporate and Premium Sales Department at 1-800-221-7945, extension 5442, or by e-mail at MacmillanSpecialMarkets@macmillan.com.

First Edition: July 2016

Printed in the United States of America

0 9 8 7 6 5 4 3 2 1

To Kate — my wife, my love, my snookie, my Flying Partner.
Forever and always.

Arabella
of Mars

Prologue

MARS, 1812

THE LAST STRAW

Arabella Ashby lay prone atop a dune, her whole length pressed tight upon the cool red sands of Mars. The silence of the night lay unbroken save for the distant cry of a hunting *khulekh*, and a wind off the desert brought a familiar potpourri to her nose: *khoresh*-sap, and the cinnamon smell of Martians, and the sharp, distinctive fragrance of the sand itself. She glanced up at Phobos—still some fingers' span short of Arcturus—then back down to the darkness of the valley floor where Michael would, she knew, soon appear.

Beneath the fur-trimmed leather of her *thukhong*, her heart beat a fast tattoo, racing not only from the exertion of her rush to the top of this dune but from the exhilaration of delicious anticipation. For this, she was certain, was the night she would finally defeat her brother in the game of *shorosh khe kushura*, or Hound and Hare.

The game was simple enough. To-night Michael played the part of the *kushura*, a nimble runner of the plains, while Arabella took the role of the *shorosh*, a fierce and cunning predator. His assignment this night was to race from the stone outcrop they called Old Broken Nose to the drying-sheds on the south side of the manor house, a distance of some two miles; hers was to stop him. But though Khema had said the youngest Martian children would play this game as soon as their shells hardened, it was also a sophisticated strategic exercise . . . one that Michael, three years her elder, had nearly always won in the weeks they'd been playing it.

But to-night the victory would be Arabella's. For she had been observing Michael assiduously for the last few nights, and she had noted that despite Khema's constant injunctions against predictability, he nearly always traversed this valley when he wished to evade detection. Its sides were steep, its shadows deep at every time of night, and the soft sands of the valley floor hushed every footfall—but that would avail him little if his pursuer reached the valley before he did and prepared an ambush. Which was exactly what she had done.

Again she cast her eyes upward. At Michael's usual pace he would arrive just as Phobos in his passage through the sky reached the bright star Arcturus—about half past two in the morning. But as she looked up, her eye was drawn by another point of light, brighter than Arcturus and moving still faster than Phobos: an airship, cruising so high above the planet that her sails caught the sun's light long before dawn. From the size and brightness of the moving light she must be a Marsman—one of the great Mars Company ships, the "aristocrats of the air," that plied the interplanetary atmosphere between Mars and Earth. Perhaps some of her masts or spars or planks had even originated here, on this very plantation, as one of the great *khoresh*-trees that towered in patient, soldierly rows north and east of the manor house.

Some day, Arabella thought, perhaps she might take passage on such a ship. To sail the air, and see the asteroids, and visit the swamps of Venus would be a grand adventure indeed. But to be sure, no matter how far she traveled she would always return to her beloved Woodthrush Woods.

Suddenly a *shuff* of boots on sand snatched her awareness from the interplanetary atmosphere back to the valley floor. Michael!

She had been careless. While her attention had been occupied by the ship, Michael had drawn nearly abreast of her position. Now she had mere moments in which to act.

Scrambling to her feet in the dune's soft sand, she hurled herself down into the shadowed canyon, a tolerable twelve-foot drop that would give her the momentum she needed to overcome her brother's advantages in size and weight.

But in her haste she misjudged her leap, landing instead in a thorny *gorosh*-shrub halfway up the canyon's far wall and earning a painful scratch on her head. She cursed enthusiastically in English and Martian as she struggled to free herself from the shrub's thorns and sticky, acrid-smelling sap.

"Heavens, dear sister!" Michael laughed, breathing hard from his run. "Such language!" He doubled back in order to aid her in extricating herself.

But Arabella had not given up on the game. She held out her hand as though for assistance . . . and as soon as he grasped it, she pulled him down into the shrub with her. The thorny branch that had trapped her snapped as he fell upon it, and the two of them rolled together down the canyon wall, tussling and laughing in the sand like a pair of *tureth* pups.

Then they rolled into a patch of moonlight, and though Michael had the upper hand he suddenly ceased his attempts to pin her to the ground. "What is the matter, dear brother?" Arabella gasped, even as she prepared to hurl him over her head with her legs. But in this place there was light enough to see his face clearly, and his expression was so grave she checked herself.

"You are injured," he said, disentangling himself from her.

"'Tis only a scratch," she replied. But the pain when she touched her injured scalp was sharp, and her hand when she brought it away and examined it beneath Phobos's dim light was black with blood.

Michael brought his handkerchief from his *thukhong* pocket and pressed it against the wound, causing Arabella to draw in a hissing breath through her teeth. "Lie still," he said, his voice quite serious.

"Is it very bad, then?"

He made no reply, but as she lay on the cool sand, her breath fogging the air and the perspiration chilling on her face, she felt something seeping through her hair and dripping steadily from the lower edge of her ear, and the iron smell of blood was strong in the air. Michael's jaw tightened, and he pressed harder with the handkerchief; Arabella's breath came shallow, and she determined not to cry out from the pain.

And then Khema appeared, slipping silently from the shadows, the subtle facets of her eyes reflecting in the starlight. She had, of course, been watching them all along, unobserved; her capabilities of tracking and concealment were far beyond any thing Arabella or Michael could even begin to approach. "You leapt too late, *tutukha*," she said. A *tutukha* was a small inoffensive herbivore, and Khema often called her this as a pet name.

"I will do better next time, *itkhalya*," Arabella replied through gritted teeth.

"I am certain you will."

Michael looked up at Khema, his eyes shining. "It's not stopping."

Without a word Khema knelt and inspected the wound, her eye-stalks bending close and the hard cool carapace of her pointed fingertips delicately teasing the matted hair aside. Arabella bit her lip hard; she would *not* cry.

"This is beyond my skills," Khema said at last, sitting back on her haunches. "You require a human physician."

At that Arabella did cry out. "No!" she exclaimed, clutching at her *itkhalya*'s sleeve. "We cannot! Mother will be furious!"

"We will endeavor to keep this from her."

The pain of Dr. Fellowes's needle as it stitched the wound shut was no worse than the humiliation Arabella felt as she lay on a cot in her father's office. From the shelf above Father's desk, his collection of small automata looked down in judgement: the scribe, the glockenspiel player, and especially the dancer, still given pride of place though it no longer functioned, all seemed to regard her with disappointment in their painted eyes.

Her father too, she knew, must be horribly disappointed in her, though his face with its high forehead and shock of gray hair showed more concern than dissatisfaction. Though no tears had fallen, his eyes glimmered in the flickering lamplight, and when she considered how she had let him down Arabella felt a hot sting of shame in her own eyes.

Even the crude little drummer she herself had built, a simple clockwork with just one motion, seemed let down by its creator. She had been so proud when she had presented it to Father on his birthday last year and he had placed it on the shelf with his most treasured possessions; now, she felt sure, he would surely retire it to some dark corner.

Again and again the needle stabbed Arabella's scalp; the repeated tug and soft hiss of the thread passing through her skin seemed to go on and on. "A little more light, please," the doctor said, and Khema adjusted the wick on the lamp. "Not much longer." The doctor's clothing smelled of dust and leather, and the sweat of the *huresh* on which Michael had fetched him from his home. Michael himself looked on from behind him, his sandy hair and heart-shaped face so very like her own, his blue eyes filled with worry.

"There now," said the doctor, clipping off the thread. "All finished." Khema brought him a washbasin, and as he cleaned the blood from his hands he said, "Scalp wounds do bleed quite frightfully, but the actual danger is slight; if you keep the wound clean it should heal up nicely. And even if there should be a scar, it will be hidden by your hair."

"Thank you, Doctor," Arabella said, sitting up and examining his work in the window-glass—the sun would rise soon, but the sky was still dark enough to give a good reflection. Her appearance, she was forced to acknowledge, was quite shocking, with dried blood everywhere, but she thought that once she had cleaned herself she might be able to arrange her hair so as to hide the stitches from her mother.

But that opportunity was denied her, for just at that moment the office door burst open and Mother charged in, still in her nightdress. "Arabella!" she cried. "What has happened to you?"

"She is quite well, Mother," Michael said. "She only fell and hit her head."

"She is not 'well.'" Mother sat on the edge of the cot and held Arabella's head in her hands. "She is covered in blood, and what on *earth* is this horrific garment you are wearing? It exposes your limbs quite shamefully."

Arabella had been dreading this discovery. "It is called a *thukhong*, Mother, and it keeps me far warmer than any English-made dress."

"An ugly Martian word for an ugly Martian garment, one entirely unsuitable for a proper English lady." She glowered at Arabella's father. "I thought we agreed when she turned twelve that there would be no more of . . . *this*." She waved a disgusted hand, taking in the *thukhong*, the blood, the desert outside, and the planet Mars in general. Dr. Fellowes seemed to be trying to disappear into the wainscoting.

Father dropped his eyes from Mother's withering gaze. "She is still only sixteen, dear, and she is a very . . . *active* girl. Surely she may be allowed a few more years of freedom before being compelled to settle down? She has kept up with her studies. . . ."

But even as he spoke, Mother's lips went quite white from being pressed together, and finally she burst out, "I will have no more of your rationalizations!" She stood and paced briskly back and forth in front of Father's broad *khoresh*-wood desk, her fury building still further as she warmed to her subject. "For years now I have struggled to bring Arabella up properly, despite the primitive conditions on this horrible planet, and now I find that she is risking her life traipsing around the trackless desert by night, wearing *leather trousers* no less!" She rounded on Arabella. "How long have you been engaging in this disgraceful behavior?"

Arabella glanced to Michael, her father, and Khema for support, but in the face of her mother's wrath they were as defenseless as she. "Only a few weeks," she muttered, eyes downcast, referring only to the game of *shorosh khe kushura*. She and Michael had actually been exploring the desert under Khema's tutelage—learning of Mars's flora, fauna, and cultures and engaging in games of strategy and combat—since they were both quite small.

"Only a few weeks," Mother repeated, jaw clenched and nostrils flaring. "Then perhaps it is not too late." She stared hard at Arabella a moment longer, then gave a firm nod and turned to Father. "I am taking the children back home. And this time I will brook no argument."

Arabella felt as though the floor had dropped from under her. "No!" she cried.

Without facing Arabella, Mother raised a finger to silence her. "You see what she has become!" she continued to Father. "Willful, disobedient, disrespectful. And Fanny and Chloë are already beginning to follow in her filthy footsteps." Now her tone changed, and despite Arabella's anguish at the prospect of being torn from her home she could not deny the genuine sadness and fear in her mother's eyes. "Please, dear. *Please*. You *must* agree. You must consider our posterity! If Arabella is allowed to continue on this path, and her sisters, too . . . what decent man would have them? They will be left as spinsters, doomed to a lonely old age on a barbarous planet."

Arabella bit her lip and hugged herself tightly, feeling lost and helpless as she watched her father's face. Taking Arabella, Michael, and the two little girls to England—a place to which Mother always referred as "back home," though all of the children had been born on Mars and had never known any other home—was something she had often spoken of, though never so definitively or immediately. But with this incident something had changed, something deep and fundamental, and plainly Father was seriously considering the question.

He pursed his lips and furrowed his brow. He stroked his chin and looked to Mother, to Michael, to Arabella—his eyes beneath the gray brows looking very stern—and then out the window, at the sun just beginning to peep above the rows of *khoresh*-trees.

Finally he sighed deeply and turned back to Mother. "You may have the girls," he said in a resigned tone. "But Michael will remain here, to help me with the business of the plantation."

"But Father . . . ," Arabella began, until a minute shake of his head stopped her words. The look in his eyes showed clearly that he did not desire this outcome, but it was plain to all that this time Mother would not be appeased.

Arabella looked to Michael for support, but though his eyes brimmed with tears his shoulders slumped and his hands, still stained with Arabella's blood, hung ineffectually at his sides. "I am sorry," he whispered.

Khema, too, stood silently in the corner, hands folded and eyestalks downcast. Bold, swift, and powerful she might be in the desert, but within the manor house she was only a servant and must submit to Mother's wishes.

"Very well," said Mother, after a long considering pause. "Michael may remain. But the Ashby women . . . are going home." And she smiled.

That smile, to Arabella, was like a judge's gavel pronouncing sentence of death.

1

ENGLAND, 1813

1

AN UNEXPECTED LETTER

Arabella eased her bedroom door open and crept into the dark hallway. All about her the house lay silent, servants and masters alike tucked safe in their beds. Only the gentle tick of the tall clock in the parlor disturbed the night.

Shielding the candle with one hand, Arabella slipped down the hallway, her bare feet making no sound on the cool boards. She kept close to the walls, where the floor was best supported and the boards did not creak, but now and again she took a long, slow step to avoid a spot she had learned was likely to squeak.

Down the stairs and across the width of the house she crept, until she reached the drawing-room. In the corner farthest from the fireplace stood the harpsichord, and the silent figure that sat at its keyboard.

Brenchley's Automaton Harpsichord Player.

Nearly life-sized and dressed in the height of fashion from eight years ago, when it had originally been manufactured, the automaton sat with jointed ivory fingers poised over the instrument's keys. Its face was finely crafted of smooth, polished birch for a lifelike appearance, the eyes with their painted lashes demurely downcast. A little dust had accumulated in its décolletage, but in the shifting light of Arabella's little candle it almost seemed to be breathing.

Arabella had always been the only person in the family who shared her father's passion for automata. The many hours they had spent together in the drawing-room of the manor house at Woodthrush Woods, winding and oiling and polishing his collection, were among her most treasured memories. He had even shared with her his knowledge of the machines' workings, though Mother had heartily disapproved of such an unladylike pursuit.

The harpsichord player had arrived at Marlowe Hall, their residence in England, not long after they had emigrated—or, as Arabella considered it, been exiled—from Mars. It had been accompanied by a note from Father, reminding them that it was one of his most beloved possessions and saying that he hoped it would provide pleasant entertainment. But Arabella, knowing that Father understood as well as she did how little interest the rest of the family had in automata, had taken it as a sort of peace offering, or apology, from him specifically to her—a moving, nearly living representative and reminder that, although unimaginably distant, he still loved her.

But, alas, all his great expense and careful packing had gone for naught, for when it had been uncrated it refused to play a note. Mother, never well-disposed toward her husband's expensive pastime, had been none too secretly relieved.

That had been nearly eight months ago. Eight months of frilly dresses and stultifying conversation, and unceasing oppressive damp, and more than any thing else the constant inescapable *heaviness*. Upon first arriving on Earth, to her shame Arabella had found herself so unaccustomed to the planet's gravity that she had no alternative but to be carried from the ship in a sedan-chair. She had barely been able to stand for weeks, and even now she felt heavy, awkward, and clumsy, distrustful of her body and of her instincts.

Plates and pitchers seemed always to crash to the floor in her vicinity, and even the simple act of throwing and catching a ball was beyond her.

Not that she was allowed to perform any sort of bodily activity whatsoever, other than walking and occasionally dancing. Every one on Earth, it seemed, shared Mother's attitudes concerning the proper behavior of an English lady, and the slightest display of audacity, curiosity, adventure, or initiative was met with severe disapproval. So she had been reduced, even as she had on Mars, to skulking about by night—but here she lacked the companionship of Michael and Khema.

On Mars, Michael, her only brother, had been her constant companion, studying with her by day and racing her across the dunes by night. And Khema, their Martian nanny or *itkhalya*, had been to the two of them nurse, protector, and tutor in all things Martian. How she missed them both.

Setting her candle down, Arabella seated herself on the floor behind the automaton and lifted its skirts, in a fashion that would have been most improper if it were human. Beneath the suffocating layers of muslin and linen the automaton's ingenious mechanisms gleamed in the candlelight, brass and ivory and mahogany each adding their own colors to a silent symphony of light and shadow. Here was the mainspring, there the escapement, there the drum. The drum was the key to the whole mechanism; its pins and flanges told the device where to place its fingers, when to nod, when to appear to breathe. From the drum, dozens of brass fingers transmitted instructions to the rest of the device through a series of levers, rods, springs, and wires.

Arabella breathed in the familiar scents of metal, whale-oil, and beeswax before proceeding. She had begun attempting to repair the device about two months ago, carefully concealing her work from her mother, the servants, and even her sisters. She had investigated its mysteries, puzzled out its workings, and finally found the displaced cog that had stilled the mechanism. But having solved that puzzle, Arabella had continued working with the machine, and in the last few weeks she had even begun making a few cautious modifications. The pins in the drum could be unscrewed, she had learned, and placed in new locations to change the automaton's behavior.

At the moment her project was to teach it to play "God Save the King," as the poor mad fellow could certainly use the Lord's help. She had the first few measures working nearly to her satisfaction and was just about to start on "Send him victorious." Laying the folded hearth-rug atop the harpsichord's strings to muffle the sound, she wound the automaton's mainspring and began to work, using a nail-file, cuticle-knife, and tweezers to reposition the delicate pins.

She was not concerned that her modifications might be discovered between her working sessions. It was only out of deference to Mr. Ashby, the absent paterfamilias, that her mother even allowed it to remain in the drawing-room. The servants found the device disquieting and refused to do more than dust it occasionally. And as for Fanny and Chloë, Arabella's sisters were both too young to be allowed to touch the delicate mechanism.

For many pleasant hours Arabella worked, repeatedly making small changes, rolling the drum back with her hand, then letting it play. She would not be satisfied with a mere music-box rendition of the tune; she wanted a *performance*, with all the life and spirit of a human player. And so she adjusted the movements of the automaton's body, the tilt of its head, and the subtle motions of its pretended breath as well as the precise timing and rhythm of its notes.

She would pay for her indulgence on the morrow, when her French tutor would stamp his cane each time she yawned—though even when well-slept, she gave him less heed than he felt he deserved. Why bother studying French? England had been at war with Bonaparte since Arabella was a little girl, and showed no sign of ever ceasing to be so.

But for now none of that was of any consequence.

When she worked on the automaton, she felt close to her father.

The sky was already lightening in the east, and a few birds were beginning to greet the sun with their chirruping song, as Arabella heaved the hearth-rug out of the harpsichord and spread it back in its accustomed place. Perhaps some day she would have an opportunity to hear the automaton perform without its heavy, muting encumbrance.

She looked around, inspecting the drawing-room with a critical eye. Had she left any thing out of place? No, she had not. With a satisfied nod she turned and began to make her way back to her bedroom.

But before she even reached the stairs, her ear was caught by a drumming sound from without.

Hoofbeats. The sound of a single horse, running hard. Approaching rapidly.

Who could possibly be out riding at this hour?

Quickly extinguishing the candle, Arabella scurried up the stairs in the dawn light and hid herself in the shadows at the top of the steps. Shortly thereafter, a fist hammered on the front door. Arabella peered down through the banister at the front door, consumed with curiosity.

Only a few moments passed before Cole, the butler, came to open the door. He, too, must have heard the rider's hoofbeats.

The man at the door was a post-rider, red-eyed and filthy with dust. From his leather satchel he drew out a thin letter, a single sheet, much travel-worn and bearing numerous post-marks.

It was heavily bordered in black. Arabella suppressed a gasp.

A black-bordered letter meant death, and was sadly familiar. Even in the comparatively short space of time since her arrival on

Earth, no fewer than five such letters had arrived in this small community, each bearing news of the loss of a brother or father or uncle to Bonaparte's monstrous greed. But Arabella had no relatives in the army or navy, and had no expectation of her family receiving such a letter.

"Three pounds five shillings sixpence," the post-rider said, dipping his head in acknowledgement of the outrageousness of the postage. "It's an express, all the way from Mars."

At that Arabella was forced to bite her knuckle to prevent herself from crying aloud.

Shaking his head, Cole placed the letter on a silver tray and directed the rider to the servants' quarters, where he would receive his payment and some refreshment before being sent on his way. As Cole began to climb the stairs Arabella scurried back to her room, her heart pounding.

Arabella paced in her bedroom, sick with worry. Her hands worked at her handkerchief as she went, twisting and straining the delicate fabric until it threatened to tear asunder.

A black-bordered letter. An express. No one would send such dire news by such an expensive means unless it concerned a member of the family. She forced herself to hope that it might be an error, or news of some distant relative of whose existence she had not even been aware . . . but as the silence went on and on, that hope diminished swiftly.

Who was it who had passed? Father, or Michael? Which would be worse? She loved them both so dearly. Michael and she were practically twins, and he had many more years ahead of him, so his loss would surely be the greater tragedy. But Father . . . the man who had shared with her his love of automata, who had sat her on his knee and taught her the names of the stars, who had quietly encouraged her to dare, to try, to risk, despite Mother's objections . . . to lose him would be terrible, terrible indeed.

Every fiber of her being insisted that she run to her mother's room, burst through the door, and demand an answer. But that would be unladylike, and, as Mother had repeatedly admonished, unladylike behavior was entirely unacceptable under even the most pressing circumstances. And so she paced, and pulled her handkerchief to shreds, and tried not to cry.

And then, startling though not a surprise, a knock came on the door. It was Nellie, her mother's handmaid. "Mrs. Ashby requests your presence, Miss Ashby."

"Thank you, Nellie."

Trembling, Arabella followed Nellie to her mother's dressing-room, where Fanny and Chloë, already present, were gathered in a miserable huddle with their mother. The black-bordered letter lay open on her mother's writing-desk, surrounded by the scattered fragments of the seal, which was of black wax.

Arabella stood rooted, just inside the door, her eyes darting from the letter to her mother and sisters. It was as though it were a *lukhosh*, or some other dreadful poisonous creature, that had already struck them down and was now lying in wait for her. She wondered whether she was expected to pick it up and read it.

She ached to know what the letter contained. She wanted nothing more than to flee the room.

Nellie cleared her throat. "Ma'am?" Mother raised her head, her eyes flowing with tears. Noticing Arabella, she gently patted the settee by her side. The girls shifted to make room for her.

Arabella sat. Each of her sisters clutched one of her hands, offering comfort despite their own misery.

"The news is . . . it is . . . it is Mr. Ashby," Mother said. She held her head up straight, though her chin trembled. "Your father has passed on."

"Father . . . ?" Arabella whispered.

And even though the distance between planets was so unimaginably vast . . . even though the news must be months old . . . even though it had been more than eight months since she had seen him with her own eyes . . . somehow, some intangible connection had still remained between her and her father, and at that moment she felt that connection part, tearing like rotted silk.

And she too collapsed in sobs.

2

AN UNCOMFORTABLE DINNER

Five weeks later, Arabella arrived at Chester Cottage, the home of her cousin Simon Ashby in Oxfordshire. She stepped from her carriage, handed down by William the footman, and was greeted by Simon and his wife Beatrice.

Simon, a barrister, was a nervous man, thin and pale, with watery eyes and light brown hair worn a bit longer than the current fashion, but as he was her only living relative on her father's side of the family she felt quite tenderly toward him. "We were so very sorry to hear of your loss," he said.

"He was a very good man," Arabella replied, "and I miss him dearly." She blinked away tears.

The last five weeks had been very hard. Even though Father's passing, so distant in time as well as space, had not affected the family in any immediate or practical sense, the loss had affected Arabella greatly. Inconsolable, she had taken to her bed for days at a time, refusing food, water, and solace.

Beatrice, a plump girl with tiny hands, offered Arabella a handkerchief. "When your mother wrote to us of the depth of your grief," she said, "offering our humble home for a brief respite was the least we could do."

"I thank you for your kindness, and I extend my mother's thanks as well." Arabella took a deep breath and looked about herself. Chester Cottage was, indeed, quite humble, and rather far removed from town, but it was at least a fresh locale lacking any memories for Arabella.

Every thing at Marlowe Hall reminded her of her loss. Whenever she managed to forget for a moment that her father had passed away, she would immediately catch a glimpse of Fanny all in black, or the shrouded mirrors, or the black mourning wreath that hung over the front door, and grief would come flooding back.

Even the automaton harpsichord player, the one thing that had kept her sane in the last few months, now served only to remind her of her father. The very sight of it brought tears to her eyes.

Arabella shook her head, dispelling the memory. "I suppose I should also extend my condolences to you," she said. "He was, after all, your uncle."

"You are too kind," Simon said, and bowed his head. But his expression, Arabella thought, was rather sour, and she wondered at this.

They led Arabella into the cottage and introduced her to infant Sophie, their firstborn, who was not yet two months old. Then they showed Arabella the room which would be hers during her stay. It was small and rather shabbily furnished, in keeping with the rest of the house, and as her things were brought in from the carriage Arabella could not help but notice that the Ashbys of Chester Cottage had only a single servant, an elderly maid-of-all-work called Jane.

But, despite the meanness of her cousins' circumstances, they had offered her hospitality, and there was nothing here to remind her of her father. Arabella determined to be grateful for the opportunity to rest her battered spirit.

"If you don't mind, Miss Ashby," William said to Arabella once she was settled, "I'd best be returning home straight away." It had been a lengthy journey, and even with the long summer days he would need to set off immediately in order to return to Marlowe Hall in time for Sunday supper.

"By all means, William. I wish you a safe journey home, and look forward to seeing you again in two weeks."

At dinner that afternoon, after Jane had taken away the bowls from the rather thin and unsatisfactory soup, Beatrice said, "I believe we shall go berry-picking upon the morrow. Would you care to join us? It will be little Sophie's first such occasion."

At the mention of his infant daughter, to Arabella's surprise, Simon's face clouded. Surely this reminder of the recent addition to his family should raise his spirits, not lower them?

"Is berry-picking a suitable activity for small children?" Arabella asked, not certain how to interpret her host's sudden change of emotion.

Beatrice smiled. "She will not be taking an active part, to be sure; she will simply be carried along, to enjoy the fresh air and sunshine."

Arabella ran a finger under the scratchy cuff of her stiff mourning costume. Even her favorite dresses had been taken away by her father's death, for Venusian silk did not accept dye. They had all been replaced by heavy, rustling outfits of black bombazine, more suitable for mourning but exceedingly uncomfortable. "Forgive me my ignorance. It is not a thing I have done before."

Beatrice tilted her head inquiringly. "Do they not have berries on Mars?"

"Not as such. We have *khula*, which I suppose you would consider a fungus, and *gethown*, which is a tuber . . . they are quite sweet and succulent, but they must be dug up, not picked from a vine." For a moment Arabella lost herself in memory, recalling happy days with her beloved Michael, digging *khula* together with pail and shovel.

She wondered, as she often did, what Michael might be doing at this very moment. Most likely he was engaged in some serious activity, directing the harvest or balancing the accounts, as befitted the head of the family. He would attain his majority in just a few months; until then his godfather Mr. Trombley, the family solicitor and a dependable man of sober stolidity, would act as his legal guardian.

No one doubted that Michael was entirely capable of managing the Ashby household and plantations as well as his father had done, but still she worried about him. He must be overwhelmed by his new responsibilities, as well as torn with grief from his father's loss. How she wished she could be with him now, to comfort and aid him in this difficult time!

"Mr. Ashby and I met while picking berries," Beatrice said, interrupting Arabella's thoughts. "Perhaps you will be as fortunate." She smiled and inclined her head coquettishly. "There are many eligible bachelors in Oxfordshire. . . ."

"Heavens no!" Arabella gasped, then immediately regretted her outburst. "That is . . . I mean to say . . . I am sure you are very happy together, but I . . . I have no interest in male companionship at this time."

"Truly?" Beatrice replied with unfeigned astonishment. Simon, Arabella noted, was silent and still appeared distracted. "I have never heard before of a healthy girl of seventeen years being uninterested in the other sex. Are you already engaged, then?"

Arabella frowned and shook her head.

"But what of your sisters? They will require you to introduce them into society."

"I am keenly aware of this." Arabella sighed. "Ever since my father's passing, my mother has made it abundantly clear that I am to be married as soon as possible, for my sisters' sake if not my own. But every suitor she has presented to me has been . . . entirely unsuitable." The best young men England had to offer were, it seemed, barely comparable to her most ordinary acquaintances on Mars, and could not begin to hold a candle to her brother. Vapid empty-headed dandies the lot of them, knowing nothing of any thing beyond horses and hunting, lacking in any spirit of adventure, and completely uninterested in automata, astronomy, or any other thing of importance. "I suppose that I must be married eventually, but I cannot imagine to whom."

"La!" Beatrice fanned herself. "You Martian girls are so headstrong!"

Arabella smiled wryly at the observation. "If you were to ask my mother, my upbringing on Mars has completely ruined me for polite society." She grimaced as she recalled the many whispered conversations she'd overheard between her parents late at night, her mother calling her a "wild child" and demanding to take her, Fanny, and Chloë back to Earth to prevent her sisters turning out as she had. Mother had prevailed in that argument, in the end, and Arabella supposed that she would eventually have her way in this one as well. "Truly, I am not suited for England. How I wish I could return to the land of my birth!"

At this Simon finally joined in the conversation. "I cannot imagine pining for Mars," he said. "It seems a horrid place, cold and dry and crawling with those dreadful natives."

"I would much rather be there than England," Arabella countered. "It is so warm and damp all the time here, and every thing is so impossibly *heavy*! And I find the soil unbearably filthy, unlike the clean dry sand found on so much of Mars. The first time I saw an earthworm I was horrified."

Simon seemed about to reply with some heat, but Beatrice stayed him with a meaningful glance. "Have you ever met a Martian native?" she asked Arabella brightly.

"Oh, yes. I was practically raised by Martians! My nanny, or *itkhalya* as we call them, was a Martian named Khema."

Simon frowned even more deeply. "A great crab as a nanny? Surely it would rouse up nightmares in the child."

"It is an insult to compare a Martian to a crab," Arabella snapped. But when she saw the shocked expression on Beatrice's face at her outburst, she realized that once again she had committed a faux pas. English manners were so very easily bruised! "However," she continued in an attempt at conciliation, "now that I have seen a crab, I must agree that there is some slight resemblance around the eyes and mouth-parts, and like the crab Martians are covered in a hard carapace. But Martians do not scuttle about in such a lowly fashion as the Earth crab; they stand tall, as we do, and like us they have but two arms and two legs. And they are as possessed of intellect, morals, and judgement as we." She stared out the window at the clear blue sky, remembering. "What adventures we had together!"

As well as her duties of care, protection, and companionship, which she had always performed without fault, Khema had educated Arabella and Michael in Martian culture, history, geography, and all the practical arts. Many days and not a few nights had been spent in the trackless desert, learning how to find one's way, identifying edible plants and animals, and springing ambushes upon each other.

Arabella loved Khema dearly, but she often wondered if she might still be on Mars if her *itkhalya* had demanded less of her. After Arabella had fallen into the *gorosh*-shrub, she and her sisters had departed for Earth within the month, leaving Michael behind as his father's assistant.

"So you speak their language?" Beatrice said, interrupting Arabella's reminiscences.

Arabella blinked away memories and returned her attention to her cousin. "You say that as though there were only one Martian language. They have their nations, clans, and tribes just as we do, each with its own language or dialect. I did learn to speak a few words of my *itkhalya*'s tribal language, though it is frightfully difficult for us to make the *kh* sound properly. But most Martians who work with Englishmen speak quite passable English."

"How wonderful it must be," said Simon in a bitter tone, "to have so many Martian servants at your beck and call."

"I consider Khema more of a friend and companion than a servant," Arabella replied. "It is true that she was in my family's employ, but the bond between us was quite sincere and affectionate."

"Money," Simon shot back with a resentful tone, "can create the appearance of affection."

At that statement, Arabella noticed that Beatrice's face fell momentarily into rueful contemplation. But then she brightened—albeit somewhat artificially—and said, "I am sure your nanny's tender feelings were entirely genuine. But what of the male of the species? I have heard that Martian warriors are fierce and savage."

"Though war is a frequent occurrence between the Martian nations," Arabella replied, "there has been peace between Martians and English for many years. In any case," she continued with a small smile, "among the Martians, it is the females who are the warriors." Simon and Beatrice both expressed shock and disbelief at this. "I swear to you that what I say is true," Arabella reassured them. "The Martian female is larger and more powerful than the male, and—though the English often refuse to believe this—Martians consider the female to be more suitable by temperament to the warrior's life. Indeed, my own *itkhalya* is well known among her people as a strategist." To herself, Arabella reflected that this was one of the ways in which Martian culture was superior to that of the English. Sometimes she even thought that, if she had no alternative but to be born female, she would rather have been a Martian.

At that moment Sophie, in the next room, began to wail and fuss, and Beatrice excused herself to tend to her. Arabella, seeing an opportunity to converse with her in private, excused herself as well.

Once Sophie's immediate needs had been tended to and Beatrice had begun to rock and comfort the child, Arabella seated herself on the sofa next to her. "Forgive me if I am being impertinent," she said, "but I cannot help but notice that Mr. Ashby seems . . . rather vexed. I hope that my presence here is not a burden to you."

Beatrice gazed contemplatively out the window for a time before replying. "I am afraid that your father's recent passing has revived old grudges about the estate."

"How so?"

"I gather he resents that his father did not receive a share of the inheritance when your grandfather died."

Arabella placed a hand upon her bosom. "Let me assure you that it was not my father's choice, nor my grandfather's, to do so. They both loved my late uncle, Mr. Ashby's father, dearly, but the estate is entailed. . . . It *must* pass entirely and without division to the eldest son."

"And thus it passes now to your brother Michael, and again we are left with nothing." Mrs. Ashby's voice was more resigned than aggrieved.

"If there were any thing I could do . . ."

"It is the way of the world, I suppose." Beatrice sighed. "I am sure that he will be much more himself in the morning. We will pick strawberries together, and all will be well."

By now Sophie had drifted off, burbling contentedly in her sleep, and Beatrice laid her down in her crib. She and Arabella returned to the dining table, where Simon sat staring off into space and drumming his fingers on the table's edge.

The two women seated themselves, with apologies for the interruption, and without a word Simon began to carve the roast. Arabella received her portion with thanks, but after she had eaten the first few bites she was forced to deposit a large lump of gristle on the side of her plate.

Though she had done it as discreetly as possible, the act did not escape Simon's notice. "I must beg your pardon for the quality of the roast," he said, quite testily. "I know that your side of the family is accustomed to finer fare, but this is the best possible under the circumstances."

Beatrice gave him a withering look, then with a rather forced smile turned to Arabella. "Tell us about your voyage from Mars," she said. "How did you survive the absence of gravity and atmosphere?"

Arabella sighed and closed her eyes for a moment. The scientific ignorance of English women, and most of the men as well, was appalling, but as her mother had repeatedly cautioned her, expressing her true opinion of her cousin's lack of knowledge would be a gross breach of etiquette. "It is merely a common misperception," she explained, "that there is no gravity between planets. The sun's gravity is quite substantial, even as far out as Mars. But the ship is in orbit, you see, which means that she is circling the sun at exactly the same rate she falls toward it, so that those aboard the ship do not *feel* any gravitational attraction. We call this a state of free descent." Beatrice's vacant smile told Arabella that her words were falling on stony ground, and she resolved to simplify her account still further. "And as to the atmosphere, although the interplanetary atmosphere is . . . of different composition from that of Earth or Mars, I assure you it is entirely breathable and quite healthful."

"That is . . . fascinating," Beatrice said, blinking rapidly. "But do go on. Did you see wind-whales, or asteroids? Were you attacked by pirates?"

"We were fortunate enough to avoid pirates, as well as the French navy. As to the rest, I am afraid there is little to tell." She took another careful bite of her roast. "I spent most of the journey in my cabin."

She did not confess the reason for this, which was that her mother had kept her forcibly confined there for almost the entire voyage—at first to prevent Arabella from attempting to escape

the ship and return to Mars, and later, or so she had said, to protect her from the unwelcome attentions of the airmen.

"Surely you cannot have spent the *entire* time in your cabin?
Does the trip not take a year or more?"

"That depends upon the positions of the planets." Arabella paused,
then pointed to her place setting. "Suppose my dinner-plate is the
sun, and my bread-plate the Earth. My wine-glass, then, would
be Mars; both orbit around the sun, but Mars is further away
than Earth, do you see?" She picked up her glass in her right hand
and held it above her lap so that the glass and the two plates
were all in a line, with the large plate between the small plate and
the glass. "Now, when Earth and Mars are on opposite sides of the
sun, as you see here, the trip does take well over a year, and
because of the expense and difficulty very few ships undertake it.
We call this 'conjunction.'" She shifted her wine-glass to her left
hand and set it down just beyond her bread-plate, so that the glass
and the two plates were again in a line, but this time with the
small plate between the glass and the large plate. "But when the two
planets are on the same side of the sun—we call this 'opposition'—
they are much closer together, and the voyage from one to the other
takes as little as two months. This is our situation at the moment,
as it happens."

Suddenly Simon brightened, taking a keen interest in the
conversation for the first time. "Two months, do you say?"

But Beatrice appeared puzzled. "Why is it that when the planets are far apart it is called 'conjunction,' but when they are close
it is 'opposition'? This seems contrary."

"It is because of Mars's position in Earth's sky—a rather pa-
rochial point of view, in my opinion. Conjunction is so called
because Mars and the sun are very close to each other in the sky
when seen from Earth; at opposition, they are on opposite sides
of the sky."

But Simon seemed uninterested in details of astronomy.
"You say that few ships will undertake the long voyage because

of the expense. Is the cost of passage on the short voyage more . . . reasonable?"

"Oh, yes! Much more so." This, as it happened, was a subject very close to Arabella's heart. Ever since her arrival at Marlowe Hall, whenever a newspaper should happen to fall into her hands she eagerly perused the shipping news, taking especial note of ships accepting passengers to Mars. Though the expense was, of course, very far beyond her means, she eagerly drank in every detail, stoking her impossible fantasies of running away to London and returning to the land of her birth. "At the moment one could take passage for as little as two hundred pounds."

"Two hundred pounds!" gasped Beatrice.

"Two hundred pounds . . . ," mused Simon.

"The accommodations at that price would be Spartan, to be sure, but with so many ships departing at this time, you would find no difficulty in obtaining a berth."

The conversation went on in that vein for some time—Arabella being amazed, once again, by the degree to which most Englishmen were ignorant of even basic astronomy—but only Beatrice participated, Simon having again fallen silent and pensive. His gristly roast lay untouched upon his plate, and he stared at it with pursed lips and tense shoulders.

Suddenly, with only the briefest of courtesies, he rose and excused himself from the table. Beatrice's eyes followed his retreating back with an expression of deep concern.

"I . . ." Arabella stammered. "Have I said something improper?"

"I do not believe so. He has been more than usually troubled these last few days, but I know not what might be the matter."

The two women ate their dinner in silence for a time, while various sounds of motion and activity echoed down the hall. Beatrice became increasingly anxious as Simon's absence lengthened, and finally she excused herself to see what might be keeping him.

Alone at the table, Arabella was left to examine her dinner-plate, bread-plate, and wine-glass, which sat where she had left them at the end of her astronomical disquisition.

The bread-plate and wine-glass were so very close together. . . .

Suddenly she had a frightful thought. Casting aside all she had learned of the courtesies a guest should extend to her hosts, she rose from the table and followed the sound of voices in hushed and urgent conversation to Simon and Beatrice's bedroom.

There she found Simon frantically cramming clothing into a valise, which lay open on the bed between him and Beatrice. The valise also contained a pair of silver candlesticks, a silver tureen, and a collection of cutlery.

"Wherever could you be going in such a frightful hurry?" Arabella said, though she feared she knew the answer. "And with the family silver?"

Simon looked up, his eyes wide and staring. "How dare you intrude upon us in our bedchamber!" His attitude, however, was more suited to one who had been surprised in the midst of a shameful activity than to one offended by an intrusion.

"I could not bear the thought of letting you depart without giving you my best regards. Might this have any thing to do with the relative positions of Earth and Mars?"

Simon gaped at her for a long moment, seemingly searching for some response and failing to find one. Then, with a sudden motion, he reached into the valise and brought out a dueling-pistol, which he leveled directly at Arabella. "I—I beg your pardon, but I must depart immediately. And I must insist that you remain here." He drew back the pistol's hammer with a definitive click.

Arabella shied away from the pistol, but found her back against the wall. The opening of the barrel, directed toward herself, seemed as big as the world. Her hands pressed the rough wallpaper to either side. "What is the meaning of this display, Cousin?" Though Simon's expression was diffident, the pistol did not waver, and she could see that the pan was primed with powder.

"I . . . I beg your pardon," he repeated. "But the last mail-coach to London departs within the hour, and I must be upon it, and I . . . I cannot allow you to prevent me from doing so." Without taking his eye or his weapon off of Arabella, he brought another dueling-pistol from the valise and handed it to his wife. Trembling and uncertain, she nonetheless accepted it. "Dearest, I must ask you to lock Miss Ashby in the pantry. Do not permit her to depart, or to have any communication with the outside world, for at least the next two days."

Awkwardly Beatrice directed her pistol at Arabella. "Of course, dearest," she said, her eyes flicking from her husband to Arabella and back. "But . . . but *why?*"

Simon, breathing rapidly, swallowed and pressed his eyes closed for a moment before speaking. "My dear, I must confess that for the last several weeks I have . . . I have withheld confidences from you, and for this I apologize. I have made some . . . imprudent decisions. Financial decisions." Beatrice stared at him in dismay, and her pistol sagged toward the floor, but Simon's gaze and aim remained steady upon Arabella as he spoke. "You knew when you married me that my, my pecuniary situation, was not of the highest degree. I had thought myself inured to this situation, but with Sophie's birth . . . I became ashamed." He blinked away tears, and Arabella steeled herself to spring, but now Beatrice's weapon was again trained upon her. "I determined that my daughter should not be forced to endure the penury which circumstance has forced upon me, and so I . . . I invested my inheritance . . . my *entire* inheritance . . . in a projected copper mine. A scheme which promised great and rapid returns." He shook his head slightly, with a wry smile. "I should not, I suppose, have been surprised by the outcome."

"Your *entire* inheritance?" Beatrice asked, but Arabella could see that she, too, was unsurprised by the outcome of Simon's investment, and though her voice quavered her pistol remained firmly pointed at Arabella's heart.

"I am afraid so, dearest." He swallowed. "Only the family silver remains. And if nothing intervenes, before the year is out I
shall be lodged in the sponging-house, and you and Sophie . . .
you shall, I suppose, be cast upon the mercy of your parents."
Beatrice's expression left little doubt as to how little mercy she
expected from that quarter. "But now it seems an opportunity has
presented itself." He straightened, firming his jaw and his grip
upon his pistol. "And so, my dear cousin, I must ask you to retire
to the pantry." He gestured curtly to the door.

Warily, keeping her eyes upon her cousins and watching for
any opportunity of escape, Arabella sidestepped in the indicated
direction. "I do not understand what you hope to accomplish by
this."

Simon gave a grim smile. "I suppose I should thank you,
Cousin. Until this afternoon I had thought all hope lost. But your
presence here—a living reminder of the entailment which has
stolen my rightful inheritance from me—together with your very
helpful explanation of our current astrological situation with respect to Mars . . ."

"Astronomical," Arabella corrected automatically.

"The *point* is," he fumed, "that with a mere two hundred
pounds—which can be obtained as a loan, with the silver as
collateral—two months' time, one dueling-pistol, and an entailed
estate . . . I can very shortly correct my financial circumstances
for good and all." Then, quite improperly, he grasped Arabella's
arm and propelled her out of the room, pressing the pistol's muzzle to her side.

Simon marched Arabella to the kitchen, silencing the maid
Jane's enquiries with a stern expression, and shoved Arabella roughly
into the dark and noisome pantry, slamming the door behind her.
She immediately pressed her shoulder against it, but with his
greater strength and weight he held it shut. Simon shouted something to Beatrice, and a moment later Arabella heard a scrape and

thud as something heavy was thrust against the door, followed by a clatter as of chains.

"Cousin, you cannot!" Arabella shouted through the door while impotently rattling its handle. "This is *murder* you are contemplating!" For she was now certain exactly what Simon planned. As the only remaining male in the line of succession, in the event of Michael's death the entire Ashby estate would pass to him.

"I am sorry," he replied, "but I have no alternative. Goodbye." And then, after a brief whispered colloquy with Beatrice, his footsteps beat a hasty retreat.

3

ESCAPE

Arabella tried the door again and again, but no matter how hard she pressed against it, it would not shift even half an inch.

"Pray do not continue in your efforts, Cousin," came Beatrice's voice from without. "The door is securely shut, and even if you should succeed in opening it, I remain here with the pistol. And I *will* use it, if necessary. Please do not require this of me."

"This mad scheme cannot succeed!" Arabella cried. "To put an end to one's own relatives for personal gain would surely render the inheritance invalid!"

"You underestimate my husband, Cousin. Despite his occasional follies, he *is* a barrister, and very clever. He will find some way to avoid suspicion."

"Murder will out," Arabella said, but even as she spoke she realized that platitude was not always true. Mars was but thinly peopled; many had met their end there in lonely circumstances, with no witnesses and no evidence. If a cousin from Earth were to pay a visit, a convenient hunting accident could easily be arranged, and accusations of foul play would be difficult or impossible to support. "If nothing else, *I* will not let him escape blame."

"And who are *you*?" Beatrice gave a nervous little laugh. "A seventeen-year-old girl—a wild child known for headstrong, intemperate actions—a jealous cousin deprived of her inheritance and ten thousand miles away from the court where the issue would be tried. Even if you could make your opinion known, who would listen to you?"

Arabella leaned against the door, breathing hard.

Though she did not want to believe what Beatrice said, she feared her cousin might be correct.

Hours passed. The light in the tiny window near the ceiling faded and dimmed as the sun sank toward the horizon. From time to time Arabella tried the door, but on each attempt Beatrice's voice dissuaded her from further effort.

Simon had said that he would be on the last coach to London. She *must* find some way to stop him. But how? Her reticule contained nothing but minor toilette articles and a bit more than nineteen shillings—not nearly enough to bribe her way past Beatrice or even the maid. The tiny pantry had but a single window, quite high up, and the shelves held nothing more than a paltry selection of bread, potatoes, and other foodstuffs. Not even a butter-knife could be found.

Whatever could she do?

Arabella removed the silver locket which hung on a chain around her neck—the locket which had never once left her person since her exile from Mars—and opened it. Up from her trembling palm smiled a miniature portrait of her brother, painted by an itinerant artist when he had been fifteen years of age. The companion portrait, of herself at age twelve, rested in Michael's watch-fob.

The youthful face in the portrait seemed so gay, so happy, so unconcerned. Arabella was the only one in all the worlds who knew how much danger he was in, and she seemed helpless to prevent it.

Even if she could somehow manage to make her way home before Simon reached London, she could not imagine Mother doing any thing to prevent him from carrying out his plan. So mired in propriety was she that she would never make an accusation, much less take action, against him until it was far too late.

No. It was up to Arabella, and Arabella alone, to prevent Simon from carrying out his dreadful scheme.

Decisively, she snapped the locket shut and looked around, seeking a fresh perspective upon the situation. What, she asked herself, would Khema do if similarly trapped?

The door was blocked and guarded. The rough plaster walls and wooden floor seemed too strong to be defeated without tools. The single window was far too small for escape.

Or was it?

As quietly as she could, Arabella climbed up to it, stepping up the shelves from one side of the tiny pantry to the other. The window was no more than a foot and a half wide and nine inches high; it was not made to open, and its cracked and bubbled glass was too filthy for a clear view to the outside.

But the frame . . . the frame was old, the paint cracked and peeling. And under the paint . . . the black of dry-rot.

Bracing herself awkwardly across the topmost shelves, Arabella pried at the splintered, rotted wood with her cuticle-knife. Though splinters abraded her skin and lodged painfully beneath her fingernails, a few bits and slivers came away, revealing still more rot beneath.

With grim determination she kept at her task, sending a shower of wood chips sifting down toward the floor. She worried that Beatrice might hear her, but no protests came from without. Her toes and calves began to ache from holding herself pressed against the ceiling, and the shelf pressed painfully against the backs of her thighs.

And then, suddenly, a large sliver came free all at once and the frame collapsed!

Arabella gasped and pressed the cracked glass, now free, into place before it could fall and shatter, nearly losing her footing on the shelves beneath her in the process.

Once she had caught her breath and stilled her beating heart, she gingerly picked the three large pieces of glass from the ruined frame and set them down upon the top shelf.

The cool air of a summer's evening came through the opening, its blessed breath drying the perspiration which her efforts had brought to her cheeks and forehead, and for a moment she relaxed. But she was still a long way from escape.

She was, she knew, quite tall and exceptionally straight and slender for a girl of seventeen. How her mother had despaired of her daughter's figure! "It is all on account of this planet's inadequate gravity," she had complained to Father. "It makes children grow up weak and spindly." But in this case her shape might prove her salvation, for she estimated that she might just be able to squeeze herself through the opening.

But what would she find beyond it?

Cautiously she put her head through the window and looked about. The sun had fully set, but the light of Earth's enormous moon revealed clearly that the window was only ten feet above the ground. And a large bush lay directly beneath, which would break her fall. She thought she might chance it.

But could she trust her instincts?

The force of Earth's gravity was greater than that of Mars, as had already been demonstrated to her on numerous painful occasions. A leap which seemed entirely reasonable to her might here be sufficient to break her leg, or her neck.

"For Michael," she whispered, and touched the locket.

She squirmed about, seeking to maneuver herself into a position whereby she would not plunge headfirst from the window as she exited, but very quickly realized that, while her hips might be able to pass through the opening, her black bombazine mourning dress would not.

She paused, breathing heavily, and considered her options.

Her mother would be appalled. But the night was dark, and her brother's life was at stake.

How she wished she had her *thukhong*!

Quickly, but as quietly as possible, she descended to the pantry floor. Removing her dress without assistance in the confined space was maddeningly difficult, but she finally managed it. The shift, petticoat, and stays beneath she left on, to protect her skin from the shattered window frame as well as for modesty; the reticule she tucked securely beneath the stays at the small of her back.

Then, staring up at the moonlight that stole through the window opening, she had an idea. She balled up the dress and tossed it onto the top shelf. Then, hitching her shift and petticoat up to her hips, she climbed back up to the top.

Straightening the dress to its maximum length, she removed one of the upper shelves from its brackets and tied the sleeves firmly about it. The remaining fabric extended less than a yard and a half, but she hoped it would make a difference.

Twisting about until she lay face-down across the remaining shelves, she maneuvered her feet out the window, then her legs, then her hips . . . her hands clinging to the shelf brackets with desperate strength. Once her hips were clear of the opening— with her knees against the outside wall's rough plaster, and the cool night air caressing her thighs—she hauled on the black dress, drawing the wooden shelf up to her collarbone.

This was as far as she could go without committing herself to the drop.

"Now or never," she breathed, and with her knees she pushed

her stomach through the window. Her weight took her the rest of the way.

The splintered window-sill rasped painfully against her bosom. She felt herself falling.

And then the shelf slammed into the window opening, halting her progress so rapidly her teeth clacked together.

The noise was tremendous. Immediately she heard Beatrice call her name, and chains rattling against the pantry door.

Quickly Arabella lowered herself as far as she could, her feet scrabbling against the wall, hands gripping the black dress. Soon she hung from the dress's end, arms fully extended, gasping from the effort. Her feet swung in the air, feeling nothing beneath no matter how she stretched her toes.

From the window above came the sound of the pantry door opening, a light from the kitchen, and a gasp from Beatrice.

Arabella closed her eyes tight and released her hold on the dress.

With a shriek and a crash she fell into the bush, its branches tearing at her legs and arms, then tumbled out of it and onto the hard ground.

From within the house came the sound of Beatrice's voice: crying out alarms, calling for Jane, and casting imprecations on Arabella even as she rushed through the Ashbys' little house.

Arabella pulled herself to her feet—panting hard, heart hammering. Her dress hung from the window above, far out of reach.

At least she still retained her reticule.

She gathered up her petticoats, turned, and ran.

She was a hundred yards or so down the lane when Beatrice rounded the corner of the house, shouting, "Stop! Stop! Stop or I shall shoot!"

Arabella did not stop. Surely Beatrice would not—

A loud *crack* came from behind. But though the sound nearly stopped Arabella's racing heart, a *zing* and crash from the shrubbery to her left showed that, though Beatrice might be willing to pull the trigger, she had aimed wide—or else her skill as a marks-man did not match her intent.

Arabella risked a glance over her shoulder. Beatrice stood panting, winded, the smoking pistol still in her hand, her eyes desperate. "Please, Cousin!" she cried. "Come back! Simon will regain his senses, I am certain of it!"

"I am not!" Arabella called back. "You must help me to stop him before he commits murder!"

Though the expression on Beatrice's face held nothing but mis-ery, she shook her head. "For the sake of my child," she replied, "I cannot." She then cried out, surprisingly loud, "Help! Oh, help me! Madwoman! Madwoman!"

Lights flickered to life all around, and voices were raised in alarm.

Arabella turned and ran.

Dodging through copses of trees smelling of loam and leaf-mould, scrambling over stone fences damp with moss, stumbling across plowed fields stubbled with wheat-stalks, Arabella fled headlong, caring for nothing other than to evade pursuit. Though the moon was setting and only half-full, it was so very much larger than Phobos that its light was still sufficient to keep her feet from roots and other obstacles. Strange chirruping noises—from birds or frogs or insects, she knew not what—came from the shadows, reminding her just how unfamiliar this landscape was to her; her desert skills availed her not at all.

From time to time she paused, gasping, peering in every direc-tion. But Beatrice was nowhere in sight, and any sounds of pur-suit were inaudible over her pounding heart.

After she knew not how long a time, exhaustion compelled her to stop. She crept into the darkness in the shade of a rock wall and lay panting on the cold ground there for just a moment's rest.

A moment later, or so it seemed, she woke with a gasp from sleep. The moon had entirely vanished, and the sun's wan light had begun to illuminate the horizon. Somehow, despite the excitement of the chase, fatigue had gotten the better of her.

Immediately she began to shiver from chill and weariness. The earth beneath her felt cold as ice, and besides the effort of escape she had barely slept or eaten in the last two days. She hugged herself miserably and bunched her sodden, soiled shift beneath herself as best she could.

What could she do? She had nothing—no family, no friends, hardly any money, not even decent clothing. Only the locket with Michael's picture, and a grim determination.

The rising sun limned a farmhouse on a rise not far away. Arabella levered her stiff and protesting body to its feet, and began walking toward it.

———————

The kitchen door creaked open a crack and a wrinkled, suspicious face peered out. "Who might you be?" the old woman said.

"Arabella Ashby, ma'am," she replied. Her voice, after a cold night sleeping on bare earth, was little more than a croak.

The woman snorted. "What d'yer want?"

For a moment the apparently simple question vexed her completely. What *did* she want? To report the terrible crimes that her cousins had perpetrated upon her, and planned to perpetrate upon her brother. To send word to her mother of her situation. Most of all, to prevent Simon from traveling to Mars and carrying out his monstrous scheme. But that could all come later. Just now she was cold, and weary, and hungry. "Please, ma'am," she rasped, "I've been the victim of a horrible crime. If I might come in, and warm up for a bit, and—"

"Strumpet!" the old woman interrupted. "Away with ye." And with a firm, harsh motion she shut and latched the door. A moment later her eye reappeared at the window nearby, fixing her with a hostile glare.

Arabella stood motionless, stunned and appalled by the woman's inhospitality.

A hand joined the eye at the window, gesturing unequivocally: *Go away.*

Arabella spat at her—or tried to, her mouth being so dry that only a tiny drop of spittle escaped her lips to fall ineffectively on the dirt before the door—turned, and walked away.

She cursed herself for her naiveté. A filthy, disheveled, bloodied young woman, in a scandalous state of undress, with a mad story of imprisonment, betrayal, and murder? She should never have expected to be believed. And even if she should somehow find someone who accepted her outlandish tale, it might be hours or days before they took any action. In that time Simon could easily take passage to Mars, and once the ship had launched he would be beyond the power of any one to stop him.

Arabella gritted her teeth and turned her steps toward the rising sun.

Toward London.

She could not walk all the way to London, of course—not if she wished to catch up with her cousin in time. Simon had taken the mail-coach, but no such option was open to Arabella. Even though she had what she hoped was sufficient money for the fare, for a woman of quality to travel on a public conveyance without male accompaniment was completely inconceivable.

If only she had not been born a woman. . . .

Arabella stopped dead in the path, appalled at the notion which had just occurred to her.

She shook her head and walked on.

As she proceeded, she debated with herself whether theft and deception could truly be justified by necessity. At the same time, she kept a sharp eye out for an opportunity to commit those very sins.

Finally, as she topped a rise, she came upon a small but prosperous farm. Wheat waved in the fields, chickens scratched in the yard, cattle grazed contentedly. . . .

And clean clothes hung on a fence, apparently having been left to dry overnight.

Arabella looked all around. There was no one in sight.

To steal was a sin. But at this very moment Michael might be rising from his bed, yawning and stretching, unaware of the doom that approached him. . . .

"I have no choice," she whispered to herself, touching the locket.

Moving as quickly and as quietly as she could, she descended from the rise and scrambled over the low stone wall marking the edge of the property. From the wall it was only a few steps to the fence on which the clothing hung.

There were several complete sets of clothes here, men's and women's both.

After only a moment's hesitation, she selected breeches, hose, a shirt, a coat, and a soft cap which seemed to be about the right size for her. She attempted to assuage her guilt by taking only those articles which seemed the most worn, which she hoped would be missed the least and might also provoke the least suspicion. Finally, from her reticule she drew a single shilling, leaving it where the clothing had been—a token payment to be sure, but she knew not what other expenses might come her way.

Gathering up the clothes into a compact packet, she took one last guilty look back at the farmer's cottage before running away across the field.

Secreting herself behind a hedgerow which blocked the view from the farmhouse and the nearby road, Arabella clothed herself in her stolen garments. The coat was too broad across the shoulders, she had neglected to obtain a neck-cloth, and there seemed to be several other minor articles missing, at least to judge by the buttons in the breeches which attached to nothing she could find. The space in the front of the breeches she filled with a wad of fabric torn from her tattered shift.

She left the rest of her ruined garments rolled up in the hedgerow, along with the reticule, whose contents she distributed among her pockets. From her previous clothing she retained only the shoes, sturdy Mars-made half-boots which she hoped would not appear too girlish.

Now there remained only the problem of her hair.

On Mars Arabella had never paid much attention to her hair, wearing it short enough to keep out of her eyes and combing it only when her mother insisted. But since arriving in England, the formerly occasional demands of fashion had become constant, and Arabella had been subjected to interminable rounds of combing, brushing, braiding, and fussing that left her extremely vexed. Thus it was with great satisfaction that she pulled back her hair and cut the majority of it away with her cuticle-knife, leaving the discarded strands in the hedgerow for birds to make their nests of.

The result was, even she had to acknowledge, extremely untidy, being executed with an instrument only middling sharp and without the aid of a looking-glass, but as she pulled the cap low on her brow she reflected that it was not much worse than the rest of her outfit.

But still . . . worn, ill-fitting, and stolen though her clothing might be, what a relief it was to have her legs properly covered again! No more would she suffer the indignity of a skirt catching on a protruding branch, nor be forced to concern herself with the prying eyes of the public upon her exposed flesh.

Her outfit was no *thukhong*—how she missed that warm, comfortable leather garment!—but in it she nonetheless felt ready for any eventuality.

Half an hour later, Arabella swaggered along, hands in her pockets and arms a-kimbo, aping her brother's confident stride as best she could. Ahead on the path lay an inn, where she hoped she might obtain something to eat and perhaps directions to a mail-coach or stage-coach. To cover her anxiety, she whistled loudly in what she intended as a manly fashion. She hoped she had made no dreadfully obvious mistakes with her unaccustomed garments.

The inn still lay some five hundred yards distant when she heard, and then saw, a black-and-scarlet mail-coach approaching along the road. She burst into a run, holding on to her breeches at the waist to keep them from sliding down to her ankles and hoping the wad of fabric that filled out the front did not fall too badly out of place.

As she rushed along, her brains rattling in her head from each blow of her heels on the path in Earth's heavy gravity, she saw the coach come to the inn, draw to a halt, and the guard at the rear of the carriage hand down a packet of mail to the innkeeper. The coach seemed to be just on the brink of departing.

But finally, stumbling, panting, and catching at her falling breeches, she leaned heavily against the side of the coach before it left. "I should like," she gasped, pitching her voice as low as she could, "to take passage, to London."

"You are in luck, my lad," the driver said, hooking a thumb over his shoulder. "There's one seat open inside."

"Bless you, sir." But as she reached for the door handle, the driver blocked the door with his hand.

"Seventeen shillings sixpence, sir."

"Sev—!" Arabella's mouth hung open at the shocking fare.

"Outside's cheaper, but there's none left." The four dusty and miserable-looking men seated on the coach's roof regarded Arabella with red-eyed indifference. "Or you could take the stage tomorrow for half the price. But this here's the Royal Mail, and we waits for no man. So what's it to be, lad, stay or go?"

Seventeen shillings sixpence was nearly all the money that remained in her pocket. But one day's delay could make the difference between intercepting her cousin in London and watching in helpless despair as his ship sailed away into the interplanetary atmosphere. "I shall go," she said, and counted out the coins.

Before she had even properly seated herself, the coach jolted into motion, slamming her into the wall on one side and her neighbor on the other in irregular alternation. She felt rather like a hat being rattled about in a hat-box, and the noise precluded all conversation.

It was not until the coach was halfway to Tetsworth that she realized she had successfully posed as a boy without being questioned.

———

The day passed as though in a fever. She slept fitfully as the coach jolted along, often waking with a fellow traveler's elbow in her ribs or coat-button in her eye. She had no idea where they were; from where she sat she had only a sliver of a view through the tiny window. In the darkness and noise of the lurching coach, conversation was impossible even if she had desired it.

Her stolen clothing itched at her conscience as badly as the worn and rustic fabric itched at her body. For the hundredth time she told herself that she had had no choice—that, despite the great hardship she knew her theft would cause some unknown farmer, the risk to her brother's life was greater still. Yet she knew her beloved Khema would be terribly disappointed in her.

She remembered the automaton dancer—a tiny doll, less than two feet tall, which had leapt and pirouetted most realistically when its key was wound. It had been her favorite of all her father's automata, and very dear to him as well.

Until one day she had, in a foolish excess of enthusiasm, turned the key one too many times. The mainspring had snapped with a hideous metallic twang, leaving the dancer frozen in mid-leap.

She had been in the dunes behind the drying-sheds, desperately shoveling sand over the broken device, when Khema had found her. "What is this, *tutukha*?" she'd said.

"It's my father's automaton dancer," Arabella had replied, her voice quavering. "It . . . it broke, and I thought that if I took it away and buried it he wouldn't notice it was gone."

Khema's eye-stalks had curved back in skepticism. "It broke, did it? And I am sure that you had nothing to do with this?"

Exhausted and still all a-flutter from her frantic rush to conceal the damaged automaton, Arabella had been able to do nothing more than shake her head.

Khema had bent down to Arabella's level, her black and subtly faceted eyes fixed on Arabella's. "We Martians have a concept we call *okhaya*," she had said. "In English you would say 'personal responsibility,' though that does not quite convey how very important *okhaya* is to us. We believe very strongly that if one does something wrong, one should immediately admit it and make amends. To conceal a bad action, or even worse to lie about it, brings very great dishonor." She had sat back on her heels then, the sand crunching beneath the complex carapace of her knees. Silently waiting.

Arabella had withstood that calm, expectant gaze for no more than a few seconds before bursting into tears and admitting her crime.

The automaton had not been repairable, and she had had no desserts for a month. But, though he was terribly cross at the damage, her father had said he was proud of her for her confession.

Suddenly the coach halted and the door was flung open, making her blink in the unaccustomed light. "London!" cried the driver. "All out!"

Arabella stumbled out into a vast confusion. Horses, men, and ladies milled all about in a riot of gaudy colors, the noise of hoof-beats and shouted conversations adding to her bewilderment. Buildings of brick and stone towered three and four stories on every side. A terrific smell of soot and dust and offal assaulted her nostrils.

"Get out there, you!" someone shouted. She turned to see a coach-and-four thundering down upon her, and threw herself from its path only to collide with a woman in a fashionable green dress. "Take a care, you guttersnipe!" she cried, and shoved Arabella rudely away.

Heart pounding, Arabella scrambled to the nearest wall and pressed herself against it, trying her best not to be trampled.

It was the most people she had ever seen in one place in her entire life. The whole population of Shktetha Station, a small town north of Woodthrush Woods, could have fit into this one street without crowding, but this mob of people filled the street and the next one and the one after that . . . on and on to the limits of the vast metropolis.

The very thought made her giddy.

This was not the first time she had been in London, of course; she had passed through the city when she had arrived on Earth last year. But on that occasion, weak and debilitated after a four-month aerial journey, she and her mother and sisters had been carried from the ship directly into a private carriage and conveyed immediately to Marlowe Hall. Too enervated to even raise her head, her impression of London had been little more than a blur.

And now she found herself in the thick of it. Lost, bewildered, friendless, nearly penniless, dressed as a boy in a suit of stolen clothes, she had to find her cousin Simon somewhere in this enormous crowd and stop him before he could take passage to Mars.

The coach had deposited her in front of an inn called The Navigator, whose sign showed a man seated at a writing-desk with a map spread out upon it. If the mail-coach from Oxford always arrived here, Simon might have spent the night here. He might even still be here, awaiting passage to Mars.

Arabella drew herself straight, pulled up her breeches, and took a deep breath before entering. Then she paused and adjusted her padding, which had slipped down to her knee. This business of being a boy was not easy.

The inn was as bustling with people within as the street had been without. Raucous conversation babbled at every table, adding up to a terrible din. Looking around, she identified a lean and unfriendly-looking fellow stacking dishes behind the bar as the likely proprietor.

"If you're looking for a room," the barman said as she drew near, "we're full up."

"No, I am looking for my cousin," she said. It was difficult to pitch her voice low, like a boy's, while at the same time raising it to be heard above the tumult of the crowd. "Simon Ashby, from Oxford. He would have come in on the mail-coach yesterday." She could only hope that Simon was not traveling under an assumed name; if he were, the chances of finding him were slim indeed.

With an annoyed sigh, the barman set down his dishes and shifted to the other end of the bar, where he drew out an account-book from a cupboard. "No one by that name," he said after running his eye down the last page.

Arabella's heart fell, but only a little. It would have been unreasonably good fortune to have found Simon in the first place she looked. "Thank you for looking, anyway."

The barman shrugged. "I hope you find him." He stuck out his hand. "Best of luck, Master . . . ?"

Awkwardly Arabella took the proffered hand, which gripped her own with crushing force. "Ashby," she stammered as her hand was briskly pumped. "Ara . . . *Arthur* Ashby."

Arabella spent the rest of that day calling at inn after inn looking for her cousin. Sometimes she received concerned, solicitous aid, other times a brusque rebuff, but no one admitted having seen any one by that name.

What would she do, she thought as she walked, if she did find him? She was smaller than he, and weaker, and he might be carrying his pistol, so she would be foolish to attack him physically. She could denounce him to all the people around when she found him, and importune them to assist her in detaining him. But all she had against him was an accusation—she held no proof that he had imprisoned her, nor that he planned to murder her brother.

But still . . . the accusation, together with the pistol, might carry some weight with the local magistrate. When she found Simon, she would have to make enough noise that the two of them would be detained by the constables; once she had explained herself, surely, as the Gospels promised, the truth would make her free.

As plans went, she had to confess, this was not much of one.

A merry sound of chimes distracted her from her concerns, and she looked up to find herself in front of a clockmaker's shop. A clockmaker's shop that also sold automata.

Prominently presented in the shop window was a fine specimen of an automaton—an artist seated at a drawing-desk, about three feet high. A display model, designed to demonstrate the maker's skills, only the right half of its body was clothed. The left half lay open to the air, displaying its gears and works.

But though the mechanism was impressively complex and finely made, it was flawed. The automaton bent and dipped its pen and scratched out its work with a cunning and lifelike motion, but the drawing that emerged—a ship at sea, its sails flying—had a long horizontal line drawn right through the middle of it. Several more copies of the same drawing were visible within the shop, on sale for a penny apiece, and each one was marred by the same error.

The fine automaton was damaged, just as her life had been damaged by Simon's perfidy.

With grim determination she turned from the shop window and continued to the next inn.

4

THE AERIAL DOCKS

Arabella awoke the next morning to a brusque kick and an order to "move along" from the keeper of the shop in whose alley she had spent the night. Stiff, cold, and miserable, she parceled out a few coins from her nearly empty purse for a stale bun and a drink from a shared water cup.

At some point to-day, she reflected as she gnawed on the tough bread, she would have to find some way to send word to her mother about what had occurred at Simon's. But her prime concern was to find and stop Simon.

———

Having finished her paltry breakfast, she determined that she would concentrate her attentions on the inns nearest the aerial ship docks. If Simon were still in London, she thought, he would no doubt have taken lodging there.

The docks were not difficult to find. With Mars in opposition, dozens of Mars-bound ships were departing each day, floating up into the sky like Newton's Bubble—the soap bubble in the great man's bath which had led him to the principle of aerial buoyancy. All she had to do was follow their path down to its origin.

The Mars Docks, once she arrived, proved to be a riot of clamor and noise that made the London streets on which she had spent the previous day seem bucolic by comparison. Men and beasts labored, hauling boxes and barrels to and from the docks; sweating stevedores walked in treadwheels, powering the cranes that lifted bales of cargo to the ships' decks; hawkers cried the virtues of their products, ships, and services; and under all rumbled the ever-present roar of the great furnaces.

But it was the Marsmen—the ships themselves—their masts swaying as they bobbed on the tide, that drew Arabella's attention. Smaller than the seagoing ships they resembled, they differentiated themselves by being constructed of honey-blond *khoresh*-wood, which gleamed like gold in the early morning sun.

Without *khoresh*-wood, or "Marswood" as the English styled it, Marsmen would be tiny ships like the fragile little *Mars Adventure* in which the brave Captain Kidd had been the first Englishman to reach Mars. Kidd had been very lucky to survive his arrival on Mars, and if not for his discovery of the *khoresh*-tree he would not have returned. Stronger than oak but lighter than wicker, *khoresh*-wood was now both the major item of Martian export and the material that made interplanetary travel practical.

And with that thought, the sough of wind in the spars and rigging made her ache with homesickness, reminding her as it did so painfully of the similar sound made by the Martian wind in the *khoresh*-trees of Woodthrush Woods. Perhaps some of these brave ships might be built of wood from her family plantation . . . the very plantation where, even now, Michael might be taking toast with *guroshkha*-jam and planning his day.

Her stomach clenching at the responsibility that had fallen to her, she continued down toward the docks, hoping against hope that she might not be too late.

———————————

The inns of the Mars Docks were mostly on Rotherhithe Street, grand imposing structures with names like The Asteroid, The *Khoresh*-Tree, and The Thork, whose sign depicted a Martian warrior, properly a *thorakh*, with the traditional oval shield and forked spear. The Martian shown on the sign had clearly not been drawn from life; though his spear and shield were reasonably authentic, his carapace—painted as a hard, unnatural red—was far shorter and wider than any actual Martian's, and his hands were simple two-pincered claws like those of an Earth crab. Also, he was naked as a savage, lacking the true *thorakh*'s colorful battle dress.

Simon's purse, Arabella reflected, would be heavy with the money obtained from pawning his family silver, and he planned to return richer still, so she selected the largest and most luxurious inn of them all, The Martian King, to begin with. The inn's sign depicted a figure having a Martian's eye-stalks and mouth-parts, but otherwise human, in the garments of a Medieval English monarch; the wide and solid door was of *khoresh*-wood, a pointless luxury.

The keeper of the inn affected a buff coat, aping those of Company ships' captains, and a haughty attitude likewise. "We've no need of errand-boys today," he said as Arabella approached.

"I am looking for my cousin," she replied, undeterred. Dozens of similar encounters in the last day had inured her to any amount of hauteur. "Simon Ashby, from Oxford. Have you a guest by that name?"

The innkeeper's expression showed clearly that he did not believe any cousin of such a shoddy-looking figure as Arabella could possibly be a guest at his fine establishment, but he did consult his guest-book. "No, we have not . . . ," he said without looking up.

"Thank you anyway." She turned to leave.

"He departed just this morning."

That stopped Arabella where she stood. "What?"

"Are you deaf as well as ill-mannered, young man? I said that he departed this morning."

Arabella's heart hammered in her chest. "Did he say where he was going? I have . . . I have some important news for him."

The innkeeper peered at his guest-book. "It says here that he booked passage on the Marsman *Earl of Kent*."

At this news Arabella's pounding heart seemed to stop cold.

"*Earl of Kent!*" Arabella shouted as she ran toward the docks, the cobbles slick under her feet. "*Earl of Kent*! Where is the Marsman *Earl of Kent*?"

Passerby after passerby gave her no reply save an annoyed or disdainful glance. On she rushed, dodging dray-carts and stevedores rolling heavy barrels. "Where is the *Earl of Kent*?" Finally one stranger pointed, saying something about the Heron Place dock.

But this new intelligence seemed only to make her search the harder, as she now sought two targets rather than one. Again and again she doubled back, chasing up and down the sea-wall, importuning strangers for directions and trying to sort out contradictory advice. No one seemed to know where the *Earl of Kent* might be found.

At last she found herself on a stinking, filthy wharf at the foot of Heron Place. Surely this was the dock the stranger had indicated, yet the ship that bobbed nearby was no Marsman at all, merely a nameless cargo barge, and the area was practically unpopulated.

"What might ye be seeking?" called out a one-legged airman, who sat at the base of a nearby wall with his hat upended on the cobbles before him.

"The Marsman *Earl of Kent.*" She sorted a farthing from her much diminished purse and tossed it into the unfortunate man's hat.

"I know her well," the airman replied. "A fine ship, a soft berth. She were docked just here this very morning."

Arabella swallowed. "And where is she now?"

An agony of waiting as the airman sucked his few remaining teeth, squinting and contemplating. "I calculate she'll be well above the falling-line now."

"Which means?"

"Just furling her envelope and swaying out sidemasts."

"Swaying out . . . ?"

"Just so, sir. A soft berth, the old *Earl*, but no air-clipper. Now, you want a *fast* ship, there's better. *Royal York*, or *Diana*, she'd be halfway to the moon by now. Depending on the winds."

"So the *Earl* is still nearby?"

"Nearby?" Again the old airman sucked his teeth. "Closer than the moon, aye, but above the falling-line. . . . Well, there's nothing between her and Mars now save clean air and sweet winds, the good Lord willing."

"I see," Arabella said, though in truth she understood little of what she had heard . . . save that the ship was well departed. "Is there any chance she might be forced to return to port? By storm or foul winds, perhaps?"

The old airman shook his head. "She'd never have taken to the air in such case."

Arabella's shoulders slumped. "I see," she repeated miserably, and gave the airman another farthing for his help.

"Thankee, mate," he said, tucking the coin away in his pocket.

Stunned and dejected, Arabella wandered up from the docks, lacking any destination, letting the waves of humanity wash across her without feeling them. Her feet moved without volition, carrying her unseeing and uncaring though a dark fog of despair.

Simon had gone. Vanished into the air, Mars-bound, with his pistol and his envy and his greed. In two months he would arrive at Mars, meet with Michael, and find some way to work himself into his cousin's confidence. Plenty of time to work out a convincing story as to why.

Michael could be so trusting sometimes. He would never suspect, until some supposed hunting accident or other artificial tragedy had already befallen him. And then Simon, all feigned distress and forged tears, would inherit Marlowe Hall and all the rest, and Arabella and her mother and sisters would be tossed out onto the street.

Arabella knew the fate of women who lost the protection of their family fortune. They were thrown upon the kindness of relatives—not that Simon could be expected to offer any such kindness, nor were there any other relatives upon whom they might depend—or, failing that, must make their own way in the world, taking in washing or selling matches to earn their daily bread.

Mother, for all her flintiness, was accustomed to a soft life. And Fanny and Chloë were barely more than infants. None of them would survive if they were forced upon their own resources.

It would be up to Arabella herself to save her family. But how could she do so? She was only a girl . . . friendless, nearly penniless, and a hundred miles away from them.

She must send a letter, she thought. The *Earl of Kent* was not a fast ship, the old airman had said. A letter, carried on a fast packet-ship, might reach Michael before Simon did.

"Excuse me, sir," she asked a passing stranger, "where might I find a receiving house for a letter to Mars?"

The nearest receiving house proved to be a stationers', which among many other services received letters for conveyance to the penny, general, and aerial post. Her gracious bow to the proprietor, a thin and sour-looking man with pince-nez spectacles perched upon his nose, was met by a disapproving glare.

Arabella was suddenly very aware of the appearance she must be presenting. She was filthy, her ill-fitting clothes had been stolen from a poor Oxfordshire farmer, and they had been traveled in, slept in, and subjected to extremely hard service for the last several days without proper cleaning or care. Even she had to admit that her odor was extremely unpleasant.

Again she bowed. "If you please, sir," she said in her politest tone, "I should like to send an express to my brother on Mars." The cost of an express, she well knew, was extravagant, but when he read the news the letter conveyed she was sure her brother would be happy to have paid it. "My news is exceptionally urgent, and I wish to convey it immediately and by the fastest possible ship."

Apparently her fine diction managed to outweigh her rough appearance, for the shopkeeper's disdainful expression softened somewhat. "You are in luck, then, boy," he said. "The next collection for the aerial post is in only half an hour." He extended his hand.

Arabella stared blankly for a moment at the man's open hand before realizing what it meant, then cursed herself for stupidity. "I'm sorry, sir, I have not written my letter yet." She looked about at the stacks of creamy paper displayed behind glass on the shop's walls. "And I fear that I lack paper."

The shopkeeper sighed, opened a cabinet, and drew out a sheet of fine cream laid. "Eighteen pence and a half," he said. "And ha'penny for the use of pen and ink, if you should require that, as I suspect you do."

Arabella's purse contained only three farthings—less than a penny all told. "Have you any thing more . . . reasonable?"

He stared down his long nose at her, then sniffed. Slipping the fine paper back onto the stack, he reached below the counter and brought out a small, battered box. "Penny a sheet," he said, "and you'll find no better price in London."

Arabella swallowed. She had no doubt the man was correct in that. "I thank you for your time, sir," she said. "I shall return with the money as soon as I can."

Arabella's hands gripped each other behind her back as she paced away from the stationers'. Tuppence might be sufficient to save her brother's life, but even that modest sum was far beyond her now.

She tried not to regret the money she had spent so far. The coach-fare, the shilling she had left for the clothing, the ha'penny she had given the old airman, the few pence she'd spent to assuage her hunger and thirst . . . all had been practically or morally necessary.

Surely she could perform some small service for a farthing or two.

But the metropolis's bustling crowds cared little for the needs of a tattered, filthy young man. All those she importuned, on the streets or in the shops, rebuffed her entreaties—some with a kindly expression of regret, others quite brusquely, but none with any charity or offer of employment.

Already the sun had passed its zenith. Increasingly frantic, she charged from street to street, her eyes scanning shop windows in search of one that might require her particular skills. . . .

And then she recalled what she hoped might be the answer to her prayers.

The clockmaker's shop.

The automaton artist.

It took her some hours to locate the shop again. She had nearly given up hope when, finally, she found herself before the shop window with the flawed automaton.

Eagerly Arabella peered at the exposed mechanism. It was complex, yes, especially being so much smaller than her father's harpsichord player, but it lacked subtlety. Every gear and wire was connected, directly or indirectly, to the drawing hand; there was no attempt to counterfeit breathing or make the device's head seem to follow its hand. And having understood this, the source of the problem became obvious. A simple bent rod, just one among the brass fingers that read the pins on the device's controlling drum. Easily damaged, easily fixed.

Hands trembling, she pushed her way into the shop.

The shop's dark and ticking interior was crowded, nearly filled by the shopkeeper and his one customer, a tall dark foreigner in a buff coat.

"May I help you, young sir?" the shopkeeper said, sliding his spectacles down his nose as he leaned to peer around the customer. The *sir* came weighted with a heavy freight of irony.

Arabella swallowed, and again bowed with the greatest grace she could muster. "I wish to speak with you concerning your display model, sir," she said. "The automaton artist. I see what is wrong with it, sir."

"What's *wrong* with it?" the shopkeeper replied with a note of incredulity. "What's *wrong* with it? There is nothing whatsoever *wrong* with it, my dear boy. Clarkson's Clockworks sells only the very finest products, and I personally guarantee the function and performance of each and every one." This last was clearly directed at the customer rather than Arabella.

"It—it is but a small flaw, sir," she stammered, her nervousness making it difficult to pitch her voice low like a boy's. "It puts an, an extraneous line across the middle of the picture, sir. And I can repair it, sir, for a very reasonable fee of sixpence."

"An . . . *extraneous* line?" His already-sour expression soured still further. "It was Hodge who put you up to this, wasn't it?" He turned his attention to the customer again, all obsequiousness. "My competitor, sir. He'll stop at nothing. Day in and day out, spreading false rumors about the quality of my automata." Now he returned to Arabella, and his words burned with scorn. "And I'll tell you what I've told all the others who've complained about that line, and that is this: it is an artistic decision, a decorative flourish."

"No, sir," Arabella insisted. "It is only a bent rod, sir. One of the pickups from the control drum. I can fix it, sir!"

"*You?*" he scoffed. "A ragged, beardless gutter urchin?" Now he came out from behind his counter, begging the customer's pardon, and stomped up to where Arabella stood trembling. He was a big man, and though his hands were very white and delicate, the forearms exposed by his rolled-up cuffs were thick with muscle.

The shopkeeper grabbed her roughly by the collar and twisted. Choking out a squawk, she heard and felt fabric tear. "You are nothing more than Hodge's creature," he growled in her ear, "sent to humiliate me before my clientele. You will return to him, you will give him back whatever he has paid you, and you will tell him not to try this sort of stunt again or he'll get from me himself what I give to you now!" Then he cuffed her hard across the ear and shoved her through the door, sending her sprawling across the cobbles and into the path of a passing gentleman, who cried out and gave her a good kick. Pain exploded in her midsection, joining the pain in her bruised ear and abraded hands.

Eyes blinded with tears, she dragged herself around the corner and lay gasping against a wrought-iron fence, trying to recover her wits. But a few moments later she heard the shop door open and a loud voice calling, "Where has that boy gone? That ragged boy?" A man standing in the street immediately pointed in her direction.

She had no idea why the man who had just thrown her out of his shop might now be seeking her, but she had no wish to find out, nor to endure any further abuse or humiliation at his hands.

She ran.

5

THE MOON AND SIXPENCE

Arabella ducked and weaved frantically between irate passersby in an attempt to evade the man, but no matter how many woolen-clad elbows she jostled or fine shoes she trod upon, his shouting and footsteps continued to dog her heels.

After several frantic minutes—the thudding boots now nearer, now farther, but never completely eluded—she dodged into an alley, pressing herself against the wall.

Her pursuer passed the alley mouth, his rapid footsteps pounding past and vanishing around the corner.

Panting, exhausted, she slid down the rough bricks to the alley floor. The man had been diligent in pursuing her; she could not rest long.

And then, pasted to the wall across from her, she saw a recruiting poster.

GOD save the KING.

To all Loyal British Subjects,

Our beloved SOVEREIGN, seeing his Majesty's AIRLANES
threatened by FRENCH PRIVATEERS both rapacious and bold,
has caused to be built and commissioned

THE AERIAL CLIPPER
ATHENA
of Sixteen Guns
a fine and exceptionally fast Ship

Which now lies ready for MARS
lacking only a few good Hands

CAPTAIN
SIR HIRAM WALTER
who was not killed at Ceres as some have reported

Commands her.

The following BOUNTIES will be given by his MAJESTY,
in Addition to Two Months Advance.

To Able Airmen . . . Five Pounds.
To Ordinary Airmen . . . Two pounds Ten Shillings.
To Landsmen . . . Thirty Shillings.

REPAIR,
All who have good Hearts, who love their KING and COUNTRY,
to Lieut. J. F. CONNOR
at his Rendezvous, at THE MOON AND SIXPENCE

MAKE HASTE!

G. BONDHAM, Printer, Carrow-Street

As she read the poster, Arabella recalled the old airman's words: the *Earl of Kent* was no clipper. But here *was* a clipper, Mars-bound, a "fine and exceptionally fast ship," and not only was she calling for volunteers, but offering a bounty as well!

Even a landsman—into which class Arabella assumed she herself fell, owing to want of experience—would receive a bounty of thirty shillings, thus providing a solution to her financial problems . . . as well as passage to Mars!

The game was not yet lost. She might be able to do better than send a letter . . . she might be able to beat Simon to Mars herself!

"Excuse me, sir!" she called to a passerby, a tall gentleman with a shockingly long knitted scarf. "Do you know where I might find The Moon and Sixpence?"

———————————

The Moon and Sixpence, located in a narrow side way only a few streets distant from the poster, was a dark and low-ceilinged public house of a type Arabella had never before entered. Raucous conversation rattled the beams, rough tankards clattered against the tables, and a stink of sour ale pervaded the atmosphere.

Hesitantly Arabella stepped down into the space from the stairwell, blinking from the light outside. Here, at least, her ragged and unwashed clothing would be no impediment.

A serving-girl, carrying three brimming mugs in one hand and showing an indecent amount of bosom, came swaying past. "Excuse me?" Arabella said to her.

"Aye? What's yours?"

"I am looking for Lieutenant J. F. Connor. Of the *Athena*."

The serving-girl looked her up and down. "The Air Service won't take you before sixteen."

"I am seventeen years of age, miss." That much, at least, was the truth.

Suddenly the serving-girl reached out and drew a finger down

Arabella's smooth and beardless cheek, then laughed aloud. "Aye, and I'm a Martian."

At that Arabella laughed in return. "Indeed? Well, so am I, miss. A Martian born and raised."

The serving-girl tipped her head and grinned. "Cheeky little b——d. Well, you wouldn't be the first to join the navy under false colors." She jerked her thumb toward a table near the fireplace. "Connor's there."

"Thank you, miss."

But as Arabella turned away, the serving-girl touched her shoulder. "Take care, now," she said, her expression serious. "'Twould be a shame for a sweet young face like yours to get blown to bits by some pirate off Ceres."

"I will, miss."

———————

Connor lounged against the wall, drinking from a glass-bottomed tankard and talking with several companions. He wore a blue navy coat with airman's red piping, but his neck-cloth was loose and stained; above it, his cheeks were ill-shaven.

Arabella pushed down her fears and stepped forward. "Lieutenant Connor?"

The airman looked up over the brim of his tankard, but said nothing.

"My name is Arthur Ashby, sir. I saw the recruiting poster for *Athena*. I would like to volunteer."

At that the lieutenant immediately excused himself from his conversation, drained and set down his tankard, and walked over to Arabella. "Delighted to meet you, Mr. Ashby." His handshake was exceptionally rough and strong, like being gripped by a great twist of rope. "Allow me to stand you to a drink." With a great show of cheer and camaraderie he ushered Arabella to the bar, where he ordered two pints of ale, handed one to Arabella, and raised the other. "The king's health!" he cried, and drank off a great swallow.

"The king's health!" chorused all those in earshot, and Arabella chimed in, slamming her tankard down on the bar afterward along with the rest. Ale sloshed out, disguising the fact that she had not swallowed any. She felt she should keep her wits about her.

"So, tell me why you wish to become one of His Majesty's airmen."

"Mars, sir. I am filled with a great desire to visit the red planet. And such a fine fast ship as *Athena* is said to be, well, I figure she will get me there sooner than any other."

"That she will, lad, that she will. She's a fine ship." He took another drink. "Now, before you accept the king's shilling and appear before the magistrate to take your oath, I have a few questions I must ask you. Are you a loyal subject of His Majesty the King?"

Arabella straightened. "Absolutely, sir!"

"Are you at least sixteen years of age?"

"Indeed I am, sir! Seventeen in March."

He did not appear convinced, but seemed to decide not to press the matter. "Are you rated able airman?"

"No, sir." On this point she felt sure that lying would get her in endless trouble, by raising expectations about her capabilities that she could not fulfill.

"Ordinary airman?"

"No."

"Well then, can you reef, hand, and steer? Do you know the ropes, at least? There's plenty of use for a sailor's skills on an aerial ship."

Arabella ducked her head sheepishly. "I am afraid I have no idea what those even mean, sir."

The lieutenant did not seem surprised, nor even particularly disappointed. "Right. Landsman, then. But we've a place for you, have no fear." He reached into a pocket and produced a freshly minted shilling. It gleamed in the lamplight. "D'ye know what this is, and whose face is on it?"

Was this some kind of test? "It is a shilling, sir. And that is the king, George the Third." She did not mention his madness, or the fact that his duties were currently being performed by his son the regent. The king was still the king, and his face was still on the money.

"Exactly." The lieutenant's expression grew serious. "Now, a shilling ain't much." That might be so, though Arabella reflected that it was far more money than she owned at the moment, and more than she had any other prospect of obtaining any time soon. She felt as though her purse were salivating for it. "But for many years, English soldiers were paid a shilling a day. The pay's quite a bit more today, I assure you! But for tradition's sake, we still do place a great ceremonial value upon the acceptance of, as we say, the king's shilling. Now, by taking this shilling, with the king's picture on it, you pledge yourself to serve His Majesty, in whatsoever capacity he may choose to use you, for whatsoever period he may choose to employ you. In exchange you will be fed, housed, equipped, transported, and provided many fine opportunities for enrichment and advancement." He held the shining coin up between them. "Do you accept this shilling?"

Arabella swallowed. It was a terrific commitment. Not only was war ongoing with both Bonaparte and the Americans, but French privateers swarmed the airlanes between Earth and Mars—joining a warship could put her into the thick of the fighting.

But she had to do it. It was her foolish tongue that had put the notion of Mars into Simon's head, and now she was the only one who could stop him from carrying out his fiendish plan, save Michael's life, and preserve her family fortune.

She closed her eyes, took in a breath. "I do, sir."

At that the lieutenant broke into a broad smile. "Then welcome to the Aerial Service of His Majesty's Navy." And with his thumb he flipped the coin toward her.

But though Arabella reached for it, she did not catch it. For a stranger's hand—lean, dark, and swift—darted from the dimness behind her and snatched the spinning coin in midair.

6

CAPTAIN SINGH

"What the d—l!" shouted the lieutenant at the interloper, raising a fist in anger. "This is the king's business!"

Arabella turned. The coin had been snatched by a tall, lean foreigner in a buff coat. "I have been chasing this man for over an hour," he declared in a clipped, precise accent. Though he was breathing hard, and his face shone with perspiration, somehow he managed nonetheless to give an impression of imperturbable calm. "I desire him for my crew, and wish to present my case to him before he makes his final decision."

Arabella gaped at the stranger in astonishment.

"You're too late," the lieutenant sneered. "He's already taken the king's shilling."

"This shilling?" The stranger held it up and grinned, his teeth showing very clean and white against the dark brown of his skin, and Arabella realized that she had seen the man before: He had been the customer at the automaton shop. "It seems that it is I who has taken it. But, sadly, I am disqualified for your service, so I must return it to you." He handed the shilling back to the lieutenant.

The lieutenant refused to take the proffered coin. "He accepted the conditions of service," he growled.

"Such acceptance is not final until he takes his oath before a magistrate." The stranger turned his attention to Arabella. "Are you aware that you could be earning two or three times as much aboard a Marsman as you could in the navy?"

"Navy pay's not much," the lieutenant admitted. "But there's prizes for captured ships! One action could make you rich!"

"Possibly. Eventually. But the navy will withhold your pay until you return home, however long that may be. If ever."

Arabella looked back and forth between the two men. Whom should she trust, the red-faced English officer or the well-spoken foreigner? Or should she run from them both?

The lieutenant might be a good English seaman, but he stank of rum and his uniform coat was filthy and disheveled. The foreigner in the buff coat of a Mars Company ship's officer, meanwhile, had the calm cool bearing of a gentleman . . . even an aristocrat.

"Furthermore," he continued, "the navy may chain you into your hammock in port, as a deterrent against desertion."

"Don't listen to him!" the lieutenant roared. "Foreign b——d will say any thing to get a good English seaman. Marsman? Go with him and you'll wake up halfway to Shanghai, and never see a penny!"

The stranger drew himself to his full height. "I am a captain in the service of the Honorable Mars Company, and I will not stand for any more such insults!"

The lieutenant's mouth curled into a snarl, and Arabella realized that he was very likely about to say something that might lead to fisticuffs.

And if these two men fought, her chance for Mars on either of their ships might very well be the victim.

"Is that true?" she asked the lieutenant, all in a rush. "About chaining men into their hammocks in port?"

He hesitated before responding, his gaze darting from the stranger to Arabella. "Absolutely not," he said eventually, but his vehemence had died away.

Arabella knew a lie when she heard one. She turned to the foreigner. "And your ship, sir, is she a fast one?"

The man grinned broadly. "The very fastest, sir."

Arabella looked from one man to the other, considering, then returned to the foreigner. "I do not believe I have had the pleasure," she said, and extended her hand. "Arthur Ashby, sir, of Oxfordshire."

"Captain Prakash Singh of the Mars Company airship *Diana*," he replied, and took it.

––––––––––––––

"You said you had been chasing me for an hour?" Arabella said to Captain Singh as they walked down the street toward the docks, leaving the ranting lieutenant behind.

"Indeed I have, sir," the captain replied, stepping around barrel-toting stevedores as neatly as a debutante at a ball. "Ever since you left Clarkson's Clockworks. And quite a merry chase you led me, sir. If I had not by chance encountered a man with a very long scarf, of whom, as it happens, you had asked directions, I would have lost you completely." His head waggled from side to side on his neck, neither rotating nor tilting . . . a rather disturbing motion that Arabella had never seen any one perform before, and whose meaning she did not know. "That man Clarkson is an ignoramus. All the automata in his shop are built by others; he himself understands only how profitably they may be sold. You are not the first to identify the flaw in the automaton artist's work, and receive nothing but scorn for your sharp eye." The captain stopped walking, and perforce Arabella did as well, not knowing where she was being led. The captain looked down at her with a steady gaze. "You are, however, the first I have seen to identify the source of the problem and suggest a solution."

His deep brown eyes were so filled with intense intelligence that Arabella had to drop her gaze. "It was obvious, sir."

"And there we have it," the captain replied, and set off again. Arabella had to hurry to keep up with his long-legged stride. "This ragged boy who sees so easily what others not only miss, but deny." He contemplated Arabella for a moment. "Where is it that you were educated? I cannot place your accent."

"My father has a plantation in . . . in the country, sir, quite far from town. He taught me himself, mostly." In point of fact, Father had shared with her only his interest in automata. As far as formal schooling, Father had taught only Michael, leaving Arabella to be educated by her mother. But her *itkhalya*, Khema, had taught her much on the subject of Mars and Martians, constantly questioning and prodding her to greater comprehension. "I also had a . . . tutor."

"I myself, despite the many tutors provided by my own father, am mostly self-taught in all areas of significance." Again he waggled his head in that unusual way. "In any case, after you departed, I paused and inspected the malfunctioning device, and satisfied myself that you were correct. So I said to myself, this is exactly the man I need for my crew, and I sought you out."

Arabella could barely believe her luck. "You would take me on as a member of your crew? To *Mars*?"

"Subject to certain qualifications," he replied.

Arabella swallowed. "I must confess, sir, that I can neither reef nor hand nor steer, whatever those things may be."

"These things can be learned. However, the Company imposes strict standards for its airmen, so I may not bring you aboard with that status. Would you object to the title of captain's boy?"

Arabella was keenly aware just how much she did not know about naval titles and the running of a Mars-bound merchant ship. "I suppose not."

"In any case, those are not the qualifications to which I referred. Ah, here we are."

They rounded a corner. There, floating serenely in the Thames beneath three enormous white balloons, lay the largest and most beautiful airship Arabella had ever seen.

On her stern was painted and gold-leafed the name *Diana*.

On several occasions Arabella had visited the shipyards at Fort Augusta on Mars with her father, to observe at first hand the construction and fitting-out of airships built from the wood of his plantation. This *Diana* was at least a third again longer and broader than any she had seen there; her single visible mast towered more than a hundred feet in the air, and each of her three globular balloons loomed at least as large. Tiny airmen swarmed over the gleaming white balloons, clinging to the netting stretched taut over each one.

The ship's lacquered *khoresh*-wood gleamed honey-blond in the afternoon sun. Beneath the quarterdeck at the stern end, closest to Arabella, a broad, paned window spanned the width of the ship; behind this window, she knew, lay the captain's cabin. The wood of the stern to either side of this window was fancifully and dramatically carved with allegorical figures: on one side the goddess Diana, of course, with her quiver of arrows and her dog, and on the other side a leaping stag. These were tastefully accented with gold leaf and highlights of red and black paint, which only served to emphasize the natural beauty of the wood.

Arabella and the captain walked out onto the dock nearest the ship, where five airmen immediately leapt to attention. One, a boy younger than Arabella in a buff coat like the captain's, directed them with shouted commands; the other four, burly men in matching flat caps, first stood ramrod-straight with oars held high, then descended with alacrity into a small boat tied up at the dock's end. "Take us across, Mr. Binion," the captain said to the young officer, and with smooth dignity he too climbed down into the boat.

Arabella herself took what seemed like forever to make her way down into the pitching, bobbing little craft, finally succeeding only with the little officer's assistance. His smug, cocky smile at Arabella's discomfiture did not endear him to her, but she supposed that in time she too would learn to bound with swift assurance from dock to boat.

"Out sweeps," the little officer cried once the captain and Arabella were seated, and with swift strong motions the four airmen rowed toward the anchored airship. They seemed eager, disciplined, and well-fed, with the enormous thighs and calves typical of their profession matched by broad bands of muscle twining across their backs and down their arms as they stretched out and pulled. They moved in easy unison, the rhythmic commands of the officer seeming to acknowledge rather than to direct their actions.

Surreptitiously, Arabella also inspected the captain, who sat beside her, facing forward as she was. He was an odd sort, a foreigner in command of an English ship, with his own distinct accent. In some ways he was even farther from home than she was. She watched his eyes as the boat rowed across the water, rocking with each surge of the oars. Even as the boat tilted with each strong stroke, his eyes stayed level and fixed on the windows of the captain's cabin.

Something of great interest to the captain lay within. Something that consumed his entire attention. But what?

The boat came up alongside *Diana's* bows, rippling with the sun that sparked from the river water. The ship's bowsprit lay nearly horizontal, rather than being steeply raked like the seagoing ships nearby, and her figurehead was another carving of Diana, with her quiver across her shoulder and one arm outstretched, holding a bow and a pair of arrows. Unlike the crude little figures she had seen on some other ships, this figurehead was larger than life and very finely carved. Diana's eyes seemed full of intelligent intensity, like her captain's.

As they approached the ship, the captain seemed to quiver with . . . no, it could not be fear. Suppressed excitement. But he said nothing, and Arabella did likewise.

"Ahoy the boat!" came a cry from the forecastle.

"*Diana!*" replied the little officer. His voice piped even higher than Arabella's, but it carried across the waves with a power and a degree of gravitas far in excess of the boy's size. It was a type of voice, she thought, that she would do well to emulate.

Two boys scrambled down *Diana's* side to steady the boat and assist Arabella to board; the captain, of course, required no such assistance. As his foot touched the deck, the bosun's pipe sounded a tune and all the men present snapped smartly to attention.

The captain might be a foreigner. His coat might be Mars Company buff, rather than Navy blue. But he was still a ship's captain—he might as well be a god in his little world, once under way—and clearly well respected and obeyed by his men. And this man wanted Arabella for his crew? Again she was overwhelmed by her good fortune.

"Leak test on the envelopes complete, sir," said another officer, this one a grown man with wide feathery side-whiskers. Arabella would need to learn quickly how to understand the ranks and responsibilities of the ship's officers from the details of their coats. "Two leaks found and patched."

"Excellent work, Mr. Kerrigan. I will forgo inspection at this time. You may strike the envelopes at your discretion. Is all in readiness for departure at first light?"

"Aye, aye, sir!"

"Very well. Send the call for inflation at eight bells, set the ballast for rising trim, and dismiss the boats . . . all save one." He looked at Arabella. "We might need to return this one to shore, if he does not meet qualifications."

Arabella gulped.

———————————

The man the captain had just spoken to turned and bellowed, "Strike the envelopes!" This command was echoed and reechoed down the length of the ship, sending men scurrying up ropes and swarming across the vast balloons that loomed overhead like great lowering clouds. But Captain Singh paid them no mind, instead leading Arabella toward the stern and down a narrow set of stairs.

They emerged in the captain's cabin. The afternoon sun streamed in through the broad, paned window she had observed from out-side, illuminating a space that combined luxury with cramped conditions and odd materials. Fine brass fittings gleamed every-where, including lamps of a peculiar design fixed to the *khoresh*-wood walls, but most of the furniture was woven of wicker or rattan; the ceiling beams were so low that even Arabella had to duck, and the captain bent over nearly double. But clearly he had long experience with the situation, as he somehow contrived to move about the cabin with the same long-legged grace he displayed in the streets outside.

The captain moved to a figure seated near the window, silhou-etted against the bright light from outside. Despite the man's large and rather outlandish hat, Arabella had failed to notice him at first, so quiet and still was he. "How do you do?" she said, and slightly raised her cap. But to this greeting the seated figure made no reply.

The captain chuckled slightly. "He does well, Mr. Ashby, quite well indeed." He reached over and turned up the wick of one of the lamps.

The seated figure was a Turk, dressed in the most extraordinary garb of that nation, complete with a silk turban, flowing sleeves, and a red waistcoat embroidered with metallic thread and spangled with sequins and tiny mirrors. But as he turned to face Arabella, she found his motion even more extraordinary.

The Turk's head tilted, his surprisingly bright green eyes glittering in the lamplight as he silently regarded Arabella. Then his entire upper body rotated as a unit, starting suddenly, turning with a smooth uniform motion, then halting just as abruptly.

He was an automaton!

Arabella approached more closely. Never had she seen an automaton so lifelike. Its face and hands, painted in dark but quite natural-looking skin tones, included eyelashes and lacquered fingernails. Its chest rose and fell in a very convincing and subtle simulacrum of breathing. And its eyes, which she saw now were finely crafted of glass, seemed to be inspecting her carefully. "It is amazing," she breathed.

The automaton inclined its head in seeming acknowledgement.

Startled, Arabella looked to the captain, and saw that he had one hand on a bank of levers on the side of the desk at which the automaton sat. She chuckled nervously, acknowledging that she had been taken in by the trick.

Bending to inspect the desk, she saw that the automaton was not merely seated at it, but was built into it. The desk, which was mounted on small wheels, enclosed the entire space which would normally hold the user's chair, and the automaton's legs merged into the desk at that point. He seemed to be a sort of centaur— half Turk, half desk. The desk's *khoresh*-wood top was bare and smooth except for a regular grid of small holes, one per inch; all four of its sides were completely covered with brass levers, ivory pointers, and wheels displaying numbers and letters. "May I see inside?"

The captain smiled broadly. "Not one person in ten chooses that as his first question." He snapped open a pair of catches, then swung one of the complex side panels aside.

Revealed within was a dense array of gears, cams, springs, rods, levers, and wires, many of them ticking and twitching in regular motion. So many parts, so closely packed, that Arabella feared she would never be able to understand what they all did. She leaned in close but kept her hands behind her, and even breathed shallowly through her nose, for fear of damaging the delicate mechanism.

"You see that cam there?" the captain said, pointing at a bit of brass the size of a sovereign, shaped rather like a comma.

"Yes . . ."

"What is its function?"

Arabella began to protest that she had no way of knowing, but the pressure of the captain's gaze closed her mouth. Instead, she peered closer.

The indicated item was clearly built to pivot around a shaft that pierced its center, the two being joined together by a small set-screw, and a thin finger of brass at the cam's edge would cause it to rotate. No, on second thought, it would not. . . . The angle was wrong, and the brass finger too fragile. It must be instead that the *shaft* rotated, causing the finger to move as the cam's curved edge turned. Tracing the finger with her eyes, she saw that it attached to a wire which tugged on a cylinder painted with numbers. "When the shaft rotates," she said, "the cam causes that lever to move, which makes the numbers change."

"What happens when the shaft turns clockwise ten times?"

Arabella chewed her lip as she stared into the gleaming mechanism. "The number increases by one."

"And when it turns anticlockwise ten times?"

She opened her mouth to provide the obvious answer—that the number decreased by one—but then looked closer. The numbered cylinder's edge was notched, and a small pawl with a spring would drop into each notch as the cylinder rotated. "Nothing. It only goes one way."

"Very good."

"But what is it *for*?"

"That is what is known as an arithmetic accumulator. It is a very useful component in the calculation and display of trigonometric operations."

Arabella blinked, sitting back on her heels. "No, I mean the whole machine." She gestured, taking in the half-Turk and the desk, packed with clockwork, at which it sat. "What does it *do*?"

"He is our navigator," the captain replied, and swung the panel shut over the fascinating, ticking mechanism. "Many airships employ clockwork navigators, but Aadim is the finest, most complex, and most accurate of any in the Company's fleet." He lay a proprietary hand on the automaton's shoulder. "Aerial navigation is far more complex than its Earthly equivalent on sea or land, having six cardinal directions rather than four. In addition to north, south, east and west, with which you may be familiar"—as he spoke, he pointed up, down, left, and right—"we have sunward and skyward." For *sunward* he pointed behind himself, to where the sun shone through the window, and for *skyward* he pointed in the opposite direction, toward the cabin door. "Add to that the vagaries of the interplanetary atmosphere, with winds of up to ten thousand miles per hour which may come from any of those six directions with little warning, and the fact that our ports of departure and destination are moving relative to one another, and I hope that you can understand how much of a help a first-rate navigator can be. It is Aadim who is responsible for *Diana*'s well-deserved reputation as the fastest ship in the Company's fleet. And, if you will accept the lowly position of captain's boy, I would like to train you in his operation and maintenance."

Suddenly the intellectual game that Arabella had been playing, herself against the gears and wheels, fell away and she remembered the true stakes in play. Her mouth went dry. "You will take me to Mars? And allow me to leave the ship when we arrive?"

"I will take you to Mars," the captain replied solemnly. "And, unlike the navy, the Honorable Mars Company does not indenture its men indefinitely. Though I do hope that you will return to the ship voluntarily, as most of my men do."

Arabella swallowed. "Then I will accept your offer."

"I am most delighted." They shook hands, Arabella's pale moist palm enveloped by the captain's long dry dark fingers. "The work is hard, but I believe that you will find it rewarding."

7

DIANA

Leaving the navigator, they returned to the deck. The three huge balloons had vanished from the sky above the ship; instead, acres of billowing Venusian silk lay on the deck, lines of airmen chanting a rhythmic work song as they heaved and folded the fabric into a box the size of a carriage.

"Envelopes struck, sir," said the same officer who had greeted them as they boarded, touching his forehead with a knuckle. "They'll be stowed shortly. Furnace-men will be by at eight bells, and the harbormaster's cleared us for departure."

"Very good, Mr. Kerrigan. Ashby here will be joining the crew, so you may dismiss the last boat." He turned to Arabella. "Unless you have some possessions on shore to retrieve?"

Arabella swallowed. "No, sir."

"I had thought as much. Welcome aboard, Ashby." The captain turned to Kerrigan. "He will be serving as captain's boy. Have Faunt show him where to stow his hammock." Then he turned away.

"Excuse me, sir—"

"Pipe down!" Kerrigan cried, and with a start Arabella shut her mouth. "You'll speak only when spoken to!"

But the captain turned back. "That is the general rule, but as you have come aboard at my particular request I will make an exception"—he held up one long lean finger—"in this one instance. Be aware, though, that I treat all my people equally and fairly, and you will not receive any special dispensation in future. Now what is it that you wished to say?"

Arabella had a thousand questions, but just one leapt to the forefront of her mind. "Why *me*, sir?"

The captain regarded her levelly for a moment. "An excellent question, Ashby. You are untrained, pale, weak, and spindly. However, very few men show the affinity for automata that I have seen in you this day. In this one area, I believe you have exceptional promise. And also, very significantly, Aadim likes you."

Arabella blinked as the captain turned away. Was he *serious*?

What kind of ship had she just signed on to?

"Pass the word for the captain of the waist," Kerrigan said to one of the airmen nearby, who immediately scurried off. He then stood with his arms folded behind his pristine uniform coat, inspecting Arabella coolly. Not knowing what else to do, she stood where she was, following the officer with her eyes as he paced around her.

"Eyes front!" he bellowed suddenly. Wide-eyed, she stared straight ahead, reduced to listening as the booted footsteps plodded steadily around behind her.

"Captain's boy, eh?" he said. "Never had one of them before. Perhaps the captain's getting soft in his old age." By now he had come around in front of her again. "How old might you be?"

She paused, uncertain, but eventually decided that it must be acceptable to answer a direct question. "S-seventeen, sir."

"Old for a boy. I hope you're up to it." He crossed his arms on his chest, seeming to look down at her though they were nearly the same height. "You'll be the most junior, lowest-ranked, lowest-paid member of the entire crew. Except and unless you are engaged in some specific task assigned to you by the captain—and there'll be no shirking on that score—you'll do whatever any one senior to you tells you to do. And that's *any* one, even the cook. *Especially* the cook. You'll clean, polish, mend, and paint. You'll fetch and carry. You'll kindle the fire and keep it going. You will do your turn at the pedals, oh yes you will. And if you are very, very fortunate, you may be allowed to haul on a line from time to time. D'ye understand?"

Trembling, Arabella nodded fractionally.

"The correct response is 'aye, aye, sir.'"

"Aye, aye, sir," she barely squeaked out.

Just then an airman appeared, knuckling his brow to Kerrigan. "Ah, Faunt," the officer said, all cool professionalism again. "This is Ashby. He's just joined the crew as captain's boy. He'll be messing with the waisters; please be so good as to get him situated. Ashby, this is Faunt, the captain of the waist." He paused, considering Arabella for a moment. "I wish you luck."

"Aye, aye, sir." It was the only thing she knew to say.

Mr. Faunt was an older fellow, weathered and gray-bearded, with a knitted watch-cap pulled low over his eyes. "Ashby, is it?" His hand, hard and brown and seamed from sun and wind, had a grip seemingly capable of crushing a pewter tankard into a wad of scrap.

"Aye, aye, sir," she replied, wincing.

"None of that guff," Faunt said, and set off down the length of the ship. "I work for a living."

Arabella scrambled to follow. "How shall I address you, then, sir?"

"Faunt will do." He glanced over his shoulder at her. "Awfully high-spoken for a ship's boy, ain't ye?"

She had no reply to that.

"Ye'd best watch yer mouth around the men," the airman continued. "Most of 'em don't take so kindly as I to one who puts on airs."

"I shall do my best." She swallowed the *sir* that tried to follow.

They had to pause while a gang of men ran past, bearing a large crate. "Ye've never served on an airship afore, have ye?"

"No, I have not. I mean, I haven't."

"That way's fore," he said, pointing to the front of the ship. "Aft. Starboard. Larboard. Aloft. Below."

"Six directions," she muttered.

"Eh?"

"Nothing."

Faunt led her forward and down a narrow stairway—"This here's the fo'c'sle, and we call this a ladder"—to a tiny cupboard where Mr. Quinn, the ship's purser, had her sign the ship's muster-book.

Most of the other crewmen had marked nothing more than an X. Mindful of Faunt's advice not to put on airs, she simply printed the name "Arthur Ashby" in a plain, unadorned hand.

"Welcome aboard, Ashby," the purser said. "Now, d'ye have a hammock?"

"No, sir."

The purser tut-tutted and opened a cabinet. "Here's a hammock for ye." He tossed her a wadded ball of canvas and rope half the size of her torso. As she struggled to untangle the ungainly thing, he examined her coldly. "And those slops'll never do."

"Slops?"

"Clothes," Faunt clarified.

"Here's the scran-bag." The purser handed her a heavy canvas bag, which stank of mildew and unwashed airmen. "Take what you need."

With Faunt's help, she found a pair of duck trousers, a shirt, a kersey jacket, and a knit cap that would fit her slightly better than the ones she'd stolen. "These'll do ye as far as Mars," Faunt said, "in this season. Ye'll be wanting warmer later."

"Thank you."

The purser cleared his throat. "That'll be one pound, eight shillings, and ten pence."

Arabella goggled. Almost a pound and a half, for these malodorous rags? But before she could protest, Faunt poked her shoulder hard and gave her a warning look. She pushed down her indignation and instead confronted the simple reality of the price. "Um, I am terribly sorry, sir, but I haven't that much."

"No matter," the purser said with a shrug. "We'll take it out of your pay."

"Which would be . . . how much?"

"How old are ye?"

"Seventeen."

She should be getting used to that dubious look by now, but at least he did not question her statement. "Boy second class . . ." he muttered. He flipped through his muster-book and ran his finger down a column of figures. "Here we are. Eight pounds per annum."

Arabella gulped. "I see."

All she needed to do, she reminded herself, was to get to Mars before Simon.

———————————

Faunt led her from the purser's cubby and down another ladder to the lower deck, a long dark space crowded with cargo in crates and barrels. He pointed out hooks in the ceiling beams—"the overhead"—where she could hang her hammock. "Can ye read?"

"I can," she acknowledged. "And do my sums, and I've been tutored in French."

"Hunh," Faunt scoffed, giving her a sour eye. "Well, there's a number by each hook, d'ye see? Ye'll be number seventeen." But as she began to unfold the hammock, he held up a finger. "Not now."

Back up on deck, he showed her a long narrow shelf into which dozens of tidily rolled hammocks were crammed. "Stow it anywhere ye like. Just don't forget where."

She rolled up the hammock and shoved it in amongst the others. She would have to find some private place in which to change her clothing later. Which reminded her . . . "Where do we, um, do the necessary?"

"That'll be the head."

The "head" proved to be a filthy, odorous, dark, narrow space at the very front of the ship, just below the bowsprit, equipped with a variety of incomprehensible bars and handles fixed to the walls. She did not look forward to using this facility in any kind of foul weather, but at least there was a tiny modicum of privacy.

She amazed herself by managing to change into her new clothes in the tiny, cramped space without smearing them with her own soil. "How do I look?" she asked Faunt when she emerged. "More like an airman?"

He did no more than grunt in reply. "Ye want yer old slops?"

She looked down at the small, pathetic bundle of stolen clothing that had seen her from Oxfordshire to London. In a way, it was her last tenuous connection to her old life . . . a life of ease, and boredom, and wealth, and stifling restriction.

A life which, if she did not prevent Simon from killing her brother, would be taken away from her mother and sisters as well as herself.

"No," she said, and handed the bundle to Faunt.

After a whirlwind tour of the rest of the ship, during which Arabella was exposed to more new airfaring concepts and words than she had any hope of absorbing, Faunt took her back to the lower deck, the place where she would be hanging her hammock. "Ye'll be messing with the waisters," he told her. "Which is to say, ye'll eat yer meals with them as works in the waist of the ship."

The space was completely transformed from the afternoon, when it had been unoccupied save for clouds of dust shaken down from the overhead by many trampling feet on deck. Now it resembled a boisterous public house, with airmen seated on every available box, barrel, and bag. Most of them were engaged in shouted conversation at the tops of their lungs; the rest busied themselves in eating and drinking from square wooden plates and rough wooden cups.

"This'll be yer mess," Faunt shouted in her ear, indicating a group of five men who sat holding empty plates. "This's Young, Hornsby, Snowdell, Taylor, and that's Mills. Ye'll eat with them every day. Where's Gosling?"

"He's mess cook today. Just got called up."

"Right. Men, this is Ashby."

They were all rough, surly-looking men, who regarded Arabella with what she considered a judging expression: not actively hostile, but not particularly friendly either. She felt as though she were a fresh horse that was just about to be broken. "Evening, sirs," she said, raising her cap.

Young, paradoxically, was the oldest, a thin pale man whose sunken, gray-stubbled cheeks betrayed a severe lack of teeth. But he smiled nonetheless. "Evening t'ye," he said, and the others did likewise, except for Mills, the black African, who merely nodded and handed her a plate.

Just then another man appeared, carrying a steaming covered bucket. "Fresh meat, boys!" he cried, to general sounds of delight.

"This'll be Gosling," Faunt explained. "Now I'll leave ye to yer dinner."

To Arabella's surprise, Gosling seated himself on a barrel facing away from the rest of the men. He placed the bucket between his legs, drew a large and well-used knife from a sheath tied to his leg, then leaned down into the bucket. After repeated sawing motions, he called out, "Who shall have this?" without looking up.

"Snowdell," said Young. Arabella noticed that he had a hand clapped across his eyes.

Snowdell, a muscular young man with a long plait of hair down his back, passed his plate to Gosling, who filled it with a cut of some kind of meat, a dollop of stewed cabbage, and a big wedge of bread. Snowdell immediately picked up the meat with his hands and began gnawing with vigor.

"Who shall have this?" Gosling called again, and again the blind distribution was repeated. Arabella came third, and Young last.

The whole process had been a kind of Punch and Judy parody of the way Arabella's father had always carved the Sunday joint for the family. "Why do you not look at the men as you cut their meat?" she asked Gosling after he'd turned around with his own plate.

"It'sh the fairesht way," he said, chewing a mouthful of meat, then swallowed. "No one knows who'll be getting each bit, so it's all even-like. And we each take our turn as mess cook, t' mix it up even more."

Arabella took a bite. The meat was tough, grayish, and had an unfamiliar flavor.

"Good, innit?" said Taylor, the youngest, a lean fair-haired fellow with tattoos all over his arms.

"I have never tasted the like," Arabella admitted neutrally. "What is it?"

"Horse, I think. And look a' this! Greens! An' fresh bread!" He tore off a hunk of bread with his teeth and chewed noisily. "Enjoy it while you can—once we leave port it'll be naught but salt beef, salt pork, and ship's biscuit."

Arabella did her best to enjoy it.

"Ye've not touched yer grog," Young said. "I'll take it, if ye don't want it."

Every one laughed heartily at that, though Arabella had no idea why. To be polite, she grinned and took a sip from her cup.

The drink was not nearly as bad as she had feared—a little sour perhaps, a little bitter, but actually quite nice after a day spent running around in the sun. She was sure she would appreciate it even more once she really started working. She took a deep refreshing draught.

Then she noticed the sensation of warmth spreading down her throat and through her stomach.

At her expression the men all laughed again. "What is *in* this?" she asked.

"Four parts water, one part good Navy rum, and a bit of lime juice," said Young. He raised his cup to her and drained it off.

Four to one . . . this stuff was nearly as strong as Madeira! And her father had only let her have a sip of that at Christmas! "Is there any thing else to drink?"

"You can have it with small beer instead of the water."

"Oh."

She would have to be careful. If she allowed herself to become at all tipsy, her secret would surely be undone.

———————

After dinner, Arabella was sent to the kitchen, which was called the "galley," to clean up—a greasy, smelly, backbreaking task. The cook, a one-legged man called Pemiter, took what she felt was entirely too much pleasure in having someone who ranked even lower than himself to order about, and by the time she was finished scrubbing the last wooden plate she was nearly dead with fatigue.

The sun had already set when she emerged from the galley, and the lights of London shimmered in the Thames. Carriages with their lanterns clopped across a bridge nearby.

She took a moment to regard the view before searching for her hammock. London! How she had wondered what that shining capital city might be like, reading a book by the fire before bedtime in the manor house at Woodthrush Woods. And now here she was, about to depart it, having seen practically nothing of it.

She wondered when, or if, she would see it again.

Then, suddenly, she remembered that, despite her best intentions, she had not sent word to her mother about her situation. A sharp pang of guilt ran through her at her preoccupied self-absorption.

Though the deck was nearly deserted, one elderly airman sat quietly nearby, smoking a pipe. "Excuse me, sir," she said to him, "but might there be any way for me to mail a letter before we depart?"

The man glared from beneath his wild, gray brows, seemingly annoyed at her polite query, and she realized she had forgotten her station and slipped into an inappropriately elevated diction. She would have to take care not to do that again. "Last boat's already gone," he grunted, and turned away.

Her eyes threatened to spill over with tears, and she wiped them quickly with her rough sleeve. But now there was nothing to be done about it.

The lights of London suddenly seemed ten thousand miles away.

The hammock was right where she had left it, alone on the shelf. She gathered it up and returned belowdecks, which had again transformed itself in her absence. All lights had been extinguished, but as her eyes grew accustomed to the dark she perceived that the space was now filled with dozens of bundles—airmen in their hammocks—slung from the overhead beams. Many snored with great vigor; a few engaged in low, muttered conversation.

Ducking beneath the sleeping men, she made her way to the space she had been told was hers. And, indeed, though the room was too dark to read the numbers, she found a pair of unoccupied hooks in the right place, with nearly a foot and a half of space clear between the snoring bundles to either side. Standing on a barrel, she looped the ropes of her hammock over the hooks.

Getting herself into the hammock was another problem altogether. She found herself nearly glad of the close press of bodies, for without them to lean on she would certainly have tumbled unceremoniously to the floor—or "deck"—below more than once. As it was, she was forced to apologize repeatedly to those she had jostled.

Finally she found herself, fully clothed, settled and stable in the hammock's tight embrace, and tried to sleep. But, tired though she was, the sound and movement of so many men sleeping nearby, not to mention their warmth and smell and the rocking motion of the ship, were too unfamiliar and sleep refused to come.

Had it really been just five weeks since that horrible blackbordered letter had arrived? The time since then seemed an eternity crowded with dreadful people, hideous food, filth, stink, and endless wearying labor.

And she would never see her beloved father again.

Lying in the swaying, odorous darkness, Arabella wept.

2

IN TRANSIT, 1813

8

DEPARTURE

The next thing Arabella knew, she was being roughly shaken awake. Heart pounding, she immediately sat up, determined to get the better of her assailant.

But it was her hammock that got the better of her. As soon as she sat up, it turned over and dumped her unceremoniously on the hard and filthy deck.

Shaking her head, spitting out sawdust, she struggled to her feet and raised her fists. But there was no assailant. Instead, the pitch-dark deck was crowded with airmen, yawning, stretching, and scratching themselves with vigor.

"Out or down, lads!" came an enthusiastic cry. "Rise and shine! Cosmic tide waits for no man!"

Lamps guttered to life down the length of the hold, helping every one to find his way as he took his hammock down and rolled it into a tight little bundle. Arabella, blinking, did her best to follow their example, but her hammock wound up little more than an untidy tangle of rope and fabric.

Once the hammocks were stowed on deck—it was a chill morning, the sun not yet risen and the city lights mostly extinguished—and most every man had taken his turn at the head, they all returned below and divided into their messes for a breakfast of porridge oats and good strong tea. Famished, Arabella shoveled more than half of her oats into her stomach before she realized they were actually quite tasty.

Arabella again drew clean-up duty in the galley. Though the one enormous pot was heavily encrusted with oats, cleaning it or "hogging it out" was not nearly as bad as the previous night's cabbage and horsemeat. And the cook let her have a small portion of raisins left over from the officers' breakfast.

As she came out on deck, munching her raisins and watching the eastern horizon begin to lighten, Arabella mused that perhaps this life was not as bad as all that.

———————————

"Ahoy the boat!" came a cry to Arabella's left. From across the water came the reply, "Furnace-men!" She turned to see, making its way across the Thames in the pale light of the rising sun, a most extraordinary sight.

A huge boat, very wide and shallow, was being rowed toward *Diana* from the riverbank by two dozen grunting, heaving men. At the center of the boat, swiveling atop a sort of plinth, was a barrel the size of a hogshead, closed with a lid at one end, and at the other . . .

An enormous canvas tube, three or four feet in diameter, stretched from the bottom of the barrel down to the water on the far side of the boat. From that point the tube, bulging and trembling as though it were stuffed with fidgeting mice, floated on the Thames from the boat all the way back to the bank, where it entered a gaping door in the sea-wall. Above that door loomed a square brick building, atop which four huge chimneys belched out vast quantities of smoke.

Arabella gaped at the extraordinary craft. The laboring oarsmen were all black with coal-dust, and the grime on their faces was streaked with sweat though the morning air was quite chill.

She understood why as the boat drew alongside and was made fast to *Diana* with stout cables. Once the boat was secured, the oarsmen unscrewed the lid from the barrel . . . and a great wind, hotter than the sultriest August day and smelling of coal-smoke, roared from it with tremendous force. The canvas tube wilted slightly, yet so great was the rush of air that it remained mostly inflated. Arabella, fifty feet or more away, had to hold her cap on to her head with both hands.

Two men leapt down from *Diana*, bearing a similar canvas tube with them, and attached it to the open end of the barrel. At once the tube from the ship snapped taut, and the roar of wind from the open barrel was replaced by a thrumming through the deck beneath Arabella's feet.

A rough hand smacked Arabella's shoulder. It was Faunt, his expression stern. "Bear a hand, man!" he said.

"Aye, aye, sir!" she said without thinking.

The enormous box, the size of a carriage, into which the balloon envelopes had been stowed the previous day had been opened again, and from its top emerged a gradually inflating mass of Venusian silk. Glowing in the light of the rising sun, the three huge balloons resembled white fluffy clouds drifting in over some far horizon.

But they were not clouds, they were not fluffy, and they were not far. They were gigantic masses of fabric, as huge and ungainly as a thousand wet bed-sheets, and as the furnace-hot air began to fill them it took every bit of the entire crew's strength and skill to keep them from tangling with each other and with the net of silk ropes that caged them and tethered them to the ship. Light and smooth though the Venusian silk was, tugging and hauling on it soon left Arabella's hands red and sore and blistered.

An hour later, Arabella lay panting on the deck, watching the balloons as they firmed up and grew taut so high above her. The sun was well up now, and the bright white Venusian silk gleamed like a trio of full moons brought down to Earth. Unlike the previous day—when, she knew now, they had been filled only with cold air, to test for leaks—the balloons not only swelled against the constraining nets, but strained upwards as though desperate to reach the sky. The ship, too, seemed to feel the upward pull, riding high in the water and rocking in a new and unsteady motion bearing more kinship to the wind than the wave.

"Trim ballast and prepare to cast off!" came a command from the quarterdeck. It was Kerrigan, the chief mate, and was echoed, reechoed, and amplified down the length of the ship. Airmen sprang into action, many hurrying below, others hauling on ropes. Arabella had no idea what to do, but her messmate Young sat unmoving on the deck, so she did the same.

The ship began to shudder and lurch as Kerrigan called out command after incomprehensible command. Each one was repeated, or expanded into a series of other commands, by lesser officers, who relayed it to the airmen designated "captains" of the waist, the fo'c'sle, and other parts of the ship, who in turn directed their men to perform whatever task was desired. This Arabella knew in theory . . . in practice, it meant that she did whatever Faunt, the captain of the waist, told her to. And when, as was so often the case, she had no idea what his aerial gibberish meant, she could only watch the other members of her mess and try to do the same.

The captain stood beside Kerrigan, arms folded behind his back, the calm in the center of the storm of activity. He watched

every thing, though, and from time to time he would mutter softly
to Kerrigan, a word or two immediately translated into a fusillade
of shouted commands.

He had not spoken to Arabella once after handing her off to
Kerrigan. She hoped he had not forgotten her.

Now Kerrigan cried "Cast off the furnace-gut!" and the already feverish activity of the men grew still more agitated. Young
poked her elbow. "This'll be a sight," he said, and moved to the
rail. She followed, and with him she looked down at the gray
Thames where it lapped *Diana*'s hull. The ship was riding much
higher now, five feet or more of dripping *khoresh*-wood showing
above the waterline.

The furnace-men now unfastened *Diana*'s tube from their barrel, blasting Arabella with a gust of hot smoky air that rippled the
balloons high above, and put their oars in the water, backing
away from the ship with what seemed considerable haste. Two
of *Diana*'s airmen hauled the sagging tube from the water and
out of sight below the curve of her hull.

The ship seemed to pause. Arabella looked to the captain, whose
eyes scanned the length of the ship, seeking any fault or error or
she knew not what. Then he nodded briskly and spoke one word
to Kerrigan.

"Ballast away, fore and aft!" Kerrigan cried.

With a creak of wood and a great rumbling rush that made the
rail vibrate against Arabella's chest, several small ports opened in
the hull below her, each discharging a square column of frothing,
filthy water.

The whole ship trembled.

Then, suddenly, she burst aloft.

Arabella's stomach seemed to drop below her rope belt as the
ship flung herself into the air, and she found herself whooping
with surprise and excitement. So did all the other crew, a great
wild "Hurrah!" that echoed off the Thames rapidly receding
below.

Arabella leaned as far as she could over the rail. The river immediately below churned, a great ship-shaped roiling welt in the water showing the space *Diana* had just vacated. Water continued to pour from the ballast-ports; more water ran down the ship's sides, flowed along the keel, and fell in a great stream from the rudder.

In moments the ship rose as high as a tall house, as a church-steeple, as a soaring bird, giving Arabella a view she had never before even contemplated. The whole dockside area spread out below her like some huge and complex toy, the river crowded with boats and ships and barges. Nearby another airship was just filling its envelopes, the great tube running to the furnace-house on the shore seeming little larger than a shoelace.

Threads of smoke rose into the air—rose up *below* her!—from a hundred chimneys. A few early-morning promenaders and milk-men with their carts trod the streets, the horses looking absurdly like mice when seen from above. Some of the people waved hands or hats at the rising ship, and Arabella waved her hat at them in turn. Others ignored the miracle above them, plodding along head-down and oblivious. One fellow shouted and gestured rudely as a trickle of falling water cut across his courtyard.

As *Diana* rose higher, Arabella's view expanded. Now she could make out the great double curve of the Thames, as plain as any map. From here she could see not just the dockyards, but the crowded center of London: rank on rank of houses, shops, and great public buildings. That pencil laid across the Thames must be London Bridge! And the large building and park just to its north, Bedlam Hospital.

Diana's shadow sailed across Arabella's view. She followed it with her eyes, watching as it skimmed silently across streets, parks, and rooftops. Immediately surrounding it, panes of glass and puddles of water glinted the rising sun back into her eyes, ringing the airship's silhouette with a glittering halo of light.

The whole teeming metropolis was visible now, seething with

the motion of ten thousand early risers . . . maybe even a million. A great human anthill filled with busy workers.

A hand clapped onto her shoulder. "Impressive view, eh lads?"

Arabella looked back to see Faunt, his hands on her shoulder and Young's. Young stood at stiff attention, eyes staring rigidly ahead, and Arabella realized she might be in trouble. "Aye," she said in a neutral tone.

"Well, if *somebody* don't start shoveling coal pretty soon, we won't have that pretty view very much longer." Young seemed to wilt under Faunt's hand.

"I suppose that would be us, then?" Arabella asked.

"It would indeed. Now get below."

———————

Although the great blast of hot air provided by the furnace-gut had gotten *Diana* started, the air in the envelopes was already cooling, and a great quantity of coal had to be burned to keep the ship aloft. By the time their relief arrived, Arabella and Young were as grimy as the furnace-men and bone-weary from endless shoveling.

Arabella came out on deck after her mid-day meal, still sneezing and blowing black coal-dust from her nose, to find the world had fallen away from *Diana*, the ship hanging suspended in blue air scattered with white, fluffy clouds. The air around the ship lay still and clear, with a clean dry scent that brought to mind the high plateaus of the Kthansha region. A few birds flapped lazily nearby.

But when she peered over the rail, expecting an infinity of blue, her stomach dropped. The Earth lay far below, her curvature plainly visible.

Arabella had expected the planet to resemble a map, with continents and oceans easily distinguished, though she knew not to expect to see national boundaries. What she saw instead looked more like a huge, rounded globe of decorative glass, the blue of oceans swirled with white sweeps and streaks of cloud, the sun's light winking brightly off the clouds and sea so very far below. "Where's England?" she asked Young, who leaned exhausted on the rail beside her.

"My eyes ain't what they once was," he said, shading them as he peered downward. A moment later he pointed. "Y'see that big shiny white patch? That'll be the North Pole. And the terminator?"

"Which would be?"

"The line 'twixt dark and light. It's just past one bell, so you should look for England in the middle of the lit part, 'bout halfway down from the pole."

She peered and searched, but though she made out the shining threads of rivers and some areas of cloudless light brown that she thought must be deserts, she could not puzzle out the continents and countries.

Her failure disappointed and worried her. If she could not even find England with the globe spread out below her, how could she expect to understand aerial navigation? And if she failed at that, what would the captain do with her?

———

Just then the bosun's pipe trilled, and a voice cried out, "All hands on deck!"

All the men lined up, chivvied into untidy lines by the captains of their divisions and facing the quarterdeck. The captain waited there, looking out over their heads, peering into the distance beyond the figurehead.

When every one was reasonably settled, the captain stepped to the rail. "Who here has never sailed above the falling-line before?"

As Arabella had no idea what the falling-line might be, she remained silent. But Taylor, beside her, called out, "We've a new fish here!" and shoved her forward. She joined a group of some dozen or so nervous men, most of them older than herself, all peering about themselves with curiosity and concern; plainly none of them knew what was to come.

The captain held out an arm above the deck. In his hand he held a gold sovereign. "May I have a count, gentlemen?"

"Aye!" cried the assembled men.

The captain released the coin.

Slowly, slowly, glinting in the bright sunlight, the sovereign tumbled toward the deck some ten feet below. Arabella had never seen the like. Certainly nothing like this had occurred on the trip to Earth from Mars.

"One!" came the cry.

Gradually the falling coin began to gain in downward speed, still turning lazily over. It was now at the level of Arabella's eyes.

"Two!" the men chorused.

Still faster the coin fell.

"Three!" the men all cried, just at the moment the coin struck the deck. The sound of its impact was lost in a loud hurrah, and Arabella felt a hard shove between her shoulder blades.

"Get it get it get it!" came the cry from all around her, and Arabella and the rest of the "new fish" scrambled to catch the coin as it rebounded into the air. But though the sovereign rose as lazily as it had fallen, she found it nearly impossible to lay a hand on it, for her feet skidded without purchase across the deck and whenever she reached for the flying coin she found her hand passing half a foot or more away from it.

Great was the mirth of the assembled crew as Arabella and the other new men scrambled about after the coin, grunting and scuffling, colliding with each other. Despite the apparent ease of the task, the lot of them seemed incapable of the simple action of catching a falling coin.

It was the gravity, she realized. The ship had risen far enough from the Earth that her attraction was substantially reduced;

indeed, the gravitational attraction of Earth was now even less than the Martian gravity she had grown up with. She stopped and held herself still, observing the coin as it flew.

Every thing about the coin's movement was wrong. It moved too slowly, bounced too high after each impact with the deck. But if she placed her hand just *there* . . .

The spinning coin was just about to strike her open palm when another hand, the wildly flailing hairy-knuckled paw of a massive red-bearded Scotsman, happened to snatch it away. The Scotsman held the coin aloft to a general huzzah, and a golden mantle was placed upon his shoulders.

"Now, as to the rest of you," came Kerrigan's voice—and it had a nasty edge to it—"you line up along the larboard rail."

Arabella and the others were driven into line at the rail, where two of the burliest topmen waited with broad grins.

Just as Arabella realized she had been shoved to the front of the line by the other new men, the two brawny airmen grabbed her by her shoulders and hips and lifted her over their heads . . .

. . . then hurled her over the rail!

Arabella screamed. She could not have prevented herself from doing so any more than she could prevent her heart from beating. The scream was pulled from her lungs as though it were attached to the ship by a stout rope.

She tumbled end over end, sun and clouds and Earth and rail spinning dizzily all around her. What had been her crime, to deserve such a death?

And then the breath was driven out of her as she was caught up again by the same hands that had just released her. The two topmen hauled her back aboard, dumping her without ceremony onto the deck, and grabbed the man in line behind her. Despite his forewarning, he screamed nearly as high as Arabella herself as he was tossed over the rail. But so slowly did he fall that the topmen had no difficulty catching him again before he had descended more than two feet.

As she drew herself, trembling, to her feet, Taylor came over and thrust a cup of grog into her hand. "That weren't so bad, now, were it?"

She merely gave him a withering look.

He laughed and clapped her on the back. "Well, you're a real airman now in any event." He took a great draught of his own grog. "And the coin struck the deck just at the count of three."

Arabella sipped her drink, noting that the shaking in her knees was beginning to subside. "What does that mean?"

"It's a good omen, innit? Any less than three means the captain's too eager, wants to sway out before it's safe. Much more and he's being too cautious. But our Captain Singh always catches it right on the dot."

Again the bosun's pipe sounded. "All hands prepare to sway out!"

Taylor shrugged and drained his grog. Arabella took one last sip of hers and offered the remainder to him. "Much obliged," he said with a grin, and drained it as well.

Arabella and Taylor joined the other waisters at the starboard rail, where at Faunt's command they busied themselves untying a spare mast from where it was lashed at the ship's side. Why this should be needed she had no idea, as there was no sign of any problem with the ship's one standing mast.

"Clap on, lads!" Faunt cried as the mast, now fully released, began to roll downward, and they all bent down and held it against the ship with their hands. Though the force of gravity was greatly reduced, the mast was more than a hundred feet long and still pulled heavily against the men's grip. Arabella, with her spindly arms, felt as though she was barely contributing.

A cry came from above: "Ahoy the deck!" Arabella looked up to see a weighted line snaking down from the mast high above, where several topmen clung to the rigging. Faunt caught the end of the rope before it struck the deck, and proceeded to make it fast to the end of the spare mast. A second line shortly followed, and was affixed to the other end.

The entire crew, officers and men alike, now wrestled the mast away from the ship's side, tugging and hauling on the mast itself and the lines attached to it until it projected horizontally away from the ship, its thick end closest to the rail. "Lower away," Kerrigan cried.

Arabella now found herself one of a long line of men from every division, all hauling on a line that ran through a block at the masthead to the head of the spare mast, while another gang of men did the same for the mast's foot. Gently, inch by inch, they lowered the mast until it was well out of sight below the rail. Kerrigan, leaning over the rail and carefully observing the mast's progress, directed the two gangs with commands and hand signals. "Handsomely now," he said. "Steady . . . steady . . . ease up on the head a bit . . . that's well! Make all fast!"

While several of the men busied themselves fastening the two lines to the rail, Kerrigan peered about the deck, looking for Arabella knew not what. Then his eye fell on Arabella. "You're a scraggy little thing, you are. You'll do." He turned to the officer beside him. "Put this one in harness."

Another weighted line came hurtling down from the mast, and several men converged on Arabella. Before she knew what was happening, Arabella found herself with a loop of rope around each leg and another around her waist, hanging just above the deck. She'd been too busy keeping her softer parts away from their hands to wonder *why*.

Faunt pressed a wooden peg, the size of her arm, into her hands. "All ye need do is guide the mast-foot into the keelson-plate, then peg it in place with this fid." He clapped her shoulder. "Hoist away!"

Thoroughly baffled, Arabella felt herself hauled up into the air, then pushed sideways, past the rail, until she hung dizzily over nothing at all. The Earth gleamed far, far below, like a great glass marble floating serenely in the blue sky that lay all about.

Desperately she clung to the rope, which ran taut from the great knot at her navel to her collarbone, while trying not to lose the peg. "Lower away!" came the distant cry.

A moment later she saw what she was to do. The mast hung beside the ship, projecting downward at an angle, with its large end near a round, black hole in the lower curve of the hull. Barnacles and weed clung to the planks, and a few drops of river water still dripped from the hole's lower rim.

She was gently lowered until she was just next to the hole. "Is the mast in position?" came a faint voice from above.

"Two inches aft!" she called back as loudly as she could. Then, as the mast shifted, "One inch up! Not so much! Back a little! That's it!"

After a series of indistinct cries from the deck, the mast moved slowly toward the hole. At the last moment, though, she saw that it would need a little help, and gave it a shove with her foot.

It slipped right in. And kept going. Fully ten feet of the hundred-foot mast disappeared into the ship's hull before, with a deep wooden *thunk*, it bottomed out.

She looked up, grinning, to see Kerrigan cupping his hands to his mouth and calling down to her. "Belay the mast!"

Belatedly she remembered the peg still clutched in her arms. Swallowing with a mouth gone completely dry, she reached out with one foot and drew herself close to the seated mast.

A hole the size of her arm—the very size of the peg—had been drilled through the hull at an angle, where it met up quite tidily with a matching hole in the mast.

Clinging with her left hand to the rope, using her feet to steady herself, she shifted the peg to her right arm and began to guide the narrow end to the hole.

But just as it was about to slip in, a drop of water from the hull above fell *splat* into her eye. She gasped in surprise.

The peg slipped from her grasp!

Without thinking she reached for it. But the motion overbalanced her, and she turned topsy-turvy, swinging head-down over a thousand miles of empty air.

Spinning about its axis, the peg began to fall . . . slowly, but rapidly gaining speed.

Still hanging upside down, Arabella clung to the rope with her left hand and reached out her right to snatch the falling peg. But her initial motion had set her swinging, and it was now well out of reach.

Heart pounding, she tightened her grip on the rope. She was already beginning to swing back. She would have one chance to grab it before it fell away forever, probably to knock senseless some innocent on the planet below.

Slowly, slowly, she swung toward the falling peg, even as it tumbled Earthward.

As she reached the bottom of her swing, she reached for the peg and missed. "D—n it!" she cried, astonishing herself.

But the peg was not yet completely out of reach. Not quite.

She reached out her hand . . . she stretched her entire body as far as she possibly could . . . she extended her fingers to the utmost . . .

. . . and she caught it!

Here above the falling-line, even a spindly-shanked landsman such as herself had enough strength to pull herself vertical with one arm.

By the time she righted herself, she had swung back to the mast, which she caught between her feet. From here it was a simple matter to jam the peg firmly in place.

She looked up to see more than two dozen heads peering over the rail at her, gazing down in astonishment.

"Will that be all, sir?" she called up to Kerrigan.

Once hauled back on deck and untied from the harness, Arabella received a clap on the shoulder from Faunt and a grudging nod of acknowledgement from Kerrigan. She and the other waisters were then put to work on the other side, swaying out the larboard mast. This time she had no difficulty with the fid.

When Arabella returned to the deck the second time, she found it a hive of activity, with men and ropes and lengths of wood and huge swaths of Venusian silk running every which way. Arabella was immediately thrown into the maelstrom, helping to drag and haul and carry whatever was needed to wherever it was needed.

The topmen and riggers busied themselves like spiders, leaping over the rail and scrambling out to the end of each new mast with hundreds of feet of line—called "stays" fore and aft, "shrouds" to either side—to hold each mast firmly in place. They then rigged yards and booms, timbers set at a right angle to each mast, and attached sails to each. Hundreds more feet of ropes of various thicknesses, lines and sheets and halyards, were added to keep the sails taut and control their position and attitude.

"What's the great rush?" Arabella asked her messmate Hornsby as they lay gasping together during a brief lull. They'd been laboring without pause for hours and hours, though the sun had not budged in the sky.

In response Hornsby raised one weary arm and pointed silently forward.

Ahead and above lay a great curving bank of gray roiling cloud shot with lightning. Arabella had been so busy she'd failed to notice it before, but the ship was plainly heading directly toward it.

"She needs must be full rigged afore we round the Horn," Hornsby said.

Arabella swallowed, then roused her aching body to haul yet more rope and sailcloth.

9

ROUNDING THE HORN

"Ye'll be wanting this," Faunt said, handing her a loop of line. The end of the line trailed away behind him.

Arabella made fast the line she'd been hauling on and took the loop, but then stared blankly at Faunt. In his other hand he held the loop ends of several more lines, and he moved with the high bounding lope of one whose weight has been reduced to no more than a few pounds. "It's a safety line," he said, annoyed. "Cinch it tight round yer ankle when yer on deck. And remember: one hand for the ship, one for yerself. *Never* let go with both hands when we're rounding the Horn." He waved ahead at the surging gray maelstrom of cloud that now loomed above, below, and far to either side. Only behind the ship could pure blue sky be seen, and a bit of the Earth so very far below.

She raised one foot, bouncing lightly off the deck as she did so, and began fitting the loop around her foot. "But I have a question," she said before he could move away.

Faunt glared at her from beneath his profuse gray eyebrows.

"Why don't we just go around that storm?"

"'Cause we'd never get to Mars without it, would we?" he thundered. But at her stricken expression, his voice softened a bit. "Look, ye need a good hard kick to get on yer way. The trick is to catch the right wind with all sails set, then strike 'em all down afore it changes. Else ye'll just blunder about like a lubber, and take a year and a day to get to Mars."

"That doesn't sound easy." How would she ever manage to understand all of this?

"Don't be afeared. The cap'n's the best." Then his expression returned to its usual severity. "But every man jack must do **his job**. Now shake a leg."

"Aye, aye."

———————

Arabella shivered miserably in her hammock while the ship twitched and shuddered in every direction around her. Despite her exhaustion after an endless day of labor—a literally endless day, in which the sun never budged in the sky—and despite the dark and humid warmth of the belowdecks space, she found herself unable to sleep: the motion of the ship, the snores of the airmen close-packed all around, and the strange sensations brought on by lack of gravity were all too distracting.

Though the state of free descent was not completely foreign to her, as she had experienced it once before on the trip from Mars to Earth, it was still disquieting: her head felt stuffy, as though she'd caught a cold, and there was a dizzy sensation of falling at all times. At least she was not afflicted by aerial nausea, as some of the other "new fish" were.

There must have been a time when the gravity had fallen away to the point that it was equal to that of Mars. She must have been shoveling coal at that moment, she supposed, and she was sorry to have missed it, because it would have been a moment of familiarity in between the uncomfortable heaviness of Earth and the different discomforts of shipboard floating.

But at the moment, she felt unimaginably distant from any familiar thing, any comfortable place, any person who cared about her.

How she wished she had managed to send a letter to her mother! Though the two of them had often been at odds, she still felt tenderly toward her, and after Arabella's sudden and unexplained departure—and what story had Beatrice concocted to explain her absence?—Mother must be completely overcome with anxiety. And poor Fanny and Chloë would be entirely bereft.

Another gust, feeling like a hard shove on the end of her bed, made Arabella's hammock thrum like a low harpsichord string between the hooks on either end. They'd begun rounding the Horn some hours ago, and since then the ship had been nudged and jerked by capricious winds from every direction. Winds that had been steadily growing in strength.

The Horn, she had learned, was the airmen's term for the place where the daily-rotating atmosphere of Earth met the yearly-rotating interplanetary atmosphere, the two great masses of air grinding against each other like a pair of millstones. It was a place of constant turbulence, but as Faunt had explained, an experienced crew could make good use of the ever-shifting winds to send the ship rapidly in any desired direction. This pummeling wind was a *good* thing.

Then a sudden massive jolt hammered the ship, accompanied by a loud protesting groan of wood, and Arabella shrieked aloud.

"Shut yer yap!" cried a nearby airman. Arabella clapped both hands across her mouth, but the sensation of being pushed hard from one side and the creak of stressed timbers went on and on. A low whimper escaped from behind her hands.

Dear Lord, she prayed, *preserve me.*

With another loud and sudden jerk, the ship slewed upward,

then was slammed down. Each motion was accompanied by unexplained creaks, groans, and rattles from every direction. The
creaks and groans, she told herself, were nothing more worrisome
than the sounds of Marlowe Hall as the ancient house shifted in
a strong wind; *Diana* had made this passage many times and was
surely well built for it. As for the rattles, she supposed that a few
beans or nails might have slipped from a cask and were now rattling about the hold.

Then the ship jerked again, and Arabella stifled another scream
as a large dark rat scuttled along an overhead beam not two feet
from her face, its claws rattling on the *khoresh*-wood. The rat ran
nimbly along the beam's lower surface, apparently untroubled by
the lack of gravity.

Arabella squeezed her eyes tight and prayed harder, feeling
like a die in a cup being shaken by God in some enormous game
of backgammon.

Suddenly the hatch was thrown open, letting in a gust of wind
and throwing harsh and shifting light directly into her face. Her
eyes blinked open and then squeezed shut against the glare. "Rise
and shine, lads!" came the cry, which was greeted by groans from
the men. Had it really been four hours? She hadn't slept a wink.

Breakfast was a quick, cold bite of hard ship's biscuit, but Arabella
was glad of it—any thing hot or more substantial would have
been dangerous in the constantly shifting ship.

She came out on deck to find the ship embedded in bright,
thrashing cloud. All around the tempest roiled, white and gray
and black with not a trace of blue, here and there shot with occasional bursts of lightning. The sound of thunder was lost in the
constant rush of wind and groan of the ship's embattled structure.

"Ashby!" came a shout from the quarterdeck. It took Arabella a
moment to register the name as her own, and when she finally did

she saw it was Kerrigan who had called. He was waving pointedly at her and looking very cross in the harsh and shifting light.

Arabella checked that her safety line was well attached at both ends before working her way hand by hand along the rail to the aft end of the waist. All around her, more experienced airmen leapt from deck to mast to yard with hardly a care; many of them did not even wear safety lines like hers. Some day, she vowed, she'd be as brave as they.

"Yes, sir?" she called from the foot of the ladder when she reached it.

"The captain requests you bring him his tea!"

Tea? In this weather? But "Aye, aye, sir," was what she said.

She made her way down to the galley, where two of the other waisters were working the bellows that kept the stove alight. For some reason, the lack of weight made the fire go out. "The captain wants his tea," she told the cook, expecting a snide remark or possibly even a thrashing, but without a word of complaint the cook set to work, squeezing water from a huge skin—apparently made from a whole cowhide—into a stout iron kettle, which he twisted firmly into a fitting atop the stove to keep it from floating away. In minutes the kettle was boiling, the rumbling sound incongruously homely against the rush of wind and moan of timbers.

"Watch out, boys," the cook said to Arabella and the other two waisters. "This's hot." He twisted off the kettle's lid, then used a pair of wooden paddles to shepherd a seething, roiling glob of boiling water out of the kettle and into a plain white china teapot.

Arabella gaped in astonishment at the floating blob of water. For the cook to manage this dangerous, unpredictable fluid in a state of free descent, in the middle of a turbulent storm, was an amazing performance, and Arabella's respect for the one-legged old man suddenly grew tenfold.

The lid of the teapot also fastened with a twist, and the spout was plugged with a cork. "Get this up to the old man straight away," the cook said, thrusting the pot at Arabella. "He don't like it if'n it's too strong."

She drew in a sharp breath at the pot's heat, and juggled it from hand to hand. Were the cook's palms made of leather?

As she came up on deck with the teapot, Arabella held it to her chest with one arm—bunching up her shirt to keep the pot from burning her arm and side—so as to keep the other hand free. And she was most glad of that free hand as the wind assailed her, threatening to whip her away immediately; she clung to the guide ropes and shuffled along, not letting either foot leave the deck, for fear of being swept overboard.

Though there was no rain as such, the rapidly moving air was filled with stinging tiny drops of water, which half-blinded her eyes and made the footing treacherous. At least it was fresh, not salt.

At last she reached the quarterdeck, requested and received permission to ascend, and approached the captain with her steaming burden. But just as the captain was turning to face her, she felt a jerk on her ankle and fell forward.

The teapot flew from her hands, bounced once upon the deck, and sailed away into the roiling heavens. In moments it was lost to sight.

Furious and ashamed, Arabella looked behind herself to see what had tripped her. The young officer who'd led the crew that rowed her and the captain across from the dock to *Diana*— Binion, that was his name—stood nonchalantly by the rail, with his foot several inches from where her safety line snaked across the deck. But the line, she noted, extended dead straight from her to Binion, then curved away from his position, as though it had a moment ago been drawn taut by some force in his vicinity.

"Ashby," the captain said, and she snapped her attention back to him.

"Sir?"

"I requested you bring my tea to me," he remarked mildly, "not fling it over the side." But his face was very serious.

Arabella took a breath to explain herself, but the captain interrupted her before she could speak.

"On this ship, Ashby, we do not lay blame or make excuses. Each man must perform his duty. Upon occasion, circumstances intervene; in such a situation, we are judged by our ability to do what is required *despite* any obstacles. Do you understand, Ashby?"

Arabella swallowed her excuse and her pride. "Yes, sir."

"I am still waiting for my tea, Ashby."

"Aye, aye, sir." She turned, with as much dignity as she could muster in a state of free descent buffeted by winds from every direction, and hurried back to the galley.

As she passed Binion, he gave her a nasty, knowing smirk. "Captain's boy, eh?" he muttered, so low that no one else could have heard it. "Captain's *bum*-boy, more like it. It's clear you're no airman."

She glared hard at him, but though he was her junior by several years, he did outrank her and she dared not raise her voice to him.

He met her gaze with a nasty, knowing smirk. "Don't get above your station, bum-boy," he whispered. "You'll be smacked down, and don't think you won't. And don't go running to the captain neither."

She glanced quickly at the captain, who stood in conference with the other senior officers just as though they were not all floating in a near-weightless state. The captain's eyes met hers, and he flicked one finger in a clear gesture: *Go.*

She went.

And she'd show that snotty little Binion that she was too good to rise to his bait.

———

Days passed. As *Diana* drew further round the Horn, the constant buffeting of the winds grew stronger and even more capricious. The captain kept the topmen busy watch after watch, constantly raising and striking and adjusting the sails to catch the favorable winds and coast through the unfavorable ones.

When the wind was in *Diana*'s favor and all sails were set, life was calm; the ship seemed to simply drift along, the sails billowing gently and a mild breeze blowing across the deck from astern. But this seeming tranquility belied the ship's actual velocity, for she was embedded in a mass of moving air whose speed might exceed eight thousand knots.

But when the wind blew contrary, the captain struck all sails and *Diana* flew with bare poles, doing her best to glide through with the speed and heading she'd built up during the last favorable wind. Winds might come whipping in from any side, above, or below, and could shift dramatically at any moment. Even seasoned hands wore safety lines, and the men of the watch on duty scrubbed the deck or polished the brass with one eye on the weather. For at any moment a favorable breeze might pick up and the captain call all men aloft to set sail, or equally likely a new and even more inimical wind might suddenly begin to blow from another quarter, tumbling men set too firmly against the old wind over the side.

And then came the times when no wind blew at all.

These times were rare at the Horn. But when they did occur, *Diana* must needs move quickly and nimbly, lest she find herself becalmed in an atmospheric eddy, losing all the momentum she hoped to build up at the Horn for the long swing to Mars. Without that momentum, the voyage to Mars might take not just two months, but over a year . . . . a year for which the ship's stores of food and water would be sadly inadequate.

Arabella was filling and winding the lamps in the captain's cabin—a fascinating small clockwork mechanism advanced the wick and provided a draught to keep the flame alive—when the bosun's pipe sounded, followed by a chorus of voices: "Idlers and waisters to the pedals!" Sighing, she carefully capped and stowed the oil canister before reporting to her duty station.

As she arrived at her station belowdecks, pulling herself through the air hand over hand along the guideline, the other waisters had already cleared away most of the cargo from the ship's central line and opened the panels in the floor, exposing fifty or sixty wooden seats. Each "seat" was a hard, narrow, massively uncomfortable saddle, really nothing more than a board whose hard edges had been softened by years of pedaling thighs, and as Arabella raised her seat and locked it into place with a peg her legs and bottom began to ache preemptively. She could not imagine how men, whose natural equipment occupied the same space between their legs as the wooden seat, could possibly pedal without doing themselves serious injury, but somehow they managed.

Arabella positioned herself on her seat, tied herself into place with a stout cord across her lap, then slipped her feet into the pedals' leather straps and awaited the command to begin. All around her the other waisters and idlers—any one else who was not currently occupied in the handling of the ship—grumbled and sighed as they did the same. "Step lively, now!" Binion called from his station near the bow. "Time's a-wasting!"

Finally all the men were settled. "By the right," Binion shouted, "pedal!" The command was accompanied by a *thud* from the drum fastened to the deck before him, which he struck with a large wooden mallet.

Arabella grunted as she pressed hard with her right foot on the wooden pedal, the strain transmitting itself through her body to the stout horizontal rod she grasped in her hands. Most of the other pedalers grunted as well, but the sound was lost behind the groaning creak of wood and leather as the whole complicated system of cogged wheels and perforated leather belts beneath the deck moved complainingly into action.

A long, creaking moment later Binion called, "By the left!" and struck the drum again. Arabella and all the others leaned to the right as they pressed with their left feet, the awkward protesting pedals moving slowly in a circle beneath each man, returning to the point where they'd started. "Right!" and another drumbeat began the cycle again.

Before the pedals had gone around ten times Arabella was already streaming with sweat—sweat that in the close warm dark of belowdecks refused to evaporate, and which in a state of free descent did not even have the decency to run down her face. Instead, it clung to her forehead and temples and cheeks, stinging and blinding her eyes no matter how much she blinked and shook it away. Not that there was any thing to see here in any case. Grimly she set her jaw and pedaled, pedaled, pedaled to the incessant beat of the drum.

Beneath the deck, she knew, a series of creaking shafts and belts transmitted the force of the men's pedaling feet to the propulsive sails, or "pulsers," at the ship's extreme aft. These five triangular sails, unlike any others on the ship, turned in a circle like a windmill's blades, and somehow—Arabella didn't quite grasp the philosophical principle—rather than catching the wind that usually pushed the ship forward, they actually *created* a wind where no natural wind existed.

But the pulsers' wind, the product of mere human effort, was but a pale imitation of God's own wind, and for all the men's labor it pushed the ship at a comparative snail's pace. But still, from what Arabella had learned, it was better than drifting hopelessly, and after some hours or days of work might serve to move the ship from an area of calm into a favorable wind.

At least, that was the men's hope. Arabella had heard tales of ships thoroughly becalmed, crews pedaling day upon day for weeks, men dying of thirst and of cramp while fruitlessly praying for the faintest breath of breeze.

On and on the drum pounded, the men grunted, the pedals

creaked, the belts wailed like tortured cats. The carpenter and his men were kept busy anointing the many moving parts with grease, and from time to time a halt was called so that a broken or misaligned part could be repaired. The complex mechanism that transmitted the men's effort to the pulsers was balky and unreliable but, again, better than drifting hopelessly. Arabella gritted her teeth and tried to ignore the burning in her upper thighs.

And then—oh, God be praised!—a new sound intruded upon the dark and groaning space between decks, a faint whispering rush, and Arabella felt the ship shift with a new and tentative life that issued from a source other than her and the other men's pedaling efforts. A weak cheer sprang up at that, and a few men slacked off their labors, but Binion cursed them and pounded his drum still more insistently. "You'll pedal till I tell you to stop!" he said, and so weary were the men that none could spare even a mutter of complaint at that.

Finally, as the whisper of wind grew to a constant, comforting waft accompanied by a gentle yet insistent pressure, one of the other officers appeared and whispered in Binion's ear. "Leave off pedaling!" Binion called, and with a great sigh the men obeyed.

Arabella floated, gasping, in her seat, her burning legs twitching like a pond full of agitated frogs. Sweat stung her eyes and pooled beneath her arms. The smell was of the Augean stables.

"Stow pedals!" Binion shouted then. Wearily, with fingers numb from hours of gripping the rod before her, Arabella began to untie the cord that bound her to the hateful seat.

10

LIFE IN MIDAIR

"You wanted to see me, sir?"

Captain Singh turned from where he sat staring out the wide, paned window. The roiling gray clouds of the Horn lay well abaft now, and the sun streamed in from a clear blue sky. The ship's constant shifting and jerking had been replaced by a smooth, imperceptible drift that felt like no movement at all, though the other members of Arabella's watch assured her that the mass of air in which *Diana* was embedded was moving at some thousands of miles per hour, carrying the ship along with it.

"Yes, Ashby." The captain swiveled himself about, his body twisting in the air to face her, though he did not touch the wall or deck with either hands or feet. Arabella had grown far more comfortable with weightlessness, but this elegant demonstration of experience and skill brought home just how much more she had to learn. She hoped that some day she might move as handsomely as he. "Now that we have rounded the Horn, I have time and attention to devote to the education of the ship's young gentlemen. And in that number, for certain purposes, I include yourself."

"Thank you, sir." She bowed in the air, which caused her to begin a tumble which she checked with a hand to the door frame.

The captain, to his eternal credit, appeared to take no notice of Arabella's clumsiness. He moved to where Aadim, the clockwork navigator, sat fixed to his desk, facing out the same window. "Please come over here and observe these dials."

Arabella pushed off from the door frame and drifted across the cabin, bringing herself to a halt beside the captain. For a moment she nearly brushed against his buff-clad shoulder, and the sudden effort of controlling her motion in the air to prevent that contact made her heart race.

Suddenly, with a soft creak and a whir of gears, the navigator's head swiveled to face Arabella and inclined in a slight nod.

Arabella gaped in astonishment. "Did he just . . . notice me?"

"An interesting question." The captain smiled. "Aadim is, in effect, the face of the ship. His mechanisms extend throughout *Diana*, from the forward anemometer beneath the figurehead to the rotational counter on the pulser drive shaft. Within this cabin he has several components that affect the actions of his head and eyes." He gestured to a small, unobtrusive lens in a brass fitting on the bulkhead to his left. "Sunlight from the window falls upon that lens. When it is interrupted, the change in temperature causes a cam to shift, transmitting power to the shafts that turn the head."

Arabella couldn't look away from the green glass eyes that seemed to meet her own. "It's rather . . . disquieting."

At that a small line appeared between the captain's bushy black brows. "I'm sorry you find it so."

For some reason the captain's disapproval, however mild, bit deeply at Arabella's heart, and she quickly amended her position. "Well, it's all a bit strange now. I am certain I shall become accustomed to it."

The captain's face betrayed no emotion. "I hope so."

For a moment longer the automaton's eyes remained still, then with a click and a whir the eyes and head swiveled back to face out the window. Arabella strove to focus her attention on the ingenuity of the mechanism rather than the somewhat disturbing effect the action had upon her sensibilities.

The captain pointed to one of the dials on the front face of the desk. "This dial indicates our current air speed, as determined by the anemometer I mentioned earlier."

Arabella turned herself in the air for a better look at the dial. "Twenty knots?"

"Twenty-one, to be precise. But, of course, we are traveling much faster than that relative to the Earth." He pointed to another dial.

"Seven and a half . . . . *thousand* knots?"

"Indeed. Would you care to speculate how the two figures are calculated, and why they differ?"

"Well . . . an anemometer measures the speed of wind, so this must measure the ship's speed relative to the air mass we are passing through. But the other . . ." She frowned, concentrating. "The ship's speed relative to Earth is largely determined by the speed of the air mass itself, but how to measure that?" She thought a bit more. "Could one determine the distance to Earth by measuring the angular distance between, say, London and Paris, as seen through the telescope?"

The captain shook his head, though he smiled—and that smile warmed Arabella's heart far out of proportion to its slight extent. "An interesting guess, and not entirely incorrect." He opened a cabinet, revealing several cylinders of gleaming brass. "These devices form part of the actual solution." He removed one of the devices from the cabinet. It was a small brass telescope, perhaps ten inches long and an inch in diameter, attached by a swivel onto a wooden shaft about two feet long. He pointed out that the bottom end of the shaft was a brass fitting with a cross-shaped point. "This fits into one of several sockets in key locations throughout the ship." Drifting across the cabin, he indicated a brass disk set into the deck with a matching cross-shaped hole in it. He inserted the pointed end of the telescope's shaft into the hole, where it seated with a precise click, then swiveled the telescope back and forth. From this location, she noted, the telescope had a view of nearly half the sky through the broad stern window. "The horizontal angle, which we call lambda, is transmitted to Aadim through cables. The vertical angle, or phi, is measured on this scale here"— he pointed to a brass scale etched onto the telescope's swivel— "and set by the operator through the dial next to the socket."

Struggling to follow the demonstration, Arabella asked, "The angle between what and what?"

The captain grinned and held up one finger, then put his eye to the telescope and swiveled it back and forth for a time, first with large motions and then with careful, precise adjustments. "Observe," he said then, and gestured Arabella to take his place.

Careful not to jostle the telescope out of its alignment, Arabella put her eye to the telescope's eyepiece. Swimming there, pale against the blue of the sky, lay the planet Saturn, seemingly large as a penny, his broad ring plainly visible and the pinpoint lights of two moons gleaming nearby.

"An excellent view for such a small instrument," she mused.

The captain quirked an eyebrow at her observation. "You are familiar with telescopes?"

Arabella's mouth went dry and she began to stammer, then blurted out the truth. "I . . . my father, he, he . . . was an amateur astronomer." Silently she cursed herself for letting slip her opinion of the instrument. Though this bit of information could not, she hoped, lead to the discovery of her true identity and sex, she knew that she must keep as many secrets as she could. The more the captain and the other crew members knew about her, the more likely it was that they could puzzle out who and what she really was. "But what," she said, hoping to change the subject, "does the observation of Saturn have to do with the ship's speed?"

The captain tapped the scale on the telescope's side. "Why do we measure these angles?"

Why did he always answer her questions with a question? "As the ship moves through the air," she thought aloud, "the planet appears to fall astern." She considered the question for a moment more. "The changing angle of the telescope over time can be used to determine how fast it is receding."

"Very nearly correct. Consider, though, that the ship does not travel in a straight line, nor does Saturn or any other planet stand still. What could be done to compensate for these issues?"

Arabella closed her eyes, her mind wheeling. This was so much harder than the simple household economics she'd had from her mother! If it hadn't been for Michael, and the lessons in trigonometry he'd passed on from their father, she'd be completely lost.

At that reminder of her late father, and her beloved Michael who was even now, unknown to himself, in such danger, the worry and exhaustion of the last week seemed to fall upon her from a great height. Suddenly she could barely breathe, and hot tears squeezed out between her closed eyelids.

But she could not show such weakness in front of the captain! She sniffed and shook her head hard to mask the tears. "I'm afraid I don't know, sir." Silently she cursed her quavering voice.

The captain gave her a smile which was not quite condescending. "Do not be too disturbed at your own limitations, young man. These problems are rather difficult, but I have confidence you will comprehend them in time." He extracted the telescope from its socket and replaced it in the cabinet with the others. "The answer is twofold. First, we take observations of several stars and planets and use triangulation to determine the ship's position, independent of her heading. And second, the motions of the planets are incorporated into Aadim's workings."

He unlatched the side of the automaton's desk and swung it

open, pointing out the complex shapes of several notched wheels and explaining how they worked together to calculate the motions of the planet Jupiter. But as he did so, Arabella could not help but notice that he laid a hand on the machine's shoulder, as though reassuring it that this exposure was necessary and would not go on too long.

Arabella nodded and tried to concentrate on the captain's descriptions of the mechanisms. But though the automaton's head faced the window, it still seemed to be regarding her from the corner of its glass-and-ivory eye.

On the seventh day after rounding the Horn, all hands were called to action stations for a gunnery drill. "Ye'll be a powder monkey," Faunt told her, and directed her forward to the gun deck.

The gun deck, where the ship's cannon were housed, didn't seem to Arabella to be a "deck" at all. The other decks—defined by the deck, or floor, between each—were long flat spaces like the storeys of a house, but the gun deck was a nearly cylindrical space just behind and beneath the figurehead, the massive *khoresh*-wood timber of the ship's stem running through its axis. Three brass cannon, each the size of a man, clustered close around the stem like huge, deadly fruit. The space stank of metal and powder.

Kerrigan had positioned himself near the forward end of the deck, where a stout square door in the hull stood open before the mouth of each cannon, and looked over the twenty or so men who now crowded the space. He floated with hands clasped behind his back, looking, Arabella thought, rather like a shopkeeper in Fort Augusta awaiting his next customer.

"Most of you have been through this drill before," he said. "You new men"—and here his gaze flicked across Arabella as well as several others—"are mostly seamen. You probably think a four-pound gun is just something you'd brush your teeth with, and even three of them add up to less than a mouse fart in a hurricane." He laid a hand respectfully on the black brass barrel of the nearest cannon. "But in the air, properly handled, these weapons are just as deadly as any of His Majesty's naval broadsides."

The experienced crewmen then separated themselves among the three guns, followed by Kerrigan sorting the "new men" into the remaining positions. "You'll be number three powder boy," he said to Arabella, "reporting to Gowse." He indicated a burly airman, who nodded an acknowledgement of the assignment to Kerrigan. "Run down to the magazine and bring back a charge, then do as he tells you."

Arabella had to ask where the magazine was. It proved to be belowdecks and well aft, and like the gun deck it was positioned at the ship's stem in the very center of her body—a small, dim room whose walls were sheathed in copper, stinking of saltpeter and sulfur. There a thin, nervous man whose name Arabella did not catch handed her a flannel bag packed tight with gunpowder. She tucked it under one arm and hurried back to the gun deck, nervously eyeing every lamp as she passed for fear her burden would explode before she reached her destination.

When she arrived back at the gun deck, she found it a hive of activity, reeking with the smell of freshly burned powder. Most of the men were stripped to the waist, and Arabella's gun had been hauled back away from the open port, though a network of ropes and tackle held it fast in place.

Gowse glared angrily at her. "Ye took yer sweet time," he shouted, snatching the bag from her and tossing it through the filthy air to another man. This second man shoved the bag into the cannon's mouth and then, hooking his feet through two of the ropes that held the gun in place, rammed it the rest of the way down the cannon's throat with a stout oak ramrod. Gowse, who had shoved some kind of tool through a hole at the cannon's base, shouted "Home!" as he felt the bag touch down. The bag was followed by an iron ball a bit bigger than a cricket ball and then a wad of cloth, each packed tightly in place with the ramrod.

Then all the men, including Arabella, hauled on the lines until the gun was snugged up against its port, joining the rest of the guns, which had been waiting in that position for some time. One of the other men then grabbed Arabella by the shoulders and hauled her roughly away, leaving her to sail through the air until she bounced off the wall. Flailing in midair, she snagged one of the cannon ropes and held fast.

Kerrigan, frowning grimly at his pocket watch, immediately cried, "Fire!" At once, all the men around Arabella put their hands over their ears, and she strove to do the same without letting go of her rope.

Gowse blew on a smoldering match and touched it to the hole at the cannon's base.

Then there came a cataclysmic triple crash as all three guns went off at once. The sound was so great that the breath was crushed out of Arabella's lungs and, despite her hands pressed tightly to her ears, it felt as though her eardrums were meeting in the middle of her head.

For a moment Arabella floated stunned in midair, the brimstone stench of burnt powder the only sensation that penetrated her rattled brain. Hearing had been replaced by a vast sourceless ringing, vision was blurred, even the sense of touch was muffled by that terrible sound.

And then, out of the ringing dimness, could barely be heard Kerrigan's voice: "Five minutes, eight seconds! That was appalling, lads! Again!"

A rough hand shook Arabella's shoulder. It was Gowse, who shouted in her face, the spittle spraying her cheeks, but she could not make out a word. She shook her head. Again he shouted at her, and this time she barely heard: "Get down there and bring us a charge, and make f——g haste! Ye should have left the moment the last shot was done!"

For that entire watch, Arabella ran back and forth from the gun deck to the magazine, nearly the entire length of the ship, over and over and over again. The terror of carrying a highly explosive powder bag soon faded, replaced by exhaustion and annoyance at every obstacle, human or otherwise, that stood in her way. She became adept at flinging herself great distances down the length of the deck, springing off a bulkhead with the full strength of her legs and then twisting in midair to stop herself with her feet. Then, when she arrived at the gun deck with powder in hand, she joined in the preparation of the gun and then dashed away immediately for another charge, increasing her speed as well as avoiding the worst of the guns' mighty noise.

She was almost disappointed when, after hours of endless labor, she brought back yet another bag of gunpowder only to find the gun deck's ceaseless activity stilled. "That's enough for today, lads!" Kerrigan cried, glancing at his watch. "Three minutes, fifty-eight seconds. Better, but still not good enough! More drill tomorrow!"

Arabella felt in her chest, rather than heard with her ringing ears, the men's groans in response.

After every cannon had been cleaned and every ramrod, swab, and handspike properly stowed, Arabella hauled herself wearily hand over hand along the guide rope toward her berth. All she could think of was the simple pleasure of her hammock. But as she entered the lower deck, she found her way blocked by Gowse, the captain of her gun crew. Still grimy, red-eyed, and bare-chested from the afternoon's gunnery drill, he stood at the ladder's base like some malevolent troll from a fairy tale.

"Ye've made me look bad, Ashby!" he shouted. After so many hours of the crash and thunder of guns, his voice grated hoarsely, but even so he had to shout to be heard over the ringing in Arabella's and every other airman's ears. "Ye've made us all look bad, and now ye'll pay!"

"Please, sir, I did the best I could." Arabella looked around for support, but every airman in the vicinity was another member of Gowse's gun crew, and none of them seemed in the least sympathetic. "And I did get better with time."

"It's thanks to you we'll be drilling again tomorrow!" Gowse's hands twisted into fists, and the ropey muscles of his arms bulged. "Ye need to be taught a lesson!" With that he lunged toward Arabella, flinging himself up the ladder toward her with a great thrust of his massive legs.

Arabella's hand still lay on the ladder's guide rope. Without thinking she twitched herself out of Gowse's path, just as though he were some obstacle she'd encountered while running bags of powder back and forth. Gowse hurtled past the point she'd recently occupied, growling as he collided with the coaming above the ladder.

Arabella turned in the air and pushed off the ladder's lowest step, rocketing through the crowd of airmen that had surrounded Gowse. Other men scrambled out of her way as she flew, until she stopped herself with a hand on an overhead beam. "Do you think if I'm beaten black and blue I'll be able to go *faster*?" she cried.

Gowse made no reply, save another growl as he pushed through the crowd.

Arabella turned and prepared to push off the beam. But all the other airmen had gathered in a ring around her and Gowse. No direction offered an easy escape.

Twisting in the air, panting, she stared in every direction, hoping that some member of her mess, or an officer, or *any* friendly person would appear to save her. But every man in the watching crowd, even airmen she'd thought friendly, merely waited, looking up at her with an attitude of grim expectation.

Gowse floated in the center of the ring of men, fingers flexing, a determined scowl on his face. "So, Ashby, are ye gonna fight?"

Arabella swallowed.

She could bend her knee to Gowse, acknowledge her failure, beg forgiveness. And he would beat her senseless, after which her sex would almost surely be revealed.

She could cry out for help. And every man present would know her to be a coward, one who could not be depended upon if the ship did happen to fall into battle with pirates or the French. She'd lose the respect of the captain, who'd emphasized that in his ship every man must take responsibility for his own actions and his own failures. And Gowse would probably still beat her senseless.

She could fight like a girl. She'd seen many a hair-pulling, scratching altercation in the fields and paths near Marlowe Hall, and even been drawn into a few. Girl fights produced much noise and little serious injury. If she fought like that, Gowse would overpower her, and beat her senseless.

Or she could fight to win.

And Gowse, though a huge, muscular man, showed no under-standing of the unique challenges and opportunities of free descent. Every tactic he had displayed thus far would have been perfectly at home on the floor of some tavern on Earth.

With a sudden shriek, Arabella pushed off the beam with both feet, hurling herself downward into Gowse's face. They met in midair with a stinging thud. Taking advantage of his momentary surprise, she tore into him with all she had, thrashing at his face with both fists.

Gowse recovered his wits quickly, grabbing Arabella's wrists and squeezing until the bones ground together. She cried out at the pain, struggling in his grasp, but all her strength was not enough to pry herself loose. He grinned at her, an evil leering thing that promised far more pain to come. Desperate, fighting for her life, she twisted and writhed, lashing out with feet and knees and elbows, any thing at all—as hard as she could, but to little effect.

But then, by chance, one flailing foot caught the man between his legs. Gowse winced and his grip lessened. Immediately Arabella bent herself double, bringing up her legs between herself and Gowse, then kicked out with all her might.

She missed her target, but caught Gowse in the stomach. His foul breath came out in a grunt and he let go!

The momentum of the blow carried Arabella away. She collided with a few of the surrounding airmen, who immediately shoved her back toward Gowse. Now she was flying feet-first. Again she brought her knees up to her chest, and struck out with her heels at the last moment, connecting solidly with Gowse's nose. She felt a sickening crunch, like the carapace of a *shikastho* breaking beneath her heel, as she ricocheted away. Gowse cried out and clapped both hands to his face.

This time Arabella caught herself on an angled stanchion. She hung there for a moment and assessed the situation.

Khema had often conducted mock battles with Arabella and Michael among the crags and rilles beyond the plantation fence. "Aren't you going to finish me, *tutukha*?" she'd taunted once, lying panting in the dust after a solid blow to the leg. "Or are you too soft-hearted?"

Arabella had blinked at the weapon in her hand—in reality nothing more than a lightweight bundle of *thukathi*-reeds— marveling that she had finally managed to land a proper hit on her *itkhalya* after so many months of sparring. "I've just cut your leg off," she'd said. "You're no threat to me now." She'd tossed the reeds aside.

"No threat?" Khema had said. And with one swift motion, not using the supposedly severed limb at all, the Martian had pivoted herself upright and brought her own bundle of reeds down on the leather at the junction of Arabella's shoulder and neck. "Now we're both dead."

A few beads of blood squeezed out from between Gowse's fingers, tumbling in the air as they drifted away. Arabella cried out, a wordless howl of rage, and pushed hard with her legs against the stanchion, driving her outstretched fists with all her strength into the hands that clutched Gowse's injured nose.

Gowse shrieked in pain, scrabbling ineffectually at Arabella as she collided with him, wrapping her legs around his waist and seizing his shirt in her left hand for leverage. She raised her right fist, preparing to drive it down a third time upon the already broken nose.

"That's enough," came a firm voice from behind her.

Not releasing her grip, Arabella risked a quick glance at the voice. It was Young, the eldest member of her mess. "Ye've beaten him," he said. "Now let him go."

With one last hard glance at Gowse—he seemed to cringe from its impact—she shoved the man away. He bounced off the floor as she caught herself lightly on an overhead beam, leaving a bloody handprint.

She looked around at the sphere of airmen. Her whole body trembled from exertion and late-arriving fear, but she worked hard to keep it from showing.

Several of the men nodded appreciatively, then turned away. The sphere melted away in moments, as quickly as it had assembled, the men drifting off to their hammocks or the head.

Gowse remained, floating near the deck, grasping the ladder's lowest rung with one hand and holding his nose with the other. "I think ye've broken it," he said, wincing, his words indistinct.

"You said something about a lesson needing to be taught," Arabella observed.

"Aye," Gowse muttered. "Aye, that I did. And someone got hisself schooled, a'right." He reached out with the hand that was not holding his nose, sending himself slowly tumbling. "Would ye be so kind as to bring me some water, lad?"

Leather sacks of water were kept in a net at one end of the deck. Arabella brought him one, tossing it to him from some distance away in case of a ruse.

"Thanks," Gowse said, pulling the stopper with his teeth. He swigged down half the water and used the other half to wet his shirt-tail and mop up some of the blood from his face. Droplets of reddish water drifted everywhere.

After cleaning himself up a bit, Gowse looked up to where Arabella still hung near the overhead. "Good fight, lad." He nodded. "Good fight."

"Thank you," Arabella said, not knowing what else to say.

"We'll do better with that gun tomorrow."

"I'll do my best."

"That's all a man can do."

Airmen, Arabella reflected, were a strange lot.

After the fight, the men treated Arabella differently. Before, she'd felt tolerated—the weak, unskilled new hand—and had thought that good enough, for now. But after her defeat of Gowse she seemed accepted as truly part of the crew. When she had problems or questions, the other men provided answers and assistance without the air of annoyance or opprobrium they'd displayed before; she was now treated as merely inexperienced. It was as though, by showing skill with her fists, she'd demonstrated her potential to perform any other task.

As for Gowse himself, to Arabella's great surprise his relations with Arabella grew highly cordial. She'd feared retaliation, expected incivility, and hoped for merely being left alone, but despite his two black eyes and visibly off-kilter nose—about which every one, including the officers, studiously avoided any comment—Gowse now treated Arabella as the greatest of friends.

Of course, she was still the most junior member of the crew, still given the filthiest and most tedious jobs. And if in gunnery drill she was slow in delivering a charge of powder, which did still occur from time to time, Gowse could be sharp with a rebuke. But the same was true of any other man whose performance displeased him, and during the few hours of each day when they were neither asleep nor employed in their duties he would often invite her to share a chew of tobacco (which she declined) or join in a game of cards.

Paradoxically, now that the men had accepted her as one of their own, Arabella worried more about keeping her sex hidden. Before, when no one had paid her the least mind, she'd been free to slink off to the head while the men were gaming or carousing together, when she was less likely to be caught with her pants down. Now that she was engaged in those games and carousals herself, her absence was more likely to be noticed.

But even at those times when she was not alone in the head, she still managed to keep her private parts private. The space was dark, close, and vile; visibility was poor, and no one wanted to do any thing other than to get in, do his business, and get out. Only during a few days of the month was there any need for Arabella to spend any more time in the head than that herself, and even then she could plead the flux or some other, more sordid, medical condition. These excuses were greeted by a sympathetic nod or knowing wink, and seemed to raise no suspicion. Certainly no airman would even consider consulting the ship's surgeon for any condition less serious than a direct and immediate threat to life or limb.

Outside of the head there was rarely any threat of exposure. The men slept in their clothing, almost never washed—water was too closely rationed to do otherwise—and even when a man was injured or ill and had to visit the surgeon, clothing was removed only from the affected part. Some men would strip off their shirts during gunnery drill and when working the pedals, but not every one did, and no one ever questioned Arabella's modesty. And as the ship drew farther and farther from the sun, the warmth of the air diminished and hardly any man went shirtless.

But there was one incident in the head that made Arabella's heart pound.

The incident came in the middle of Arabella's time off-watch, when a dire pressure in her gut roused her from her well-earned slumber. She rushed to the head, and was in the middle of doing her business when she realized she was not alone. Two other men were there with her.

This company was not unusual; the space could accommodate as many as five, in a pinch. Nor was it strange that, the head being so dark, she had no idea of their identities. What *was* unusual was that they were conversing in the head—unlike women, men generally did their business in silence—in voices so low they no doubt thought themselves inaudible. But, after many years of gunnery drill, many airmen were somewhat deaf, and often spoke more loudly than they knew.

"So," rasped one, "are you with us?" His voice was low and grating, quite distinctive, but not one she recognized. Perhaps, she thought, he was deliberately disguising it.

"Maybe," came the response. This voice was not familiar either. "All I know is, I'd rather see a white face on the quarterdeck."

"John Company does love our Captain Singh," the first man replied with hard irony. "He makes the owners a tidy profit, him and that witchy machine of his, so they put up with his heathen ways. But there's plenty of good English airmen on this ship, and officers too, who agree with you."

A pause. "I'm in."

"Good man." There was a rustle of cloth—the sound of a handshake? "We'll contact you again when we're just about ready to move. Until then, just do your duties, and don't tell a soul. But be warned—there's no changing your mind now. We're watching you, we're everywhere, and if you even *try* to tell an officer we'll slit your throat in your hammock, and don't think we won't."

"Mum's the word." The sound of a hand clapping another man's shoulder, and then the door opened and closed as the two men slipped out. Try as she might, Arabella could still not discern who they were.

She floated, trembling, for a long time in the stinking darkness before she returned to her hammock. And then, despite her exhaustion, it was yet a longer time before she slept.

11

SAIL HO

Weeks passed, and the work grew routine. Arabella learned her duties well, became conversant with the strange terminology used by airmen, and developed cordial relations with the men in her mess.

She overheard no further conversations in the head, nor were there any rumblings of mutiny among the crew on deck. Even the conversation she *had* heard might be no more than dissatisfied grumbling. Yet she feared that insurrection was brewing, and viewed every man with suspicion. She never found herself alone with the captain, and with no knowledge of which officers or men might be involved in the plot, she dared not share her worries with any one else.

Despite her caution and concerns, she gradually became more comfortable with her tasks and the other members of the crew. From time to time she was given new duties, which kept her on her toes.

The one aspect of airmanship she could not seem to master was that of tying knots, which for all its seeming simplicity proved far more complex in execution than her mind was capable of encompassing. She had never dreamed there were so many ways of tying two ropes together! But one day, as she struggled in vain to fix a loop in the middle of a line, her messmate Mills floated up to her with a raised eyebrow, his pink palms raised in a clear offer of assistance.

The man spoke little—his native language was some West African tongue he shared with no one else on the ship—but Arabella was sure he understood English as well as any man aboard. When he did speak, his words, though not always grammatical, were carefully chosen and to the point.

"I am to tie a bowline here," she confessed, "but I simply cannot fathom how to do it when both ends of the line are secured."

"Bowline on bight," he said. With clear deliberate gestures he demonstrated the knot, his pale yellow eyes firm and kind upon hers as he made certain she understood the process.

She tried it herself then, and though the resulting knot was far more untidy than his, his bright white smile showed that she had tied it correctly.

"Thank you, sir," she said, and with an amiable salute he returned to his duties.

The most interesting part of her day was the time she spent in the captain's cabin, learning about navigation and the use and maintenance of Aadim the clockwork navigator. These lessons were nominally for the benefit of Binion and the other midshipmen, with herself as only a guest, but it soon became abundantly clear to all that she was by far the most adept student of the lot. Even Binion, resent the situation though he might, plainly could not deny its truth.

Though the lessons were hard—the trigonometry of sextant and compass was a particular challenge—Arabella applied herself to them with vigor and joy. Here she could exercise her mind in a way her mother, indeed all of English society, would never tolerate in a girl or even a grown woman. In these moments all shame at her continued deception fell away, replaced by anger at the opportunities denied her by her sex.

As the captain lectured patiently, Arabella could not fail to be reminded of her father, and she often reflected that he would have very much admired the captain if they had met. The two men shared a keen interest in automata, of course, but the affinity ran deeper than that—both had an actively curious intelligence, a tenacious persistence when confronted with a difficult puzzle, and a warm heart beneath a sometimes gruff exterior. But the most complex automaton in her father's collection was a mere toy by comparison with Aadim. The more she worked with the navigator, the more impressed she became with the many clockmakers who'd designed and built his workings.

But far more impressive than those clockmakers, she realized, was the captain himself. Captain Singh's knowledge of automata ran deep and broad as any aerial current, and he himself was responsible for much of Aadim's design. Though the captain was no clockmaker himself, his understanding of the clockwork navigator's mechanisms was complete and intimate. Aadim's technical draughts were kept in a chest in the captain's cabin, tightly rolled in a protective leather case, but the captain himself never consulted them; he knew every cog, gear, and shaft as well as he knew the names and duties of his crew.

The captain, in fact, seemed to treat the automaton *as* a member of the crew. He always called it "he" or by name, and in cases where the ideal set of the sails or course correction was less than certain, he seemed to respect its solutions far more than the advice of Stross, his sailing-master. This habit caused some small amount of grumbling from his fellow officers, but their complaints were muted because Aadim's navigation was invariably swifter, more accurate, and more efficient than any of theirs.

But not only the captain's mind was admirable to Arabella. He was handsome, to be certain, with fine symmetrical features and piercing dark eyes, and as she aided him to don his always impeccable jacket she could not fail to notice how broad and firm were the shoulders beneath his shirt. And though, as captain, he perforce held himself aloof from the men, he never failed to treat even the least of them—which would, of course, be Arabella herself—with any thing other than respect, kindness, and patience.

Under other circumstances, he might have been a man whose company she would have sought out for its own sake. But, sadly, those circumstances were not hers, and so she kept her observations of him to herself.

One day Arabella was engaged in holystoning the deck—a tedious and common chore which involved hooking herself to the deck with a leather strap, scrubbing the wood with a pumice stone, and wiping up the resulting dust with a damp washing-leather before it could float away—when a cry of "sail ho!" came up from the lookout on the starboard mast. Immediately every man rushed to the starboard rail, including the other men holystoning, so she too unhooked herself and did likewise. But peer though she might, she saw no sign of any sail.

The men around Arabella fidgeted and murmured uncertainly. "What are we looking for?" she asked her messmate Hornsby, who floated beside her, shielding his eyes from the sun.

"'Nother ship," he muttered, still staring off into the distance. "Rare in these parts, and troublesome."

"Troublesome? How so?"

"There!" he cried, pointing downward. Arabella looked in the indicated direction and this time managed to discern a tiny, wavering speck, barely visible against the blue of sky and small, scudding clouds. It might be a hundred or a thousand miles off; without landmarks, she had no sense of distance.

"What's so troublesome about that?" Arabella asked again. "It's much too far away to bother us."

"Aye, and if she *keeps* her distance, there's no worry. But it's her angle on the bow I'm worried about." Arabella knew from her lessons with Aadim that "angle on the bow" referred to the angle between the line of *Diana*'s course and a line drawn from *Diana* to the other ship. "No Marsman would come at us from below like that; she'd be ahead or astern, on the same course as we." He pointed again, measuring with his eye. "If the angle changes with time, we can all breathe easy. But if it don't . . . that means our courses intersect."

"But surely we can easily avoid a collision, with so much warning and so much space to maneuver?"

Hornsby took his gaze from the distant speck and fixed it upon Arabella. "Unless she *means* to engage us. And who'd want to do a thing like that?"

Suddenly the reason for the crew's agitation became clear. "Pirates," she breathed.

"Or worse," said Hornsby.

"What could be worse than pirates?"

"Could be a French frigate. Our little guns haven't a chance against a full-blown man of war." Again he peered into the distance. "Mind you, she don't swim like a frigate. Might be a corsair, though. Nearly as bad."

"What kind of ship is that?"

"No particular rig. Corsair's just what the French call a privateer."

The naval terminology was making her head spin. "What might be the difference between a privateer and a pirate?"

"Pirates take honest men's cargo for their own profit, and if they're caught they hang. Privateers do the same, but they have a license—a letter of marque, it's called—from the French, and they share what they take with Bonaparte, all legal-like. They're better funded, better equipped, and just all around more dangerous."

"Avast that lolling about!" cried Kerrigan from the quarterdeck. All the men returned to their duties, along with Arabella. But though she did her best to concentrate on her holystoning of the deck, a part of her attention was always directed to the men and officers peering over the starboard side, eyes and telescopes trained on the unknown airship.

It seemed to her that the direction of their gazes—the angle on the bow—was not changing with time. And the expressions on the officers' faces betrayed concern.

———————

During the midday meal, Arabella's mess talked of nothing but the approaching ship and what might occur if she did prove to be an enemy. Of the group, only Gosling and Young had seen action, and the others peppered them with questions.

"There's no sinking a ship in the air," Gosling declaimed, stabbing the air with his finger. "No battle is over until every man on one ship or t'other's dead or captured."

"Nay," said Young. "When I were in *Columbine* we met with a French frigate. Cap'n Clive shot away her pulsers and we got away clean." He took a bite of his biscuit, chewed noisily. "Nary a casualty on either side."

Hornsby shook his head. "It's a dangerous tactic, getting in close enough for a shot like that. Ye might find yer own pulsers shot to h—l. And if *neither* ship can pedal away, well then it's hand-to-hand combat, with the survivors left to piece together one good ship from whatever's left."

"But *Diana*'s such a fast ship," Arabella said. "We are traveling at a rate of over seven thousand knots! Why can't we simply outsail them?"

Young grinned, though without humor. "It's not so simple, lad." He carefully placed two bits of biscuit in the air above the mess table. "This is us, and that's them." Then he blew a puff of breath at them, causing both bits to waft gently in the same direction. "We're both in the same current of air, ain't we? *That's* what's moving at seven thousand knots, carrying both of us along with it. For either ship to outrace the other, both being in the same wind, means pedaling. And though she's fast for a Marsman, *Diana* can't out-pedal a corsair with one-tenth the tonnage."

"Can't we change course? Find some other wind?"

"This ain't the Horn, lad, where the winds blow every which way. We're in the trades. Nearest other wind might be a hundred mile off."

Taylor angrily punched the air. "It's the g———d *waiting* I can't stand! On the sea, ye can't see another ship until she's hull-down on the horizon." As his tattoos attested, Taylor had served as a seaman for years before joining *Diana*. "But out here . . . it could be weeks from first sight until she gets within cannon range."

"Be careful what ye wish for," Gosling admonished. "From what I hear at the scuttlebutt, she's closing fast. We could be in battle within five days."

At that all the men, including Arabella, fell silent, morosely chewing their salt pork.

———————————

As the other ship drew near, they drilled and drilled, spending hours each day at gunnery practice. While Arabella's and the other gun crews strove to increase their rate of fire, the topmen dashed from sail to sail, and all the other men slaved at the pedals. The other ship was now clearly visible to the unaided eye, though not yet close enough to make out her provenance.

"What is the point of trimming the sails while pedaling?" Ara-

bella asked the captain during one of their increasingly rare sessions together. She understood enough of aerial navigation now
to know that the trim of the sails was normally adjusted only
when passing through an unfavorable wind or to catch a favorable
one, but now there was no hope of finding any wind better than
the one in which they were embedded.

"When we pedal," the captain explained, "the ship gains a bit
of way, which the sails can use to change her course. A good ship,
with a strong and experienced crew, can turn one hundred and
eighty degrees in less than ten minutes. And we must turn the
ship smartly and accurately if we are to bring our cannon properly
to bear upon the enemy."

Arabella swallowed. "So she is indeed an enemy?" The other
ship's behavior, drawing directly closer and closer, had been seen
by all the men as an ill sign, but some still held out hope she
might be another Marsman, bending her course to match *Diana*'s
out of a need of supplies or succor.

"She is no Company ship," he replied, his expression grim.
"We've signaled with cannon, and she has failed to respond in
kind." He stared past Arabella's shoulder, his gaze directed through
the hull at the other ship's location. "And, as such, I am sorry to
tell you that this will be our last session together until . . . until
after we are well clear of her."

"I see," Arabella said, and swallowed hard.

That night, swaddled in her hammock between the warm and
snoring bodies of the other men, Arabella could not sleep despite
her body's exhaustion.

What would the coming days bring? Would there be battle, or
merely an encounter with another, albeit strangely uncommuni-
cative, merchant ship? And if there was battle, what then?

It was not only concern for Arabella's own safety that kept her mind awhirl with desperate trepidation. After so many weeks aboard *Diana*, she had formed good working relationships with most of the crew, and despite her continued deception of them she considered many of them friends or at least comrades. The captain, too, had earned . . . her trust and professional loyalty, she told herself. If the other ship did indeed prove to be a pirate or corsair, any of them might be injured or killed in the coming action.

But worst of all, if Arabella was killed, or if *Diana* was delayed or thrown off course, she might not reach Mars in time to prevent her wretched cousin Simon from carrying out his nefarious scheme. He would deceive the gentle-hearted Michael and do him in . . . and then, by the inexorable laws of entail, Mother, Fanny, and Chloë would be left penniless. As well as Arabella herself, of course.

From beneath her stiff and grimy shirt she drew the precious locket with her brother's portrait. Though the portrait was barely visible in the slivers of light that crept in through gaps in the decking above, still in the dimness that well-loved and well-remembered face seemed clear, and she thought with fond reminiscence of the warm and happy day on which the portrait and its fellow had been painted. "I *will* save you, Michael," she whispered. "Somehow."

She kissed the locket gently before secreting it away.

Suddenly a thunder of drums startled Arabella awake. Despite every thing, she'd managed to drift off.

"Action stations!" cried a voice—Kerrigan's—as the drums' booming rattle continued to echo throughout the ship. A clamor of other voices repeated the command. "Action stations! Action stations, ye lubbers!"

Heart pounding, Arabella scrambled from her imprisoning hammock. All around her other men did the same, a confusion of limbs and scattered clothing flying every which way through the dimness. Warm and pungent bodies struck her from every direction as she struggled to roll up her hammock at the same time as every other man.

Suddenly the confusion and clamor stilled, every man stopping with bated breath. Arabella too paused, straining her ears toward the sound she thought or feared she'd heard above the men's noise.

And then it came a second time.

The ringing distant boom of cannon.

With renewed vigor the men scrambled to ready themselves for battle.

Arabella fought her way through the tumbling crowd of floating men, up the ladder, and on to the deck to stow her bedroll. She emerged into a scene of furious chaos, topmen scrambling up the masts while most of the crew milled about on the deck. Despite all their drill, in the actual event they were acting more like a herd of frightened *shokari* than seasoned airmen.

For Arabella's own part, though she knew where she was needed, as she shoved the tightly rolled bundle of all her possessions in beside the others she paused for a brief moment to glance at the sky.

The other ship now hung well above the beam, twice as big as even Earth's enormous moon. A sleek four-master she was, the great cross of her sails showing she was pointed directly toward *Diana*, and rippling at her stern Arabella saw the French colors—blue, white, and red—marking her as no mere pirate but a deadly corsair. Even as Arabella watched, a quadruple flash and burst of smoke showed at the crux of that cross—four guns to go with her four masts. A long moment later came the rolling *bang-ba-bang-bang* of the report.

Someone shouted, "Hit the deck!"

Arabella dove below the rail, holding firmly to the edge of a scupper. A long, howling wail marked the passage of a cannon-ball through the air somewhere above her head, with others a bit farther off.

She had just time to think they'd gotten lucky when the deck gave a violent jerk beneath her hands and a monstrous shattering crash assailed her ears.

An incoherent babble of shouts and screams followed, including a long high shriek of pain that made the hairs stand up on the back of Arabella's neck. She could not stop herself from looking.

The ball had struck not fifty feet from where she cowered beneath the rail, tearing a long splintering gouge across a stretch of deck that Arabella had holystoned just ten hours earlier. Fragments and slivers of golden *khoresh*-wood, some longer than her arm, sped tumbling through the air in every direction.

One of them had impaled an airman, the jagged splinter thrust like a sword right through his stomach. Screaming, his face contorted in agony, he rotated in midair, grasping tight to the splinter with both hands as though this could somehow halt his tumble.

His name was West. He was proud of his fine white teeth, and he carved the most delightful little figures from Venusian scale-wood.

Red drops gouted from the wound, scattering into the air as he twisted and tumbled in pain.

Paralyzed by this horrific sight, Arabella could do no more than gape, holding firm to the edge of the scupper. She knew her place was on the gun deck. Her crew needed her. Yet to budge from this spot would expose her to a fate as bad as West's, or worse. Her fingers clamped trembling to the wood.

But one voice made itself heard above the chaos: Kerrigan's.

"Action stations!" he called, firm and clear. "To your posts, d—n you!" Arabella looked to the quarterdeck.

The captain stood there, feet planted on the deck as firmly as though *Diana* were a ship of the sea, long brass telescope fixed to his eye. A stout leather belt at his waist, fixed by straps to two turnbuckles abaft the wheel, held him in place against whatever maneuvers the coming battle might bring.

If any one could carry them through this chaos, it would be he. If any one could.

The captain lowered the telescope and cast a stern glance across the deck, assessing the condition of his ship and crew. For a moment he and Arabella locked eyes. The message of his stark expression was plain: *Get to your station!*

She leapt with alacrity to the forward ladder, hauling herself hand over hand down the guide rope to her action station in the gun deck.

The situation in the gun deck was chaotic, all three gun crews struggling to free the cannon from the chains and bindings which kept them secure when not in use. Not one of the three gun crews was entire; West, the captain of number two, was now writhing on the deck above, leaving that crew floundering and leaderless. For her own part, Arabella hung back, recognizing that adding another body to the scrum around the guns would slow rather than speed the process.

Another bang and jarring shudder ran through the ship's frame. Arabella risked a glance through the nearest gun-port, but the corsair was nowhere to be seen. Plainly the other ship had the advantage; Arabella prayed that situation would not continue long.

At last one of the officers, not Kerrigan, appeared on the gun deck and began chivvying the men into some semblance of order.

At his command Arabella clapped on to one of the hawsers and helped to haul the number three gun into position to be loaded. As soon as it was ready she sprang away for the magazine.

Her traversal of the length of the ship had a nightmare quality. Shattered fragments of *khoresh*-wood spun and tumbled everywhere, a deadly litter of aerial flotsam. Men cried out in pain or floated limp in the air. Drops of blood spattered every surface; the very air tasted of iron. *Bang-bang-ba-bang*, came the quadruple report of the French guns, followed shortly by the howl of cannonballs through the rigging. A clean miss, this time, but as the ships drew closer together *Diana* could not continue that luck.

At the magazine a new man worked nervously with the wooden scoop and bucket, filling the charges much less rapidly than his predecessor. Arabella, wondering what had become of the previous man and hoping the new one would learn his job quickly, grabbed a charge from the loose floating pile and leapt away.

Returning to the upper deck from the magazine, she was shocked to find sunlight streaming in through a ragged hole in the hull. Smoke and slivers of wood made the sunbeams seem as sharp and hard-edged as the rough fragments that tumbled in the air within them, seeming to glow and flicker as they passed from shadow into light. A knot of frightened, confused men were trying to tend to the several wounded, their pandemonium of shouts and screams making the scene still more infernal.

Then Higgs, the boatswain, appeared, sticking his head down from the main-deck above. "Get those wounded clear!" he shouted. "Where there's one ball, a second won't be far behind!"

At once the men changed tactics, dragging the screaming wounded aft to the sickbay, and Arabella dashed down the ladder to the lower deck, hoping to find a clear path to the gun deck. A moment later, true to Higgs's word, a second ball came crashing in behind her.

Most of the crew on the lower deck were laboring at the pedals, grunting and straining more feverishly than she'd ever seen before. Binion exhorted them to still greater effort, hammering the drum brutally, but she paid him no mind as she shot the length of the deck and made her way to the gun deck.

"There you are, d—n you!" cried the officer as she tossed the charge to Gowse. "Where are the others?"

Arabella looked around. All three guns were now unshipped and awaiting their charges, but she was the only powder monkey in sight. "I don't know, sir!" she cried, even as Gowse and the rest of his crew rushed to load the number three gun.

"D—n!" the officer swore again. "Well, hop to your duty, lad!"

Arabella hopped, speeding off to the magazine again. Behind her she heard the officer shouting to someone to find him two more powder monkeys.

———————

Back and forth Arabella dashed, gun deck to magazine and back again and again. Forward, the gun deck was a sunlit Hades of smoke and noise and furious shouting, three hard rectangular shafts of light from the gun-ports sweeping the scene as *Diana* swerved and tumbled in her attempt to avoid the corsair's shots. Abaft, the magazine was a dark Hades of quiet, desperate activity, two ill-trained crewmen gingerly scooping the dangerous powder into measured charges as quickly as they dared. Between, the upper and lower decks were a raucous Hades of flying fragments, tumbling casks, and airmen slick with sweat or blood scrambling hither and yon. A dozen holes or more pierced the hull, each a deadly forest of smashed timbers which had to be navigated past.

On each traverse Arabella was forced to find a new route, as new damage or crowds of men or debris blocked her path. At one point she was nearly crushed by two crates that floated free, knocked from their lashings by cannonballs when the ship suddenly changed course and sent them crashing toward the starboard hull. Only her sharp eye and the fortunate presence of a heavy floating barrel, which she could use to change her course with a strong kick, had saved her then. Another time she collided with an airman who'd fallen unconscious at the pedals—struck in the head by flying wreckage or simply passed out from exhaustion— and drifted from his station unexpectedly.

When she arrived at the gun deck, she joined with her crew to get the number three gun loaded and aimed. It was hot, furious work, full of shouting and swearing and peering through the ports in hopes of spotting the other ship. And when the corsair did appear, pulsers whirling as she moved rapidly against the clouds beyond, a great wordless growl burst from the gun crews as they strove to haul the heavy guns into position before she could get away again.

To Arabella's eye the French ship did not seem damaged at all.

"Fire!" cried the officer, and Arabella leapt away to fetch another charge of powder. Behind her the immense triple crash of *Diana*'s guns was followed by a groan of disappointment— another miss.

Exiting the gun deck she found her way blocked by a tangled knot of splintered wood, with a deadly cloud of nails spewing from a shattered cask like an angry swarm of *chakti*. A harsh, sharp smell of sawdust and iron assaulted her nose. Quickly she sprang off the coaming of the gun deck hatch, sailing with tucked arms and legs up the companionway to the upper deck just as the nails clattered against the bulkhead behind her.

———

Arabella shot out of the companionway into a bright, airy, screaming maelstrom. Blinking against the unaccustomed light, she caught herself on a stay and took a moment to orient herself.

The deck was a tangled mess of spars, sails, and rigging that smelled of gunpowder and blood. One of the main yards lay diagonally across *Diana*'s waist, a shambles of rope and Venusian silk that blocked her passage and her view. Above, the mainmast still seemed whole, though several topmen floated limp and bleeding against a background of roiling smoke.

And then, rising above the larboard rail like some malevolent moon, the corsair hove into view. Near enough that Arabella could easily make out the rapacious grins on the faces of her crew, she turned as she climbed, yawing about to bring her guns to bear on *Diana*'s midsection. The French ship was not undamaged—one mast was little more than a mass of splinters held together by shreds of silk—but plainly she was still very much able to maneuver. Abaft, her pulsers whirled like a windmill in a gale.

The corsair's four gun-ports gaped, black and malevolent, seeming to grow larger as the ship swiveled herself to point directly toward Arabella.

With a shriek, Arabella flung herself away from those four hideous maws, flying aft, hiding herself in the tangled silk of the fallen yard. A moment later the corsair's quadruple report sounded, the flash of her guns just visible through the waving silk, almost immediately followed by a shattering crash as the balls struck *Diana*. The ship jerked at the impact like a wounded living thing.

Arabella disentangled herself from the imprisoning fabric, finding herself on the far side of the wreckage. She was near the quarterdeck now. Abaft, officers on the quarterdeck orbited the sun of their captain, who stood, still strapped in place, pointing and calling out commands.

Arabella looked over her shoulder. From here the French ship could not be seen at all.

The quarterdeck was officers' country, inviolate—no mere airman could enter that sacred space uninvited. Nevertheless, Arabella sprang from her position immediately, sailing through the stinking, littered air directly toward the captain. "The corsair!" she called as she flew, pointing behind herself. "She's right over there!"

Kerrigan whirled to face her, anger showing on his blood-spattered face, but the captain called back, "Where?"

Catching herself on a stay, Arabella pointed through the obscuring silk. As though to confirm her observation, the unseen corsair's cannon sounded again, directly in line with her pointing finger.

For a moment Captain Singh's brow furrowed in furious concentration. Then he said, "Ashby, report to the magazine. Tell them to provide you with an explosive charge. Carry it to your gun and instruct your captain to target the enemy's magazine. I will endeavor to provide him with a clear shot."

Before she could even reply "Aye, aye, sir!" the captain had already turned away, barking commands to his officers.

Arabella hauled herself down the rail to the after hatch, squeezing past two men armed with cutlasses against an anticipated boarding attempt, belowdecks to the magazine. There she relayed the captain's order to the wan and trembling men in charge.

"This is the only one left," said one of them, handing her a ball equipped with a ropy fuse. "Best make good use of it."

"Aye, aye," Arabella said, and took the precious, deadly thing, along with a charge of powder.

Recalling the nails and other wreckage in her path, Arabella realized she'd have to return via the upper deck. Tucking the ball under one arm and the charge under the other, she propelled herself with legs alone back up the after companionway and out into the light.

The scene here was little different than before—scrambling airmen below, smoke and wreckage above, the corsair still hidden from sight by the fallen yard—but even as she made her way forward she heard a repeated call of "Hold fast! Hold fast for maneuvers!"

She was just then passing the mainstays, thick diagonal ropes that held the mainmast in position, but with the ball and charge under her arms she had no hands free. At the last moment she reached out one foot, snagging the last stay and bringing herself to a sudden halt. Juggling her deadly cargo under one arm, she twined her legs and the other arm around the tense and heavy cable and held tight.

"Strike all starboard and larboard sails!" came the captain's next command. "Strike mains'l! Sheet home main royals and t'gallants! Pulsers full ahead!"

All around topmen scrambled to obey. First the main-sail vanished, then with fierce and rapid action the sails far above snapped into position, bellying backward against *Diana*'s forward motion through the air. A deep thrum sounded through the stay to which Arabella clung, making her whole body vibrate, and the mainmast creaked alarmingly from the great pressure placed upon its upper reaches.

And then, with a mighty groan, the whole ship pivoted around the remaining sails of the upper mainmast.

The clouds above wheeled dizzyingly past. Arabella felt herself slide down the stay until her feet pressed against the deck with a force nearly as great as Earth's accustomed gravity. The French ship rotated into view above Arabella, the crew staring back, astonished at *Diana*'s unprecedented maneuver.

In just a moment they would be in *Diana*'s line of fire. And Arabella held the explosive charge.

Arabella released her hold on the stay and began making her way forward. Pressed against the deck as she was by the ship's rotation, it was almost like walking on a ship at sea—a pitching, yawing ship, under attack, on a heaving sea. Yet she knew she must reach the gun quickly or the whole perilous maneuver would be for naught.

Rushing from mast to rail to hatch, dodging flying spars that clattered against the deck in a flutter of silk, Arabella reached the forward companionway with the corsair not quite yet in the line of fire. She flung herself down the companionway and into the gun deck. "Explosive shot!" she shouted to Gowse, handing him the ball and charge. "Target the enemy's magazine!"

Grimly he nodded, then began shouting to his crew to load and aim the gun—no easy task with the ship's rotation still pressing them against the deck. Arabella hauled and sweated along with them, getting the charge well seated and the gun aligned to face the corsair, even now rotating into view.

Gowse peered out the gun-port, eyeballing the distance to the target. "Fifteen hundred feet?" he shouted, to which his second assented with a nod.

Carefully Gowse trimmed off six inches from the shell's fuse, then lit the end with a slow-match. Even as it began to sputter sparks and smoke, he rammed the ball down the gun barrel, followed by a wad. "Run up, boys!" he called, and Arabella and the rest of the crew hauled on the ropes that snugged the gun tight against its port.

Now Gowse sighted carefully along the gun's barrel, calling out instructions to haul it right or left, up or down. Exhausted though they were, Arabella and the crew obeyed.

Through the gun-port, they looked down upon the corsair's deck, the leering upturned faces of her crew peering back with rude malevolence.

"Fire!" cried Gowse. His second brought the slow-match to the touch-hole.

With an almighty bang and a gout of smoke, the gun jerked back against its stays.

This time Arabella remained with the gun. Ears ringing, the tang of burnt powder on her tongue, she peered out the gun-port and through the smoke, hoping against hope. . . .

Just for a moment the smoke cleared, showing the still-sputtering ball as it crashed through the corsair's deck, well aft. . . .

And then a great ball of flame came rushing out of the hole, followed almost immediately by a roaring crash so loud that even Arabella's already deafened ears rang.

A gust of black smoke rushed through the gun-port, making Arabella choke and completely obscuring her view. Shouts, screams, and confusion followed, men coughing and colliding in the sudden dark. Heedless of exposure, Arabella pulled up her shirt and breathed through the fabric.

Gradually order returned. The force which had pressed them against the deck eased, then vanished. The smoke began to clear, and Arabella quickly tucked her shirt under her belt again. All the men gathered around the gun-ports, peering through the filthy, cluttered air. . . .

And then someone called, "Huzzah!"

Soon all the rest joined him, including Arabella. The corsair had been blown completely in two, smoky flames guttering in the wreckage. The Frenchmen, stunned or dead, floated everywhere. The only sound that penetrated the ringing in Arabella's ears was the crack of small arms fire, *Diana*'s marksmen and the few surviving privateers trying to finish each other off.

The men on the gun deck cheered and clapped each other upon the back. From somewhere a flask of whisky appeared and was passed around. Even Arabella took a swig of the harsh, burning stuff.

And then Watson, one of the young midshipmen, appeared in the hatch. "Damage report!" he called in his small piping voice. "How many casualties?"

Gowse and the two other gun captains tallied the men and materiel lost or damaged during the battle. The gun deck had caught only one ball from the corsair, which had wounded three men but not killed any. "The captain'll be pleased to hear that, I'm sure," said Gowse.

At that the midshipman looked grave. "Haven't you heard?" he said.

Arabella's heart, so recently lightened by victory, suddenly felt as heavy as lead.

"Quarterdeck took a hard hit just before that last shot," the midshipman continued. "The captain was struck in the head by flying wreckage."

He swallowed. The whole gun deck fell silent, all the men focused on his small pale face.

"We don't know if he'll make it."

12

AFTERMATH

After the battle, Arabella's mood resembled the air around the ship, still fogged with dense, stale smoke and cluttered with wreckage and clumps of black, clotted blood. Any joy that might have remained from the victory over the French, and Arabella's small part in it, was extinguished by the reality of that victory and its aftermath.

The captain still lay in the cockpit, under the constant eye of the surgeon. The ship rattled with rumors as to his condition, but even when real news could be had it was inconclusive at best, discouraging at worst. The bleeding had stopped, it was said, and his injuries were supposed to be survivable, but he was still completely unconscious and his prognosis was uncertain.

The situation made Arabella sick with worry. If the captain were to die . . .

No. The idea was too terrible to contemplate, and so she would not do so. She would instead continue on, just as she had before the French attack, so that he would be proud of her when—*when*—he returned to command.

Fourteen of *Diana*'s crew had been killed, including Arabella's messmate Hornsby. Though she hadn't known him well, he had been kind to her, always willing to share his considerable knowledge of the air, and his absence from her mess was like a missing tooth—an aching gap that would never be filled again in this life.

Hornsby and the other dead were given a traditional aerial burial: wrapped in canvas, splashed with lamp oil, set alight, and cast away aft, where the wind from the pulsers would keep the flame going until the body was consumed or drifted beyond sight.

Another of those whose flaming carcass had vanished abaft was Kerrigan, who'd been killed by the same final shot that had knocked the captain unconscious. Arabella's feelings on this loss were mixed. The man had been harsh to her personally, but the captain had plainly respected his talents as an officer, and she had to admit that he'd been no more demanding of her than he had been of any other crewman, even himself. Even though she'd never liked him, the lack of his strident voice from the quarterdeck somehow made *Diana* feel like less than herself.

So, with the captain incapacitated and Kerrigan dead, it was Richardson, the second mate, who found himself in command. Arabella had barely even met the man, a thin pale Irishman with dark eyes and a stammer, but from the other members of her mess she learned he was considered competent but inexperienced. And though he did his best to emulate Captain Singh's firm demeanor, even the most decisive command delivered in his reedy Irish tenor sounded rather like a question.

The ship Richardson commanded was in a sorry state. Every deck, every mast, every sail had suffered some degree of damage. One in three of the surviving men was injured, some very seriously; the surgeon had cast three amputated legs and two arms overboard.

One of the arms still drifted along with the ship, caught in an eddy off the starboard beam, which some in the crew called a bad omen and Arabella found deeply disquieting. Whenever she was on deck, or on the starboard hull, laboring with the other waisters to cut away the shattered wood so the carpenter could replace it with spare or salvaged timber, she could not prevent herself from glancing at the arm, now black and twisted, which tumbled slowly in the air like some ghastly pub sign swinging in the wind.

As for the corsair's crew, only one had survived. Most of those who had not been killed in the explosive destruction of their ship had been picked off by sharpshooters; three who had hidden in the wreckage had died in a pitched cutlass battle with *Diana*'s salvage crew. Their bodies had been sent abaft along with *Diana*'s dead.

The lone survivor had been found unconscious in the corsair's wreckage, and though he had regained his senses shortly after the battle his condition had quickly worsened. Now, according to the scuttlebutt, he lay moaning incomprehensibly in the surgeon's cockpit and was not expected to live much longer.

One day as Arabella was sanding smooth a repaired section of deck with a pumice stone—a sweaty task that generated huge quantities of choking dust—Faunt came and tapped her on the shoulder. "Report to the surgeon," he said, jerking a thumb aft.

Arabella grimaced even as she wiped the clinging *khoresh*-wood dust from her face and made her way down the ladder to the cockpit. Of all her dreary tasks, those dealing with the ship's surgeon were among the worst. She might be called upon to empty bedpans, or change stinking bandages, or even hold down a thrashing airman while an arm or leg was sawed away. In that last case, she had barely retained her breakfast. The only good thing about a trip to the cockpit was that she might catch a glimpse of the captain—who still lay insensible, though at least his condition was not worsening.

The surgeon, a portly bespectacled man called Withers, seemed to smell of blood even when there were no spots of it upon his coat. "Ah, Ashby," he said as she entered the dark and noisome cockpit. "Faunt tells me you've been tutored in French."

"I have, sir."

"Good." The surgeon hesitated, his eyes glancing downward. "Our prisoner's condition is deteriorating, and I fear that he may not survive much longer. My own command of the language is not sufficient to . . . to convey this intelligence to him, and ask if he has any last requests."

Arabella swallowed hard, recalling her French tutor's impatience with her. Yet she had found French more straightforward, and much easier to pronounce, than Khema's tribal language. "I will make an attempt," she said.

The survivor thrashed weakly in his hammock, moaning, eyes darting about beneath their lids. His skin was pale and mottled, and his blood-soaked bandages stank of rotting meat. "*Monsieur?*" she asked, laying a hand on his uninjured shoulder.

One eye pried itself open. "*Oui?*"

For a moment Arabella's breath caught in her throat. This was a conversation she would have great difficulty beginning even in English. Yet her duty to the ship, and mere human kindness, demanded it of her. "*Le médecin . . . il dit que vous êtes très malade.*" The surgeon says you are very sick.

At that the prisoner gave a weak chuckle, which quickly devolved into a hacking cough. "*J'y sais,*" he managed at last. I know that.

"*Il dit . . . il dit vous peut-être pas vivre.*" He says you might not live. She knew her statement was far too direct for politeness, and feared she had mangled the grammar, but hoped that she had at least gotten the point across.

Apparently she had, as the wounded Frenchman's already

doleful face grew still more dire. *"Ah,"* he said at last. *"C'est dommage."* That is a pity.

Despite the seriousness of the situation, Arabella nearly smiled at this example of the famed nonchalance of the French. Then she composed herself. *"Avez-vous des . . . demandes finales?"* Do you have any last requests? Or some approximation of that.

He seemed to consider for a moment, then said, *"Je voudrais les derniers sacrements catholiques."* I would like Catholic last rites. Not a surprising request.

"Je vais voir . . . que je peux faire," she told him, and gently squeezed his shoulder. I will see what I can do.

She conveyed the man's request to the surgeon, who nodded with pursed lips. "I believe we may be able to accommodate him," he said. "Thank you. You are dismissed."

Before she left the cockpit, she paused briefly at the captain's hammock. Though he did not seem to be in quite such bad shape as the French prisoner, he still lay pale and sweating and insensible. "Come back to us," she whispered.

He made no response.

Two hours later, one last corpse was set adrift, with acting captain Richardson muttering in Irish-accented Latin as it went over the gunwale.

As Arabella watched the fitfully burning bundle of rags float away toward the sun, she realized she had never even learned the Frenchman's name.

It was nearly a week—a week filled with the hard work of chopping and hauling and scraping and painting to bring the ship back to some semblance of her previous condition—before Arabella saw the captain again. Still under the surgeon's care, he had been moved from the cockpit to his own cabin.

Withers laid a weary arm across Arabella's shoulders before she was allowed to enter the cabin. "I've brought him up here in hopes that the air and light, along with the familiar surroundings, will help him recover himself. But he's not sensible, and requires constant care. As you are the captain's boy, I will be relying on you to help minister to his needs, and you must report to me *immediately* upon any change in his condition. Any change whatsoever, d'ye understand?"

Arabella nodded, not trusting her voice. Imagining the captain lying injured and insensible made hot salt tears pinch the corners of her eyes and the back of her throat, and she feared that any attempt to speak would instead bring forth nothing but a gush of sobs.

They entered the cabin. Half the great window had been smashed in the battle, the shattered panes now covered with rough planking, and the space was still disordered and stank of smoke. Aadim sat in his accustomed position to one side, face and clothing besmirched with soot but otherwise apparently unharmed. And in the middle, sprawled in his hammock, lay the long dark body of Captain Singh.

His head was tightly wrapped in a bandage, blood seeping through at his left temple. The face visible below that bandage seemed racked with pain, or perhaps merely bad dreams, and twitched at irregular intervals. His whole body, in fact, twitched and spasmed frequently, explaining the disordered state of his bed-clothes.

Every twitch seemed to tug at her heart. To see this fine, brave man reduced to so miserable a state raised such strong emotions in her breast that she could barely breathe. She knew at once that if there were any task she could carry out, any thing at all she might do which would aid his recovery, she would perform it unhesitatingly.

She had not, until that moment, realized just how deeply this man had fixed himself in her sentiments.

"The motion is a positive sign," the surgeon explained, breaking into Arabella's brooding abstraction. "It indicates that all the connections between his brain and limbs are intact, awaiting only the return of consciousness. Until that occurs, you must keep him lightly covered, so that he remains cool but not chilled. Here is a sponge; you must squeeze a little water onto his lips every half an hour. Mark that he licks it off and swallows it, and take care that he not breathe it in." He gave her further guidance as to the care of his bandages and other needs, and adjured her again to summon him immediately upon any change in the captain's condition.

"H-how long," Arabella managed to stammer out, "will he be like this?"

The surgeon gave a small sigh. "The Lord alone knows." He then excused himself to tend to his other patients, promising to return before the end of the watch.

After the surgeon left, Arabella stared into the captain's face—the dark, piercing eyes now hidden behind trembling lids—and gently stroked the sweating brow beneath his bandages. "You *will* recover your senses," she whispered reassuringly. "You *will.*"

After one last glance at her unconscious captain, she busied herself in tidying up the cabin. Hundreds of tiny bits of glass still floated in the corners, and had to be swept from the air with a damp washing-leather. Even as she worked, though, she could not stop her eyes from straying to the captain as he lay insensible in his hammock. But though he still twitched and thrashed at intervals, he seemed neither better nor worse off.

She did notice that a lock of his hair had dislodged itself from under his bandage and now rested against his closed eyelid. Perhaps it tickled, causing at least some of his restless motion.

Tenderly she brushed the lock aside and tucked it back under the bandage.

And then came a sound—a brief whirring of gears, somewhat reminiscent of the clearing of a throat—that made her look up.

The sound had come from Aadim, the navigator. His head had turned to face her, so that the green glass eyes sparkled in the sunlight slanting in through the unbroken panes of the cabin's great window.

Dismayed by the automaton's apparent attention, Arabella quickly drew back her hand from the captain's forehead.

For a moment longer the shining green eyes seemed to lock with hers. Then, with another sound of gears, the head swiveled back to its previous position.

Heart pounding, Arabella cast her gaze about the cabin. Amidst the clutter and damage, the automaton's lenses still glittered intact in their brass fittings. Surely the turn of the navigator's head was only a reaction to her own rather sudden motion, a purely mechanical response.

Surely.

———————

The surgeon having expropriated Arabella to the captain's care, she was largely excused from her other duties, and for the next several days she spent most of her waking hours in the great cabin. Yet, despite the seriousness of the task and the diligence with which she performed it, it still occupied no more than half the day.

The time she spent changing the captain's dressings, mopping his fevered brow, and rearranging his disordered bed-clothes was heartrendingly difficult, for many reasons, but also very dear to her. Yet she could not spend nearly as much time at these tasks as she might wish, for no matter what her feelings, her prime consideration was to maintain her identity as Arthur Ashby. No captain's boy, however loyal, would moon over his superior officer as much as Arabella, left to her own devices, might do.

And so Arabella wound, cleaned, and fueled the lamps. She restored books, charts, and instruments to the places from which they had been dislodged by the ship's violent maneuvers and the impacts of the French cannonballs. Every item of brass or bright-work she polished until it gleamed. She assisted the ship's carpenter in the repair of the cabin's bulkheads, fittings, and furniture.

She even cleaned and inspected Aadim. Hesitantly at first, as though approaching an unfamiliar *shokari*, she brushed soot from his face and clothes, but like the inanimate object he was he did not react. Soon confidence began to return, and she made sure that his springs were wound and all his workings were free of splinters and grit. His other parts, too, which extended throughout the ship, she inspected and repaired as much as she was able.

So diligent was she in her care of the captain and his cabin that the ship's officers seemingly began to accept her as part of its furniture, taking little notice of her when they came to visit. Apart from their frequent appearances to assess the captain's condition and to extend their best wishes to his unconscious, but perhaps still receptive, ears, they also used the cabin as a meeting-place for private conferences away from the crew's hearing. And though they often shooed Arabella out for the most confidential of these discussions, occasionally they seemed to forget that she was there, and when that did occur she did her best to ignore their muttered conversation. But on one such occasion, acting captain Richardson conferring with the other officers on some point of navigation, Arabella overheard something that made her ears perk up.

"Though I'm loath to suggest it," said Stross, the ship's sailing-master, "we could try the clockwork navigator."

Upon hearing this, Arabella glanced toward Aadim, who still sat stiff and unmoving in his accustomed place. After cleaning and inspecting him, Arabella had wound his springs daily, and to the best of her knowledge he was entirely functional. Why would the master imply he was not available?

Surreptitiously she edged closer to the officers' conversation.

"We do have its draughts," the master continued, "and the instructions Captain Singh wrote up. . . ."

"No," said Richardson, with a sad shake of his head. "I can't count the number of times he tried to teach me to work the d——d thing, and no slightest bit of it ever stuck in my brain. Even with written instructions, I'm sure I'd never trust any course that came out." He sighed. "I wish Kerrigan had lived. The man was a lout and a martinet, but he was better with the automaton than I."

Even as she continued to quietly polish the lamps behind the captain's hammock, Arabella quivered with tension. She felt that she should volunteer her knowledge of Aadim's workings . . . yet she feared calling attention to herself, for any additional attention could reveal her sex. Furthermore, she lacked confidence in her own, only somewhat trained, skills with the automaton.

"Well, then," the master began, but then fell silent, peering out the window with a distant, considering expression. "Well, then," he began again, "I suppose I shall just have to do my best with ruler and compass. But I must warn you that it will be a near thing, and if we fail to intercept this asteroid . . ." He blew out a breath. "Well, I cannot tell you what we'll do then."

"Do what you can," Richardson said, clapping the master on the shoulder, "and put your trust in God."

"I shall endeavor to do so," the master replied, closing his eyes and dipping his head.

The conversation stuck in Arabella's head, especially because of the unanswered questions it raised. For the whole rest of that day, in between her other chores, she did what she could to remain within earshot of the master and the other officers, trying to over-hear and piece together some idea of the ship's situation.

If nothing else, the task distracted her from the captain's dete-riorating condition. Despite all her attentions and the surgeon's care, he seemed to be growing thinner; though his twitching and trembling continued, its frequency and strength were diminish-ing; even his mahogany brown skin, now dry and clammy, had paled to a weathered gray.

Every half an hour she dribbled water on his lips and waited for the dry and leathery tongue to lap it up. At these moments the captain's face seemed at its most animated, merely asleep rather than unconscious, but when the water was gone it returned to a disturbing, ashen mask of himself.

The sight struck daggers through her heart. "You *will* recover," she whispered again and again, in as reassuring a tone as she could muster.

Though she did not know, in truth, whom she was trying to reassure.

All that day she fretted over him, doing all that she could, hoping for the best and fearing the worst. As she tended him she kept one eye on Aadim, but though the automaton did move from time to time it never seemed to be responding to her actions as it had on that first day.

It was after supper, when the officers gathered in the captain's cabin to drink their grog, that she finally learned that the ship was in even more peril than she'd feared.

Richardson and the others floated above a chart of the region, spread out and tacked to the floor. From her studies with the cap-tain, Arabella recognized the great aerial current in which *Diana* was now embedded, denoted by a series of arrows, along with its side-currents, eddies, and cross-winds. The ship's position was marked with a pin, but all the officers' attention was directed to a tiny spot, labeled Paeonia, in the far corner of the chart. The spot rested at the center of a long, looping figure-of-eight, which Arabella knew represented its motion relative to the current over time.

"At this time of the solar year," the sailing-master said, "the asteroid should be here." He peered at the tiny lettering inked on the figure-of-eight, then placed a second pin about an inch from the inked spot. "And, according to my observations, our current wind speed is eighty-one hundred and a bit knots." He measured out a distance of about four inches on his calipers, laid a straight-edge against the pin representing *Diana*, lined it up with the ar-rows on the chart, and walked the calipers along it. "Here's where we'll be in eight hours."

The caliper's pointed tip rested near the straight-edge's closest approach to Paeonia, still at least five inches upstream from the pin.

"With the men in the shape they're in, we can pedal at no more than six or seven knots." Stross adjusted the caliper to a tiny gap, walked it eight steps from the straight-edge toward Paeonia, and placed a third pin there.

All the officers stared at it. A gap of nearly four inches sepa-rated the third pin from the second.

"Seven thousand miles short," breathed Richardson, then cursed quietly.

"More like ten thousand, actually," the sailing-master said in an apologetic tone. "Accounting for the third dimension."

Richardson cursed again, more vehemently this time.

All the officers floated quietly, contemplating the chart. Ara-bella, too, stared hard at the lines and pins. It was exactly like some of the navigation exercises the captain had set her, except that this time the situation was not merely theoretical. There was a cross-current on the chart that would carry them much closer to the asteroid, but to reach it would require them to cover a distance far greater than they could pedal in a mere eight hours.

"You've found no other asteroids in our path?" Richardson said.

Stross shook his head. "There's two or three we might reach, but according to the charts none of them is wooded to any degree. There's always the possibility of a wandering comet, of course, but those so seldom have any plant life at all."

Richardson sighed. "So it's Paeonia or nothing. And in eight hours it'll be behind us."

Still Arabella stared at the chart, thinking about something she'd read in one of the books the captain had loaned her. The arrows began to move in her mind's eye, flowing across the chart, air currents meshing and colliding like gears in a complex mechanism.

"Perhaps," suggested Higgs, the boatswain, "we'll meet up with another Company ship."

"Aye," Richardson scoffed sarcastically. "We'll pull right alongside and say 'Pray, neighbor, might ye lend us five hundredweight of coal till Thursday next?' And they'll be happy to do so, as they will through sheer happenstance be loaded down with twice the amount required for their own landing."

The boatswain's face darkened. "No need to come it ironical."

Richardson sighed. "I suppose we'll have to burn the cargo, then."

"All them fine linens?" moaned Quinn, the purser. "And the furniture and rugs, up in smoke just to fill the balloons?"

"They tried that in *Earl of Wessex*, remember?" the master cried. "Fat lot of good it did 'em! Burned up every stick of cargo they did, and half the decking too, and still scattered themselves all over the Juno Plain." He sighed. "No, lads, it's coal we need, five hundredweight at least, or else half a ton of fresh charcoal."

"Might as well wish for a flying pony!" the boatswain shouted. "H—l, a flying coach-and-six!"

In reply the master growled and clenched his fist. Richardson's eyes darted, all in a panic, from one angry officer to another, but only a series of ineffectual blubbing sounds emerged from his lips.

And then Arabella burst out one word: "Drogues!"

All at once the officers' argument cut off. They stared at her as though she'd appeared from nowhere.

Arabella clapped her hands across her mouth.

She hadn't meant to speak. She had not even realized at first that she had spoken aloud. It had only been the suddenness of the realization that had forced the word from her mouth.

"How long have you been hiding there?" Richardson snapped, straightening in the air, his expression cold. The other officers skewered Arabella with their gazes, pinning her to the spot where she floated. "What's your name?"

This was Arabella's worst nightmare. "I—I'm Ashby, sir. I'm, I'm tending to the captain, sir." As she spoke, she realized that she had positioned herself between the captain and the quarreling officers, as though to protect him from the knowledge of his crew's disarray. "Surgeon's orders, sir."

"Surgeon's orders or no, you are *not* to intrude upon my private conferences with—"

"Just a moment, sir," Stross interrupted. Richardson fixed him with a hard glance, but he stood his ground, glaring back just as hard for a moment before turning his attention to Arabella. "Did you say 'drogues,' lad?"

Arabella swallowed. "Aye, sir, I did."

Stross licked his lips, staring upward in concentration, then peered down at the chart. "Mr. Quinn, did you mention linens?"

The purser stammered for a moment before replying. "W-we've fifteen crates of fine linens, yes, bound for Fort Augusta."

"Tablecloths, that sort of thing? Good sturdy Ulster linen?"

"What the d—l does—?" cried Richardson.

Stross held up a hand in Richardson's face, quite rudely.

"Tablecloths!" he demanded of the purser. "Do we have some? At least ten or twenty?"

"Yes!" the purser squeaked. "Sixty, in fact, I think."

Stross nodded slowly, scratching his chin, contemplating the chart. He reached out one finger and tapped the cross-current Arabella had spotted, then took the calipers and measured the distance from there to the pin representing *Diana*. "Drogues," he repeated, and looked Arabella right in the eye.

"We'd have to start right away, sir," Arabella said.

"Aye," Stross said. "And the calculations will be tricky. Very tricky indeed, without the navigator."

In for a penny, thought Arabella. "I can work the navigator, sir. A bit."

All the officers looked at her.

"The captain was teaching me, sirs. Before the French attacked."

Richardson's glance darted from Arabella to Stross and back again. "What in blue blazes are you contemplating?"

Stross glared balefully at the acting captain. "You *do* know what a drogue is, don't you, sir?"

For a long moment Richardson blinked rapidly, lips pressed together, jaw set hard. "Refresh my memory," he spat at last.

Stross grinned and nodded toward Arabella. "I'm sure Ashby can explain it."

Richardson looked at Arabella with an expression of undiluted malevolence. She glanced toward Stross for assistance, but his face held nothing but a studied, beatific calm. The other officers looked on with a mixture of shock and frank curiosity. Trembling, she closed her eyes. *It's no worse than reciting Martian history for Khema*, she thought, and began to speak, quoting from *Thompson's Guide to Aerial Navigation*. "An aerial drogue is a construction of sturdy, windproof fabric, typically conical or hemispherical, whose open end is fastened to a cable attached to an airship. The drogue is generally propelled downwind by means of a gun, catapult, or other mechanism. The ship can then employ the drogue as an anchor point so as to proceed in a direction nearly perpendicular to the wind." She swallowed and opened her eyes. All of the faces but Richardson's had changed to expressions of amused satisfaction. For his part, Richardson ignored Arabella and glared at Stross. "That is the general principle, at least."

"Nicely done, Ashby," said Stross, who then nodded pleasantly to Richardson.

With a visible effort, Richardson controlled his anger. "Very well," he said through gritted teeth, then turned to the boatswain. "Mr. Higgs, you are ordered to requisition a quantity of fabric, and any other necessary materials, from the cargo, in order to create a drogue or drogues sufficient to change the ship's course and intercept the asteroid Paeonia. Mr. Quinn, you are ordered to assist Mr. Higgs and to keep proper records of all materials requisitioned. Mr. Stross, you are ordered to plot an expeditious course to the asteroid Paeonia, using any available means to do so, and bring the ship directly there forthwith. And Ashby, you are ordered to assist Mr. Stross in his efforts." He straightened in the air, doing his best to look down his nose at the others present, though as it happened they were all floating above his eye level. "Are your orders clear?"

"Aye, aye, sir," they all chorused.

"Come on, lad," said Stross. "We've much to do, and little time to do it in."

As the other officers left the cabin—Richardson favoring Stross with a withering look as he departed—Stross unpinned the chart from the floor and spread it out on Aadim's desk. While he was doing this, Arabella tended to the captain.

The poor man, unconscious though he might be, seemed distressed by the sounds of the argument. He had thrashed off almost all of his bed-clothes, and beads of sweat had burst out on his wrinkled brow. Arabella gently tucked the captain's blanket back in place and patted away the sweat with a soft cloth. "All will be well, sir," she murmured low. "We'll get *Diana* to Mars safely, you'll see."

The sound of Arabella's voice, the touch of her hand, seemed to calm him somewhat. His face relaxed a bit, though it still retained the quietly pained expression it had held ever since the battle with the French, and he lay still beneath his blanket. "Rest well, sir," she said, and patted his shoulder.

"Ashby, come here!" Stross said, and she joined him at the desk. "Here's the situation."

The three of them made an odd conference. Arabella trembled beneath her shirt, frightened as much by the responsibility that had been placed upon her shoulders as by the fear of discovery. Stross, the sailing-master, was a man she'd barely even encountered before the current crisis. Balding, with dark hair and eyes, his rather portly torso contrasted with the hard hands and strong arms of an experienced airman; his attitude of bluff confidence and attention to duty nearly masked the worry that lurked behind his eyes. And Aadim, though his eyes gazed woodenly out the window, seemed nonetheless to be paying close attention to the discussion, the mechanisms within his desk ticking and whirring beneath the chart.

The situation, as Stross put it, was grim. Two of the French cannonballs had shattered the hull of *Diana*'s coal-store, and over half the coal had drifted away before the breach could be repaired. This coal, carefully budgeted because of its great weight, was intended to fill the ship's balloons with hot air upon arrival at Mars, allowing her to drift gently downward to a landing. Without it, once the ship entered the influence of Mars's gravity she was doomed to smash upon the surface. Returning to Earth, where they would be more likely to encounter another ship that might have coal to spare, was out of the question—the ship's stores of food and water would never stretch so far.

"So we're bound for Paeonia," Stross concluded, tapping the pin on the chart. "It's a substantial asteroid, uninhabited but forested; there we can cut timber and make charcoal. Not so good a fuel as coal, to be sure, but adequate to the task."

"How much time will it take to make the charcoal we require?"

Stross considered, rubbing his chin. "Some weeks, I should imagine."

"I see." Arabella's heart grew heavy at this news. Any delay might allow that dastardly Simon to reach her brother before she could warn him. But she must not give up hope.

"You say you have some facility with the navigator," Stross said, breaking into Arabella's distressing train of thought. He grasped Aadim's right hand and wrenched it toward the pin representing *Diana*, the sudden rough motion making the navigator's gears shriek in protest. Arabella cringed as though she felt Aadim's pain in her own shoulder. "I know how to plot a course from here to here"—he hauled the hand across to the pin representing Paeonia—"but not how to tell the d——d thing to use drogues."

"I believe it is done thus," Arabella said. She returned Aadim's hand to *Diana*, moving it slowly and evenly to respect the gears and levers, then pressed down on the index finger to indicate the start point. A click sounded from within Aadim's mechanism. Next she opened a panel on the side of the desk, where several brass levers were labeled with the letters of the Greek alphabet.

She paused for a moment in thought, then raised the beta lever and lowered the lambda lever. Then she contemplated the gamma lever. For a transit by drogue, should it be set up or down? Down, she thought. She laid her finger upon the lever and pressed it gently downward.

The lever seemed to resist her finger, quivering gently from the motion of the gears behind it. Aadim's whole body joined in this motion, his head seeming to shift fractionally from side to side.

Curious, she thought, and tried raising the lever instead. This time it moved smoothly, locking into position with a soft click, and Aadim's head remained still.

Upon reflection, this combination of settings made the most sense.

Arabella moved Aadim's hand to the side current and pressed the index finger again to indicate the destination of the transit. Finally she returned the three levers to their initial positions and moved the hand to Paeonia, carefully setting the dial indicating displacement in the vertical dimension before pressing the index finger for a third time. Immediately a series of whirs and ratcheting sounds began to vibrate from inside Aadim's desk. "It may take some time for the calculations to complete," she said. "The use of drogues adds quite a bit of complication to the course."

"A very tidy bit of work," Stross said admiringly. "How many years did it take you to learn all that?"

"I've only been studying with the captain since I came on board," she admitted. "But my father—" She stopped herself, wary of revealing too much about her past. "He owned a great many automata," she concluded feebly.

"I must thank the man when we return to England! What might his name be, and where might I find him?"

Suddenly the nervousness which had vanished while Arabella was working with the automaton returned in full force. This line of questioning probed perilously close to secrets which must not be revealed. "My—my father has passed on," she said, which had the benefit of being true. "I would prefer not to discuss him any further. It pains me to do so." Which also, she realized, was true.

"I'm sorry, lad," Stross said, and clapped her on the shoulder so hard that she began to tumble in the air. "Well, now. You stay here, look after the captain, and let me know straight away when the course is plotted. I'll go see how Mr. Higgs fares with the construction of the drogues." He paused in the doorway before departing. "I won't lie to you, lad. This is as nasty a situation as any I've faced. But with your work on the navigator, I think we may have a chance."

Arabella could only hope that his trust in her was well founded.

13

DROGUES

Arabella was giving the captain his water when a bell sounded, indicating that Aadim's calculations were complete. She took a slate and chalk and recorded a series of numbers from the dials on the front of his cabinet, double-checking her work because there were many more figures than usual. She then consulted a book of tables—this part was something she knew the captain would have done from memory—and wrote down the sailing order and navigation points required to implement the course. When she was done with that she again double-checked her work, then copied it out quickly but neatly on a sheet of vellum.

As she sanded and blotted the sheet, she was forced to admit that she had only a theoretical understanding of how this plan would be implemented. As an airman, her skills were limited to hauling on a rope when instructed; as a navigator, she was keenly aware of the great size of the field of navigation and the tiny proportion her own command of it encompassed. It was as though she knew how to lay out the major blocks of color that made up a portrait, and understood the general principle of two eyes, a nose, and a mouth, but must rely upon others to execute the actual brush strokes.

She was deeply concerned about Richardson's abilities in this area. The man was plainly more interested in maintaining his own authority than he was in the actual running of the ship. The other officers, and the men who reported to them, were doing their best to work within the constraints that the acting captain laid upon them, but she feared that at some point their practical knowledge and Richardson's orders would collide. Arabella hoped that would not occur in the middle of a difficult navigational maneuver.

She gently laid a hand on the captain's shoulder before leaving the cabin. He looked even more thin and pale than he had even that morning. Despite her best attentions, and the nourishing broth that the surgeon fed him several times a day from a kid-leather squeeze bag, he seemed to be fading rapidly. "The head wound is healing well," the surgeon had said. "I've seen men recover from worse. But whether or not he regains his senses . . . that's in the Lord's hands."

Fighting to keep the tears from her eyes, Arabella silently pledged to do every thing in her power to keep the ship and crew alive until he returned to his proper place on the quarterdeck.

She emerged on deck to a scene that would have been humorous in its domesticity, had not the situation been so perilous. Dozens of airmen, rough-handed muscular men, worked closely and diligently with needle and thread, plying their needles through heaps of shining white linen tablecloths instead of the usual sails or shore-going clothes. Other men were employed in bending canes of rattan into hoops and pounding out brass grommets. And the ship's carpenter, assisted by two of the most senior airmen, was busily cursing over a strange assemblage of wood, iron, and cordage.

"Have you the sailing order?" Stross called out from where he hung by the rail in close conference with the purser.

"Aye, sir," Arabella replied, and with a kick propelled herself across the deck to hand him the paper. He looked it over with a skeptical eye. "It'll be close," he muttered. "Very close." He tapped the page. "If that cross-wind isn't exactly where the charts say, we might miss the asteroid completely."

Arabella floated at attention, unable to reassure Stross. Although she had confidence in Aadim's calculations and her own transcriptions, she had no idea how practical the resulting course might be.

Stross peered hard at the paper, then shook his head. "We'll need five drogues, lads," he called out, "not four!"

The men with the needles groaned at this new intelligence, but the purser cried out as though in pain. "Lord's sake!" he said. "At this rate we'll go into the red for sure!"

"Better that than dead," the sailing-master replied. He folded the paper and tucked it into his jacket pocket. "Ashby, can you ply a needle?"

"Aye, sir," she admitted. Though she despised needlework, thanks to her mother she had considerable experience with it.

"Report to Mr. Higgs, then, and be sure to make every stitch tight!"

"Aye, sir." But, despite the direct order, she did not leap to comply, finding it very difficult to tear her gaze from the great cabin's door.

Stross must have seen her reluctance, because he reassured her, "The captain will get along without you for a few hours." Then he pursed his lips and shook his head. "If it's much longer than that . . . well then, it won't really matter."

Arabella was somewhat embarrassed to discover that many of the men were both faster and tidier with needle and thread than she was. Her mother, she knew, would be terribly disappointed in her. She soon shook off this attitude, though, and concentrated her efforts on working as rapidly as possible. Stross and the other officers continually admonished them to work faster, faster, for they had only a few hours until the current carried them irrevocably past the asteroid. But at the same time, they must be sure to make the seams as strong as possible, for the drogue would bear the entire weight of the ship.

Richardson, she noted, remained imperiously on the quarterdeck, looking out over the work but not taking any part in it.

Soon they had the first of the drogues completed. A great cone of white linen, its open base was formed of a ten-foot circular loop of bent rattan, and it measured twenty-five feet from base to tip. Two of the topmen quickly lashed together a rope harness to attach it to a sturdy cable, the other end of which they carried below.

The carpenter and his men, meanwhile, had managed to cobble together a sort of crossbow from a long, springy plank and several yards of cordage. This they had fastened to the forecastle deck, arranged to fire its projectile just larboard of the figurehead.

Arabella, still stitching as fast as she could, stole an occasional glance over one shoulder as Stross and Higgs packed the drogue into as compact a bundle as possible and placed it in the improvised crossbow's basket. They then called all available waisters—those not currently occupied with stitching—to the forecastle, while a series of commands from the quarterdeck sent the topmen scurrying aloft.

Only Arabella and a few other waisters were left to continue fashioning drogues. Some of the idlers, including the surgeon and Pemiter the one-legged cook, took the topmen's places. She helped them to understand what needed to be done, and they set to their sewing with a grim determination entirely unlike any thing Arabella had ever seen on land or in the air. The cook's technique had only enthusiasm to recommend it, but the surgeon worked with astonishing precision and rapidity, his long pale fingers flying.

While Stross conferred with the waisters gathered in the forecastle, all the sails came down, leaving *Diana* completely bare-masted for the first time Arabella could recall. Soon a stiff breeze began to ruffle the billows of fabric around her, as the wind current was now able to slip past the ship nearly unimpeded. After so many weeks of near perfect calm on deck, other than when the pulsers were being employed, it was a very strange sensation, which pointed out how very unusual this maneuver would be.

Stross sprang to the masthead. "Listen up, lads!" he called. "If this works, there'll be a h—l of a jerk. Be prepared to hang on tight!" He then descended to the quarterdeck for a muttered conference with Richardson and the other officers.

Arabella made sure her safety line was snug about her ankle and there was a solid handhold nearby. She kept stitching; the second drogue was nearly complete.

"Crossbow men, haul away!" came the command from the quarterdeck. The waisters in the forecastle, bracing themselves against capstans, masts, and pinrails as best they could, began to haul on a line, drawing the crossbow's string with the bundled drogue back and back. Soon the line was quivering with tension, the men groaning and sweating with the effort.

"Away drogue!"

The waisters released the line, which whipped hissing along the deck, and with a great deep thudding vibration the crossbow flung the bundled drogue away downwind. The cable behind the drogue paid out rapidly as the package of linen and rattan diminished in the distance.

And then, suddenly, it reached the end of the cable. Immediately the drogue snapped open.

The deck jerked out from beneath Arabella, sending her and

the rest of the drogue-makers crashing into the quarterdeck's forward bulkhead in a great untidy pile of men and rope and linen. With many shouts and curses—and Arabella using her arms to fend away any hands that approached her chest—they began to untangle themselves.

She shook herself free from the imprisoning fabric. A torrent of commands was flowing from the quarterdeck; in the rigging above, topmen scrambled to sheet home sails and bowse up the yards. Soon the force that had propelled her against the bulkhead changed direction, sending her and every other loose man and object sliding to starboard. Unaccustomed winds buffeted her face and threatened to whip the linen away into the blue.

The ship was swinging from the drogue, she knew—swinging like a vast pendulum, moving crosswise to the great current that still carried her forward at a speed of thousands of knots. Arabella hoped the linen, the stitching, the rattan, the cables, the knots would hold. The whole ship thrummed like a bowstring.

Arabella fetched up against a coaming and made herself fast there. As quickly as she could, she found her work and resumed her sewing. The second drogue must be complete, and well made, very soon. At one point she drove the needle all the way through her thumb, but though she cried out from the pain she drew it right out and kept working.

"Cast away drogue!" came the command. A moment later the cable zipped away across the deck; the pressure on Arabella's back vanished. Even as she floated up into the whipping air she kept stitching.

"Ready drogue number two!" came the cry from the quarterdeck. Nearly done!

Stross appeared above Arabella. "Come *on*, lad!" he cried, holding out a desperate hand. "We're falling free!"

She bit off the last stitch. "Here it is, sir!" She wadded up the ungainly package and thrust it at him. He and Higgs carried it away, while Arabella joined the cook in his work on the third drogue.

And so it went with the second drogue and the third and the fourth and the fifth. After she handed the final drogue to Stross, who looked as weary as she felt, she could do no more than float nearly insensate near the quarterdeck. The final thrum and jerk, still an impact though no surprise, barely impinged upon her consciousness as she fell heavily against the bulkhead below her. Only a few remaining scraps of linen cushioned her fall. She didn't care.

For the fifth time the ship swung through the air, hanging impossibly from a great bag of linen. The force on Arabella's back grew, changed direction, then slacked away.

She opened her eyes. The cable stretching away to the final drogue now pointed well to starboard, no longer taut and straight but slack, a long gentle curve that grew more and more pronounced as the drogue at its end began to fold and tumble like a flower losing its bloom.

The air calmed. The ship drifted.

Diana floated, turning slowly, in the immense blue bowl of the air.

"Where's that d——d cross-current?" cried Richardson from the quarterdeck.

Stross, floating beside the acting captain, turned to face Arabella, annoyance on his face warring with fear welling up from far below.

The other officers, and then the men, followed Stross's gaze.

It seemed that every man on the ship was staring at Arabella. Her breath seemed to catch in her throat. "I——" she began, then choked off. "I checked the figures twice. . . ."

"We should never have trusted that godforsaken machine!"

Richardson shouted. "Useless f——g thing! Now we're stranded in midair!"

"At least we tried," Stross said. The annoyance and fear in his face had faded, replaced by weary resignation.

"This is *your* fault!" Richardson shrieked, rounding on Stross.

"I don't recall hearing any better suggestions from you!" Stross replied with considerable heat.

"We might've tried the pedals at least!"

So this is how it's to end, Arabella thought. *Drifting and bickering until we smash upon the Martian sand.* She closed her eyes against the unpleasant sight and touched the locket at her throat. *I'm sorry, Michael, I did what I could. Please don't trust Simon. . . .*

And then something changed.

It took her a moment to realize what had happened. The arguing had stopped. Even the muttering of the men had ceased, leaving a silence in which the gentle sough and creak of the rigging could plainly be heard.

Arabella opened her eyes.

Captain Singh hung in his cabin hatchway. Thin—oh, so painfully thin—with his skin still ashen and his head still bandaged, he floated with his night-shirt tail drifting above his bare feet and his hands gripping the coaming on either side. But though his face was sallow and drawn, his eyes were bright and alert.

She was so very, very happy to see him so that her breath caught in her throat. If only she could embrace him, to properly express her joy!

"Gentlemen," the captain said, his voice no more than a whisper but plainly audible in the stillness, "what was all that banging-about just now?"

Stross swung himself over the quarterdeck rail, stopping himself with one foot on the deck exactly in front of the cabin. He drew himself up to attention in the air and saluted smartly. "We are attempting to intercept the asteroid Paeonia so as to make charcoal, sir. We have deployed drogues in order to reach a cross-current; however we are currently stranded."

"Glass," the captain whispered, and extended a hand. One of the midshipmen immediately appeared with a telescope.

The whole crew waited as he peered about in all directions.

"Observe, gentlemen," he said, and pointed off the larboard beam.

Stross accepted the glass from the captain. Richardson and the other officers on the quarterdeck used their own instruments.

Then Stross laughed aloud. "Aha!" he cried, pointing. Other men with telescopes began to shout and cheer, clapping each other upon the back.

Arabella shaded her eyes and peered in the indicated direction. At first she saw nothing.

And then she realized what she was seeing.

Motion in the air. Scraps of cloud, tiny bits of drifting matter, even the shimmering air itself, all whipping past so rapidly the eye could barely perceive it.

The cross-current.

"To the pedals, lads!" Stross cried. "We'll be set in that current in less than half an hour!"

But though the men streamed past her, laughing and jostling, toward the lower deck, Arabella forced her way through the crowd to the captain's side. The surgeon was already there, peering into the captain's eyes and feeling with his fingers for the pulse in his neck.

"I'm very glad to see you up and about, sir," Arabella said. Though this small expression of sentiment seemed entirely inadequate, it was, she thought, what Arthur Ashby the captain's boy would say. "If you please, sir, I could fetch you some broth from the galley."

"Thank you, Ashby," the captain whispered. "I should like that very much."

14

PAEONIA

Diana was soon safely moored at the asteroid Paeonia.

Arabella had never seen an asteroid before. Asteroids, she knew, were the islands of the air, great floating mountains of rock ranging in size from less than a mile to hundreds of miles in diameter. Thousands of them drifted in the skies between Earth and Mars, yet so great were the distances involved that to encounter even one in a voyage was a rarity. If not for the French attack, *Diana* would not have come close enough to this one to make it out with the naked eye.

Paeonia proved to be a highly irregular sphere some ten miles across, but from where *Diana* floated nearby it seemed more a ball of foliage than of rock, the solid surface entirely invisible beneath a tangled canopy of branches and leaves at least fifty yards deep.

"I thought asteroids were rocky," she said to Stross one day after she had assisted him in sending off a work crew. Eight men pedaled an aerial launch—little more than an open wickerwork frame with a small pulser at the back and a pair of sails for steering—away from *Diana* toward the great green expanse of Paeonia.

"Most small asteroids are entirely barren," Stross explained, "but the ones over five miles or so carry a small force of attraction, and draw drops of water and bits of organic matter to themselves from the atmosphere. Over time these build up into a layer of soil, loose and sandy to be sure, but if any seeds should happen to be carried into the air from the surface of Earth or Venus they may find purchase there. Once established, they generally colonize the entire surface." He gestured to Paeonia. "Fortunately for our purposes, this one bears a fine crop of oak and elm, both of which make tolerably good charcoal."

Arabella herself, unlike the rest of her mess, was not detailed to charcoal-making duty—as captain's boy, she was tasked with caring for him through his recovery. Though she would have liked to visit the asteroid, with its endless net of twining branches playing host to twittering birds and birdlike things, she was not too sorry to be missing the work of sawing, stripping, and hauling vast quantities of wood, the piling up of damp sandy soil around a stack of logs, or the endless pedaling of the air-pump which kept the slow-burning logs in their caul of soil just barely alight. The work crews returned at the end of each shift weary, exhausted, and filthy.

She had to admit that she took a certain malicious pleasure in seeing Binion covered with soot and half-dead from fatigue. When he saw her smirk, he spat "bum-boy" at her, but seemed too exhausted to do any thing else.

Richardson continued as acting captain. But with the real captain now awake and improving, he seemed paradoxically less concerned about asserting his own authority, and his relations with the other officers grew much more cordial. It was as though the weight of the mantle of responsibility had caused him so much discomfort that he'd snapped at his subordinates.

Though conscious, the captain was still extremely weak, and even in a state of free descent he could not bear to remain on the quarterdeck for more than an hour or two. He spent most of each day in his cabin, slowly building up his strength and sleeping frequently. From time to time Arabella noticed him gripping his head with an expression indicating severe headache, but she never once heard him complain of it.

Arabella continued to tend to the captain's needs, changing his bandages, bringing him soup from the galley, or doing any other thing he required. But, paradoxically, now that he was conscious their relations became more distant than they had been while she was caring for his unconscious body. For as long as he was awake, she must work to maintain the fiction of Arthur Ashby, captain's boy. It was only while he slept that she could gaze upon his face and entertain fancies entirely inappropriate to her supposed sex and station.

And so they discussed the theory and practice of aerial navigation, the workings of Aadim and automata in general, and the sights he had seen during his travels. But though she gently inquired into his personal history, the captain proved as resistant as Arabella herself to discussing his family and his early life. All he would say was that he had joined the Honorable Mars Company at the age of eighteen, sailing on *Swiftsure* as navigator's mate.

She wished that he would reveal more details about his inner life. Perhaps, she sometimes dared to hope, beneath his smooth professional veneer he might harbor some warm feeling toward herself. But though she must respect the captain's desire to keep his life private—he certainly offered her the same courtesy—she realized that his reticence only made him more intriguing and mysterious, and seemed to draw her into wanting to know more.

The man was already intriguing enough, with his deep brown

eyes, his musical accent, and his charming and very polite man-
nerisms. Some of the crew, she knew, considered him little more
than a sort of performing ape, resenting his rise to the position of
captain. But though she'd encountered this attitude toward for-
eigners as much on Mars as she had in England—her own mother
harbored a particularly virulent strain of it—she herself had spent
so much time among Martians that she held no predispositions
against *any* thinking being, no matter their birthplace, color, or
shape.

Indeed, so far was she from prejudiced against Captain Singh
because of his race that sometimes, in idle moments, she found
herself musing on what sort of life they might build together. He
was in every way, she reflected, far superior to the foppish dandies to
whom her mother had insisted on presenting her back in England. . . .

She shook herself and returned her attention to her duties.
Such a gulf separated them—a gulf of status and breeding and, of
course, hidden gender, as well as of color and creed—that such a
notion could never be any thing more than a distracting fancy.

She needed to bend her thoughts toward *Diana*. All her efforts
must be dedicated to getting the ship, captain, and crew back into
peak operating condition, so as to resume the journey to Mars
with all possible dispatch. Every day that passed put her further
behind Simon.

Above all, she must not despair. Even if Simon arrived at Mars
days or weeks before she did, it would take him some time to
convince Michael to leave off the running of the plantation and
go hunting with him. There was still time for her to warn her
brother of the deadly danger their cousin posed. But that time
was slipping away with every turn of *Diana*'s spring-wound glass.

Arabella was far from the only one who felt the pressure of passing time. *Diana* and all her sister ships of the Honorable Mars

Company made their money by speed, by the swift conveyance of cargo from the place where it was produced to the place where it was needed. The officers and crew, too, must be fed and watered, and the ship's stores were far from inexhaustible. Every man knew in his bones that *Diana* must finish her repair and resupply and be on her way as soon as ever she could, and the officers drove them hard.

So it was that the men, exhausted though they might be from their labors at charcoal-making, grew restive, muttering direly to each other about short rations and lost bonuses. The exhilaration that had followed the corsair's defeat bled away, as day by weary day the men pedaled back and forth to Paeonia with load upon load of charcoal. They ate their diminished meals in sullen silence, and whispered complaints passed from hammock to hammock among the watch below.

Even the charcoal, the very substance that ensured their survival, served only to worsen the crew's foul mood. The filthy stuff, far bulkier than the coal it replaced, soon overfilled the coal room, and lumpy burnt-smelling bags of charcoal had to be stowed in every unused corner of the ship. Every man and every thing smelled of it; greasy black powder drifted into every corner and begrimed every bodily crease. The biscuits and salt beef came from the galley seasoned with the gritty stuff. It crunched between Arabella's teeth.

The very air, it seemed, tasted of charcoal, and the weary, filthy, red-eyed men smoldered beneath its smoky pall.

As the mutterings increased, Arabella's earlier concern about a possible mutiny returned. Though she had neither heard nor seen any further sign of dissent in the ranks since that overheard conversation in the head, she feared the conspiracy had continued unseen. But who were the conspirators?

She tried to investigate without seeming to do so, asking veiled questions and straining to overhear muttered conversations, but learned nothing concrete—if there was a plot in train, the plotters were very good at keeping quiet about it. And though she kept an attentive ear open at all times for that grating voice she had overheard in the darkness, never did she hear it upon the deck or below it.

Perhaps, she thought—she *hoped*—the rumblings of mutiny she'd overheard had been nothing more than talk.

She should tell the captain, she knew. But the man had such a strong respect for personal responsibility—in fact, a nearly Martian sense of *okhaya*—that she knew any report of questionable behavior from a member of the crew would be met with sharp skepticism. And as she had no certain knowledge of *which* member of the crew it might be . . . serious charges should not be brought up lightly, and if she told him of her fears without absolute, objective evidence it might diminish her in his eyes. And that was something she devoutly did not wish.

So she continued to wait, and watch, and listen.

At last the master and the purser judged that nearly sufficient charcoal had been chopped and burned and carried and stowed for a safe landing on Mars. The carpenter and his mates had long since repaired *Diana*'s battle scars; patches of pale fresh *khoresh*-wood gleamed on every deck and bulkhead, torn sails had been neatly stitched and patched, and fractured spars had been "fished" with splints and wrapped tight with cordage.

The officers met each day in the great cabin, at six bells of the afternoon watch, to assess the ship's progress. Arabella, now tacitly accepted in the officers' company, filled and wound the lamps as they conversed.

"One more load ought to do it," Stross said, and sucked a great draught of grog from his drinking-skin. Weeks of unceasing labor had made him nearly as thin and weak as the captain, and great dark circles stained the cheeks beneath eyes reddened by the ever-present charcoal dust. "The last clamp should be well-cooked by two bells in the forenoon tomorrow. Figure another two watches to dig it out, haul it aboard, and stow it."

"Well done, Mr. Stross." The captain looked around the floating circle of officers. "Is all else in order?"

"Aye, sir," they all replied in turn, though the boatswain added, "As long as we don't encounter another corsair, nor any foul weather. Starboard mast's nothing more than splinters held together with whipcord."

The captain's already-drawn face grew still more serious. "We will do our best to avoid any untoward stress upon the masts."

That night Arabella awoke with a filthy, charcoal-stinking hand pressed against her mouth. Though she struggled, it very quickly became apparent that she was outnumbered, her arms and legs and shoulders pinioned by several pairs of silent hands. The darkness around them lay still, save for the sleepy mutterings and snores of the exhausted, hungry men.

"Hello, bum-boy," came a voice in her ear—the same anonymous, grating voice she had overheard in the head so long ago.

No . . . no longer anonymous! For though her assailant pitched his voice unnaturally low, and added a grating growl to disguise it, his use of that sneering insult revealed his identity.

Binion!

"We know you've been nosing about," he said. "Trying to suss out who's with us and what we're going to do. Well, here's the plan: We're going to mutiny, sell the ship, cargo and all, on the black market, and split the proceeds. We'll all be rich!" She glared in the midshipman's direction, clenching her jaw, for all the good that might do. "We're nearly ready to make our move. Soon's we cast off from this d——d asteroid with a full load of charcoal, we'll take the ship. We've more than enough men to do it." The hand tightened on her cheeks. "But we've one small hitch. Kerrigan was our navigator." A cold, sharp pressure appeared at the side of Arabella's neck: Binion's rigging knife, sharp as a razor. She tried to squirm away from it, but the imprisoning hands held her fast. "We need someone who can run the clockwork man."

Binion leaned in closer, his foul breath rasping in her ear. "You *will* work with us," he said, the knife cold and hard against the vein that pulsed in her throat. "We'll be fair—you'll get the same share of the spoils as every other man." The blade pressed still harder. "Now tell us that you accept our offer, or we'll end you right now." The hand clamped over Arabella's lips loosened just enough to allow her to speak.

"You can't kill me," she whispered. "You need a navigator."

Hands tightened all over her body, especially Binion's, which gripped her jaw. "Don't think we haven't thought of that, lad," he said, and she swore she could *hear* his malicious smile in the Stygian blackness. "We've seen how much you dote on that darkie captain. So once we take the ship we'll keep him alive—but if you don't cooperate, or if we think you're steering us wrong, his journey will be cut short." The knife slid a fraction of an inch along its length, and Arabella felt a trickle of blood begin to well up. "So . . . do we have an agreement? Just nod."

Arabella swallowed, the motion of her throat bringing a sting of pain from the knife blade. How could she possibly agree to help these harsh, cruel men in their campaign of mutinous larceny? But if she said no, or if she tried to struggle free, Binion in his self-centered cruelty would surely end her life. They'd kill the captain, too, no doubt, and without her warning Simon would do Michael in and leave her mother and sisters penniless. But if she acquiesced, they'd leave her alive—for now, at least—and she might have a chance to thwart the mutiny.

Gritting her teeth, Arabella nodded, her head barely moving in Binion's grip.

"Now say it." The hard fingers that pressed the bones of her jaw and cheek relaxed just slightly. "Swear on your life that you will join and support our cause."

"I swear." Just for the moment she was glad of the darkness, which hid her expression of anger and disgust.

"Well, lad, that weren't so hard now, were it?" said Binion, and he slapped her cheek lightly like a doting uncle. "Welcome to the brotherhood of independent airmen." He muttered to the other men, who released Arabella and melted away into the darkness, then leaned in close to Arabella's ear. "Mind you, now," he whispered, his foul breath assaulting her nose, "we'll be watching you close. If you make one move to warn any one or interfere, the deal's off, and you *and* your precious captain go over the side . . . in pieces." He pressed the knife hard against Arabella's throat, making her gasp. "Don't think we won't." Then he pushed himself away, making her hammock vibrate like a plucked harpsichord string.

She lay staring into the darkness for a long time, trying to calm her hammering heart. Her throat was dry, her head pounding with headache. Her clothing was soaked with sweat, now growing cold.

What would she do now?

What *could* she do?

Tears came then, hot stinging tears of fear and rage and shame, and she stuffed her fist in her mouth to stifle the sobs.

15

MUTINY

Arabella had not slept when the call to "rise and shine" sent her and all the other men tumbling from their hammocks. "Big day, boys!" cried the boatswain's mate. "No more charcoal-makin'! Today we set sail for Mars!"

At this declaration a weak, ironic cheer sounded across the deck, but a weary and fearful Arabella could not join in. Instead she peered about, examining each face in the guttering lamplight, trying to discern which men were conspirators in Binion's mutiny. An overly cheerful expression might be as suspicious as one with hooded, shifting eyes. But in this light, to Arabella's worried eyes the exhausted, red-eyed men all looked like potential mutineers.

After breakfast, Arabella was called into the great cabin to observe as Captain Singh and Stross worked with Aadim to plot out the ship's course to Mars. Her heart leapt up when she heard the call, thinking that this would be the perfect opportunity to warn them of Binion's plot, but as soon as she arrived it sank again. Binion was there ahead of her, along with several other midshipmen, all seemingly attentive to the captain's navigation lesson. Seeing the dismay on Arabella's face at his presence, Binion favored her with a nasty smirk.

The rest of the day passed in a blur. She hauled on lines to raise sails, scrubbed black charcoal grit from decks and bulkheads, and spent weary hours slaving away at the pedals like any other airman, but all her attention was fixed on the officers and the men around them, alert for any opportunity to slip a word into Stross's ear, or Higgs's, or even Richardson's. But whenever an officer was near, so were dozens of ordinary airmen—men whose hard eyes and set jaws marked them as possible mutineers. And if any of the traitors should overhear her imparting her intelligence, her life and the captain's would be forfeit.

She tried to leave a note in the great cabin where the captain might find it. But she lacked pen and paper to prepare such a letter in advance, and even the minute it would take to scrawl a note in the cabin was one more minute of privacy than she could obtain there. Binion was seemingly as inevitable as her shadow and twice as ominous, and when he himself was not present some other midshipman, one whom she'd seen Binion laughing and smirking with, was always nearby.

Perhaps not all the midshipmen were mutineers. But she could not be certain who was a member of the conspiracy and who was not. The only thing she could be sure of was that no one with any skill in navigation was part of it, or else they'd never have need of her.

Weary, fearful, and paralyzed by lack of information, Arabella kept a sharp eye on every man and awaited an opportunity to take action.

The mutineers struck just before eight bells of the afternoon watch, when the men on duty were tired, hungry, and inattentive. Arabella and Mills had been sent to haul a cask of water from the hold for the men's supper, and were just engaged in the slow manipulation of the heavy, awkward thing—bigger than two big men—up the hold's aft ladder when they heard a great commotion from the deck above. Shouts and thuds were interrupted by a sharp *crack*, then silence.

Arabella looked to Mills. "What was that?"

Mills's dark eyes narrowed. "Pistol."

Arabella moved ahead of the water cask, still pressing inexorably forward, and braced her back against the bulkhead to bring it to a halt. She and Mills paused, straining their ears, but could make out little more than muted voices and the occasional thump. Then one voice rose above the others, a high and strident one, delivering a long and impassioned speech. Though the words failed to penetrate the wood above their heads, the speaker's voice was far too familiar.

Binion.

"I'm afraid it's mutiny, Mills," Arabella said. "And I need to know which side you're on—the mutineers', or the captain's."

Their eyes met over the cask. Mills's eyes, the nearly black irises floating in pale yellow whites, gazed steadily into Arabella's, his expression revealing nothing.

Arabella swallowed. One or the other of them would have to take sides, or they'd still be here staring at each other when the mutiny reached them. "I'm . . . I'm with the captain," she said, knowing that with her words she might be signing her own death warrant. "He's been good to me."

Mills blinked. "Been good to me too," he said. "No telling what them mutineers might do."

Arabella blew out a sigh of relief, but then realized her peril had been only slightly reduced.

Mills maneuvered himself around to her side of the floating cask and spoke low. "So we do what, now?"

A sudden, sharp scuffle from abovedecks was brought to a halt by another pistol shot, which caused both their heads to jerk up like a pair of puppets. "We can't just hang about here waiting for the action to come to us," Arabella said.

Mills frowned, then ducked back down the ladder. He returned a moment later with a heavy belaying pin, which he handed to Arabella. A second pin was tucked into his rope belt, next to his rigging knife.

Arabella took the pin and worked it beneath her own belt. She had no knife of her own. "We should bring the cask with us, as though we didn't know that any thing was wrong. It might stop a bullet."

They put their shoulders against the cask and began the long, slow process of nudging it into motion.

As they reached the lower deck, they were met by a topman, one not well known to Arabella. "Belay that hauling," he said. "It's all hands on deck."

Arabella held tight to the cask, which continued its stately progress upward, keeping its bulk between herself and the topman. The bulkhead behind her brushed against her shirt-collar. Mills, she noted, had positioned himself similarly, the great muscles of his shoulders bunching in anticipation. "Why?" she asked the topman, pretending ignorance.

"Change in course," he sneered, revealing his allegiance.

Mills's eyes met Arabella's, she jerked her chin toward the topman, and without a word they braced their backs against the bulkhead and pressed the heavy cask toward the mutineer with all the strength of their arms and legs. Such a maneuver was strictly against the rules for normal operations—a full water cask was never to be allowed to move rapidly, on account of the danger of its great weight.

For a moment the airman did not notice the cask's change in course and speed. For a second moment he failed to appreciate its implications. By the time he took action, attempting to scramble out of the way, Arabella and Mills were already halfway up the ladder to the upper deck.

The drifting cask, moving with stately inevitability, pinned the topman between itself and the mainmast with an audible crunch, rebounding away with an equally unhurried pace and only a slight tumble.

He began to scream just as they had reached the upper deck. But the screams soon faded away, to Arabella's mingled dismay and relief.

One mutineer down. How many more were there?

They paused at the top of the forward ladder, peering from the darkness of the hatch out onto the sun-washed deck. But even as they watched, the sunlight rippled and dimmed—a storm was on its way.

Clearly something unusual was afoot. Men drifted in clumps here and there, laughing or chattering nervously without any display of discipline. And on the quarterdeck, no officers were visible. Only Binion and two other midshipmen—two midshipmen whom Arabella had heard the captain describe as the least capable students of navigation. Binion held a cocked and loaded pistol in each hand.

"Where are the officers?" Arabella whispered to Mills.

He shrugged. "Overboard?"

Arabella's throat tightened at the thought. "We can but hope not." She paused, thinking hard. "Binion told me he'd keep the captain alive, as a hostage to force me to navigate for them. He's probably tied up somewhere." The upper deck, from which they had just come, was mostly one large room and currently empty of airmen. Surely if the captain were still alive he would be under heavy guard. And if he were further below, on the lower deck or in the hold, they'd have seen some evidence of it as they'd ascended. "Must be in the great cabin," she muttered.

And, indeed, two stout airmen floated before the great cabin's door, truncheons in their hands and their arms crossed on their chests. One of them wiped at his eye, where a drop of rain had just impacted, and Arabella realized with a start that he was Gowse. Surely the captain was imprisoned there, and perhaps the other officers as well. "We must creep in there somehow and free him."

Mills glanced at her quizzically. "How?"

Arabella peered with trepidation across the vast open expanse of deck between her and the two guarding airmen. Once she and Mills emerged from the shadow of the hatchway they would be in plain sight of every mutineer. The only alternative route involved the aft ladder, which emerged immediately between the two guards.

"I don't know," she admitted, then looked behind and below herself in case some other mutineer might be approaching from behind. At the moment no such threat was imminent, but that situation surely could not last.

Binion's harsh high voice caught Arabella's attention then. "Where's Westphal?" he called.

"He went below to roust out the last of the fish," someone replied.

Arabella and Mills exchanged a worried glance. Westphal must be the topman they'd crushed with the water cask.

"He's been gone too long," Binion said. "Bates, Parker—go follow him up. Take truncheons." Two burly airmen immediately separated themselves from a group and launched themselves through the air toward Arabella and Mills.

"We need to hide!" she hissed to her companion, and quickly scrambled back down the ladder.

But the upper deck, though dark by comparison with the cloudy day above, was well illuminated by lamps at this hour, and with all the hammocks taken up it was essentially one large open space. Cargo and bags of charcoal, lashed firmly in place against the hull on each side, offered no hiding place. Scrambling down the ladder to the lower deck would leave them just as trapped.

At least during the battle with the French, Arabella thought with grim humor, she'd known that every one on the ship was on the same side. . . .

Suddenly she had an idea. "The gun deck!" she whispered, and leapt down the length of the deck. Mills immediately followed, the great strength of his legs propelling him so quickly that he reached the gun deck hatch first, undogging it just as she arrived. They slipped through and dogged the hatch behind themselves just as the sound of voices announced the arrival of the two airmen on the deck they'd just vacated.

The closing hatch cut off the lamplight, leaving Arabella and Mills in near-darkness. "What now?" Mills whispered. "Sure they find us here, and no exit."

"There *is* an exit," she replied, and pointed. "Three of them."

There, beyond the vague bulking forms of the three cannons, gleamed three square outlines: the gun-ports.

Moving as quietly as they could, they made their way forward and eased the number one port open, letting in a rush of air and light that made Arabella squint.

Cautiously, she poked her head through the port and peered around. Directly ahead, in the path a cannonball would travel, she saw roiling clouds and a flash of lightning; other than that, her view was largely blocked by the bowsprit and its rigging. But what little she could see revealed no mutineers, or indeed any men at all. "No one's about," she said as she ducked her head back inside. "We'll make our way along the keel and enter the great cabin through the window."

"Tight fit," muttered Mills. Thunder rumbled low without, as though in agreement with him.

Indeed, the port was not much more than one foot square. "I'll help you through it," she said.

Arabella, with her lean boyish frame, slipped easily enough through the port—the wood of its frame stank of gunpowder and hot iron, even more so than the rest of the gun deck—but it refused to pass Mills's broad shoulders. "One arm at a time," she said, but though he tried first the right and then the left, the bulk of his chest was still too great, no matter how she tugged and Mills pushed. Cold, heavy drops of rain had begun to spatter her back and hair, but the small lubrication they offered was not sufficient. "We could get some grease from the galley. . . ."

Suddenly the eyes in Mills's straining face snapped open. "They're here," he said.

Behind him, they could both hear the gun deck hatch being undogged.

She had never before seen the stoic airman's expression so grim. She was sure her own face bore a similar look of anguish and dismay.

"Try to hide in the shadows," she said. "I'll come back for you as quick as I can."

Though his eyes were filled with misery, Mills nodded. Quickly he pulled his head and arm back through the hatch and shut it, leaving Arabella clinging to the bowsprit rigging and breathing hard. The rain was coming quite hard now, and she wiped it from her eyes. Lightning flashed again, and then the thunder rolled, much closer now.

Then, through the hull, she heard the gun deck hatch open. She held her breath.

A shout: "You there! Both hands in sight!"

Another voice, equally loud: "What're ye hiding from, laddie?"

Mills's response was inaudible over the patter of the rain on the thick hull. Arabella tensed, preparing to spring away if the port opened.

"Ye'll be coming with us, laddie," came the second voice, followed by the loud smack of a truncheon on flesh.

Arabella hung, shivering with cold, in the rigging. Mills had been captured, for certain. Perhaps he had been struck; perhaps that sound was only a prod or a threat. Would he give her up?

She pressed her ear to the hull, stopping her other ear with her hand against the sound of the rising storm. Only silence from within.

And then came the dull thud of the gun deck hatch closing, followed by indistinct receding voices.

She let out the breath she'd been holding.

Safe—for the moment. But the whole length of the mutineer-controlled ship lay between her and the captain, even if he was where she thought she was, and Binion would notice her absence soon if he hadn't already.

Licking her rain-wet lips with a dry, sandpapery tongue, she crept out along the bowsprit.

Moving slowly and keeping close to the wood in hopes that any watching eye might pass over her, Arabella inched out to where she could see the masts. But as the mainmast began to appear above the figurehead, it seemed empty of men; as she peered around the bowsprit, she saw that the upper reaches of the starboard and larboard masts below were equally unpeopled. Only a loose end of sail flapped in the growing rain-lashed wind.

She let out a breath, then worked her way around to the bowsprit's lower side. Gusts made her sodden shirt flap against her torso, and she clung hard to the wood in fear of being blown from her precarious perch.

From here the hull curved down and away in a grand smooth expanse of golden *khoresh*-wood, silhouetted against the roiling, lightning-shot clouds beyond. The underside of the hull had been scraped clean of barnacles in the first week after departure from Earth and was now smooth as a baby's bottom, bare of any handhold. There was no work to be done here between launch and landfall. That, and naval tradition, explained why this part of the ship was so inhospitable to the traverse she was about to make.

The one feature that offered any purchase to Arabella's hands was the keel, a broad projection of copper-clad wood some eight inches wide. She gripped the keel's edges and began guiding herself down and around the curve of the hull, frequently pausing to wipe the cold rain from her eyes or dry her hands on her trousers for a tiny bit more traction.

As she crept along, orbiting the hull's vast round bulk like some tiny, low-hanging moon, her stomach began to clench as it had not since the day of the falling-line ceremony. Weeks of free descent had inured her to the constant feeling of falling that was the airman's lot, but now, disoriented by the rain that seemed to pelt in from every direction, she felt herself unmoored from any attachment. It seemed as though at any moment she might go drifting off into the churning sky. And if she lost her grip on the rain-slick keel, that fate would indeed be hers.

She clenched her jaw and gripped the keel's cold metal as firmly as she could with hands and feet, inching along with deliberate speed. She must arrive at the great cabin as soon as she could, but if she moved too quickly she risked sailing off into the air.

She tried to build up a rhythm, first pulling with her arms, gripping the keel between her palms while bringing up her legs, then pushing with her legs, pressing the keel with her heels while extending her arms.

Soon, despite the chill water that soaked her clothing to the skin, her every muscle began to burn. She kept inching along.

Ahead of her, the starboard and larboard masts came further and further into view as she moved, rising above the horizon of the hull like two great towers festooned with lines and dark, sodden sails.

And men.

She brought herself to an immediate halt, heart pounding, the keel's cold wet copper skidding between her palms.

Three topmen were clambering quickly up the rigging of the larboard mast—the one to her right, as she moved toward the stern—making good time. She had no idea what their orders might be. Had they been sent to raise some sail, trim some sheet, or simply look out for other ships? Or were they searching for missing airmen . . . or specifically for her?

Surely if Binion had ordered men into the rigging to look for her, he would have sent only one? That implied that the three men were on a mission to adjust the sails, in which case she should hold still in hopes of slipping past later while they were busy with their task. But trimming the sails usually required a larger crew than three. Perhaps they had been sent in a group to seek out, leap upon, and overpower any reluctant airmen. In which case she should move now, move as quickly as possible, in hopes of reaching the cabin before they could spot her and sound the alarm.

Panicked, indecisive, she looked left and right, but the smooth round hull offered no hiding place. But she did see one thing that offered a tiny hope: no men were climbing the starboard mast, at least none that she could see as yet.

Quickly Arabella moved to the left, pressing herself against the hull as best she could, hoping to hide herself behind the keel. At this point it rose nearly a foot and a half from the hull, though it met the hull in a curve that left less than a foot to conceal her body.

She could not tell from here, as she trembled with her cheek pressed against the cold, wet wood, whether or not she had managed to hide herself completely. But she had to move, somehow— to put as much distance behind herself as possible before she was noticed.

Gingerly, with tiny touches of finger- and toe-tips, she began to edge herself toward the stern. Making forward progress without pushing her body away from the hull and into plain sight seemed nearly impossible, but soon she worked out a technique where, pulling with the flat of her palm against the rain-wet surface of the hull, she could move—slowly—without exposing herself.

At least she hoped she was not exposing herself. Lacking eyes in her elbows and hips, she could not be sure. But no shouts of discovery came to her ears.

Grimly, hauling herself along foot by foot, she moved some twenty or thirty feet under cover of the keel before poking her head up again. The men on the larboard mast seemed engaged in some adjustment of the rigging, their hair and clothing whipped by the storm; the starboard mast was still unpeopled.

Judging by the angle of the masts, she had barely made any forward progress.

She peered over the keel at the larboard mast. Were the airmen there sufficiently occupied that they might not notice one small figure moving along the keel?

Perhaps. They were so far away that it was difficult to be sure. But, by the same token, she was so far from them that they might not see her. And the storm, still growing in intensity, might serve to hide her from their view.

She wiped her streaming eyes and peered down the length of the ship to where the rudder loomed from the hull. It seemed a very long distance to creep at her current pace, but it could in fact be no farther than the length of the upper deck.

A distance she had covered in one leap on many occasions, during gunnery practice and the battle with the French.

Keeping one eye on the larboard mast, she slowly edged out onto the keel . . . now fully visible to the topmen, though they did not seem to notice.

She swallowed, drew up her knees to her chest, took a deep breath, gripped the keel hard with her heels, and pushed off hard.

Arabella's heart pounded as the keel's copper surface flew by just inches below her chin. Cold rain battered like hail at her face and shoulders.

A flash of lightning limned the rudder ahead, drawing rapidly closer.

Too rapidly.

She reached out her hands to slow herself.

And then a projecting flap of copper caught her hand! Pain tore across her palm and stabbed up her arm as she tumbled away, stifling a cry of pain and alarm. The world spun around her—hull and keel and masts and black, roiling clouds tumbling crazily past in rapid succession. Thunder boomed, disorienting her still further.

Arabella flailed in the air, straining her blood-smeared fingers toward the keel as it flashed past again and again. The first time she missed. The second time she brushed it with her fingers, serving only to send herself tumbling in a different direction. Disoriented, she missed the keel again on its next pass, and again.

On the next pass, stretch though she might, the keel flew by beyond her fingers' reach.

And again.

Panic flooded her throat. The ship was receding from her, farther and farther on each rotation. Thunder and lightning disoriented her still further.

She stretched out a leg, reaching with her toes, but the keel only smacked her foot, adding a nauseating spin to her existing tumble.

And then something slammed into the back of her head.

Stunned by the pain though she was, she quickly groped behind herself for the offending object. One hand found rough, wet wood and gripped it with panicked strength.

With a painful wrench of her shoulder, her dizzying tumble slowed; a moment later the wood struck her across the hips. She folded herself across it, clinging like a desperate monkey.

Her head still spun, though her body's rotation had stilled. Her right hand throbbed with pain. She tasted blood.

She was clinging to the rudder, a massive plank of *khoresh*-wood which creaked ponderously in her arms, swaying slowly from the impact.

Looking around, she saw that both masts were bare of people. Had they completed their task and returned to the deck without seeing her? Or were the mutineers rushing toward her even now?

She wiped her eyes, shook her head to clear it, and began clambering up the rudder.

Climbing the rudder was far easier than moving along the keel, as the enormous black iron hinges, attached with bolts, that connected it to the keel provided many handholds.

At the top, two mighty chains floated free, their links clinking in the roaring wind. Arabella pulled herself along the larboard chain, where great blasts of wind-driven rain tried to pluck her from the ship, but as each gust came she clung tightly to the chain until it passed. At last she reached the ledge below the great cabin's window.

Carven vines, highlighted with gold leaf, bedecked the window's lower edge. Cautiously, keeping herself out of sight, she pulled herself along the vines, leaving behind herself a series of bloody hand-prints quickly erased by the storm. When she reached the window's lower starboard corner, she slowly put her head over the edge so as to peer into the cabin.

Her first view was of nothing but a buff coat.

Moving her head to one side and wiping the rain from the window with her sleeve, she had to suppress a gasp. Every one of the officers was crammed into the great cabin, with hands bound behind them, eyes covered with blindfolds, and mouths stopped with gags. Even Aadim had a cloth bag pulled over his head.

One midshipman, a very young boy by the name of Watson, floated in the center of the cabin, slurping from a bottle of Captain Singh's very best wine. The butts of two pistols projected from the waist of his trousers.

Arabella bit her lip. Watson's participation in the mutiny surprised her; he'd seemed a pleasant enough sort. But here he was. How could she get past him to free the captain and the other officers?

Just then the hatch to the maindeck burst open and one of the two men outside stuck his head in. "Watson!" he cried, wiping rain from his face. "Get yerself and them pistols on deck! That blackamoor Mills is kicking up a fuss!" Behind him, Arabella heard shouts and growls of anger.

Watson hastily corked the wine and departed, leaving the bottle spinning in the air behind him. The hatch slammed closed, and she heard it being securely dogged.

Thank God for Mills!

The great cabin's window was not designed to be opened from outside, but neither was it intended to be secure, and in a few moments she had worked one casement free from its catch, swung it wide, and slipped inside. The cessation of the pounding rain on her back was a small relief. "It's Ashby, sir," she muttered in the captain's ear, and slipped off his blindfold. One eye was swollen and purple, which filled her heart with compassion toward him and anger toward the mutineers. "I'll have you free in a moment."

But as soon as she reached behind the captain to untie his hands, she regretted that rash promise. Rather than merely being tied, the captain's hands were locked to the bench with iron shackles. The other officers were similarly secured.

Panic squeezed Arabella's chest. Watson or one of the other mutineers would surely return soon. She untied the captain's gag. "Do you know who has the key, sir?"

"Binion," he replied, his one good eye narrowing. The single word seemed more packed with loathing than its two syllables could accommodate.

Arabella swallowed. Getting the key from the head of the mutiny would be difficult indeed. "I'll try to get it, sir."

"Hurry," said the captain. "And put the gag and blindfold back. In case they return, they will not suspect you are still at large."

"Aye, aye, sir," she said, though it pained her to put the stained and filthy rag back into her captain's mouth and tie it behind his head. At least it was not so tight this time. The blindfold, too, she intended to tie but loosely.

But as she was pulling the cloth across his eyes, a sound came from behind her. She turned to see the hatch swinging wide, and a figure entering the cabin.

Binion.

The expression of surprise on his face was quickly supplanted by a sneer. "Well, well, so *here* you are. We've been looking for you." He drew a pistol from beneath his shirt—it was, she could see, quite dry—and pointed it squarely at Captain Singh's head, drawing back the hammer with an emphatic click. "Now yield, or the captain dies."

Arabella grimaced as she was hauled onto the deck by Gowse and the other airman who'd been guarding the captain's hatch, and not only because the cold rain began to pelt her face once again. Her arms were shackled behind herself—oh, how her heart had ached when the keys had rattled from Binion's pocket!—and the belaying pin, never used, had been taken from her belt.

The first thing she noticed as she emerged from the cabin was Mills, who had been lashed to a grating fastened to the mainmast. He was breathing hard and grimacing, and blood seeped from a cut over one ear. Clearly he had put up a considerable fight, though, as many of the airmen gathered around him sported injuries of their own.

"Look here, lads," Binion called, and the heads of the men on the storm-lashed deck swiveled to face him. "We've caught our last missing fish!"

A rough cheer greeted this news.

Binion turned to Arabella. Putting a solicitous expression on his face, he shook his head and tut-tutted.

"I'm terribly disappointed in you, Ashby," he said. His words were directed to Arabella, but his voice was pitched to be heard above the storm by every mutineer. "You gave your solemn word to join and support us in our endeavor, and yet, as soon as we took rightful possession of our ship, when we went looking for you . . . you were nowhere to be found! And as though that weren't bad enough, when we did find you, you were attempting to free our darkie former captain from the shackles in which, after a fair trial, we had placed him!"

Arabella did not dignify this tirade with any response. She merely glared at the man, blinking the rain from her eyes. But the mutineers on deck, looking to be less than a third of the original crew, laughed and jeered, the thunder seeming to laugh along with them. Arabella wondered where the rest of the crew might be.

"But we are magnanimous, are we not?" Binion called to the men. "And despite Ashby's violation of his solemn oath, we would happily accept him into our number." The men's reaction to this news was mixed—as many grumbled as cheered. "Now, now, lads, do keep in mind that Ashby is quite conversant in the usage of the clockwork navigator, a skill which, in the absence of our dear departed Kerrigan, we lack." The grumbles stilled.

"And yet . . ." Binion grabbed Arabella's shirt-front and pushed his spotty face into hers, though he still spoke loudly to the assembled mutineers. "And yet, Ashby has shown we cannot put our trust in his oath." He turned and faced the men, still gripping Arabella's shirt. "How then shall we ensure his cooperation?"

"The lash!" chorused the men. "The lash! The lash!"

At this, Binion laughed. "Just so, lads." He turned again to Arabella, putting on a contemplative expression. His hair whipped in the wind. "Ten lashes for now, just to show we mean business. If you don't follow orders after that, twenty lashes for the first offense, thirty for the next, and so on."

Though Arabella's heart raced, she set her jaw and raised her chin. "Lash me if you wish, but I'll never aid you," she declared, though her quavering voice belied her brave words. All she could do was hope that her resolve would prove firmer than her elocution.

Binion stroked his beardless chin. "Very well . . . twenty for you, and forty for your precious captain." Arabella growled inarticulately and tried to struggle free, but the two men who held her arms kept her firmly pinioned. "Then thirty and sixty. Then forty and eighty, and so on, until you either acquiesce or succumb."

Arabella, straining against the hands that held her fast, spat in Binion's face. But the flying glob of spittle was lost in the driving rain.

"I see I've touched a nerve. But we'll start with just ten for you." Binion pulled the precious key from his pocket, unlocked Arabella's shackles, then gestured with his pistol to the grating where Mills was already bound. "Seize him up."

The two airmen pushed off from the bulkhead behind them, carrying the struggling Arabella unwillingly across the deck, and brought themselves to a halt just above the grating. "Hold his legs," said Gowse, and then, without ceremony, yanked Arabella's sodden shirt from beneath her rope belt.

Panicked, Arabella crossed her arms tightly across her chest before the shirt could come off any further. "I'll k-keep the shirt," she stuttered through chattering teeth. "G-grant me that much d-dignity."

Gowse leaned in close, his broken and still swollen nose just inches from Arabella's ear. "It's for yer own good, lad," he whispered, not unkindly. "Bits of shirt in the wound can fester and kill ye."

And then, in one smooth move, he broke Arabella's grip on her chest and stripped her shirt off her body. The hard, chill rain struck her exposed skin like a slap.

For a moment she managed to shield her breasts with her arms. But then, with the same great strength that had removed her shirt with barely any notice of her resistance, Gowse pulled her hands apart. "Don't struggle, lad, ye'll just make it wor . . . what the *h*—*l*?"

Arabella squirmed in the man's inexorable grip like a trapped rat, squealing incoherently, trying valiantly not to cry. But though she did her best to extricate herself, or even to cover her nakedness with elbows or knees, the wind and the rain and the men's eyes still penetrated to her soft unprotected flesh.

"Yer a *girl*!" cried Gowse.

Arabella stood exposed on the deck, the driving rain cold on her bared bosom, tears hot on her cheeks.

Time seemed to stop still in its tracks. All around her men and boys stared at her, shocked expressions frozen on their faces. Even Gowse, still holding her arms, seemed paralyzed where he stood.

Arabella herself was the first to break the moment, yanking her arms from the man's grip and folding them across her chest. But having accomplished that much, she could manage no more. All she could do was hang miserably in the gusty, soaking air, hugging herself, blinded by tears. After a moment the man holding her legs released her as well, and she curled sobbing into a ball, a tight little knot of abject wretchedness.

She was ashamed. Ashamed of her nudity, ashamed of her femininity, ashamed of herself for being too weak to prevent this moment. What would become of her now? A half-naked girl, exposed on an airship full of mutinous airmen?

"I won't whip a girl," came a voice. Something brushed her hand. Wet cloth. Her own shirt. It was Gowse, who'd stripped it off, now handing it back to her.

She took it and clutched it, wadded up, to her chest. Putting the sodden, stained, and ragged thing back on was entirely beyond her.

As her shuddering sobs subsided, she began to be able to pay attention to what was happening around her. She wiped her streaming eyes and nose with her shirt-tail.

"I won't whip a girl," Gowse repeated. He floated between Arabella and Binion, arms crossed on his chest; she couldn't see his face, but the set of the shoulders beneath his sodden shirt indicated grim determination. The other man, the one who had held her legs, had drifted to one side, his eyes flicking indecisively between Gowse and Binion. The other mutineers also seemed to be hanging back, watching the situation. Distant thunder rumbled uncertainly beneath the roaring wind.

"Girl or not," Binion replied with some heat, "she's still the only navigator we've got." A flash of lightning froze his face for a moment in a sneering rictus. "You'll whip her, Gowse, or I'll whip her myself, and you as well!"

"I'd like to see ye try," growled the airman, the great muscles in his shoulders bunching as the thunder rolled.

Binion glared at Gowse, then, without taking his eyes off the man, extended a hand behind himself. "Watson," he called, "bring me the lash."

Behind him Watson, the young midshipman who had been guarding the officers, floated trembling and uncertain.

"Watson!" Binion snapped, and turned to face the smaller boy. "The lash!"

Recoiling from the force of Binion's command, Watson moved

in the direction of the red cloth bag, floating attached to a peg on the quarterdeck bulkhead, that held the loathsome item.

"Y-you don't have to do it," Arabella said.

Her voice shook as she forced the words past the sobs that clogged her constricted throat. Her eyes were blinded by tears and rainwater, and her nose stuffed. Yet she spoke, and loud enough to be heard above the storm.

All eyes turned to her.

Arabella wiped her eyes again and tried to straighten herself in the air—to take up again the airman's bearing which had been stripped from her along with the shirt. It was hard to draw herself upright while still clutching the wadded shirt in front of her nakedness, but she did the best she could.

"You don't have to do as he says, Watson," she repeated.

"Yes, he does," Binion countered. He drew the pistol from his shirt and leveled it at Arabella. "Or you'll get worse than a whipping."

The black O of the pistol's mouth gaped directly at her. But despite Binion's harsh words and the rain and the lightning, she saw the pistol tremble and knew that the man was afraid.

"He's nothing but a bully and a martinet, Watson," Arabella said. Even as she spoke, she realized the truth of her own words, and she found strength returning to her voice—shouting into the teeth of the storm. "He's a petty, insecure boy, and if you let him whip me now, sooner or later you'll find yourself at the end of that same lash."

The airman who had held her legs now moved toward Binion. "Really, Binion," he said, "this ain't what we signed on for. Taking from the Company's one thing, but I'd rather make my way by dead reckoning than put an innocent girl to the lash."

Binion's pistol swiveled rapidly between Watson, Arabella, Gowse, and the second airman. "You're all fools," he declared in a low and deadly voice, though the pistol hand now shook so hard that all could plainly see it. "She's no innocent! She had you all thinking she was a man! I'll wager she's been diddling the captain the whole time!"

"Now I've heard just about enough," said Gowse, and lunged toward Binion.

Binion aimed the pistol at Gowse and drew back the hammer.

And Watson slammed into him from the side, the two midshipmen tumbling together in a sodden, spinning midair ball. The pistol fired, a thunderbolt of smoke and flame shooting off harmlessly upward.

A moment later Gowse joined the tumble, his massive arms pinioning Binion's arms to his sides while Watson plucked the pistol from his fingers.

"Parker! Bates!" Binion cried. "Somebody suppress these insubordinates!"

Some of the mutineers immediately came to Binion's aid. But others rose to oppose them, and though the two groups fought hand-to-hand for a time, the mutineers fought without conviction, and the number of men supporting Binion dwindled quickly. The mutiny soon began to lose its momentum, then collapsed completely.

Nonetheless, Binion continued to shriek commands in every direction until Gowse put a gag in his mouth.

16

PASSENGER

A knock came on the cabin door, a welcome distraction from her racing thoughts. She arranged herself in the tiny space to allow the door to open. "Yes?"

It was Watson. "M-Miss Ashby," he stammered, "The captain requests your presence in his cabin."

The response "Aye, aye," tried to spring to her lips, along with a salute, but she pushed it down. "Certainly, Mr. Watson," she replied.

After the officers had been freed and the mutineers sorted out, Arabella had been whisked away to the carpenter's cabin—more like a closet—on the lower deck, so that she might clean herself up in privacy. Soon thereafter a dress had been obtained from somewhere, probably requisitioned from the cargo over Quinn's strenuous objections, and conveyed to the cabin with the captain's compliments.

Fitting herself into the dress in the tiny space had proved a considerable challenge.

The dress was quite fine, she supposed, though it was too short and the sleeves were entirely too tight. But after so many weeks in trousers, she found it nearly impossible to manage female costume in a state of free descent. The skirts billowed up and had constantly to be pushed down. On her previous trip from Mars to Earth, she had been given a sort of large garter to keep her skirt decently constrained at the bottom, but as no female passengers had been expected on this voyage *Diana* did not carry any thing in that line.

The other men—the men, she reminded herself—were more embarrassed by the sight of her legs than she was. They were the same legs as before. All of the men had seen those legs many, many times. Yet now that her sex had been revealed, the sight of them had suddenly become scandalous.

Watson knocked at the hatch of the great cabin, announced her presence, and was bidden by the captain to send her in. Watson opened the hatch and bowed her in, bending himself at the waist in midair as he gestured her to enter in a most gentlemanly way.

"Miss Ashby," the captain said, and he too bowed.

The whole situation was so very strange to Arabella's sensibilities that her eyes stung with tears. The great cabin, so familiar, compelled her to salute and snap a crisp "Reporting as ordered, sir." But the captain's deferential attitude seemed to demand a demure curtsy.

She did neither. She hung stupidly in the air and said, "You . . . you desired to see me, sir?"

She realized that her heart was pounding. Was it simple concern over the unknown reason for her summons to the great cabin?

Or was it fear . . . fear of what she might find in those dark, intelligent eyes of his?

Now that her sex had been revealed, would he think less of her, or dismiss her from his consideration entirely, as a mere girl? Or might, instead, the high esteem in which she believed he held her—in which she fervently hoped he held her—develop into another type of regard, one warmer and perhaps more intimate?

But the expression in those brown eyes did not address her concerns in either direction, showing nothing but polite respect. "Thank you for coming, Miss Ashby. Will you take tea?" He proffered the tray which she herself had prepared for him so many times, the little teapot fitted to its slots with its lid screwed on tight, a sweet biscuit held beneath the silver clip. She wondered who had laid it out for him in her absence.

The thought of Captain Singh preparing a tea tray for *her*, with his own hands, was too strange to contemplate.

"Thank you, sir," she said, if only to be polite, though as she nibbled the biscuit she realized she was ravenous.

Even so, she found herself taking gentle, ladylike bites rather than wolfing the whole thing down as she would have done when she was Arthur Ashby. How quickly expectations can change one's behavior, she thought.

"I called you in," the captain said, "to thank you for your actions during the recent mutiny."

"My actions?" She blinked. "I *failed*, sir. I did not even manage to get you free of your manacles before I was captured by Binion."

"I am referring to your actions on deck," the captain replied mildly.

Arabella dropped her gaze to her feet. "I suffered my shirt to be removed, and then collapsed in a blubbering heap."

"After which, according to the reports I have received, you faced down Binion's pistol, rallied the men, and recaptured the ship from the mutineers. No small accomplishment."

Her cheeks began to burn. "I . . . that description vastly overstates my role in the action, sir. It was Gowse who set upon Binion, and Watson who tackled him. After that, all the men took a hand. I did very little of my own accord, and nothing that any other loyal man would not have done in my place."

"Any loyal . . . man," he repeated, with slight emphasis on the last word. His dark eyes regarded her seriously. "It was Gowse and Watson themselves who told me what you did, and neither of them is of a temperament to minimize his own accomplishments. Your actions would be a credit to any officer, never mind a boy second class, and are a truly extraordinary achievement for a girl."

The captain's words raised deep and contradictory emotions in Arabella's breast. She should be proud of her actions, she knew, yet she had failed—failed to expose the mutiny before it occurred, failed to free the captain, and failed to keep her sex hidden, and now she worried about the consequences of that failure. She had lied, through omission if not explicitly, and taken employment under a false identity. Would she be punished for that deception, now that it had been exposed? "I'm concerned about the men," she said, approaching the question indirectly. "What will happen to those who took part in the mutiny?"

"Binion and the other leaders are now manacled in the hold, along with a few more who injured other men during the mutiny." Arabella cringed inwardly at the remembered sound of the topman Westphal's knees being crushed by the water cask. "The rest of the men who sided with them have sworn their loyalty to the Company and returned to their stations, though there will be an inquest and possible disciplinary action upon our return to Earth."

"And what will become of . . ." Again Arabella's gaze was drawn to her feet. ". . . of me?"

"I will be putting you in for a commendation from the Company. There are, of course, no guarantees, but I think your chances are excellent."

She looked up in shock. "A commendation? But . . . but I'm not even a . . ."

"You are far from the first to obtain employment on an airship of the Honorable Mars Company by pretending to qualifications he does not actually hold, Miss Ashby." Now it was the captain whose eyes drifted downward. "Some of these have even gone on to distinguished careers." He seemed to shake himself from an inward reverie then, and his gaze returned to Arabella's face. "There is, to be sure, the unavoidable matter of your sex. You will not be allowed to continue as captain's boy."

Though the news was not unexpected, Arabella's heart fell. "I understand, sir." But she knew that *Diana* was a tight, efficient machine with no room for nonfunctioning parts. "So what will be my position on board ship?"

"Captains in the service of the Honorable Mars Company are permitted a certain number of paying passengers as personal dunnage, so long as they can be accommodated in the captain's quarters. I do not usually exercise this privilege myself, but in this case I have instructed the purser to list you as my passenger. Although," he added parenthetically, "I have never before heard of a passenger joining the voyage in mid-air."

"Thank you, sir. At what rate?" Passage to Mars, she knew, was frightfully expensive.

"Captains are permitted to set their own tariff for passage, at whatever rate the traffic will bear." He raised a finger. "I am setting your rate at three hundred pounds. Plus forty for food and wine."

Arabella swallowed hard at the size of the sum, though Michael would surely pay it . . . if he yet lived.

"Furthermore, I am hiring you, out of my own purse, as a consultant on matters of clockwork and navigation, at a rate of one hundred and eighty pounds per week."

Her jaw dropped at the idea, then dropped still further at the impossible generosity of the compensation. When multiplied by the number of weeks remaining in the voyage . . .

She closed her mouth, a small smile appearing on her face in acknowledgement of the captain's cleverness. "Which leaves me with twenty pounds in credit when we arrive at Mars."

"Exactly. Minus the cost of your clothing, of course, including the rather fetching frock you are wearing now." He consulted a paper. "Two pounds, one shilling, and eightpence, all told."

"Of course."

"Mr. Quinn insisted." He shrugged.

Mind reeling from her many recent reversals, Arabella was left with one question. "Could you not have done this when I first signed on?"

He shook his head. "To take on a ragged, beardless boy as a consultant at such an exorbitant rate would raise questions on my judgement. But a well-bred, well-read young woman of quality?" Again he shrugged. "Such an appointment is within the purview of a captain's eccentricities." He steepled his fingers. "So . . . is this arrangement acceptable to you, Miss Ashby?"

"Yes, sir." She folded briefly in the air, a sketch of a curtsey. "Thank you, sir, for your generosity."

"You are welcome, Miss Ashby. Now"—he took a breath and straightened himself in the air—"I am afraid I must impose upon you."

"Sir?" Her heart began to flutter in her throat, and she chided herself for girlishness.

"The wretched business just concluded has put us several days further behind in our already delayed voyage, and we must proceed to Mars with all deliberate haste."

"Of course, sir," she said, ducking her head to hide her foolish disappointment. She turned to leave, wishing nothing more than to escape the great cabin as quickly as possible.

"You misunderstand, Miss Ashby." She paused, hand on the latch, and turned back to face him. His expression was serious. "I require you to work out a course for us, a minimum-time transit from our current position to Fort Augusta, whilst I appraise the readiness of the ship and remaining crew. I expect a sailing order within the hour."

To her own surprise, Arabella felt her face break into a broad grin. "Aye, aye, sir," she said—then, with a start, she ducked her head and covered her mouth. "I mean, certainly sir, I will endeavor to comply."

"Carry on, Miss Ashby." He nodded to her, then to Aadim. "Your navigator."

As was often the case, she was uncertain to whom that comment had been directed. But Aadim's glass eyes seemed to glitter with mirth.

After the course had been worked out and the ship got under way again, Arabella found herself with something she had never before had on *Diana*: time on her hands with nothing to do. Lacking duties, a station, even a bunk—the carpenter had not yet finished fitting out a corner of the great cabin as a sleeping berth for her—she was reduced to floating in a corner of the weather deck and trying to stay out of the way.

The only other time she had been a passenger, traveling with her mother and sisters from Mars to Earth, she had spent most of the voyage locked in her cabin, seething at the injustice of her imprisonment and her unwanted transportation. Lacking both information about and any particular interest in the airman's life and duties, she had learned little and experienced nothing. But now, having been an airman herself for so many weeks, she understood much of the activity that streamed past her on all sides. Decks were holystoned, sails set, brass polished in a constant smooth pavane of industry that seemed to mock her inactivity.

Though her life as Arthur Ashby had been brief, arduous, and often unpleasant, she found now that she missed it terribly.

The ship's bell sounded, eight bells in the forenoon watch, and the watch above divided themselves into their messes for dinner. With great fondness and sadness Arabella saw her former messmates—Gosling, Snowdell, Taylor, Young, and dear, dear Mills—gathering and laughing together as they descended the ladder. How she wished she could join them.

They did not even seem to see her. She had turned into something like an officer or a capstan—a piece of the ship's furniture, an obstacle to be saluted, polished, or worked around.

But, she gradually realized, one of the men did see her, and was hanging back as the rest of the larboard watch descended to the upper deck for dinner.

Gowse.

The burly, broken-nosed airman removed his cap from his head, clutching and twisting it in his meaty hands as he drifted over to Arabella. "Ashby," he said, and tugged his forelock like a footman. "*Miss* Ashby, I mean."

This was the first time they had truly seen each other since the chaos after the mutiny's end. Arthur Ashby would have clapped Gowse on the shoulder, shaken his hand, and thanked him heartily for what he had done.

"Mr. Gowse," said Arabella, and acknowledged him with a nod.

"I . . ." Gowse paused, mangling his already-beaten hat still further as he gathered his thoughts. He did not meet her eyes. "I suppose I should be shamed of meself, for bein' beat by a girl." Then he did look up. "But I'm not. Ye were very brave there, with Binion holdin' his pistol on you and all, and ye were brave in that fight too. If that's the kind of girl it takes to beat me, well then I suppose I'm still right enough."

Arabella smiled at Gowse's embarrassed sincerity. "You are quite right enough as far as I'm concerned, Mr. Gowse, and I am honored that you treated me as a friend when I needed one."

Gowse crammed his battered cap back on his head. "Ye still are a friend to me, sir," he said. "Ma'am. Miss."

"Ashby will do, I suppose," she replied. "It is still my name, after all."

"Ashby then." Gowse grinned and sketched a salute, then ducked down the ladder to join the rest of his mess.

With Gowse's departure, Arabella found herself at a loss. Surely she could no longer mess with the men, yet she had no idea where she *would* eat. But Watson soon appeared on deck, saying, "With the captain's compliments, Miss Ashby, you are invited to join the officers for dinner."

Arabella soon found herself at a table in the great cabin—a table she'd often set up, as captain's boy, but had never seen set with food. The officers gathered round, each bowing to her with a deference that would have been entirely incomprehensible even one day earlier, then fitted their legs into the leather straps on its underside to present a semblance of seated manners. After some embarrassed confusion, the straps at Arabella's place, to the captain's right hand, were fastened together into a single, longer strap that passed beneath her skirted thighs.

The cook's boy, whom Arabella had never before seen in a buff coat, now served the officers their dinner. The fare was much finer than that given to the men, but the portions were smaller, the number of courses greater, and the ceremony entirely different. Rather than the current captain of the mess calling "Who shall have this?" the captain carved the joint and portioned it out himself.

It seemed to Arabella that the system used by the men was actually superior. A captain who was less than scrupulously fair could easily create discord by apportioning the meat unevenly. But, as she'd known he would be, Captain Singh was unfailingly precise, and each one present received an equitable share of the meat, beans, and pudding.

Some part of her, she realized, had hoped that she might have a slightly larger or choicer portion, as an indication of the captain's feelings toward her. But to even hope for such a thing, she chided herself, was foolish. He was the captain of this ship, and as such could show no undue favor to any one.

The conversation was strained, at first. The officers, recently freed from imprisonment by mutineers, had much of import to discuss, but plainly held themselves back for the sake of Arabella's tender ears, restricting their talk to such safe topics as the weather and the set of the sails.

Arabella did her best to make herself small and silent, to stay out of the way as she had when she'd been captain's boy. She did not wish to interfere in the running of the ship, and she hoped by listening to understand it better. But the same frock that made her invisible to the men made her all too visible to the officers, and they continued to defer to her no matter how devoutly she wished otherwise.

Finally she could stand the situation no longer. "Gentlemen," she said, and set down her fork, fitting it into its clip on the table-top. "I appreciate your desire to respect my delicate sensibilities, but I must remind you that until very recently I served in your crew as an ordinary airman. I am just as eager as you are to see the mutineers dealt with, and as far as I am concerned you may discuss whatever topics you find necessary for the safe and efficient running of the ship without deference to me."

An uncomfortable silence followed her words. Finally Stross, the sailing master, spoke up. "Whilst we recognize that you were . . . formerly, under an, er, assumed identity, a member of this ship's company, you must understand that the situation has changed." He did not, she noticed, meet her eyes. "And we must all keep in mind that any . . . conversational liberties taken in your presence under that previous . . . pretense, were in fact inappropriate at the time, even though none of *us* were aware of it." On that word "us" he did look pointedly, perhaps even accusingly, in her direction. "So I must, on behalf of the officers and crew, apologize to you for those previous improprieties." He cleared his throat and returned his gaze to his roast. "Furthermore, I believe that we should continue to moderate our words and behavior in your presence . . . in deference to your sex, if not to your personal desires." He looked around the table. "I believe I speak for all of the officers and crew in this?" No one contradicted him, though the captain's face betrayed a great deal of discomfort.

A quiet whir and click from the far corner drew Arabella's attention. It was Aadim, whose head had tilted and eyebrows lowered in an apparent expression of negation or disapproval. But Aadim was only an automaton, and as such carried even less in-fluence in this company than Arabella herself.

If such a thing were possible.

Arabella's gaze fell to her own plate. Suddenly the lovingly prepared joint of beef and Yorkshire pudding seemed overly rich, and entirely unappetizing. "I am terribly sorry to have discomfited you," she said, looking straight at Stross's averted eyes, "and, on behalf of my *sex*, I accept your apology for any improprieties inad-vertently committed due to my *pretense*." She paused a moment to calm her breathing, though tension still clamped her teeth to-gether. "Furthermore, I find that I am no longer hungry." She undid the strap beneath her thighs and, with as much dignity as she could muster, extracted her legs and her floating skirt from beneath the table. "Good evening, *gentlemen*."

She managed to keep the tears from her eyes until the door of her little closet had closed behind her. Even then, though, with the officers just the other side of a thin partition of *khoresh*-wood, she had to keep her sobs silent.

Two days later, Arabella floated before Aadim, watching the dials on his desk as his clockwork whirred and ticked through another course correction. The map of Mars was spread out before him, his pointing finger resting on Fort Augusta; though Mars's turbulent Horn was smaller and calmer than that of Earth, navigating through it was still tricky, and frequent small corrections were required if *Diana* hoped to land at the port itself rather than hundreds of miles away.

The many corrections were, she must admit, rather a blessing to her, as they provided her an excuse to spend time alone with Aadim. The clockwork navigator might not be much of a conversationalist, but unlike the officers and men, his behavior toward her had not changed with her clothing. Even the captain, whose treatment of her had altered the least, sometimes seemed discomfited by her skirted presence.

She looked into the automaton's eyes; though they did not see, they seemed filled with a sort of animation, jittering slightly as the wheels within his cabinet spun. "I wish I could take you off the ship and show you Woodthrush Woods," she said, finger tracing an area some inches from the fort. "That is my family's *khoresh*-tree plantation." Though unmarked on Aadim's map, the spot was well-worn in Arabella's memory. The great manor house, the Martians' dwellings of fused stone, the long drying-sheds with their great coal-stores—in which she would sometimes hide, to her mother's great dismay—all sprang vividly into her mind's eye. "Khema used to take Michael and me to Fort Augusta nearly every week."

At the thought of Michael, her eyes began to sting. Her fingers crept to her throat and touched the locket with his miniature portrait.

She hoped her brother still lived. With all the delays that had afflicted *Diana*, Simon would surely have already reached the plantation and insinuated himself into its daily routine. Michael, for all his intelligence, could be naïve in his dealings with other people, and she feared that it would not take Simon long to work his way sufficiently into her brother's confidences to have an opportunity to do him in. On an isolated plantation, a moment's inattention might be sufficient for Simon to push Michael off a cliff, poison his water with *uthesh*-seed, or simply shoot him, and no one would ever be the wiser.

A bell pinged, distracting Arabella from her distressing speculations. Startled, she looked up into Aadim's face. The automaton's head was tilted, his glass eyes seeming to regard her with concern.

She took a deep breath, then let it out. "All will be well," she said, and bent to record the sailing order from Aadim's dials. "All will be well."

3

MARS, 1813

17

MARS

Two weeks later, Mars loomed ahead, a great butterscotch-colored globe the size of a melon at arm's length. Contrasting with the blue of the sky beyond—a darker, more familiar blue than that seen in Earth's vicinity—the sight raised great and conflicting emotions in Arabella's breast.

First and foremost, the approach to Mars promised an end to her time on *Diana*, and with it an end to many great annoyances. Free descent, for one, was far more troublesome in skirts than it had ever been in trousers, and she looked forward to the return of good solid gravity with a sense of keen anticipation. An alleviation of the very limited space and company on board ship was something else which she anticipated with great gladness. Most of all, though, she hoped for an end to the deep, abiding loneliness which had been her lot ever since the exposure of her sex. For her to associate with the crew on any thing other than a brief, superficial level would be entirely inappropriate given her sex, age, and station; to associate with the officers, on the other hand, was an exercise in frustration from which she had decided to abstain for every one's benefit. Her primary company for the last three weeks had been Aadim, and to a lesser extent the captain, who had continued her instruction in navigation and clockworks on an informal basis whenever his other duties permitted. She took her meals in her tiny cabin.

She would miss the captain, though—miss him very dearly. And he, she thought or hoped, would miss her as well. She knew that he spent as much time with her as he could without attracting the opprobrium of his officers, and he said that he greatly enjoyed her company and conversation. But that was as far as his sentiments toward her seemed to extend.

Perhaps, she thought, it might be for the best that she would see no more of him after the landing. But, even so, the prospect weighed heavily upon her heart.

The end of the voyage also meant, for good or ill, a return to the planet of her birth. Though she had never before examined the face of Mars with her own eyes—on her departure for Earth, she had been too outraged and despondent for more than a brief, despairing backward glance—his warm, yellow-orange color and his every visible feature were as familiar to her as the lines of her own palm, though the latter was now callused and scarred. Her father's atlas and globe had given her the English names of the forts, trading posts, major mountain chains and valleys, and primary canals, while Khema had instructed her in the Martian names of all the other geographic features—the native cities, canals, plains, and rilles.

On Earth she had felt heavy, sodden, and dull—oppressed by the thick and humid air, the smothering warmth, and of course the greater pressure of gravity. On Mars, she knew, she would leap and bound as she had when she'd been a girl, and enjoy *khula* and *gethown* and *shktumaya* and many other treats whose names and flavors she had nearly forgotten.

But most important of all, Mars meant Michael. She prayed daily that, despite the many misadventures that had delayed

Diana in her voyage, she would not arrive too late to warn him of Simon's perfidy.

Oh, how she would rejoice if—no, *when*, she reassured herself—she found Michael safe in the old manor house at Wood-thrush Woods. They would laugh and play together as they had when they'd been children in dear Khema's care, and hunt *thorek*, and steal sweets from the pantry.

Or perhaps not. Michael was the head of the family now, and she supposed he must have many serious duties to attend to. But she hoped they would still be able to steal away for a Sunday picnic of *khula*-nuts on the Shokasto Plain.

Either way, Simon would be sent packing and then entirely forgotten. Though perhaps a payment to his unfortunate wife, in recompense for the money Simon had wasted on his passage to Mars, could be arranged. Though she had helped hold Arabella imprisoned, and even discharged a pistol at her, she had done so only for the sake of her infant child.

Arabella's pleasant reverie was interrupted by Watson, who had drifted up behind her as she stood at the rail, rapt in her contemplation of the rust-colored planet that floated above *Diana*'s figurehead. "Miss Ashby?" he said, "the captain requests your presence immediately. He says it's urgent."

When Arabella arrived at the great cabin, she found the captain at the window, staring into the blue distance with hands clasped behind him. The set of his shoulders, in addition to the message of urgency that Watson had conveyed, indicated that he was deeply troubled. "What is the matter?" she asked.

He turned away from the window, a deep frown furrowing his brow. "We have just received alarming news by semaphore from *Artemis*, one of our sister ships." For the last few days, Arabella had noticed the tiny wavering specks of other ships in the distance, but had not known that any of them were close enough for sema-phore communication. "It seems that Fort Augusta is experiencing a serious native uprising."

Arabella tried not to overreact to this unpleasant news. Occa-sional native uprisings were simply part of the English experience on Mars, but Fort Augusta was the largest English settlement in St. George's Land, and the nearest city to her family plantation. "*How* serious?"

"The port is entirely closed. *Artemis* was the last ship out, and was forced to flee without taking on cargo." Arabella's heart went cold at this detail. "Her captain has elected to return to Earth empty rather than risk the safety of his ship and crew by return-ing to port." He shook his head. "*Vesta* was burned where she stood, and the fate of her crew is unknown."

Arabella's hands flew unbidden to her mouth. "Oh, dear!" A thousand horrid images crowded her mind. The Customs House in flames. Michael with a rifle at the manor house door, the house surrounded by angry Martians with their swords and forked spears. And what of dear Khema? Would she have been slaugh-tered by the rebels for working with the English? "We must go to their aid immediately!"

The captain's grim expression soured still further. "*Diana* is a ship of commerce, Miss Ashby, not a ship of war. Though Com-pany ships can be requisitioned by the government in case of con-flict, we have not yet received any such instructions. So, at the moment, we are free to choose our own course of action, but if we remain in the vicinity for long we may find ourselves conscripted."

"We cannot simply turn back!" But as soon as the words de-parted her lips, Arabella wished to draw them back. No amount of anxiety for her brother could justify such impertinence on the part of a mere passenger.

However, before she could attempt a retraction, the captain shook his head. "Indeed we cannot." He did not seem even to have noticed her impudence; instead, his gaze seemed directed inward. "We are already on short rations, after our unfortunately extended passage. An attempted return to Earth without resupply would surely end in death by dehydration for all of us." Now the captain's attention returned to Arabella. "Which is why I have asked you here."

Arabella blinked. "Sir?"

The captain straightened, folding his hands behind his back. "Despite my many passages to Mars, my experience of the planet itself is scant, and the same is even more true of my officers. Negotiations with the colonial government, not to mention the natives, are carried out by the Company's factors. But you were born and raised here." His stiff pose seemed to soften now, and a small note of entreaty entered his voice—a tiny departure from his usual masterful demeanor, which she might never have noticed had she not spent so many days in close company with him during his convalescence. "I hold out some hope that you, with your unique background, might have some insights into the situation that could resolve our dilemma."

"I . . . I see." After the revelation of her true identity, it had been with great relief that Arabella had confessed all to the captain—her personal history, her recent adventures, and her current fears about her brother. He had expressed sympathy for her plight and had promised to provide whatever help he could, so long as it did not interfere with his duties to the Honorable Mars Company. But now their positions seemed to have been reversed, and the responsibility laid upon her narrow shoulders seemed completely insupportable. She strove to bear up under the burden. "Tell me more about the problem."

"It is appallingly simple. We cannot return to Earth, or even remain in orbit above Mars for long, because we will shortly exhaust our stores of food and water. We cannot land at Fort Augusta because the port is closed. And we cannot land anywhere else because Fort Augusta is the only settlement on Mars with furnaces of sufficient capacity for an airship of *Diana*'s size."

"I thought the purpose of our stop at Paeonia was to make charcoal for our landing?"

"For our landing, yes. But no merchant ship can profitably carry sufficient stores of coal, never mind charcoal, for both a safe landing and a successful launch, even given Mars's lesser gravitational attraction. Once landed, we require the assistance of a furnace to return to the interplanetary atmosphere carrying sufficient coal for our landing at Earth."

With a touch on the bulkhead behind her, Arabella drifted over to Aadim's desk, where the map of St. George's Land was already spread out. "What, exactly, is required of the furnace?"

"The capacity of our envelopes is five hundred and twenty thousand cubic feet. With a full load of cargo, coal, and crew, they must be filled with clean hot air at an average temperature of at least ninety-three degrees in order to achieve ascent from Mars. Subject to some modification based on current conditions."

In Arabella's mind's eye, the empty stretch of map between Aadim's wooden hands became populated with the fences, crops, and buildings of Woodthrush Woods. Behind the manor house, line after line of *khoresh*-trees marched off toward the horizon. Here lay the Martians' homes, here the kitchen garden, and here the drying-sheds.

She looked up from the map into the captain's eyes. "Our plantation, located near the mines of Thokesh, has substantial stocks of coal, and the coal burners in the drying-sheds could perhaps be adapted to provide the necessary hot air for *Diana*'s ascent." Freshly harvested *khoresh*-wood was too heavy with moisture to be used in shipbuilding; progressive plantation owners such as Arabella's father had in recent years begun using coal-fired drying-sheds to accelerate the necessary seasoning process.

"Assuming your family plantation has not been overrun by the natives."

Arabella's eyes stung with tears at the suggestion, but she firmed her jaw and refused them. "That is a risk we would have to take anywhere. But if we land here"—she tapped the site on the map—"we will, at least, find sufficient coal and an owner willing to sell it for a reasonable price."

She could not, she realized, absolutely guarantee any such thing. But she knew well that Michael could deny his beloved sister nothing.

If he still lived.

Arabella held her breath, filled with fear and doubt, as she watched the captain consider her suggestion. Plainly he was torn—a deep furrow had appeared between his eyes, and his whole demeanor showed how difficult was the decision he faced. Finally his gaze, which had been directed inward, returned to Arabella. "I must . . . perform some calculations," he said. "Please leave us alone."

"Of course, sir." She nodded and let herself out.

As the hatch closed behind her, she heard the whir and click of Aadim's gears and the captain's low, muttered voice.

Some hours later, another knock came at Arabella's cabin door. This time it was the captain himself. "I have consulted with Aadim and my officers," he said, "and have determined that a landing at your family plantation offers the best hope of success. If you would, please work with Aadim to plot out a course for a landing there. Once that is done, I would appreciate it if you would consult with Mr. Stross upon the specifics of your drying-sheds and coal-stores." He fixed her with an expression of profound seriousness. "If some method cannot be arranged to fill the envelopes, *Diana* may well find herself a permanent fixture of your plantation."

"I understand, sir."

Calculating the sailing order for a planetary landing was a task
Arabella had never performed before, and in order to do so she
found herself leafing through thick manuals kept stowed behind
the stores of aerial charts. As she read, hammering and curses
sounded from without the hull as the carpenter and his mates fitted *Diana* with sand-legs for her landing on the open plain behind
the manor house, while the majority of the crew worked to haul
out and erect the envelopes.

Landing at Mars, she learned, was usually performed by a local
pilot, sent up from Fort Augusta by balloon. As difficult as navigation through the vast empty spaces of the interplanetary atmosphere might be, the last few miles—drifting slowly downward
under cooling envelopes while being blown across the face of the
planet by fickle surface breezes—were even more so, and the pilot's unique knowledge of local conditions was invaluable. But
with the port closed, as the captain had explained, they could not
depend upon the availability of this assistance.

"I do not know if I am capable of this," she admitted to Aadim
in a whisper. Manuals and charts lay open all about the cabin,
with detailed maps of the Fort Augusta area unfolded on Aadim's
desk. She moved his wooden finger, which ticked and thrummed
slightly with the motions of his clockworks, from *Diana*'s point of
entry to Mars's planetary atmosphere to the location of Woodthrush Woods. "It is such a short distance," she said, "but if we
get it wrong, by even a few miles, we will be stranded, and perhaps in the middle of a native rebellion."

She didn't remember when she'd started talking to Aadim. It
was something the captain did sometimes, she knew, especially
when performing difficult navigational calculations. He claimed
that talking the problem through helped him focus his mind
upon the task at hand and not forget any of the levers or settings.
But it certainly seemed that he sometimes waited for an answer
from the patient, sturdy automaton.

As she moved Aadim's finger along *Diana*'s curving path, she noticed that the motion was not smooth as it should be, though she kept her hand upon Aadim's wooden one as gentle and firm as before. Pausing, she checked that his shoulder joint and follower-cams were properly adjusted and oiled, which they proved to be. But still the pointing finger seemed to resist the path the manuals dictated.

"You're trying to tell me something," she said. But the automaton's green glass eyes only stared back at her, as rigid and impassive as ever.

Again she returned Aadim's finger to the beginning of its path, the entry point to the planetary atmosphere. But as she moved it gently to that point, she paid careful attention to the slight jerks and tugs the navigator's wooden hand gave to her own as the gears and mechanisms within his desk ticked and whirred away.

Was there a slight tendency to the southeast?

Closing her eyes, gentling her breath, Arabella gave the automaton's hand free rein, as though trusting a horse to return to the stable on its own.

The slight tug she felt steadied, pulling gently but firmly in a southeasterly direction. She allowed the finger to drift as it seemed to wish, until with a slight distinct click it came to a trembling halt. A slight nudge in any direction from that point met resistance.

Arabella opened her eyes. Aadim's finger had come to rest at a node on the chart where three prevailing winds of Mars's planetary atmosphere came together. From there, the combined wind current would carry *Diana* directly to Arabella's family plantation. Assuming, of course, that the charts were accurate, which the manuals had warned might not be the case in all seasons of the year.

She would certainly never have noticed the node if she'd followed the path dictated by the manuals. It was well outside the area authorized for atmospheric entry by all the charts and tables.

But the manuals were designed to bring the ship to Fort Augusta, not to a *khoresh*-wood plantation some miles away.

It would be tricky to bring *Diana* round Mars's Horn to that small node. But the more she studied the charts, the more necessary it seemed.

She could not be certain this entry point would work. But with the information available to her, it seemed the best choice.

"Very well," she breathed. "We shall try it your way."

Did Aadim's painted eyebrow quirk slightly? Did his head incline, ever so gently, in acknowledgement? Or were those simply the accidental motions of a complex and temperamental machine?

Arabella met Aadim's unblinking gaze for a long, uncertain moment. Then she shook her head and set about finding a sailing order through the turbulent Horn to the new entry point.

Of all the many strange feelings Arabella had experienced in the last few weeks, perhaps the strangest was when Captain Singh invited her to join him on the quarterdeck to observe the descent to Mars.

After many hours in the great cabin, calculating and recalculating the sailing order with Aadim and trying to remember the details of the drying-sheds for Stross—whose conduct toward her remained coldly civil, which pained her after the avuncular warmth he'd shown when she'd been captain's boy—she'd felt the ship begin to shake and jerk as *Diana* entered the outermost fringes of Mars's Horn, and had emerged to witness with her own eyes the navigational path she'd plotted so many times on Aadim's desk.

The planet loomed below them now, no longer a globe ahead, but rather a vast red-gold dome that spread out to both sides beneath the ship's keel. Already Arabella felt a slight but undeniable drift toward the deck as the planet's gravitational attraction began to be felt.

"Miss Ashby," the captain called, and she turned to see him

standing—yes, standing, not floating—near the wheel on the quarterdeck above. "Please do join us here for the rounding of the Horn."

She paused at the foot of the ladder. On her first aerial voyage the quarterdeck, whose name she had not even known, was a place she had never visited, nor even seen. Then, for the last two months and more, she'd been a mere captain's boy, and entry into officers' territory was a privilege granted but rarely and grudgingly. But now she was something other than what she had been—part passenger, part navigator, and entirely ex-airman—and apparently this new person was one to whom an invitation to the quarterdeck was extended as readily as an invitation to tea.

With mingled pride and trepidation she made her way up the ladder, an awkward action with her skirts swirling in the weak gravity. Soon she would have to relearn the old familiar habits of standing, walking, and climbing.

As she reached the deck she saw that the captain's stance was artificial. He was braced to the deck by three leather straps which extended from a broad leather belt about his waist to brass rings set in the deck—rings she'd often cursed as she'd polished them. One of the midshipmen came over to her with a similar belt, which he handed to her with great embarrassment and averted eyes. If she'd been Arthur Ashby, she knew, he'd have buckled it about her waist with brusque dispatch—or, more likely, left her to manage her own safety line or simply to hang on to whatever rail or rigging might come to hand. She thanked the man as she took the belt, and swiftly cinched herself to the deck beside the captain. "How odd it feels," she remarked, "to have pressure upon the soles of one's feet again."

"Indeed." The captain smiled and flexed his toes, the polished boots squeaking. "But it would be even worse if your legs were weakened by unrelieved free descent. This is why I insist that every one on my ship, even officers and passengers, take his turn at the pedals." He put his telescope to his eye, peering ahead at the cloudless air, then muttered a command to Richardson, who immediately called out a series of orders. Topmen scrambled up the rigging and began to adjust the sails.

Arabella flexed her own legs and toes, pressing against the leather straps, feeling the strength of her calves and thighs. She had been surprised when the captain had insisted that, even as a passenger, she must continue taking a shift at the pedals, and had been embarrassed by the great production this entailed, with screens being erected around her so that none would be forced to observe her flailing limbs. But now, with the downward pressure of her weight increasing, she found herself glad she had not protested the inconvenience. Perhaps if she and her mother and sisters had worked the pedals on the voyage from Mars to Earth, they would not have had to be carried from the ship upon arrival.

The captain was again gazing ahead through his telescope. "Horn ahead," he called to Richardson, though Arabella could see nothing but empty air between *Diana* and the planet below.

"Are there no storm clouds, Captain?" Arabella asked.

He shook his head. "Not at Mars. The air is too dry. To observe the Horn's outer edge you must look for scudding flotsam." He handed her the telescope, but even with its aid her untrained eye saw nothing. Then, conversationally, he remarked, "And here it is."

Suddenly a great jolt struck the ship. With a creaking of timber and a rattling of lines against yards, *Diana* slewed hard to larboard. If Arabella had not been strapped to the deck she would surely have been flung over the rail and into the sky in a trice. As it was she nearly lost the telescope, and immediately handed it back to the captain.

He took it with barely a nod to Arabella, being busy calling out commands to his men. Topmen bustled up and down the masts, unfurling and sheeting home t'gallants and royals, then mere minutes later furling them up again in response to the Horn's ever-shifting winds.

Amidst this maelstrom of wind and wood and voices one familiar voice stood out from the rest: Faunt, the captain of the waist, calling, "Heave away, ye b——ds! Heave away smartly!" Arabella peered over the forward rail to the deck below, wondering what task her former messmates were engaged in.

What they were doing was opening the great cabinet, fixed to the deck, into which the balloon envelopes had been packed shortly after their departure from London. Immediately the wind caught at the alabaster Venusian silk, tugging billows and folds of it into the air, but the men grabbed the first envelope before it could be whipped away and began hauling it into a large untidy circle. From this perspective, the net of sturdy cables that would hold the envelope once it was inflated gave the impression of a gigantic spider's web.

"Open the flues!" called Faunt, a command that was repeated down the forward ladder. A moment later came a great bellowing roar, louder even than the rush of the wind through the rigging, and the circle of the envelope bellied out into a great flapping disc, then an inverted bowl, then a loose wobbly sphere that nearly filled *Diana*'s waist.

A midshipman, black from top to toe with charcoal-dust, appeared and saluted the captain. The smell of burning charcoal on him was so strong that even the Horn's whipping winds could not carry it away. "Boatswain's compliments, sir," he gasped. "Charcoal stores holding steady. We're clear for descent." The men below on charcoal duty must be shoveling like fiends.

"Excellent," the captain replied with a curt nod, then returned his attention to the sails.

Soon the envelope was nearly full, straining against the net that held it down, and the men gradually paid off the lines that held it to the deck until it rose to dominate the sky abaft the mainmast. Though the roaring and swelling continued, the men immediately returned to the envelope cabinet to repeat the performance.

As she watched her old messmates struggle with the envelope's luffing fabric while topmen scrambled hither and yon and other men shoveled charcoal, Arabella felt herself nothing more than a pretty bauble, a decoration strapped safely to the deck at the captain's side. Though her life as an airman had been hard, exhausting, and often tedious, the sense of accomplishment she had felt when a sail she had helped to raise billowed out in the sun against the bright blue sky, or when a gun whose load she had carried spoke out with a voice like a vengeful god, or even when she'd cried out "Who shall have this?" and passed a greasy bit of beef to another waister had been greater than any pleasure she'd had on land.

Far below, Mars's broad dome had spread until he now appeared more landscape than ball, visible above the rail in every direction, curving off to a shimmering blue horizon. The familiar yellow-ochre of the sands below, now close enough that hills, valleys, and canals could plainly be seen, caused Arabella's heart to ache with homesickness—and with concern for her brother and the family plantation, now threatened by rebellion as well as Simon's depredations.

Trepidation over what she would find when they landed warred in her heart with impatience to finish her journey, leaving her breast feeling as buffeted by emotion as *Diana* was by the gusts of wind that even now tossed her about beneath her swelling envelopes.

Though Mars's Horn shook the ship and required many adjustments to the sails and envelopes, the captain and crew's experience brought *Diana* safely to the aerial node that Aadim had located, and soon the ship was floating serenely along beneath her three great balloons, drifting in the gentle breezes of the lower planetary atmosphere toward Woodthrush Woods.

Arabella unbuckled herself and peered over the rail, looking past the men who were even now hauling in the sails and sheets from the lower masts. Soon the masts themselves would be un-shipped, returning *Diana* to her original configuration for land-ing. All of this was, she knew, ordinary standard procedure, but the situation they would encounter upon landfall was entirely ex-traordinary and nonstandard.

A hazy bright spot on the ground seemed to pace the ship as she sailed along. "What is that, Captain?" Arabella asked, pointing.

"The light of the sun," he replied, pointing in exactly the op-posite direction, "reflected back to us from innumerable grains of sand."

More and more details appeared as they drifted toward the ground: towering rock formations, orderly ranks of sand dunes marching to the horizon, rilles of soft and rounded stone. Ara-bella's heart thrilled when they came upon a canal—the great Khef Shulash, it must be, it was so broad—which ran as straight as an arrow from one horizon to another. Tiny specks of boats floated upon its shining waters.

And if that was the Khef Shulash . . . She shaded her eyes and peered ahead, to where the canal vanished in the haze of the ho-rizon. Fort Augusta lay in that direction.

From here, she thought, she should be able to see, if not the great sandstone walls of the fort itself, at least some sign of the town that surrounded it. Even if the port was closed and devoid of ships, the forest of masts that made up the shipyard should be clearly visible from this height. "May I borrow your telescope, sir?" she inquired of the captain.

She raised the instrument to her eye, focused . . . and gasped.

The haze that hid Fort Augusta from view was not haze. It was smoke.

Great dark gouts of smoke, with orange flames flickering here and there. A few running figures were visible as well; at this dis-tance she could not tell if they were human or Martian.

"What is the matter, Miss Ashby?"

"The town is afire," she breathed.

The captain took the telescope from her numb fingers, glared through it, and grunted as though struck in the stomach. "That is . . . terribly distressing," he managed at last.

18

LANDING

Diana sailed majestically along, the canal drawing nearer on her starboard side, but Arabella could not tear her eyes from the dark column of smoke ahead, which grew more and more plain as they approached.

As the ship gradually drifted lower, Arabella could also begin to see that the boats that plied the canal were not, as usual, burdened with neat bundles of *khoresh*-logs and tidily stacked crates of other goods making their way to Fort Augusta from the provinces. They were, instead, piled high with hastily stacked heaps of household furniture, valises, and assorted boxes, and the vast majority were heading away from the town. Almost all of those on board were humans, who waved and hallooed at *Diana* as she passed overhead.

Arabella glanced at the captain at one such halloo, but his jaw was set and he kept his eyes resolutely fixed on the horizon ahead. Following his lead, the officers and men focused their attention on the running of the ship.

The few boats heading toward Fort Augusta rode high and

bore no cargo. These were poled and crewed entirely by Martians, whose reaction to the airship sailing above was entirely different: the twang and thwap of bows and crossbows came clearly to Arabella's ears through the cold dry air. Fortunately, *Diana*'s altitude and distance were too great for any projectiles to reach her, except for one arrow that bounced harmlessly off of a balloon and fell clattering to the deck. Several of the waisters immediately began to tussle over it.

"Don't touch that!" cried Faunt. "D—n thing could be poisoned!"

Arabella snorted at that, which attracted a quizzical glance from the captain. "Martians don't use poison," she explained.

"Do they not have the making of it?"

"Oh, no, they know all about it; *thuroks* and *noshti* are extremely venomous. But for one Martian to poison another would be a violation of *okhaya*—entirely unacceptable."

He arched an eyebrow at her. "And for a Martian to poison an Englishman?"

"They'd never—" But she silenced herself before concluding that thought.

Surely they'd never do such a thing. But then she'd thought that the Martians of Fort Augusta would never rebel; they were civilized and friendly, not like the savages one sometimes heard of from the outlying provinces.

And yet, Fort Augusta still burned.

Arabella pressed her lips together and stared forward at the approaching column of smoke.

They crossed the canal and then left it behind. Burning Fort Augusta beneath its column of black smoke drew nearer and then alongside, though still some two miles distant. Through the telescope Arabella watched Martians and humans in groups—each group, sadly, consisting entirely of only one species or the other—scurrying to and fro. A few groups of each type seemed to be trying to fight the conflagrations that engulfed the town, but there was no coordination between them and the flames leapt ever higher. Other groups merely dashed from one place to another between the flames—though whether plundering, murdering, or trying to help, Arabella could not say.

Eventually the flaming town too fell behind, and *Diana* sailed across country, following the road toward Woodthrush Woods, which looked like the mark of a stick drawn through the sand.

No humans or Martians were visible on the road, though it was littered with abandoned furniture, broken carts, and the occasional bodies of *huresh* that had collapsed in their traces.

Sometimes a shattered cart was surrounded by dark stains in the sand. Arabella hoped these were spilled wine.

Once a troop of Martians scurried rapidly past on *huresh*-back, the setting sun glittering from their forked spears, a cloud of dust rising in their wake. One or two raised their eye-stalks to *Diana*, but they did not pause in their rush toward the town. After they had passed, the captain drew a key from his pocket and handed it to Richardson. "Open the small-arms locker," he muttered so quietly that none but Arabella, who remained close by her captain, could have heard, "but do not distribute the rifles just yet."

"Aye, aye, sir," Richardson whispered, sweating, and hurried below.

Arabella gripped the locket with her brother's picture and tried not to cry.

Yet a few stinging tears still forced themselves into the corners of her eyes.

By now they had descended so far that roadside shrines in their rocky cairns could be distinguished with the naked eye. *Diana* had flown over most of the miles from Fort Augusta to Wood-thrush Woods in less than twenty minutes, and at this rate the manor house would surmount the last rise in just five or ten minutes more. Her hands, she realized, were gripping the rail so tightly they had gone entirely pale, and though she shook them and massaged them, the next time she thought to look down the knuckles were white again.

Young Watson appeared again, eyes red-rimmed in his blackened face. "Boatswain's compliments, sir," he gasped, "we've used up the last of the charcoal."

The captain nodded in brusque acknowledgement, then cast an analytical eye upward at the balloons.

"Cutting it too close by half," muttered Stross.

"Nonetheless," the captain replied, raising the telescope to his eye, "we retain sufficient lift for a safe landing." A moment later he handed the instrument to Arabella. "Is that the plain on which you would have us land? Between that reddish rock pillar and the three large stones?"

She peered through the telescope. "Yes . . . ," she began, but then she noticed something that made the breath catch in her throat.

"What is the matter, Miss Ashby?"

She swallowed, struggling to focus the trembling instrument upon the distant, shimmering horizon. "The drying-sheds appear to be intact, but I . . . I think I see smoke. And running figures." She handed the telescope back, realizing that the trembling was in her own hands. "I'm not certain."

The captain steadied his elbow upon the forward rail, staring carefully for a long minute. "Perhaps," he said at last. "Is there any better landing site within"—he glanced up at the balloons again—"three miles?"

Arabella and Stross exchanged a glance. They had argued long and hard over the charts and Arabella's memory of the plantation, so much so that his cold civility toward her had threatened to crack. "No, sir," Stross replied. "Anywhere else is too far from the drying-sheds, or too stony, or too steep. Even if we manage to make a safe landing at any of the other sites, we'd likely never take off again."

The captain snapped the telescope shut. "Then I fear we have no alternative but to land there as planned, and prepare to defend the ship if necessary." He nodded to Richardson. "Distribute the small arms."

Arabella stared forward, through the forest of masts and cables, hoping against all hope that she'd been mistaken.

———

How many times had she traveled this road? Hundreds, certainly; among her earliest memories was awaking on the rocking back of a scuttling *huresh*, her cheek pressed against her father's warm leather-clad flank, with the field Martians hooting a greeting as she and her father passed through the outer gate.

No one greeted them now.

The gate that drifted past beneath *Diana*'s keel lay open in silence, the great doors half unhinged and peppered with crossbow bolts. The packed and hardened sand around the gate was scuffed and marked with the tracks of many men, Martians, and beasts, and great dark splashes steamed gently here and there in the slanting late-afternoon sun.

In a moment the manor house would appear, rising like a pale square sun above the prominence her brother had named Observatory Hill. . . .

But the first sight that met Arabella's eyes above that hill was not nearly so reassuring.

A thin column of black smoke.

"No . . . ," she breathed, her hands clasped beneath her chin.

But the house, as it began to appear, was not entirely destroyed. The north wing, housing the kitchen and stores, lay in blackened ruins, but the main house with the bedrooms and her father's—no, Michael's—office still seemed intact.

She must not lose hope, she reminded herself.

"Bring her down," the captain muttered to Richardson.

"Back pulsers!" Richardson called.

From below the deck came the grunting chant of the men at the pedals, followed shortly by a low grinding sound from abaft as the propulsive sails, long silent, began to turn. Soon the grinding had risen in tone, accompanied by the low repetitive rushing sound as the sails themselves sped past. With each rush, a strong breeze swept forward, the moving air bringing the ship's forward motion to a halt.

The captain nodded, and Richardson cried, "Out anchors!"

With a great clatter of wooden pawls, the two sand-anchors, one forward and the other aft, descended rapidly on their thigh-thick ropes. The booming thuds of their contact with the Martian surface below were plainly audible.

"Belay pulsers! Set anchors and prepare to warp in!"

The chanting of the men at the pedals ceased, while two airmen hopped over the rails fore and aft and began to shinny down the anchor ropes.

Arabella looked over the rail, watching the man descending the aft rope dwindle into the distance, recalling her terror as she herself had been lowered over the rail less than two months ago. The distance to the ground had been very much greater then, and her experience very much less. She wondered if, had her sex not been revealed, she would be one of those descending now.

If she were the one clambering down that rope right now, she thought, she might not be so terrified as she actually was. The certainty of a dangerous task was better than the uncertainty of what she might find in the partly destroyed manor house.

The man on the rope had now reached the anchor far below. With hands and feet he wedged it firmly into the sand, waving his cap and hallooing.

"Warp in!"

A new chant now broke out, closer to hand, as men on deck heaved at the capstans. Bare feet skidding on the polished *khoresh*-wood of the deck as they hauled in a circle, they wound the great anchor-ropes back onto the hogshead-sized spool belowdecks, pulling *Diana* gradually down toward the sand.

Arabella clung to the rail as the deck jerked unsteadily downward, peering anxiously toward the manor house. But there was no motion visible there.

Despite the vast conspicuous bulk of *Diana* floating above, despite the creak of the capstans and the plainly audible chanting of the men . . . no one was hurrying from the manor house to greet them. "Captain . . . ," she began, but he cut her off with a gesture, barking commands to Richardson as he strode the quarterdeck.

Stross stepped to the rail next to Arabella. "Where are they?" he muttered to her, gesturing with his chin to the manor house.

"I do not know," she responded. "They should certainly be coming out by now, out of curiosity if nothing else."

Stross turned from her to address the captain. "I don't like the look of the situation, sir."

The captain's eyes flicked from the balloons to the anchor-ropes to the horizon. "Understood," he replied. Then, to Richardson, he said, "Prepare to strike envelopes."

A moment later came a long whispering crunch as the ship's keel settled into the sand, followed by the soft double thuds of the sand-legs touching down. "Strike envelopes!" Richardson cried, and a man at the base of each balloon pulled hard on a slim line that had been kept, up until now, made fast to a cleat.

A large circular flap opened at the top of each balloon, fluttering like a pennant in the shimmering draft of escaping hot air. Teams of chanting men shepherded the descending loops of fabric and rope into their cabinet as the balloons deflated and collapsed.

"Well, we're well and truly landed now," Stross said, shaking his head.

Beneath Arabella's feet, the ship seemed to sigh as she settled deeply into the red sand beneath her keel.

Just then, a great clattering burst out from the watch-tower at the northeast corner of the manor house—a clatter like the *mharesh* call with which Martians greeted the dawn, but harsher and more strident.

A moment later the clatter was joined by other sounds: the harsh rustle of Martian voices, the susurration of feet on sand, and the clash and snap of steel on armored carapaces.

A huge crowd of Martians boiled from the manor house like angry *thuroks* from their nest, surging to surround the helpless *Diana*.

19

SURROUNDED

In every direction Arabella looked, she met glaring eye-stalks, bared swords, and the wicked tines of forked spears. Hundreds of Martians, perhaps even a thousand, surrounded the ship, with more pouring out of the manor house and joining the periphery of the crowd even as she watched.

But though the Martians were fully armed, every one clad in their bright clan colors, with steel blades fixed to the joints of their carapaces and spikes on every elbow and shoulder, it was the behavior of the men aboard *Diana* that frightened her more. All along the gangways, and leaning aggressively over every rail, they held pistols and rifles at the ready; many gripped cutlasses and boarding axes. Belowdecks, she was sure, men she could not see were arming themselves as well.

"Captain," she importuned, rushing to his side, "you must tell the men not to fire."

Stross and Richardson both glared at her. "Miss Ashby," Richardson replied, "you should retire to your cabin and leave the defense of the ship to the crew. For your own safety." His dark and furrowed brow put the lie to his protestations of concern.

The captain's brow, too, was drawn, but he did not speak. He simply looked to Arabella, apparently awaiting some explanation for her statement.

"Can't you see they are not attacking?" she said.

"I can see the cowards are just waiting until they have us outnumbered twenty to one!" Stross replied with considerable heat, pointing to the Martians still streaming from the manor house.

"They are maintaining a distance of twelve *korek*." She gestured to the front of the crowd, where a broad red strip of bare sand stretched between the tightly packed Martians and *Diana*'s hull. Each anchor, as well, was surrounded by a circular bubble strictly empty of Martians. "This is traditional upon meeting a group of strangers in time of conflict. They are awaiting a formal invitation."

"A formal invi—!" Stross stammered, going red in the face.

Arabella turned to the captain. "*Please*, sir, I beg of you, do not antagonize them. Their customs and formalities are every bit as strict as ours, but a failure of etiquette in this case could result in far more than our ostracization." Behind him, she could see the mass of Martians packing tighter and tighter, their spears held aloft and quivering with rage.

"Sir, I must protest!" said Richardson, but the captain silenced him with a gesture.

"What would you suggest we do, Miss Ashby?"

"We must invite their *rukesh*—their leaders—aboard, and permit them to inspect the ship. They will be quite thorough. We must also present them with gifts. Parchment and whisky are traditional."

"Parchment!" sputtered Stross. "Sir, are you seriously considering entrusting the ship's safety to the mad advice of this *girl*? What use have these savages for *parchment*?"

Arabella turned to him and spat, "Do you not know your history, *sir*? It was Captain Kidd himself, on the very first English voyage to Mars, who discovered the Martians' fondness for it." She returned her attention to the captain. "Any form of leather will do, sir, but parchment, well-inked and well-handled, is best. I believe there are some charts of the Venusian approach that could be spared. And the whisky should be of the very best quality."

Richardson's eyes had gone wide with astonishment. "And if we do not perform this ridiculous ceremony?"

"They *will* inspect the ship, sir," she told him, "one way or another. If they are not invited aboard they will force their way inside, and their inspection in that case will not be courteous. And if they are offered violence they will respond in kind. But if we observe the proper forms, the inspection will cause no damage."

"Sir!" Richardson protested again, and again the captain gestured him to silence. But he did not speak—he merely looked out over the surging crowds of Martians, brow furrowed and lips pressed tightly together.

Finally he turned back to Arabella. "You were born and raised here?"

"Up to the age of sixteen, sir. You *must* believe me, sir."

Just then one of the Martians stepped forward into the cleared area, raised her spear above her head, and chuttered out a statement whose meaning Arabella could only guess at. Arabella's command of the language was spotty at best, she knew, and between regional dialect and excess of emotion this Martian's speech was nearly unintelligible to her.

"What's that he said?" Stross demanded of her.

She turned and looked at him. The entire quarterdeck had fallen silent, all eyes fixed on her, none more intensely than the captain's.

"She requests that a party be allowed on board to inspect the ship," she said. It was almost certainly the Martians' desire, even if not a translation of the actual words. "I don't know how much longer they will wait." That much, at least, was completely true.

For a long moment the captain's intense brown eyes inspected her face. Then he turned to Richardson. "Mr. Richardson, you will do exactly as Miss Ashby suggests, without hesitation or compromise. That is an order, Mr. Richardson. Do you understand?"

Richardson's face darkened, jaw quivering, but then, between clenched teeth, he muttered, "Aye, aye, sir."

Arabella swallowed and addressed the captain. "May I give them the charts of the Venusian approach, sir? They will . . . they will not be returned."

"Yes. And the whisky. How much will be needed?"

"One bottle will be sufficient, I should think." She looked out over the crowd, whose agitation was visibly growing. "We must make haste."

As quickly as her skirts would allow, Arabella hurried to the great cabin, where she shoved Aadim aside and extracted the rolled charts from the cubby behind his desk. "Excuse me," she whispered to him, though his green glass eyes bore no reproach.

Emerging from the great cabin, she met Stross on the deck. "Here's your whisky," he said, holding out a heavy cut-glass decanter about three-quarters full of a dark amber liquid. "It's Ledaig, from my own private stock. The very best."

"Thank you, sir," she replied. "I am certain the Martians will be duly impressed." She was surprised at the confidence she heard in her own voice.

"If this doesn't work," he muttered in her ear as he handed the bottle over, "I'll kill you myself."

She chose to behave as though she had not heard his words.

Arabella, the captain, and Richardson descended to the hold, where the cargo hatch had already been unsealed. Even as they arrived, two burly carpenter's mates knocked out the last of the wedges and swiveled the hatch open, letting in the clattering sound and dusty cinnamon odor of the crowd of Martians. Four airmen then ran out the gangplank, which raised a puff of red dust as its end thudded to the sand some yards below.

The Martians grew silent. No one moved.

The captain spoke low to Arabella. "What do we do now?"

"I believe we should meet them on the sand," she said with as much confidence as she could muster.

Arabella's knees wobbled as she made her way down the steeply canted gangplank. She tried to tell herself it was because of the unaccustomed gravity. Ahead of her, the captain's long dark hands gripped each other tightly behind the broad back of his best uniform coat. Behind her Richardson followed, muttering under his breath, the stopper of the whisky decanter rattling gently with his steps. Arabella herself held the rolled chart ahead of herself as though it were an offering, minding her footing carefully—her absurd ladylike slippers offered little purchase on the well-worn boards.

They arrived at the bottom, and finally she felt beneath her feet the familiar cool crunch of Martian sand. For how many months had she longed for this moment—her return to Mars, to Wood-thrush Woods, to the sands of her birth. And yet she had never dreamed that the situation might be any thing near as dire as this.

Four Martians stepped forward from the crowd, the blue and gold tassels on their hats marking them as the group's *rukesh*. They paused before the three humans. Arabella, the captain, and then, hesitantly, Richardson each dropped to one knee, backs straight and heads held high, a formal Martian posture of greeting which Arabella had thought might be the most appropriate under the circumstances. The Martians glanced at each other, then bowed in the English fashion, which Arabella took as a good sign.

The captain returned to a standing position. "We are aware," he said in his deep clear carrying voice, "that we are an armed group entering disputed territory in time of conflict. In accordance with ancient Martian custom, we offer you hospitality"—here he gestured behind him to Arabella and Richardson, who likewise stood—"and invite you to inspect our ship." The wording was something that he and Arabella had worked out, based on her recollections of Khema's lessons in Martian history. She hoped that she recalled those lessons better than she did the Scripture verses she'd gotten from her mother.

The Martians did not respond. They only continued to exchange glances among themselves, their eye-stalks twisting independently.

Arabella's heart pounded, and she felt a trickle of sweat run down her side. Did these Martians even speak English? If not, she feared that her small command of Khema's tribal dialect would be entirely inadequate to diplomacy.

Taking a deep breath, she stepped forward and extended the rolled chart to the nearest Martian.

The Martian took it, the worn brown vellum crinkling in her hard, jointed hands, and inspected it carefully, the other Martians watching her with great interest. Then she unrolled the chart a bit, tore a palm-sized square from the corner, and crammed the torn-off corner in her mouth.

Beside Arabella, the captain's back stiffened, while Richardson gave a small but audible gasp. But though Arabella had expected nothing else, she now waited with her heart in her throat for the Martian's response.

The black lidless eyes seemed to glaze over as she chewed, the hard champing mouth-parts making short work of the soft translucent vellum. When it had been completely consumed, the Martian tore off additional bits and gave them to her compatriots, who devoured them with equal concentration.

"The whisky," Arabella whispered urgently to Richardson, who stepped forward with the decanter. The glass stopper continued to clatter even after he came to a halt, and she realized he was terrified. The captain still exuded confidence, his back straight and chest elevated, but after so many weeks in close quarters she could see from his tight-set jaw just how concerned he was.

One of the Martians took the whisky from Richardson and, after peering minutely at the bottle, delicately extracted the stopper with two sharp pincer-like fingers. She then took a small but deliberate sip, and after contemplating the flavor passed the bottle to the others.

The decanter was returned to Richardson, who nearly dropped it in his nervousness. The chart they kept. The *rukesh* then conferred among themselves, their low susurrations and clatters meaningless to Arabella.

Suddenly they turned, as one, and bowed to the humans. "We thanks for you hospitality gifts," said the one with the purple hat in heavily accented English. "We accepts you inspecting invitation." She then turned to the mob behind her and called out a long chuttering statement, which was received with low clatters and rustles. A large group of Martians then detached themselves from the crowd and moved purposefully forward, forcing the captain, Arabella, and Richardson to step aside or be trampled.

"Be sure to remind the men not to interfere with the Martians under any circumstances!" Arabella told the captain as the Martians clattered up the gangplank.

The captain immediately reminded them of that, using the full-throated command voice that carried through storms and brooked no disobedience, ending with "and belay that lollygagging at the rail!"

Immediately the dozens of heads that had been peering over the rail vanished, the men returning to their duties.

From within the hull came clatters, clanks, and muffled thuds, along with occasional cries of despair from Quinn the purser.

"We should return aboard," the captain said, "to supervise the inspection."

The Martians were extremely thorough, but they worked quickly, and when they were done nearly every thing had been returned to its original place. Most of the Martians retreated, leaving the original four on the quarterdeck along with *Diana*'s officers. "We thanks you for inspecting," the one in the purple hat told the captain. "We welcomes you visiting our plantation."

At that statement of ownership a cold anger seized Arabella's heart, but she pushed it down—it might merely be an error in the Martian's imperfect English, or reflect their current, temporary occupation of the property.

"Thank you," the captain replied. "May we impose upon your hospitality? My crew require food, drink, and exercise. And we hope to negotiate for the purchase of coal, and the use of the furnaces in your drying-sheds, or else our visit here may well be of indefinite duration."

The Martian conferred with the other members of her *rukesh* and replied, "For this you must speaking *akhmok*."

The captain raised a questioning eyebrow to Arabella, who shrugged to indicate her ignorance of the word's meaning.

"Very well," he said after a moment's consideration. "Take us to this . . . '*akmok*.'" Like most Englishmen, he could not properly pronounce the Martian *kh*.

The purple-hatted Martian stiffened in indignation. "Not 'us.' Not all. Only *rukesh* may speaking *akhmok*."

"Only our leaders," Arabella quietly translated.

"Very well." He turned to the other officers. "Richardson, Stross, with me."

Arabella, too, stepped forward, but the captain leaned down and took her hand. "I must insist that you remain behind," he said gently, "for safety's sake."

"I appreciate your concern, sir," she replied with as much confidence as she could muster, "but for that very reason—for the safety of yourself and every other man on this ship—I must insist that I accompany you, as translator and adviser in matters Martian." Her knowledge of Martian languages and culture had its gaps, to be sure, but it was certainly better than that of any other man aboard, and she knew enough of the history of the English on Mars to know that even small misunderstandings could lead to fatal outcomes.

The captain considered her for a long moment, his brown eyes steady on hers. "You pose me a difficult choice," he replied, "but I suppose I have no reasonable alternative but to acquiesce."

The four Martians led the captain, the two officers, and Arabella below. Stross favored Arabella with a withering glance as the two of them fell in behind the captain.

It was not easy to keep her step steady as she descended the ladder. She knew that she must accompany the captain, not only to increase the chances of his safe return but also to learn the fate of Michael and the other occupants of the house. But she feared that the captain had been correct in his initial assessment of the situation—that she was putting herself firmly in harm's way.

What, she wondered as she stepped onto the gangplank, was an *akhmok*?

And what had she gotten herself into?

Arabella's heart nearly broke as she and the officers followed the *rukesh* through the dispersing crowd of Martians. The oval lawn of English grass, lovingly tended and watered twice daily, that had once stretched proudly before the manor house now lay brown and neglected, trampled under many hard Martian feet. The house, too, had suffered grievously—in addition to the entire wing lost to fire, most of the main house's windows were shattered and its clapboards bore many bullet holes and the twinned scars of forked spears. Approaching still more closely, she saw that the front doors had been smashed to flinders, with only one brave board still clinging to its hinges. The stink of smoke lay like a pall over every thing.

How could this have happened? Father had always treated his servants, English and Martian alike, with the greatest of respect, and she could not imagine Michael changing that policy. Even at times of unrest, the Ashby plantation had always before escaped harm. What could possibly have enraged the Martians sufficiently to justify this wanton destruction?

And who had survived it?

Martians armed with swords and English rifles—she feared she recognized her father's favorite hunting-piece—stepped aside as the *rukesh* approached the front door, closing behind Richardson as the humans passed.

Arabella feared the worst as they entered the house proper, but though the damage in the hall was severe, with shattered plaster and shredded carpets everywhere, there were no bodies lying about, nor even pools of blood. And as they moved deeper into the house the destruction lessened, until by the time they reached her father's office most of the furnishings, even her mother's paintings, were still intact.

One Martian stood guard at the office door, but as they approached he bowed and opened the door as smartly as any butler. So familiar was the motion, in fact, that—despite his garish clan colors and the steel blades fixed to his carapace—she recognized him immediately. It was Hoksh, who had been her father's footman!

She did not know whether to be reassured or dismayed by his presence among the insurrectionists, but in either case her heart pounded as the *rukesh* stepped aside, leaving the humans to enter the office without them.

The office itself seemed completely undamaged. Even the automata above her father's desk looked down as serenely as they always had. Which was all the more astonishing because, seated behind the desk, Arabella beheld the most enormous Martian she had ever seen.

A hulking dark-red brute nearly eight feet high and almost half that broad, the Martian's carapace bristled with spiny protrusions both natural and artificial. Wide stripes in every clan color painted the massive forearms, and a sharp-edged steel mantle of office rode atop the shoulders. Incongruously, the huge ungainly fingers gripped a feather pen, which scratched away in a ledger-book, over which the Martian was hunched in a posture of deep concentration.

As the door opened the Martian looked up.

The black, subtly faceted eyes immediately focused on Arabella.

"Arabella?" the Martian boomed in a deep, cultured voice. "Could that be you? My dear *tutukha*?"

Arabella's jaw dropped.

"Khema!?"

20

KHEMA

"My dear *tutukha!*" the giant Martian repeated, and with surprising agility and grace he—no, *she*—bounded out from behind the desk and took up Arabella in her arms.

"Khema, is it really you?" Though many Englishmen said that Martians all looked alike, Arabella had never had much difficulty distinguishing between them. And now that she looked more carefully at the Martian's broad face she could see that, beneath the heavy protective brows and prominent cheek-spines, it still bore the familiar lines of her beloved *itkhalya*. And there was a crack in the carapace of the left temple, imperfectly healed, which Arabella herself had inflicted one day in a clumsy sparring incident. "How is this possible?"

Khema set Arabella down and sighed, the air whistling through her spiracles in imitation of the human expression. "It is a long story, *tutukha*, and I regret each and every day the terrible circumstances which have brought me to this state." She rapped on the carapace of her thorax with her prominent knuckles, making a sound like two stones striking together. "But, regrets or no,

I am *akhmok* now." Her attention widened from Arabella to take in the three officers. "Tut, tut, I forget my manners. Who are these fine gentlemen?"

"This is Captain Singh of the Honorable Mars Company airship *Diana*, his first mate Mr. Richardson, and his sailing-master Mr. Stross." Then, to the officers, "This is Khema Shuthkari Tekeshti, who was once my *itkhalya*—my nanny, my protector, my instructor in all things Martian." The men bowed to Khema; she replied with a curtsey of such astonishing grace that it abolished any comedic effect that might otherwise have resulted from such a formidable figure attempting the maneuver.

"I will always be your *itkhalya*, Arabella, and you my *tutukha*."

The captain bowed again. "We regret imposing upon you at this unsettled time, but my men require food and water."

"I am given to understand that you have obeyed the proper forms of greeting in time of conflict, and therefore my people will extend to you all reasonable hospitality." At that, Richardson's lips pursed, his eyebrows rose, and he inclined his head to Arabella in a silent gesture of acknowledgement. "I am sure that some of our foodstuffs palatable to you can be found."

"We also hope," the captain continued, "to negotiate with you for coal, and the use of the furnaces in your drying-sheds."

Before Arabella could protest that his request, understandable though it might be, was directed to the wrong party, Khema said, "The stores of the manor house, including the coal-sheds as well as the larder, are not ours to share. We occupy this property only temporarily, in the absence of its legal owner."

"Where *is* Michael?" Arabella burst out.

Khema went down on one knee, bringing her enormous head level with Arabella's, and took her hands quite delicately in her own large, stony claws. "I am sorry to be the bearer of sad news, *tutukha*, but your brother is a fugitive from justice."

Arabella blinked rapidly, incapable of forming any reply to this astonishing statement.

"We are holding this property in protective trust until he either surrenders himself or is apprehended. After justice has been done, we will turn over control to his heirs, in accordance with English law."

"His *heirs*?"

"Do you not remember your lessons, *tutukha*? We are a civilized people, and obey English law in respect to the property of English persons."

Arabella forced her gaping jaw shut, and had to swallow several times before continuing. "Of what . . . terrible crime is he accused? Surely there has been some mistake!"

Khema sighed, settling back on her haunches and seeming to compose her thoughts before addressing the four humans. "Eleven days ago, the firstborn egg of Queen Thukhush was abducted from the Royal Ovary. You would not remember her, *tutukha*, as she ascended after you departed for Earth, but she is a very popular queen, well-liked by all the clans as well as the humans, and as such the Ovary was but lightly guarded. Rumors pointed to your brother, and when the empty egg-box was discovered in the stables here the *Rukesh Kthari* descended upon the property to apprehend Michael for questioning. But he refused to surrender himself, denying all knowledge of the crime. He and several other members of the household escaped in the fighting that followed, and have barricaded themselves at Corey House."

Corey House, Arabella knew, was a very substantial manor house high in the hills above the city of Fort Augusta. It had been built in the early days of colonization, when relations between English and Martians had often been unsettled, and its situation and construction made it highly defensible in case of any attack.

The captain's expression was nearly as grim as the one Arabella knew her own face must be displaying. "Was this the cause of the native uprising?"

"Sadly, yes. When my people demanded that the English authorities compel Lord Corey to surrender Michael, they refused, claiming that the evidence against him consisted only of hearsay and speculation. A protest at Government House was forcefully suppressed by the King's Guard, which led to further violence. Soon there was rioting in the streets, and I . . ." She gestured to her enormous, hard-edged body. "I became as you see me. An *akhmok.*"

Arabella was having difficulty taking this all in. "I don't understand."

Khema's eye-stalks twisted in shame. "It is a . . . a relic of our savage past, one which we do not celebrate, and which has not occurred in living memory. In situations of great distress, certain females undergo this transformation. It is similar to the ascension of a queen, but the physical changes are, as you see, even more dramatic. An *akhmok* is a formidable fighter in her own right, and she also secretes certain substances that cause even warring clans to unite under her leadership against the common foe."

"The English," Arabella said miserably.

"Not in my case," Khema reassured her. "I am as appalled by this violence as you are, and have organized my people here, away from Fort Augusta, to keep them and the plantation from any further harm. I have also sent emissaries to the other *akhmoks,* encouraging them to resolve their differences with the English peaceably. We are already having some success, and I anticipate that normalcy will be rapidly restored once Michael is brought to justice."

"*Justice?*" Arabella cried with considerable heat. "I cannot imagine that my brother would perform any act so . . . so *barbaric* as the theft of a queen's egg. The accusations against him must be false."

Khema's eyes drew together in an expression of sympathy, but she said, "His cowardly flight is considered by many as an admission of guilt."

"There must be another reason." She set her jaw. "I will go and speak to him, and find out the true story."

"You will find it hard going. Corey House is under siege. Three *akhmoks* and seven thousand of their people surround the place."

Arabella thought furiously. "You said you are sending emissaries to the other *akhmoks*. Could you send me there under a flag of truce? If I appear at the gates, alone and unarmed, Michael will surely admit me and explain himself."

"No explanation could excuse the abduction of a royal egg. But if he has kept it safe and warm, it may still be viable." Khema contemplated her, considering. "You and your brother are very close, I know. If you can convince him to release the egg alive and unharmed, the siege will be lifted, the violence will end, and the *Rukesh Kthari* may be persuaded to spare his life."

"All I ask is that you convey me to my brother."

Khema thought for a moment, then clacked her mandibles in assent. "I will provide you with a *storek*—a mark of safe conduct—that can get you as far as the gates. Every thing beyond that is up to you."

Arabella was both pleased and terrified at the prospect, but before she could manage to express her thanks another voice interrupted.

"I cannot allow this." It was Captain Singh, his deep brown eyes fixing Arabella with a stern fatherly captain's gaze.

"I *must* try to save my brother!" Arabella protested.

"And so you must." His gaze, still fatherly, now softened. "But I cannot permit you to go alone. I will accompany you."

"But sir!" protested Richardson. "The ship—!"

"The ship will be safe here, under the protection of Miss Khema's people; the men I entrust to your care. I feel I owe a personal debt to Miss Ashby, for the services she did me while I was unconscious as well as for her advice and assistance today. I will accompany her to Corey House and provide any protection and aid I can in rescuing her brother and bringing this unfortunate incident to a close."

Richardson seemed about to burst, but Stross laid a hand on

the first mate's elbow. "We'll do well enough without him for a few days, sir."

At that Richardson sputtered and deflated, then finally said to the captain, "Very well, sir, if you must."

"I must," said the captain, looking to Arabella, who was so overwhelmed that she could do no more than drop a curtsey in acknowledgement of his generosity. She hoped she was not blushing, but feared that she was.

Richardson took the captain's hand. "Take care, sir, and return safe. The ship needs you."

"I will do my best."

Then Richardson bowed to Arabella, swallowed, and said, "Best of luck, miss." A small smile then appeared upon his usually serious face. "Take care of our captain."

Arabella, too, smiled in her nervousness. "I will endeavor to do so."

Khema then clapped her hands together, with a noise like two sacks of coal colliding. "Very well, then." She put her hands to her mouth-parts, then touched Arabella and the captain on the forehead. A cool moist sensation quickly dissipated into Mars's dry air, leaving behind a strong scent reminiscent of cinnamon and horses. "This *storek* marks you as my emissary and should prevent you from harm by any Martian of sound mind. Do not wash or rub the spot."

"Thank you, *itkhalya*," Arabella said, and she and the captain bowed to her in the Martian fashion. "I will do every thing I can to resolve this conflict with honor for all."

"I have every confidence you will, *tutukha*," she replied, returning the bow. "You have already made me very proud."

Arabella and the captain returned to the ship, where each of them packed a ditty bag with the necessities for a trip of some days' duration. After one final exchange of instructions and best wishes with the officers and crew, they set off on *huresh*-back for Corey House, accompanied by three of Khema's people.

But the captain's inexperience at *huresh*-riding slowed them considerably, and by the time they drew within sight of the house—the lights in its windows far outnumbered by the fires of the Martians camped all around it—full dark had descended. Arabella's escort halted their progress at a sheltered canyon just outside the encampment. "It would be foolish to approach an armed camp in the dark," said the escort leader. "They might loose their arrows before we are close enough for the *storek* to be smelled. We should make camp for the night here, and proceed at first light."

Not having come prepared for camping, they gathered and roasted *hoktheth*-roots over an open fire for their dinner, then lay themselves down on the *huresh*-blankets under the Martian stars.

Arabella lay awake for quite some time, staring up at the bright unwinking stars and worrying about what the morrow might bring. Tiny creatures chittered in the darkness; the fire crackled as it burned down; their escort, those who were not on watch, shifted and clattered in their sleep.

But the captain, she noted, was not snoring. She turned her head to where he lay nearby . . . and saw him sitting up on one elbow, looking at her, his dark eyes reflecting the fire's embers.

"I have not slept," he confessed.

"Nor I. I am too concerned about my brother."

"All will be well, I am sure."

"I wish I shared your confidence."

He blinked, the two stars of his eyes vanishing for a moment, then said, "May I entrust you with a secret, regarding confidence?"

"Of course."

"Bravery, as I am sure you are well aware, consists not of the absence of fear but in the taking of action *as though* the fear were not felt. Confidence, likewise, consists of the presentation of assurance *as though* there were no doubt as to a successful outcome. Such presentation, however false its origin, is remarkably efficacious in its effect both on others and on oneself."

She smiled in the darkness. "Is this, then, the secret to a successful captaincy? Pretense?"

"It is perhaps the only such secret." He sighed. "Far too much of my captaincy, I fear, has been rooted in deception."

"How can you say that, sir? You are one of the most honest men I have ever met!"

"I do strive to be, when I can."

The silence stretched out, then, punctuated by the cry of a night-hunting *shoshok*. Arabella waited, feeling that if the captain were to speak about whatever might be troubling him, he should be allowed to do so in his own time.

"I am not," he said at last, "the man I present myself to be. My full name and title is Farzand-i-Khas-i-Daulat-i-Inglishia Mansur-i-Zaman Amir-ul-Umra Maharaja Dhiraj Rajeshwar Sir Sri Maharaja-i-Rajgan Bhupendra Prakash Singh Mahendra Bahadur. Or was. Or would have been."

Arabella blinked. Somewhere in that stream of syllables she thought she had heard a word from her childhood storybooks. "Did you say . . . *Maharaja*?"

"Yes. I was born to be a prince of India."

This, Arabella thought, explained his regal bearing and almost inhuman poise, yet it raised far more questions than it answered. "So . . . so what occurred to change your estate?"

He sighed deeply. "When I was a young man, I had every advantage. Fine clothes, expansive hunting grounds, beautiful women . . . all were mine for the taking. Yet the one thing I desired more than any thing else was to waste my time tinkering with automata."

"You should not disparage automata so, sir. They may be, I believe, instrumental to the future perfection of humanity."

"My opinion today is much the same as yours, yet in my youth I was even more certain of it, to such a degree that I neglected my other duties. I avoided meals with my family, went days without sleep . . . all in pursuit of my notion that an automaton navigator could be built that would reduce the lengthy and hazardous voyage to Mars to something as simple as a stroll in the park."

"And from this 'notion,' as you put it, Aadim was born."

"Aadim, in his current form, was yet many years in the future. Yet so dedicated was I to his conception that, when presented with my bride-to-be, I callously dismissed her." The twin stars of the captain's eyes shimmered, then vanished. "I called her stupid and dull, only because she did not share my passion for automata. She went away in tears."

Arabella listened in silence, wanting to reach out to this intelligent, gentle man whose memories brought him such pain.

"This insult," he continued, "to the girl, to her family, and to my own father's judgement in selecting her, was too great to be tolerated. He disinherited me immediately, and cast me out of the palace with only the clothes on my back."

"How horrible that must have been," Arabella breathed.

"I was unthinking and cruel, and received no worse in return."

"But how could you be expected to survive under such circumstances?"

"I had friends, other enthusiasts of automata, who provided me with room and board for a time. But their lodgings were not large, and this arrangement soon made all of us uncomfortable, so I sought gainful employment. A learned man of my acquaintance, familiar with my theories regarding the potential of an automaton navigator, encouraged me to offer my services to the Honorable Mars Company. But upon my approach to the company's grand and palatial offices, I suffered a crisis of confidence and decided, unwisely, to present my understanding of aerial navigation—which was, in truth, entirely abstract—as actual airship experience." Again he sighed heavily. "I will never know how

I was able to talk my way into that, my first commission as navigator. I certainly hope that, as captain, I would be able to take the true measure of such a charlatan as my own younger self. Perhaps my father, regretting his decision to disinherit me but unable to take me back without losing face, exerted some influence on my behalf. In any case, I was taken aboard—under the name Prakash Singh, the very simplest form of my own name, which is as common among my people as John Smith is with yours—and somehow managed to bring the ship to Fort Augusta without disaster."

Though the captain had obtained his first posting by deceit, Arabella could not help but sympathize with his predicament, and even admired his pluck and determination in doing so.

He continued his tale. "Using the funds obtained from that successful voyage, I began to rebuild my prototype navigator. Then, after several more such journeys, I was able to put him into practice—in parallel with traditional navigation, at first. But as his theoretical advantages rapidly proved themselves practical, and in fact highly efficacious, he and I rapidly rose in prominence. After only eight years I found myself captain of my own ship. With the considerable wealth that attends that position I have continued Aadim's development, extending his instruments throughout *Diana* so that he and the ship are, in effect, a single highly efficient mechanism of commerce. Yet my tinkering continues, for I am still not satisfied."

"But he is already so successful, sir! I have never even heard of any automaton of any variety that is capable of such complexity of calculation, such subtlety of action . . . dare I say, sir, such a close approximation to human thought and feeling. Sometimes I would swear he seems nearly alive."

He tutted. "You are too kind."

"Sir, I do not exaggerate." She hesitated, for what she was about to admit seemed highly implausible even to her. Yet the intimacy of this moment, and her uncertainty of what the morrow might bring, brought the words to her lips almost involuntarily. "From time to time, sir, Aadim seems to . . . to offer suggestions. Sometimes he seems to resist certain settings of his controls; at other times he encourages them."

The captain shifted suddenly on his blanket, causing the sands beneath to respond with a hissing crunch. "You have experienced this phenomenon yourself?"

"I have, sir. It does not happen frequently, but when it does, the impression is quite distinct. I would swear that it was he, not I, who calculated the successful approach to my family plantation."

He turned away from her then, his broad back in its buff uniform coat a slightly paler smudge against the black of the sky.

For a long time he did not utter a word. Then he took in a breath, as though about to speak, but still made no sound. Then he drew in another sharp breath, and let it out with a long, shuddering sigh.

The captain was . . . crying.

She longed to take him in her arms—to offer comfort to this brave, distant, complex man—but propriety restrained her.

"I . . . ," he began, but choked off with a liquid sob. He composed himself, then began again. "I had thought that I was only deluding myself. That my desire for Aadim's perfection was causing me to imagine his actions as more intelligent, more conscious, than they could possibly be in reality. You are the first to offer any confirmation of this impression."

"I do not pretend to understand how gears and levers can bring forth consciousness, sir, but it certainly appears that somehow they have."

He turned back to her then, the blanket rustling beneath him, and moved toward her until they were nearly touching. "If any other person had offered me this assurance," he whispered, "I would think that they were indulging me, or mocking me, or perhaps that they were merely as self-deceiving as I. But you, my dear, I know to be too intelligent to be mistaken, too forthright for flattery, and too kind for mockery. With your knowledge of automata in general, and of Aadim's inner workings in particular, I am sure that you would not make such a statement in any thing other than dead earnest."

"Indeed, sir, I would not." Her voice came out as a whisper.

He swallowed, and the two shining stars of the reflected fire in his eyes shimmered. "Thank you, my dear Miss Ashby," he said, "from the bottom of my heart."

For a long moment they remained thus, their faces mere inches apart, and Arabella's heart raced as she reflected that their only chaperones were three Martian warriors, who cared nothing for human proprieties, and in any case two of them were asleep.

But then the captain cleared his throat and sat up straight on his blanket, taking himself away from her. "We should take our rest while we can," he said, his voice slightly hoarse. "Tomorrow may be a very busy day."

"Indeed," she sighed, as the reality of the situation came crashing down upon her mind. "Still, though, I am glad to have had this conversation, and honored that you have shared your story with me. I assure you most sincerely that you may depend on me to keep your secrets safe within my breast."

"From you, I would expect nothing less. Good night, Miss Ashby."

Good night, my maharaja, she thought, but what she said aloud was, "Good night, Captain Singh."

21

COREY HOUSE

Dawn revealed Corey House in all its dour magnificence. It had been built in the earliest days of Martian colonization by a Scottish family—many of the first settlers had been Scots—and it bore the heavy, martial mien characteristic of that people's architecture: all thick walls, square towers, and fortified parapets. But unlike the gray castles of Scotland, which she had seen in colored plates, this one was built of native Martian stone, and the light of the rising sun brought out the warmth in the rock's butterscotch-orange and rust-red tones. The house was set firmly into the slope of a small mountain, and the crags all around it displayed similar colors.

But despite the warmth of the scene's color scheme, the overall sight that greeted Arabella's eyes brought a chill to her bones. For the daylight also revealed the full extent of the army of angry Martians that surrounded the house. Rank on rank of tents and huts stretched for what seemed like miles across the plain below the house, lapping like a wave on the lower reaches of the prominence upon which the house was constructed, and reaching right up to the bases of the nearest towers. The encampment seethed with Martians in their bright clan colors, their swords and forked spears glittering in the sunlight.

Most disturbing of all, several enormous catapults were under construction in the midst of the encampment. Two of them looked to be nearly complete, and large pyramids of jagged hogshead-sized red stones waited near each of them.

After performing her morning necessities, Arabella joined the captain and their escort for the short ride to the near edge of the encampment. A large troop of mounted Martians rode out to meet them, hostility clearly visible in their attitudes, but as soon as they scented the *storek* on Arabella's forehead they relaxed. After a brief but thorough inspection of Arabella's and the captain's few possessions, they allowed them to enter the camp.

Their escort did not accompany them further. "We have delivered you to Corey House, as requested," said the escort leader, "and now we return to our *akhmok*."

"Thank you for accompanying us this far," Arabella said, "and please convey my thanks and appreciation to Khema as well."

The escort leader merely tossed her head in acknowledgement and rode off toward the rising sun, accompanied by her fellows and leading the two *huresh* that Arabella and the captain had ridden.

Arabella looked upon their retreating backs with considerable trepidation. Though she had finally returned to the planet of her birth, it now seemed foreign and dangerous. Even Khema, who was more dear to her than any one save her own family, had become barely recognizable. And now even that tiny particle of familiarity was gone, leaving Arabella alone and defenseless among angry, armed Martians who wanted her brother dead.

No . . . not alone. She had the captain by her side, for which she was more grateful than she could comfortably express.

"Come," she said to him. "Let us present ourselves at the gate. The sooner my brother can explain himself, the better."

They made their way through the surging crowd, Martian warriors hurrying this way and that with weapons, supplies, and construction materials for the gigantic catapults. Most of the warriors simply glared at them, but on many occasions they were approached by angry Martians with swords or spears raised, who backed down as soon as they scented the *storek*. By the twentieth or thirtieth such occasion Arabella had learned to stand her ground as though unafraid, though her heart still raced every time.

"How long does this . . . charm last?" the captain murmured to her as yet another armed Martian angrily swished her sword at them and stalked away.

"Khema said it would get us as far as the gate," she replied. It was all she knew.

The crowd grew thicker and angrier as they approached the house, until by the time they reached the gate itself they found themselves pushing through a packed mob, many of who were hurling rocks or shooting arrows at the house's thickly shuttered windows. If not for the *storek*'s influence they might not even have been able to progress on foot.

The gate itself, a heavy double door of *khoresh*-wood some ten feet wide, was deeply set into the red stone of the wall. Both door and wall were exceedingly scarred. Arabella banged the knocker, politely at first and then vigorously, but received no response.

They stepped back a bit. "Ahoy the house!" the captain called in a carrying voice that even stilled for a moment the furious activity of the Martians packed shoulder to shoulder around them. "Ahoooy!" he called again.

For some minutes nothing more happened. Then a clattering

and a rattling sounded from the other side of the gate's thick wood. "How the d—l did you get here?" came a muffled voice.

"We have a safe-conduct from . . . from a Martian general," Arabella called back. There was a tiny peep-hole in the door, she noticed, and she directed her voice to it. "We are here to negotiate an end to this siege."

Voices sounded from inside, at least two different ones, but between the thickness of the door and the clattering of the Martians she was unable to make out the words. "There seems to be some disagreement within," the captain said, and Arabella could only nod in unhappy agreement.

"Please let us in," Arabella called again. "I am Arabella Ashby, Michael's sister. And this is Captain Prakash Singh of the Honorable Mars Company."

"Miss Ashby?" came a voice from within, a different one. "I had thought you were on Earth!"

"I took passage on *Diana*, a fine and very rapid ship," she said. "Oh, do let us in. I promise we mean you no harm."

The argument within resumed, even more vehemently, until finally the first voice cursed and called out, "I shan't open the door unless you can get those d———d savages to back away at least five yards. And if they charge when I open it, I shall shoot the lot of them, and you too if I must!"

Even with the *storek*, it was not easy for Arabella to convince the Martians to clear the area near the door as the unpleasant voice demanded. The task was finally accomplished through a combination of gentle persuasion on Arabella's part, using every bit of Martian politeness she'd learned from Khema, and a display of self-assurance from the captain, who simply spread his arms and walked slowly forward, pressing the crowd back by sheer force of personality.

Rattles, thuds, and dragging sounds came from the door's other side as whatever barricade had been erected within was laboriously disassembled. "Get in close!" the unpleasant voice called. "I'll give you a count of three to get inside."

Arabella and the captain moved in close to the gate. The crowd of Martians began to edge forward, diminishing the open space.

Suddenly, with a grinding scrape of wood on stone, the door was pulled open. It stopped when the opening was less than one foot wide. "Inside!" the voice demanded, accompanied by a pair of wild red-rimmed eyes, a rifle barrel, and a pale beckoning hand. "Hurry!"

Arabella squeezed herself through as quickly as she could, followed immediately by the captain. A moment later the door was pushed shut behind her, and she was roughly shoved aside as the door was barred and casks, crates, and heavy furniture were piled up against it. The grunts of men and the thump of wood on stone as the barricade was restored were matched by the cries and clatters of the Martians outside trying to get in.

"Come away from the door, child," came the first voice. "It's not safe here."

She turned away from the door and the three burly young men still barricading it. A lean old man, with wild white hair and an old-fashioned hunting jacket, stood beckoning with his left hand, a rifle clutched in his right. The butts of two pistols protruded from his pockets.

It was, she realized belatedly, Lord Corey, the owner of the house . . . though a much aged and diminished version of the jolly neighbor she'd left behind when her mother had taken her to Earth.

"Thank you for your hospitality, Lord Corey," Arabella said, and dropped a curtsey. They had retreated from the door, with its continued thuds and clatters, to the drawing-room, a high and echoing chamber nearly unchanged from Arabella's memories except that it was now crowded with people and stacked high with crates and boxes. Apart from Lord and Lady Corey, their servants, and her family solicitor Mr. Trombley, she recognized none of the company. Where was her brother?

Lord Corey presented to the captain and Arabella the several dozen refugees who had retreated to his manor from the flames of Fort Augusta; Arabella presented the captain to Lord Corey. The refugees, as it turned out, were mostly people of Lord Corey's elevated social stratum, which explained their unfamiliarity to Arabella, and the contrast between their fine clothes and refined accents and their current straitened circumstances was sharp. But though under other circumstances Arabella would have been honored to make their acquaintance, between introductions her eyes kept darting about, still seeking Michael.

Many of the refugees had not left the house in a week or more, and they bombarded Arabella with questions. What was the situation beyond the gates? Had she any news of their relatives, their homes, their servants? And how had she, a lone girl with nothing but a heathen foreigner for company, managed to make her way through that mob of savages unharmed?

Arabella pushed down her ire at that last remark, and responded as politely as she could. "Captain Singh is a highly respected airship captain, ma'am, and we were under the protection of one of the Martian *akhmoks*, or generals."

"And how did you obtain this protection?" begged the lady in question, raising her lorgnette and pressing forward eagerly. All other eyes also turned with desperate longing to this girl who had somehow obtained special sanction from the same Martians who had driven them from their homes.

"The *akhmok* in question had been my *itkhalya*."

"Surely you must be mistaken," said one of the men. "All *itkhalyas* are female."

"I believe it is you who are mistaken, sir," she replied, and though she felt a degree of heat entering her words she did not care to reduce it. "Among Martians it is the female of the species who is larger, more robust, and has the thicker carapace; it is only English sensitivities that restrict them to the positions of cook and nanny when we engage them as servants. Have you not noticed that by far the majority of the warriors besieging you here are female? My *itkhalya* was a prominent strategist among her people even before she became an *akhmok*, and she taught me of strategy and tactics along with all other aspects of Martian culture and history. I assure you that she is entirely suited by both temperament and training, as well as the physical characteristics of her sex, to the position."

She found herself breathing heavily, glaring at the circle of distressed and indignant eyes that surrounded her. Most prominent among these were Lord Corey's. "My dear Miss Ashby," he said, "I believe you must be overtired after your long and difficult voyage. Please allow my wife to convey you to a private room, where you can rest . . . and reconsider your words."

Just as she was about to snap a reply to Lord Corey's condescension, she noted the captain's face. His head was tilted slightly toward her, one eyebrow raised, the corners of his mouth turned down. . . . It was an expression she'd learned to recognize as preceding a rebuke. And the captain's rebukes were never, ever unearned.

She took a deep breath, considered her response, and then let it out again with a deep sigh. "You are correct, of course, Lord Corey. These last few days have been extremely taxing, and I . . . I apologize for my outburst. I thank you again for your hospitality." The captain, she saw, was not displeased by her expression of regret. "However, I must decline your offer of a place to rest until I have spoken with my brother."

The glance that Lord Corey exchanged with his wife brought a chill to Arabella's heart.

"Where is he?" she demanded.

"My dear Miss Ashby," Lord Corey said, "I regret to inform

you that your brother was seriously injured while fleeing from his home after the attack there. One of the other members of your household carried him the last mile, saving his life. However . . ." His gaze lowered. "Unfortunately, he lost consciousness shortly after arriving here, and has not yet woken."

Arabella felt as though the floor had dropped away, leaving her in a state of free descent.

"We have not lost hope," Lord Corey said. "But we fear the worst."

22

SIMON

Michael's face was pale and running with sweat, and his forehead burned with fever. From time to time he moaned and thrashed beneath the thin coverlet, but to Arabella's expressions of love and hope he made no conscious reply.

"I am very sorry for your brother's condition," Mr. Trombley said, "but it would be far worse if not for your brave cousin Mr. Ashby."

"My cousin *Simon* Ashby?" Arabella gasped.

"Indeed, miss. It happened while we were fleeing from Wood-thrush Woods. At one point I noticed that your brother and your cousin were not among us; I doubled back and found your cousin Mr. Ashby crouching quite solicitously over your brother, who had caught an arrow in the calf. He had lost a considerable amount of blood, and was unconscious." Mr. Trombley closed his eyes and shook his head at the grisly memory. "I bound up the leg, but it was your cousin who carried your brother the rest of the way here. He was very brave and determined; your brother would surely never have survived otherwise."

Arabella stroked Michael's fevered brow, not quite able to credit this tale of Simon's heroism, but unable to deny the joy she felt at Michael's survival.

"Your brother was barely alive when we arrived at Corey House," Mr. Trombley continued. "Fortunately Dr. Fellowes was here, and stitched up the wound, and we were all very hopeful. But then it began to fester, and the leg had to come off. He has not, sadly, regained consciousness since."

Arabella gazed upon the absence beneath the coverlet where her brother's right leg should have been. She felt nothing but a cold numbness. Horror, she supposed, would come later.

The captain's strong brown hand rested upon her shoulder. She patted it absently, then stood. "Captain Singh, Mr. Trombley, Lord Corey . . . I appreciate your concern and expressions of support, but at the moment I desire to be left alone with my brother."

Murmured condolences and sounds of departure followed, but Arabella simply stood and stared at her brother's troubled face, holding his hot and twitching hand.

He seemed so young to her now. Though he was still her elder, and of course nearly a year older now than the last time she had seen him, by comparison with the officers and men with whom she had spent the last few months—very eventful months indeed—he seemed little more than a child.

Then, behind her, Arabella heard the sound of the door opening.

She turned and beheld her cousin Simon, standing with his hand on the doorknob and a rather abashed expression on his face.

Simon closed the door behind himself and cleared his throat. "Miss Ashby, I . . ."

"You *nothing*," she interrupted in a harsh whisper. The others might be listening from the hall, but the fiction of privacy must be maintained. "You came here to kill him, and now it seems you have succeeded. You have won, and I and all my family have lost. So what now? Am I to beg for your generosity? I would not give you the pleasure."

"Do not speak thus of your brother," Simon replied with unctuous calm. "It is said that even the unconscious can hear words of encouragement, or otherwise, spoken at their bedsides." He turned to Michael and, raising his voice as though speaking to a slightly deaf uncle, said, "We have every confidence that he will pull through."

"You need not dissemble to me, *sir*," she hissed. "Do you deny that the entire purpose of your journey to Mars was to murder my brother?"

He turned his eyes downward, away from her accusing gaze. She waited for a response.

"I cannot deny that I considered it," he said at last, speaking to the floor. Then he raised his eyes to Arabella, his hands held out beseechingly. "Please understand, dear cousin, that when I left you in Oxford I was in a state of extreme confusion and despair. On the long voyage to Mars I confess that I entertained many different notions—of entreating your brother for funds, of demanding satisfaction for the thoughtless way his side of the family has treated mine, and, yes, of outright murder. But when I arrived here, and met him in person for the first time, I was so . . . so impressed by his unaffected charm that I found it impossible to either beg from him or kill him. And then came this . . . this *horrific* business with the queen's egg." He hesitated, took a breath, looked at his feet. "I . . . I must confess that I . . ." Another breath. ". . . I do not know whether it was indeed he who stole the egg." He looked up, his eyes beseeching. "But having met him, I am certain that he is incapable of such a dastardly act, and indeed that he is more knowledgeable of, and sympathetic to, the Martians than any man I have ever met. When your brother was wounded— and I swear by all that is holy that it was the Martians who wounded him, not I—I risked all to save him, not only out of love for my cousin, but also out of knowledge that, with his greater knowledge of Martian culture, he might be able to negotiate a settlement. But, alas, he has spent most of the time since then in an unconscious state."

He paused, as though awaiting Arabella's forgiveness or at least understanding. She gave him neither, only a cold stare. Though his story seemed plausible, something in Simon's manner and her personal experience with him suggested that she should withhold judgement.

"Alas indeed," Arabella said, and regarded Simon's face with careful consideration. His tale, with its self-centered motivations, might even be true. Even if it were not—if, perhaps, he had been discovered leaning over Michael, intending to finish the job the Martians had started, and had rescued him instead only because of the presence of a witness—it would be very difficult to disprove, especially now that every one in the house considered Simon a hero.

Simon dropped to his knees and clasped his hands imploringly before himself. "And so now, having confessed to you that which I have been unable to admit to any other soul, I throw myself upon your mercy." He looked up at her with an apparently sincere expression of supplication. "I have seen that your understanding of the Martians is greater even than your brother's. It is my fervent hope that with a full understanding of the situation, you may be able to find some way to bring this violence to a close."

Arabella looked down upon her cousin with mingled emotions of suspicion, pity, anger, and despair. Whether his story was true or not, she knew she must treat him with extreme caution, though to denounce him outright would never be believed.

Simon was correct in one thing, though: It seemed to fall to her to make peace between Englishmen and Martians. Yet even with the captain's brave and wise assistance, she had no idea how she might unravel this deadly conundrum.

She turned her back on Simon and looked to her brother, his face insensible and racked with pain. "What am I to do, Michael?" she whispered in an anguish of uncertainty.

Just then came a horrific crash from very nearby, a great grinding thud of stone against stone, followed by the tinkle of glass and the clatter of falling plaster.

A moment later, the screaming began.

23

ROCKS FALL

Arabella raced down the hall toward the sound, Simon forgotten behind her.

She soon found herself in the manor's grand dining room, whose great windows, now heavily shuttered, had once offered a magnificent prospect over Fort Augusta. But now a great swath of the shutters had been smashed to flinders by an enormous, craggy boulder of red rock.

The boulder lay atop one end of the Coreys' dining table, a precious antique brought out from Earth more than one hundred years ago, which now itself lay in splinters, two of its carved and gilt legs splayed out from the wreckage like those of a *thurok* that had been trodden upon. The massive silver centerpiece, which Arabella had always thought in ostentatiously poor taste, had slid down the length of the now-tilted table to crash like a ship upon the rock. All was covered by dust and bits of broken wood.

The screaming came from Lady Corey. But she was not the

injured party—it was Lord Corey who gasped beneath the wreckage, his face gone deathly pale beneath a coating of plaster dust. Blood was splashed everywhere.

From without, through the gap in the broken shutters, came a great clattering war-cry of triumphant Martians, accompanied by rhythmic chanting.

Arabella recalled a similar scene from the French attack, and how a second ball had come crashing in shortly thereafter. "This place is dangerous!" she cried to the men who now crowded in the door. "We must leave here at once!"

"How dare you!" replied one of the men, a prosperous plantation owner called Sykes. "Our host is injured and requires succor!"

But a long arm in a buff coat held the man back. "She is correct," said the captain. "Our defenses have been breached, and the enemy are very likely to strike again at this same spot. We must retreat."

"Unhand me, you heathen," Sykes spat, and extricated himself from the captain's grip.

"Very well," the captain said, and backed away, deeper into the house. Arabella tried to push her way past the other men to follow him, but the press of their bodies blocked the door.

Sykes ran to Lord Corey, whose eyes had fallen closed. "I will assist you, sir," he said, and picked him up by the shoulders to pull him from beneath the shattered table.

He came away easily. Too easily.

The upper half of his body, separated from the lower, left a long red smear upon the carpet.

Sykes looked up at Arabella in horror just as a second boulder came crashing in, sending glass and fragments of wood and plaster flying everywhere.

Arabella screamed, then coughed as a great cloud of dust burst from the point of impact. Strong arms grasped her and pulled her away, saving her from the trampling feet of the men who, up until a moment earlier, had been pressing to enter the room and were now trying desperately to leave it.

A moment later a huge slab of ceiling fell on the spot she had just vacated, spattering her and her protector with further stinging shards of plaster and stone. He shielded her with his body, his heavy buff coat serving to ward off the worst of the impact to himself.

It was the captain, of course. "Are you hurt?" he shouted over the continuing clatter of falling plaster.

"I think not, sir!"

"We must retreat to the drawing-room!"

———————

Arabella and the captain gathered every one they could find, servants included, into the drawing-room, which faced only the impassable crags behind the house. They soon determined that only Lord Corey and Mr. Sykes had been killed by the two catapult-stones; all the rest were present save the inconsolable Lady Corey, the unconscious Michael, and Dr. Fellowes, who was caring for both of them in Michael's bedchamber.

Simon, too, was present. He lurked at the edges of the gathering as though afraid of her—and well he might be—and yet he seemed unable to take his eyes off of her. To him she said nothing, favoring him instead with a withering glance, to which he replied by skulking away with a satisfyingly mortified expression.

For the last two months she had looked forward to the day when she would publicly denounce her cousin for threatening her with a pistol, imprisoning her, and setting off to Mars to murder her brother . . . and yet, for now, she held her tongue. For all his faults, he had indeed saved Michael's life—whether that had been his original intent or not—and the current crisis, which threatened every one in the house, seemed far too pressing for Simon's crimes to obtain the attention they deserved even if she should mention them.

And so she would wait until the crisis had passed. And if the waiting made Simon anxious as a cat, so much the better.

Another loud crash sent dust pattering down from the ceiling beams and made the whole company look nervously about. A second crash followed shortly thereafter, then a long and nervous silence. After a time they all began to relax.

"How many catapults did you say they had?" Lord Bertram muttered to Arabella.

"We saw two nearing completion," she replied, "but there were at least three more under construction. And no end of boulders."

Captain Singh called her over to where he was conferring with several of the men over a plan of the house hastily sketched by Collins, the late Lord Corey's majordomo. "The dining-room, parlor, and master bedroom suite are lost to us," the captain said, pointing. "They will certainly be destroyed by catapult soon, if they have not already been. Do we need to defend against boarders? Against Martians entering through the broken windows?"

"This house is impregnable," Collins replied, his confidence undiminished by recent events. "Those windows are at least thirty feet from the ground. And the walls are sheer, quite secure from scaling."

The captain glanced to Arabella, who shook her head. "I have seen Martians build ladders for descent into canyons far deeper than that."

"Descent is not ascent," Collins sniffed.

"But ladders are ladders," the captain replied. He squinted at the plan, then at a staircase that spiraled up from one corner of the room. "How tall is that tower?" Another crash shook the house, rattling the table around which they stood.

Collins licked his lips nervously. "Sixty or seventy feet from base to top."

The captain turned to Arabella. "Can the Martians' arrows reach that high?"

"Not with any accuracy, sir."

"Nor will it be an easy target for their catapults," the captain muttered, half to himself. "Which is not to say they will not try, once we begin shooting at them from it."

"The gallery at the tower's top is crenellated," Arabella said. "It would be extremely defensible." To the questioning looks she received from Collins and the other men, she said, "My brother and I would retreat to that tower during our parents' whist games with Lord and Lady Corey. We would often imagine ourselves to be in charge of the house's defense." Though the attackers they had envisioned in those playful days had been French soldiers, not the Martians who were their servants and teachers.

"Very well," the captain said, and straightened from the plan. "We require three volunteers," he called. "Have we any one here who is a particularly good shot with a rifle?"

Several of the gentlemen, and a few of the servants, raised their hands.

The captain pointed to three of them. "Take the best pieces you can find, and a quantity of ammunition, to the top of that tower." He pointed to the staircase. "Stay out of sight as much as you can, but keep an eye on the wall below those smashed windows. If you see Martians making any attempt to climb it, shoot them. If you see any other unusual activity, send one of your number down to report it."

As the men departed in search of rifles, another crash, this one considerably louder, echoed down the hall. "Damage report," the captain called over his shoulder. No one moved. "You!" he snapped, pointing at a man standing near the door. "Go and find out what just happened." The man stared, rabbit-like, at the captain for only a moment before bolting to comply.

"I should go to the tower as well," Arabella said, "as an observer. I am best equipped to understand what I see."

The captain relaxed from his attitude of stern command. "I thank you for volunteering, Miss Ashby," he said gently, "but your services are required here, for possible negotiations with the Martians."

He is trying to keep me safe, she realized. But, as well, she understood that he was correct—they must negotiate with the Martians, and somehow bring the conflict to a close, or the house would eventually be battered to bits around them.

But there was only one thing that she could think of that might pacify the Martians.

Pray God it still existed.

"Please excuse me," she said to the captain, and went off to find Simon.

She found Simon in Michael's bedchamber, whose location and thick walls made it one of the safest rooms in the house. Dr. Fellowes comforted Lady Corey at the side of the room, while Simon knelt at Michael's bedside with apparent solicitude.

Arabella knew not what scheme Simon might have in mind. Perhaps he intended to smother Michael at the first opportunity, though that opportunity seemed unlikely as Michael's bedchamber also served Dr. Fellowes as a private room for examination and treatment of the injured. Or perhaps Simon's attention to Michael was only an excuse for him to remain far from danger. In any case, she would have to keep a close eye upon him.

When Simon realized she was standing behind him, he quickly straightened and turned to her. "He seems no better."

Arabella regarded him for a moment, filled with anger and scorn, then dropped her gaze to Michael's face. Like the captain after Paeonia, he was unconscious, helpless, and surrounded by well-meaning simpletons.

She could—she *should*—ask the captain for his advice. He was aware of Simon's perfidy and would surely have some sage counsel to offer. But he was busy with the defense of the house, and her own knowledge of Martian culture was superior to his—superior even to Englishmen who had lived on Mars for decades, who saw only what their English eyes knew how to see. And it could only be an understanding of the Martians that would get them all out of this predicament, if such were even possible.

"I know you stole the egg," she said to Simon.

Fear, panic, anger, and despair flashed across Simon's face before he covered it with his hands. "I did," he sobbed.

Arabella had not, in fact, known with certainty that it had been Simon who had stolen the egg. But that part of Simon's earlier confession had seemed even less sincere than the rest of it, and her guess that confronting him with his lie would cause him to break down had proven correct.

"Your brother welcomed me into his household," Simon continued, "and it is to my great shame that even while I enjoyed his hospitality I continually warred within myself as to whether and how I should attempt his murder. But no opportunity presented itself for weeks, and as my indecision and frustration grew . . ." He raised his face from his hands, and it was wet with tears. "I am afraid that the strain must have driven me somewhat mad. For after we visited the new queen to pay our respects to her upon the delivery of her egg, I conceived a scheme to steal the egg and lay the blame upon your brother." He drew a handkerchief from his pocket, wiped his eyes, and noisily blew his nose. "In this way I hoped to . . . remove him from the succession, so to speak, without taking direct action, and thus to salve my muddled conscience."

"But you underestimated the Martians' reaction to the egg's abduction."

"That is sadly true." He hung his head. "And so appalled was I at the, the entirely unintended consequences of my imprudent action, that when Michael was injured I abandoned all thought of my own fortune and brought him here."

That Arabella's suspicions were confirmed was satisfying, and that Simon had undergone a change of heart was gratifying. But she was still distrustful of him—indeed, she did not completely believe his tale even now—and of course her anger at him was redoubled.

"Please tell me you did not destroy the egg."

"I did not," he said, and looked to her with dawning understanding and desperate hope. "I hid it in a safe place."

For the first time that day she felt a faint stirring of hope in her own breast. "You must return it immediately," she said.

"I cannot," he said, and dropped his gaze to the floor. "I buried it in the desert, miles from here."

"In that case," she told him, in a firm yet gentle tone like the one her father had used after Arabella confessed to breaking the automaton dancer, "you must go up into the tower, tell the Martians that you were the one who abducted the egg, and tell them exactly where they can find it. If they recover it, and it yet lives, we may receive their clemency. Otherwise, we will all certainly perish beneath their catapult stones." As if to reinforce her words, a rumbling crash sounded from the far side of the house.

"Must I admit my complicity?" He looked up at her with an expression like a cornered *khushera*. "Is there no alternative?"

She gave the question serious consideration. "Martians place great stock in personal responsibility, which they call *okhaya*. If you were, for example, to tell them that you do not know who had abducted the egg but that you know where it is hidden, they might be pleased at its recovery, but they would still be bent on the apprehension and punishment of the malefactor. Whereas if you yourself admit responsibility and offer the egg's location in a gesture of sincere atonement, they will leave off their search for the culprit and they might—I must emphasize *might*—offer leniency to you for your admission of guilt."

Simon stared into the fireplace, as though seeking some other alternative there. But there was no alternative to be had. "Very well," he said, and firmed up his chin. "I shall, like Daniel, offer up my confession for the sake of my people." His eyes took on a calculating aspect. "But I must request that you, with your greater knowledge of Martian language and customs, accompany me to wherever the admission must be made."

Arabella regarded him with frank suspicion. But she could not in good conscience deny his request. "Very well," she said, considering. "I will accompany you to the tower." Others would be present there, and they would be far from the Martians and their nimble swords.

Simon bowed deeply and proffered his elbow. But Arabella fixed him with a cold eye and gestured that he should instead precede her.

He raised one eyebrow, then inclined his head and opened the door.

They made their way down the hall toward the drawing-room in this way, with Arabella careful to keep Simon in sight at all times.

"Keep your head down, miss," said one of the men on the parapet as Arabella followed Simon through the door. "They've lobbed a few arrows at us, and they usually go clean past, but you never can tell when they might get lucky."

The view from the tower's top was as spectacular as it had ever been. The house, still grand despite the substantial damage it had sustained, spread out its roofs and corbels below them, and all around rose the craggy red-ochre magnificence of the Skatasho Hills. But the view to the east, once an appealing prospect on Fort Augusta and the pleasant town beneath it, now offered nothing but ruin, scattered with wrecked and abandoned buildings and smeared with columns of smoke. And the plain below the house was a shambles of angry, clattering Martians. At least five catapults seemed complete now, and more were rising at the back of the encampment.

"We've shot a few of the buggers off the wall below the windows," offered another man, pointing. "Not many so far."

"We think they might be massing for an assault, though," said the first. "You can see there, where they're building ladders. But when and if they do attack, you can be certain we will defend the house to the last."

"Thank you, sirs, for your service," she said. But she observed to herself that these three men and their half dozen hunting rifles had no more chance against the thousands of Martians massed below than she herself, unaccompanied, would have had against the privateers who had nearly destroyed *Diana*.

Simon merely stared down at the vast insurrection that he, however unintentionally, had provoked. "How will they even hear me?" he asked Arabella.

"Their hearing is quite good. You should begin by calling '*karaa, karaa*' to get their attention."

"Must I speak in Martian? I do not know the language."

"Most of them have at least a little English."

With Arabella's encouragement he stepped up onto a box of cartridges, raising himself into the Martians' view, where he called out a creditable "*karaa, karaa*" and waved his arms. Several of the nearer Martians paused in their work and pointed at him; soon a respectable crowd had turned their eye-stalks up to him. None, she noted, loosed an arrow at him, despite his vulnerable position above the crenellated battlements. She took this as a good sign for the potential success of their negotiations.

"You have their attention," she told Simon. "Begin by stating your name."

"My name is Simon Ashby," he called, and though his voice trembled slightly it carried loud and clear across the roofs and rocks. He swallowed and closed his eyes. "I am here to confess that it is I who stole the egg."

A chuttering rattle of consternation greeted his words, though again Arabella was pleased to note that no Martian fired an arrow or even threw a rock.

Simon opened his eyes and looked to Arabella for reassurance. She smiled encouragingly and whispered, "Go on."

"I am genuinely sorry for this . . . precipitate action," he told the gathered Martians. "To demonstrate my sincerity, I reveal to you the location in which I have hidden the egg: It is buried in the sand beneath a rough outcropping of orange stone, one mile to the west of the Ashby plantation, not far from the path. The outcrop is conical in shape, and it is marked by a diagonal vein of black stone." To Arabella he said, "Is that sufficient?"

She hoped that it was. "The egg is of utmost importance to them. They will search until they find it."

He swallowed and turned again to the Martians. "Again, let me extend my sincerest apologies for my intemperate action. I . . . I did not realize the significance of the egg, and I pray that you will forgive me. And all of us." He looked out over the Martians for a time, as though hoping for an enthusiastic response. Finding none, he simply stepped down from the box. "It is done," he said.

"You have carried that off creditably," Arabella replied, and not entirely out of politeness. "Now we must wait. Once they have found the egg, I expect that they will send an emissary."

All the rest of that day they waited. The catapults ceased their hammering of the house, but a brief essay out the gate resulted in a rain of arrows—though the Martians were no longer attempting to destroy the house, they nonetheless insisted that the Englishmen remain within it.

During this respite from the catapults' pounding, the captain directed the men in inspecting and repairing the house. The destruction was frightening—in several places bearing walls, some quite deep in the house, had been demolished by the stones, and sections of the roof had collapsed. Worse, the base of the tower from which they were observing and defending the house had taken serious damage.

They did what they could to shore up the damaged sections, but it was plain that even their redoubt at the back of the manor would not survive long if the Martians resumed their assault. Either the walls and tower would fall, allowing armed Martians to enter, or the house would simply be brought down on top of them.

While the captain and most of the men worked at reinforcing the house, Arabella sat with Michael in his bedchamber, spooning soup into his mouth as she had once done for the captain. But where the captain in his stupor had licked the soup off his lips when it was placed there, Michael seemed to actively fight it, spitting out soup and spoon and all as he thrashed in his fever.

"He's growing weaker, isn't he?" she asked Dr. Fellowes in the kitchen.

"I have seen men recover from more serious infections," the doctor replied, but his expression was grave.

Simon, too, continued to spend time at Michael's bedside. "I am so very sorry, my dear cousin," he said, though Michael showed no sign of understanding. "I hope that you can somehow find it in your heart to forgive me my trespasses. If there were any thing, any thing whatsoever, I could do to atone for my errors, please rest assured that I would do so."

Despite her deep-seated suspicions, Arabella wondered if Simon's contrition might be more than mere pretense. She longed to denounce him as a worthless, foolish wastrel who had dissipated what little fortune he'd had, squandered what remained on a fantastical and murderous scheme to wrest the estate from Arabella's branch of the family, and cost her brother his leg, his health, and possibly his life. But she could not condemn him, not entirely at least. For though he had begun the insurrection that had injured her brother and so many others, he had also saved her brother's life. And now, at least, he *seemed* repentant, and had shown himself willing to take action, quite serious action, in an attempt to make amends.

"My brother has a very gentle heart," Arabella told Simon. *Perhaps too gentle*, she thought. "I am sure that if he could see how truly sorry you are, he would harbor no grudge against you."

At that Simon smiled, the first apparently genuine smile she could recall having seen from him since long before her father's death. He opened his mouth to speak.

But before any words could emerge, their conversation was interrupted by a horrific ululation from without—a great moaning, clattering cry from hundreds of Martian throats like nothing Arabella had ever heard before. And that dreadful wail was only the beginning; it grew and grew in depth and volume of sound until it seemed the entire planet Mars was crying out in anguish.

Then the rising lament crescendoed with a tremendous crash, which was immediately echoed by another and another.

The rain of catapult stones had resumed, with even greater ferocity.

24

THE LAST REDOUBT

Arabella peered over the parapet, struggling to make some sense of what she saw and heard. The captain stood beside her, outwardly calm as ever, though she knew him well enough by now to tell his current rigid stance from his usual upright one.

The crowd of Martians below seethed like a pot of water on a low boil, warriors running hither and yon, clattering and screaming and waving their spears. A knot of feverish activity surrounded each of the catapults—at least seven were now in operation—with chanting teams of Martians hauling back each deadly arm and loading huge, jagged boulders into each waiting basket. The nearest catapult let fly even as she watched, with a great cry from its crew, sending yet another stone crashing into the already thoroughly demolished dining-room. But though the added visible destruction was not large, she knew this was not just a futile exercise—the room's rear wall, a load-bearing wall, could not take much more damage, and when it collapsed it would take a goodly portion of the east wing's roof with it.

"Lookee there, sir," said one of the riflemen, pointing. Arabella followed his outstretched finger to the distant town below Fort Augusta, which had suddenly spouted a huge, fresh gout of flames. A column of black, greasy smoke rose from the spot, soon joined in the air by several more such columns. The town, already heavily damaged, now seemed doomed to complete destruction.

"What in God's name has set them off like this?" fumed another rifleman, this one a well-fed older gentleman named Morrison, sighting along his weapon. With a hard, sharp *crack* he loosed another shot, sending a Martian tumbling down the craggy hill below the house. But others rushed forward to fill the void, jamming themselves into the crowd rushing to raise ladders beneath the gaping hole which had formerly been the dining-room windows.

Arabella thought she knew, but she could not be certain—the tumult from the crowd below was so great that individual words could not be discerned, even if they were within her limited vocabulary. "I could attempt to ask them," she said. "But you must lower your rifles."

Mr. Morrison glared at her, but put down his weapon. "Be quick about it," he muttered.

The captain dragged a cartridge box close to the parapet, and Arabella climbed up upon it—the slight additional elevation making her feel giddy and exposed—cupped her hands to her mouth, and called out *"Karaa, karaa!"* several times until she had the attention of a good number of the crowd. "Gentle neighbors!" she cried. "What is the cause of this new attack? We wish only peace!"

This brought forth an angry, muddled shout from many Martian throats which completely failed to clarify the situation. But after a moment the crowd quieted itself as a gargantuan armored form moved up through the pressed bodies to the clearing at the base of the tower. An *akhmok*.

And not just any *akhmok*. Even at this distance, Arabella recognized her beloved *itkhalya*. Somehow, despite Khema's transformation, she still moved in a familiar way. "Oh, dearest *tutukha!*" Khema called, her booming voice twisted with sadness. "I fear peace is no longer a possibility."

"Negotiation is always an option," Arabella called back, "as you yourself taught me, dear Khema."

"Indeed, *tutukha*, but in this case the options are very limited. For the kidnapped egg was simply buried in cold sand like a cast-off shell, and by the time we found it . . . it had died." A few Martians behind her wailed in grief and pounded their spear hafts upon the sand. "My people are beyond consolation, and I am afraid this regrettable violence must be allowed to burn itself out."

In the silence that followed Khema's words, distant screams came to Arabella's ears from the town beyond. Human screams.

"Surely we can find some other solution," Arabella cried— though, in truth, she could see no alternative.

"I am sorry, *tutukha*."

"Get down!" shouted one of the men, and roughly hauled Arabella down from her perch. A moment later an enormous boulder flew past the parapet, so near that the roaring wind of its passage battered Arabella's face and hair. The rock's tremendous crash upon the crag behind the house was barely audible over her pounding heart.

"That was too close!" said Mr. Morrison. "For your own safety, Miss Ashby, I must insist that you return to the drawing-room."

Though she protested this exile, even the captain was set against her, and against her will she soon found her feet set upon the descending steps.

"We are Englishmen," the portly gentleman declared behind her. "We will defend this house unto our dying breaths."

And then he closed the door, leaving Arabella in darkness.

The captain, Collins, and several of the gentlemen leaned over the plan of the house, pointing and muttering darkly, while Arabella sat dejected on a settee nearby and stared mutely at the flagstones of the hearth. The thunderous crash of another catapult-stone shook the house, sending bits of plaster pattering down, but by now this event was far from extraordinary.

Was this the end? Would all of Fort Augusta—all of English Mars—fall victim to madness and violence?

A shadow fell across the stones, and she looked up. It was the captain.

"We must retreat to the kitchen soon," he said. "Once the east wing collapses it will be our last redoubt. With luck, the insurrection will be quelled before our defenses there are overwhelmed."

She nodded miserably, knowing as well as the captain did that there was no one to quell the insurrection. "I suppose we should move Michael there as soon as we can," she said. "Assuming he can be moved."

"I will ask Dr. Fellowes." But he did not turn away; instead, he stood and regarded Arabella for a moment. "You must not blame yourself," he said. "You made your best attempt at negotiations."

"That was hardly a negotiation," she sighed, and though she acknowledged the captain's sentiments she still felt horribly responsible for their predicament. "It was barely even a plea."

"It was the best that could be done under the circumstances."

But still the responsibility nagged at her. It had been her astronomical explanation that had set Simon upon the path to Mars, her failure to arrive in time that had allowed him to create this horrific situation, her lack of understanding that had left her helpless in the face of unbending hostility. "My father would be horribly disappointed in me, if he yet lived," she said.

"If he were disappointed in you, Miss Ashby, he would be a fool. And, from my experience of you, I cannot believe that you are descended from fools."

She felt a tiny smile creep onto her face at that. "I suppose I cannot help feeling as I do. I was taught from a very young age to own up to my failings and seek to make amends."

"Your father taught you well." He sighed, fractionally; had she not known him so well she might not even have noticed it. "Yet now, it seems, it is too late for any amends to be made, and it is left to us to defend ourselves as best we can. I will speak with Dr. Fellowes about your brother."

But even as he bowed and turned to leave, something in his words nagged at her.

Was it, truly, too late for amends to be made?

Who, indeed, was it who had taught her to own up to her failings?

"Khema," she whispered.

The captain paused. "I beg your pardon?"

"Khema," she repeated. "It was my *itkhalya*, not my father, who taught me the value of personal responsibility, which Martians value so highly." She looked up at the captain. "There is, perhaps, one way this violence can be brought to a close. But it would come at a terrible price."

———————

They found Simon in Michael's chamber, kneeling at the bedside as though saying his prayers before sleep. "He seems to be resting more comfortably now," Dr. Fellowes said as they entered. "The fever has abated, and I believe he may regain consciousness soon." But despite his optimistic words, Michael's unmoving face looked waxy and gray.

With grim resolution, Arabella turned from her brother to Simon. "Cousin," she began, then hesitated. "May we have a private word with you?"

Simon stood, a questioning look in his eye, but retired with Arabella and the captain to a quiet corner of the bedchamber.

"You have said," she murmured privately, "that you would do any thing to atone for your errors."

"Any thing within my power . . . ," he replied, though his eyes narrowed in suspicion.

She swallowed, then looked away. What she had in mind to ask of him was too terrible to contemplate. During this crisis she had come to see him as perhaps more foolish than evil, but even if she still hated him as thoroughly as she had on *Diana* it would be too much for any civilized person to ask. Yet she could imagine no better solution.

She returned her gaze to Simon's. "You know that the Martians place great stock in owning up to one's mistakes."

"Yes . . ." His face showed great concern.

"You are the one who took the egg, and you have already admitted this to them. There is a chance—a *chance*—that if you . . . if you *voluntarily* turn yourself over to them, they will consider justice to be done, and bring this insurrection to a close."

"I . . . I see." His brow furrowed as his attention turned inward. "And what will they do to *me?*"

"I cannot deny that Martian justice can be severe." At that statement his already-troubled face paled. "But this is a chance to redeem yourself, in the eyes of the world and of your Creator, and perhaps even yourself."

The captain cleared his throat. "If you do not do this thing," he said, gravely but not without sympathy, "the violence will continue until every Englishman in Fort Augusta is dead."

Simon trembled miserably on the cold flagstones, eyes darting every which way. Then he closed his eyes hard and seemed to gather himself up, bowing his head and bending over his clenched fists. For a long time he remained thus and Arabella watched him, holding her breath as he held his, knowing how difficult the decision must be.

Then he let out his breath with a loud "Pah!" and collapsed onto the bed, head held in his hands. "I cannot!" he said. "I have not the courage." For once, Arabella thought, he was entirely sincere.

Arabella and the captain exchanged a long, considering look. His eyes were very hard, and he glanced to the prostrate Simon and back to her, tilting his head with a raised, questioning eyebrow.

His meaning was clear, and it appalled her. She replied to his glance with a sharp shake of her head and a stern frown. "We will leave you to consider, Cousin," she told Simon, and angrily swept out of the room. The captain followed.

As soon as the door had closed behind the captain, leaving the two of them alone in the hall, Arabella rounded on him. "My cousin *must* be allowed to make his own decision," she hissed in a barely contained whisper. "To force such a sacrifice on any one, even such a villain as he, would be inhuman."

The captain's expression was as grave as ever she had seen it. "If I am any judge of character," he replied in a low intense murmur, "if we wait for him to do the honorable thing, we will all die in the waiting."

"That may very well be." She took a breath, let it out. "But in this matter, I cannot countenance coercion. To throw him to the Martians against his will would be a violation of both *okhaya* and common human decency."

His gaze bore down on her. She returned it, refusing to back down. At last the captain blinked, and inclined his head to her. "Very well. I shall gather every one to the kitchen for our final defense." He bowed. "We may die, but at least we will die with honor."

She recognized that he, too, had been asked to sacrifice himself for the sake of others, and unlike Simon he had done the honorable thing. Even if the decision cost her her life, her esteem of him was inestimably raised because of it.

"I thank you very much for your understanding in this difficult matter," she said, and gave him a deep, respectful curtsey.

Arabella watched the captain's upright, buff-coated back as he departed, his boot heels clopping on the ancient flagstones, until he rounded the corner and vanished from sight. Then she sighed, gathered herself, and returned to the bedchamber.

Simon lay as she had left him, on his knees with his upper body splayed out atop Michael's bed-clothes. Michael, for his part, still lay wan and unmoving, though he yet breathed.

"Dear cousin," she said, and he gasped and jerked upright, relaxing when he saw that she was alone. "Dear cousin," she began again, "I do understand how impossible this request must seem. But I must beg you to reconsider. Not only all of our lives here, but the lives of every Englishman in Fort Augusta territory, could be spared by your action. Perhaps even more—who knows how far this insurrection might spread if not checked?"

"I am a weak man, Cousin," he replied. "It was my weakness that led to my poverty, and brought me to Mars, and prompted me to steal the egg." He gave a rueful grin. "It would be inconsistent for me to display any strength of character now."

"People can change." She settled herself on the bedside chair. "Just months ago I was a naive girl. I, too, took myself to Mars on a sudden whim, not considering the costs or consequences, and suffered greatly for my imprudence. Yet I have also learned from the experience." She leaned in close. "There are some tasks only one person can perform." She thought of the explosive shell, its smooth warm exterior hiding such great destructive power, and how it had been placed in her hands with a confidence she still felt she had not earned. "If such a task should happen to fall to you, you may rail against it, you may deny it, you may try to push it away . . . but in the end, you may also find that you can rise to the occasion."

"Even such a man as I?"

"Even such a man as you." She held out her hand. "Come with me, Cousin."

Mutely he took it and rose. Then, still holding her hand, he stood and contemplated her face for a time, considering. "I . . . I will make the attempt," he said at last. "I will endeavor to do honor to the family name."

Arabella's suspicion of Simon warred with her desire to assume the best of any man, but in the end her natural inclination to charity won out. "That is all I, or any one, could ask."

"I only request that I be given a moment alone in my bedchamber, so as to prepare myself for . . . for the end."

"Of course."

At the door he paused and looked back at Michael, still unconscious, his breathing shallow but regular. "I am sorry, Cousin," he said, then set his shoulders and stepped into the hall.

Arabella, too, cast a long glance back at her brother before closing the door behind herself.

They found the drawing-room, when they arrived, nearly empty of both people and supplies. Only a few servants remained, rushing in and out, carrying crates and barrels away to the kitchen, and they were all too distracted to take any notice of Arabella and the increasingly anxious Simon. Even so, as they approached the spiral stair, one of the footmen paused in his work and called out, "You ought not go up there, sir and miss! It is too dangerous! Even the riflemen have been forced to retreat."

Simon quailed at this. "Will you accompany me, Cousin?" he said, his voice tremulous.

"Of course," she murmured reassuringly.

At the second turning of the stair they found, to Arabella's disturbed surprise, bright sunlight streaming down from above, accompanied by fresh air and the chattering sound of the Martian army. One more turning confirmed her fears: The tower's top had been shattered by the Martians' catapults, and the stair ended in a ragged edge of broken stone and mortar.

Again Simon hesitated, but this time he managed to gather his own courage. "What have I to fear?" he said, half to himself, and set his trembling feet upon the step. Arabella followed.

They reached the top and stood blinking in the sunlight, a stiff breeze plucking at their hair and clothing. The Martians below toiled like ants, already beginning to flow up the house's battered sides to the rough opening smashed into the former dining-room. Plainly they would be within the house very soon.

Suddenly Arabella noticed that Simon had stepped back from the edge. "Courage, Cousin," Arabella said, turning to face him. But what she saw as she turned was not the hesitant expression of a man unwilling to face death, but the calm and confident leer she had last seen in Simon's dining-room in Oxford.

Along with the pistol from that same occasion.

"I am frightfully sorry, Cousin," he said, "but I find myself unable to perform the service you have requested, and must ask you to do so in my stead. You will confess to the Martians that it was you who stole the egg, and it is you who will surrender yourself to them."

The last time she had seen that pistol, the muzzle had seemed as big as the world. But since that time she had stared down the barrel of a French cannon, and the pistol now seemed small and ineffectual. She straightened. "I was not even on Mars when the egg was stolen."

"The Martians do not know that." Simon drew back the pistol's hammer. "You will confess, or you will die at this moment, and I will give them your body, saying that you were at fault all along. But they will more readily believe it, and more readily give up their campaign, if they hear your confession from your own lips. And you do desire to bring this conflict to an end, do you not?"

Arabella's eyes sought an opening, but Simon had carefully positioned himself so that she had no means of escape. "What becomes of my brother?"

"He will have to go, of course, sooner or later. Though I assure you that once the estate is mine, I will treat your mother and sisters at least as well as your side of the family ever treated me." He pressed forward then, and perforce she took a step backwards, finding herself upon the highest remaining step. Only a great void of air lay beyond that.

She steeled herself for what she knew must be done.

"*Karaa, karaa!*" she called, waving her arms, until the Martians took notice. "This is Simon Ashby!" she cried, pointing to him.

At the name a great howling roar sprung up from the nearer Martians, quickly spreading to the rest of the crowd. Arabella had never before heard such an expression of furious wrath.

Simon's expression was equally furious. "Confess now," he snarled, taking another step forward and thrusting the pistol toward Arabella.

This was exactly the reaction she had hoped for. As soon as Simon came within her reach, with one swift motion she seized his wrist and thrust it to the side. It went easily, for Simon was only an English dandy, whereas Arabella's arms bore the strength given them by months of honest sailor's work.

Simon shrieked and pulled the trigger, but though the shot rang in Arabella's ear and the sudden sharp scent of gunpowder stained the air, neither was anywhere near as powerful as *Diana's* cannon. The ball flew harmlessly into the air, while Arabella squeezed Simon's wrist until the pistol dropped from his hand. It bounced once on the broken step's edge, then fell spinning to the rocks below.

Simon twisted his wrist from Arabella's grasp and took a step back, glaring at her. Arabella gestured to the ravening Martians below, chattering and waving their forked spears—an enormous mob of them, seeming to stretch all the way to the horizon. "It is you who brought them all here," she said, "and only you can prevent them from killing every last Englishman on Mars. Here is your chance, Cousin. Do the honorable thing, for once in your miserable life."

In answer Simon growled and charged at her, seeking to force her over the edge. But at the last moment she sidestepped and twisted away from his thrust, just as Khema had taught her, and he sailed past her.

Past her and over the edge, his eyes shining with hatred all the while.

A moment later he landed among the Martians.

Arabella turned away from the scene, but the horrible crunching sounds would stay with her until her dying day.

25

MICHAEL

The captain and Mr. Trombley met her at the base of the spiral stair. "The footman said that you and Mr. Ashby had gone up to the tower!" Trombley cried. "Whatever possessed you to do such a thing?" He blinked, looking past her to the darkness of the stair. "And . . . and where is Mr. Ashby?"

The captain's eyes were firm and cool, expressing only an intellectual inquiry, as though he were merely curious as to the fate of some large and exotic insect that had happened to land upon her shoulder.

As for herself, though Arabella's emotions were all in a roil—her heart pounding rapidly, her breath shallow, her hands chill—she found her voice firm and steady as she replied. "Mr. Ashby has given himself to the Martians."

"Dear Lord!" cried Trombley.

"I had wondered at the sound," the captain said. And, indeed, after Simon's death the Martians had cried out in triumph, then fallen silent.

Arabella closed her eyes, but nothing could shut away the

memory of Simon's fate. "Somehow . . . somehow he found the courage to redeem himself," she said, knowing that every one still considered him a hero and not wishing to argue the point at this moment. "I only pray that his sacrifice will bring an end to the insurrection."

"Oh dear," said Trombley, mopping his brow. "Oh dear me. What horrible news. Horrible, horrible. I . . . I extend my deepest condolences upon the loss of your cousin." He bowed. "Shall I summon a servant to bring you a glass of water?"

"No thank you, sir." She curtseyed, the action coming automatically despite her inner tumult. "I thank you for your concern, but I am certain the servants are all occupied in preparing the defense of the kitchen."

"Of course, of course, how stupid of me." He bowed again, quite unnecessarily. "I shall bring you some water myself." He bowed again and retreated rapidly, his own emotions obviously in a state of considerable distress.

As soon as he had departed, she collapsed. But before she could land in a heap upon the stone floor, the captain's strong arms were beneath her shoulders. Without a word he helped her upright, holding her up until, with a gesture, she indicated that she could once again maintain her own feet. Yet despite the turmoil in her heart and the feverish tremor in her limbs, her eyes remained dry.

Still without a word, the captain led her to a nearby sofa. After she had seated herself he sat silently beside her, hands chastely folded in his lap, waiting patiently for her to collect herself.

At last she drew in a shuddering breath, then let it out all in a rush. "Thank you for your understanding," she said, her voice shaky. "If that prattling fool had kept up his jabber for one moment more . . ."

"Do not concern yourself with him," he said.

Arabella, realizing that she was on the verge of babbling herself, quieted her tongue.

After another stretch of silence, during which Arabella's racing heart steadied and slowed, the captain spoke again. "Did Mr. Ashby truly give himself voluntarily? Without coercion or . . . assistance?"

Not for the first time, Arabella wondered at his seemingly superhuman ability to perceive the truth of any situation. "Not . . . entirely." She looked up, dreading the captain's judgement. "He rushed at me, I evaded his charge, and he . . . he went over the edge. But I did not push him. I swear this to you."

His gaze was clear and steady and untroubled. "I could not imagine otherwise," he said.

"Thank you, sir," she replied with deep sincerity. "But you must not share the details of his fate with the others. Not yet."

"Of course not. It would destroy morale."

She frowned then, and added, "We must make some provision for his family. Though Beatrice assisted Simon in imprisoning me, I believe she was compelled to do so, and her daughter Sophie is an innocent undeserving of punishment for her father's misdeeds."

"You have a most generous spirit, Miss Ashby."

At that moment Mr. Trombley reappeared, though without the promised glass of water. "Miss Ashby! Miss Ashby!" he cried. "The Martians are at the gate, demanding to speak to you! And Michael has regained consciousness!"

Arabella looked to the captain. Her shock and indecision must have been plain upon her countenance, for he straightened and in a firm yet compassionate voice said, "You must tend to your brother. Go. I will treat with the Martians to the best of my ability."

"Aye, aye, sir," she said, and saluted.

She did not realize until she was halfway down the hall that she had done so.

Michael was sitting up, drinking from a glass of water, as Arabella entered his bedchamber. "Michael!" she cried, and despite the presence of Dr. Fellowes and several others in the room she embraced him with heedless enthusiasm. A moment later she realized her mistake and drew back, fearing she might have damaged his already-injured body with an excess of zeal.

But her brother's face, though ashen and sunken of cheek, showed nothing but pleasure at the sight of her. "My dearest sister," he said, gripping her hand. His grasp seemed terribly feeble. "My dear Arabella. How I had worried about you!"

Michael's voice was rough, hollow, and weak, but unmistakably, joyfully his own. It was a voice she'd feared so many times in the last few months that she would never hear again, and at the sound of it she was quite overcome with emotion. She sank to her knees at the bedside, still holding her brother's hand. "Words cannot express my relief at your recovery," she managed in a hoarse whisper.

"I am, you may be sure, astonished at your presence on Mars at all," Michael said, "never mind here at Corey Hall. The last I had heard of you was a letter from Mother, which arrived on the last packet-ship before the insurrection. She said that according to cousin Beatrice, you suddenly ran mad and vanished into the countryside. Pray tell, how came you to be here?"

For a moment she hesitated—not knowing just where to begin, nor how much of her adventure she ought to share with him in his obviously still fragile state of health. But then she recalled the verve with which he'd raced across the dunes with her and Khema, and smiled. "I did not run mad," she said, "let me assure you. Though I was exceedingly vexed. . . ."

She sketched out the story quickly, knowing that the details would be filled in over many conversations to come, but despite the shocked expressions on the faces of Dr. Fellowes and Mr. Trombley, neither of whom had heard any of it before, she felt no need to either moderate or exaggerate her tale. She simply

told it as it had happened. Michael's reactions were quite satisfying, ranging from gape-jawed astonishment to hearty laughter.

"Privateers?" he gasped.

"Privateers," she repeated, and went on to describe the battle in
some detail.

Just as she was describing the ship's arrival at Mars, a commotion came to Arabella's ears from the corridor outside, followed
by a knock at the door. Mr. Trombley opened it, to reveal the
captain.

Suddenly she recalled the continuing danger of the Martians
without, which she had quite forgotten in the excitement of her
brother's return to consciousness. But though she ached for news
of the insurrection, the forms must be obeyed. "Michael," she
said, "please permit me to present to you Captain Prakash Singh
of the Honorable Mars Company airship *Diana*. Captain Singh,
my brother, Michael Ashby."

The two men shook hands with great propriety. "I have heard
so much about you, Captain," Michael said. "I thank you for taking my sister on in your crew, though I must apologize for her
deception as to her sex."

"No apology is required," the captain replied with a bow. "Her
position was earned, and well-earned, with intelligence, skill, and
bravery."

"Please, sir," Arabella interrupted, bursting with anxious curiosity, "what of the Martians?"

He paused. "Your, ah, Miss Khema, is in the entry-way, being
too large to pass through the inner door. She says that the council
of clans has met and, having heard and considered her entreaties
upon our behalf, has decided to accept your cousin's death as
sufficient recompense for the egg's abduction."

At the words "your cousin's death," Michael's face showed
shock and sadness. "My cousin Mr. Ashby? He who saved my life
in the fighting at Woodthrush Woods?"

"I am afraid so, sir. It was he who took the egg, which triggered the insurrection, and it was his confession and death which brought it to an end."

"I should never have imagined him capable of such a thing." Michael turned his pale, stricken face to Arabella. "Nor, of course, of imprisoning you."

"He did," she replied, "and much else besides."

The captain cleared his throat and continued. "We are free to depart the house, and once the word has reached the rest of the Martians, the insurrection will be at an end." He raised a finger. "However, Miss Khema acknowledges that considerable ill will has been raised, on both sides, by the recent violence. She invites you, Miss Ashby, to consult with her on matters of improving relations between the Martians and English, and to represent the English to the council of clans."

Before Arabella could reply to this extraordinary invitation, Dr. Fellowes interrupted. "If we may depart this house, I believe we should do so, and the sooner the better." A groan from the timbers above confirmed the urgency of his suggestion. "Though I fear Mr. Ashby may be in no condition to be moved, my fear of the house collapsing about our ears is greater still."

At that Michael managed to lever himself up onto his elbows. "How did the house become so damaged?" he asked.

Arabella touched the back of his hand reassuringly. "We will explain later. For now we must put all our attentions on moving you to some safer place." She paused, considering. "But where? Surely all of Fort Augusta is in ruins."

"Woodthrush Woods," Michael said, grasping Arabella's hand. The very thought seemed to lend some strength to his tremulous grip. "Take me home."

Dr. Fellowes frowned deeply at the prospect. "It is over two miles distant!"

"The Ashby house is in much better condition than this one," the captain observed, "thanks to Miss Khema's efforts. And she might be prevailed upon to aid us in transporting him."

"We must move him there at once," Arabella said to the doctor, then turned to the captain. "Give Khema my thanks for her invitation, but tell her that my brother's health must take precedence for now, and ask for her help in moving him. After we are settled at Woodthrush Woods, I will consult with her as she requests."

"I will do so," he said, and with a brisk bow he departed.

After leaving the house, they waited on the road outside while Khema arranged for a *huresh* to carry Michael back to Woodthrush Woods. While the doctor inspected her brother's dressings, Arabella looked back at Corey House.

The house, never beautiful, was now a collapsing ruin, so battered that in places it could scarcely be distinguished from the rocks on which it had been built. Even as she watched, a section of the roof fell in, sending a cloud of dust into the air. The landscape around it, too, had been demolished, pleasant paths and gazebos completely vanished beneath piles of rubble and thousands of Martian footprints. The Martians themselves were mostly departed, leaving only a few burnt patches on the sand, and the catapults with their pyramids of stones.

This place, Arabella knew, would be honored as a battlefield some day. For now it was nothing but a waste—a desolate waste of destruction and death.

A thin stream of refugees was emerging from the gate, looking about themselves and back at the ruined house in appalled silence. Arabella glanced from them to her brother, equally battered by the events of the past few weeks, then back at the refugees.

"Go and tell those people," she said to one of the servants, "that if they cannot return to their homes they are welcome at Woodthrush Woods."

The servant looked from her to her brother, who nodded. "As you wish, Miss Ashby," the servant said with a bow, and moved off.

26

A STRANGE PROPOSAL

Some days later, Arabella was in the kitchen, supervising an inventory and considering how to feed her guests. Most of Woodthrush Woods's servants, both human and Martian, had already returned—thanks to Khema, the fighting there had been much less than at Fort Augusta, and most of them had remained nearby—and they had been joined by many others from Corey House and elsewhere. This was fortunate, as most of the other Corey House refugees were of the gentry and unable to provide for their own needs.

She turned from a count of the bags of *noreth*-flour to find one of the servants waiting expectantly. "Your brother requests your presence, Miss Ashby. He says that the matter is rather urgent."

After instructing Collins, the former Corey House majordomo, to continue the inventory, she hurried to her brother's bedchamber, where she found him lying across a heap of pillows, with Mr. Trombley in attendance. A sheaf of papers lay atop the bedclothes. "What is the matter?" she said.

Mr. Trombley swallowed and looked down. "I . . . I am afraid it concerns your brother's last will and testament."

"I see." She, too, felt a sudden need to inspect the dusty floor.

Michael gestured to the papers. "Explain the situation to my sister," he said to Mr. Trombley with weary impatience.

"Sir, I really must protest this—"

Michael stopped him with a raised hand. "Explain it."

Mr. Trombley frowned, but nodded to him, then turned to Arabella. "As you know," he said, "the Ashby family estate is entailed to heirs of the body male."

"Yes, yes," Arabella said, waving an impatient hand.

"This is important. An entail, at least an entail of this type, is, in effect, a contract between generations, ensuring that the family property is neither lost nor subdivided into insignificance. It binds the estate—the *entire* estate—to the current holder and to his next two heirs." He took a breath, let it out again. "As is typical with estates of this type, your brother's will was drawn up for him shortly after he was born." He swallowed. "As such, it was prepared by my predecessor, Mr. Beale. Mr. Beale was . . . well, let us say that he gave little consideration to the fair sex at the best of times, and in his dotage he appears to have omitted any consideration whatsoever." He picked up the papers and handed them to Arabella with an expression both disgusted and contrite. "As your family solicitor, I must apologize for not having reviewed this document before now. Your father was in, in such . . . *robust* good health, until his sudden passing of course, and, well, the months since then, they have been so hectic . . ."

As Mr. Trombley continued to stammer his apologies, Arabella took the papers and ran her eyes over the dense pages of text. They might as well have been Venusian for all the sense she could extract from them. "What does this all *mean*?"

Mr. Trombley frowned and blew out a breath through his nose. "The entail binds the estate to heirs of the body male for three generations. When this will was drawn up, that was your brother, your uncle, and your cousin. Your uncle and cousin are specified by name, but in the event of their . . . their death or incapacity, the estate is to be inherited by the next heir of the body male. Whoever that may be."

Arabella thought for a moment. Apart from Simon, she had no other male relatives on her father's side, not even distant cousins. "And who would that be?"

"That . . . is the problem." He sighed. "To the best of my knowledge there *is* no surviving male heir . . . and the will contains no provision whatsoever for this circumstance. As I said, my . . . predecessor, Mr. Beale, gave little consideration to the fair sex." He shook his head. "If your brother should . . . pass, with the will in this state . . . the estate will be thrown into probate."

"In which case . . . ?"

He shrugged and spread his hands. "In a case such as this, any one with any possible claim, however spurious, may petition the court. It could take years to settle, the estate could be . . . could be divided *any* which way. And the expense would be tremendous. In the worst case, the entire estate could fall to the Crown."

Through all this Michael had been looking at Arabella with stoic resignation. "We cannot allow this to occur."

"But Michael, surely this is no concern of ours? I am sure you will be up and about in no time."

He waved a hand dismissively. "You need not prevaricate with me, sister. I am fully aware of how precarious my health is. And if this . . . *contretemps* has taught me any thing, it is that life is fragile and easily snuffed out." His expression was now as serious as any she could ever recall having seen on him. "The estate *must* be preserved at all costs. And so the entail must be broken."

"But how? To break an entail, I have heard, requires an act of Parliament! And we could not possibly—"

Michael held up one finger. "An entail is a contract, as Mr. Trombley has explained to me in wearisome detail, and contracts *can* be terminated." He struggled to sit up, but soon gave up the effort, collapsing back upon the pillows and addressing the ceiling. "Any change in an entail requires the consent of all those involved—in this case, the current holder and the next two heirs in line. Now, under most circumstances this means that change is virtually impossible. Why would any one in his right mind consent to any change which might cost them so large an estate? But at the moment, there are no such heirs. This is our problem, and our opportunity. For the first time in heaven knows how many generations, I may change my will however I wish."

"Sir," Mr. Trombley fumed, "I cannot allow you to—"

"My mind is made up," he said, "and as I have achieved my majority, albeit by only three weeks, and am of sound mind if not body, you cannot prevent it." He raised himself on one elbow to face Arabella. "My dear sister, I intend to will the entire estate to you."

"To *me*?" Arabella laid a hand on her chest and felt her own pulse throbbing hard. "But . . . even if there are no other male heirs, surely Mother is the next of kin?"

"You and I both know that she has no head for business. The maintenance of the Ashby estate, I have learned to my sorrow, is an immense and troublesome undertaking, and you are the only one I would trust with it. Besides, Mother is in England, and much happier there. We require an heir who can take the reins at once upon my . . . demise, not one who would have to be dragged here against her will, a process that would take months even if she consented to it."

"Which she would not," Arabella concurred. "For Fanny and Chloë's sake, of course, not her own."

"Of course." Michael gave a slight, wry grin that, for a moment, made his face seem as animated and youthful as she remembered it.

But the grin fell away as Mr. Trombley cleared his throat. "Sir, your sister is not legally competent to manage the estate, being both underage and female. She must have an older male relative to handle all business affairs." He cleared his throat again, and straightened. "As there is no such relative, I would, as your family solicitor, be prepared to stand as her legal guardian."

A meaningful glance passed between the siblings. "Thank you for your offer," said Michael to Mr. Trombley. "Now if you would please step outside, so that my sister and I may discuss this matter?"

As soon as the door closed Arabella allowed the disgust she had been holding back to express itself in a rolling of the eyes heavenward. "Dear Lord," she whispered, "not *him*."

Michael shook his head sadly and replied in the same low register. "Though he is a dear man, and has served the family for many years, the events of the last few weeks have shown that in a crisis he simply cannot keep his head. And this nonsense of the unexamined will is the last straw. I would not dream of saddling you with him." His expression shifted, his steady gaze now reflecting determination, sorrow, and apology. "I am sorry, dear sister, but for the sake of the whole family, and future generations, you must be married at once, in case of my early demise."

"Oh, Michael, do not say such a thing! I am sure you have many years ahead of you."

"As Providence wills." He paused, shook his head again. "Now, as to your betrothal. I have in mind my trusted colleague Mr. Williams. He is an older man, and will surely not . . . trouble you, if you do not wish it. And, in not too many years, he will in turn pass away, leaving you the freedom to find a husband of your own choosing."

The breath caught in Arabella's throat. Though she knew her brother was correct in his assessment of the situation, and she trusted his judgement completely, the thought of being . . . *paired off*, like a matched brace of *huresh*, for the sake of the estate, was repellent to her. "I . . . I see. Have you . . . approached this Mr. Williams?"

"No, not yet. I wished to obtain your consent first."

"I see," she repeated. "Thank you for that consideration, at least."

She sat and contemplated her options, looking down into her cupped hands.

They were in terrible shape. The events of the last two months had left them rough, callused, even scarred in places, and no amount of scrubbing could completely remove the dirt ground into the lines of her palms. A tiny splinter had lodged itself beneath the skin of her left thumb, and as her mind churned in anxious rumination she brought it unthinkingly to her teeth in order to prize it out.

The errant scrap of wood came free, and she spat it into her palm. For a moment she inspected it—any thing to take her mind off of the future that Fate seemed to have in store for her. It was a sliver of *khoresh*-wood, she saw, honey-gold with a bit of black paint on one side. Most likely a piece of *Diana*'s hull. Perhaps she had gotten it while she was working her way along the keel during the mutiny. Or perhaps it had been earlier, during the battle with the French—there had been splinters flying everywhere.

And as she cast her mind back upon those tumultuous weeks, she realized that there had been one factor—one constant, calming presence—that had kept her alive and sane throughout.

She stood and approached Michael's bedside. "Although I am sure your Mr. Williams is perfectly congenial," she said, "I have another in mind."

"Who, if I may ask?"

She bit her lip, suddenly nervous. "I would rather not say," she said, "until I have spoken to him."

"Of course. You know I trust your judgement implicitly, sister, and any man you find acceptable will receive my blessing without reservation." He hesitated. "But . . . I am afraid I must insist that you do so without delay." His eyes held a deep sadness. "I do not know . . . how much more time I may have."

"Oh, Michael . . . ." Her eyes brimmed with tears and she had to turn away from him.

After a moment she felt a brush at her hip, and looked down. It was Michael's hand, silently offering a handkerchief.

She smiled sadly, shook her head, and accepted it.

She found the captain at the ship, as she had expected. He was working day and night with the ship's carpenter and the master of the drying-sheds, striving to find some way to repurpose the coal burners there to the generation of hot air for lift. Though all agreed it should be possible, the practicalities of the task had proved troublesome.

As soon as he noticed her presence, the captain turned from his work. "Miss Ashby," he said, bowing.

"Captain," she replied with a curtsey. "I . . . I was wondering . . ." Her heart, she realized, was hammering in her breast. How could she be so nervous? She swallowed, straightened, took a breath. "I was wondering if I might have a word with you. A word in private."

"Of course." He made his excuses and led her up the gang-plank.

How familiar these lower decks were, and yet how strange! Only two weeks ago *Diana* had been her home, her place of work, her whole world. Now Arabella had departed from the ship and returned to her family home, leaving her to realize just how truly extraordinary her months aboard had been. Yet her home, too, and seemingly the whole planet Mars, had been entirely transformed, leaving her with no place she could truly call her own. In a sense, *Diana* was now the only home she had.

As she ascended a ladder, she ran her hand along the rail beside it. How many times had she waxed this handrail? How many others had waxed it before her, and since?

She brought the hand to her nose and breathed in. *Khoresh*-wood and wax; brass and gunpowder. Charcoal. The sweat of honest airmen.

She continued up the ladder to the great cabin.

The captain closed the cabin door behind himself, clasping his hands behind his back and straightening as he had done so many times before. "I must thank you again for your continued hospitality, Miss Ashby," he said. "The men send their best regards as well."

"You are welcome, sir, for as long as you wish to stay."

Her heart still pounded as though she had run a mile—a hard mile across the desert at night. She had, she told herself, no right to be so anxious.

It was a simple enough request, though highly unconventional. The worst he could do would be to say no.

She had faced kidnap, battle, mutiny, and insurrection. She could face this.

"Sir, I . . ." She swallowed, took a breath, began again. "You know that I hold you in the very highest regard."

"As do I you, Miss Ashby."

For some perverse reason that encouraging statement made it even harder to continue. "I have never met," she managed after a pause, "a man so intelligent, so brave, so steadfast. I have seen you guide this ship through every manner of crisis without ever once losing your aplomb, never mind your temper. And, despite my . . . necessary deception, with regard to my sex, you have never failed to treat me with any thing less than honor and respect."

He bowed. "It was, I assure you, far less than you deserved. Your own intelligence and, especially, creativity are far in excess of my own. You have found solutions to problems of navigation and, dare I say, administration that I can imagine no other man . . . no *man*, I should say, could have conceived. Your handling of the mutinous Binion resolved the mutiny without the loss of a single additional life. And as to bravery, your simple presence in the crew from day to day speaks to a degree of bravery that most men never find within themselves even in battle."

She would not cry. She would *not* cry. "Captain Singh," she began, then paused.

He looked at her, his deep brown eyes so calm and intense.

"I . . . I know this is . . . quite an extraordinary request to make. But my, my . . . situation, is quite extraordinary." She stopped again, took a breath, then spat out, all in a rush, "Would you be so kind as to do me the honor of becoming my husband?"

He raised one eyebrow. Then the other.

"I—" He paused and looked away.

Somewhere among her many strong emotions, Arabella found a tiny particle of pride that she had managed to crack the captain's inviolable composure.

He stared out the window for a long time, contemplating the house, the rolling sands, the stands of *khoresh*-trees. Every thing that could be seen from this window, all the way to the rocky horizon, was part of Woodthrush Woods.

"As you know," he said at last, "it was because of a . . . refusal of betrothal that I found myself in the Honorable Mars Company in the first place." He had not turned to face her.

Arabella's breath caught in her throat. "I do recall that."

"The life of an airship captain's wife is not an easy one," he said. "She does not see her husband for months, or years, at a time. And if you were *my* wife . . ." Now he did face her. "I . . . I have faced . . . certain difficulties, within the Company as well as without, because of my . . . race." He gestured to his own face, the warm dark eyes, the deep brown skin. "I have . . . weathered these difficulties, through diligence, patience, and perseverance, but they do continue. And if you were my wife, they would redound upon you a hundredfold." He stepped closer. "I . . . I am sorry, Miss Ashby. I have chosen this life for myself, and I have no regrets. But I cannot ask any other person, especially one I hold in such high esteem, to take on such a heavy burden." He hung his head. "Therefore I must, with very great regret—"

He was interrupted by a loud clatter from the corner, which drew his eyes as well as Arabella's.

It was Aadim. His head was moving, very slightly, from side to side.

That small movement might, conceivably, have been a stray motion from a maladjusted cam or sprocket—though Aadim was never in any thing other than the very best of adjustment. But then, with a smooth whir of gears, Aadim's head turned decisively to the left, his green glass eyes locking on the captain's brown ones. At the same time his hand rose from its position on the map, pointing directly at Arabella.

The head nodded. Once, twice, three times the chin rose and fell. Firmly. Deliberately. Unmistakably.

Then head and hand returned to their previous positions, and with one final click the automaton fell silent.

Arabella and the captain turned to each other. Her face, she was sure, reflected the baffled wonder she saw upon his, though certainly in much greater degree.

"Well—," she began, and at the same time he said, "I suppose—"

They both stopped. The captain's expression was so serious that Arabella was forced to suppress a fit of hysterical giggles.

"For many years," the captain began again, "I have depended upon Aadim in matters of navigation and direction."

"His . . . his judgement in these areas is generally quite . . . reliable," Arabella managed to reply.

Then, in one smooth motion, the captain crossed the small distance between them and descended to one knee. For the first time she could recall, his intelligent brown eyes looked up to hers. "Miss Ashby," he said, his voice entirely level, "will you be my wife?"

Arabella swallowed past a lump in her throat. "Yes," she managed. Then, more firmly, "Yes, I will."

They blinked at each other for a time, both clearly uncertain as to how to proceed. Arabella smiled nervously. "This must be the most unusual proposal in the history of romance."

"It might well be. Though I fear we will never be able to share the story with any one."

"Perhaps our children," she said, and suddenly her eyes filled with tears.

The captain rose and embraced her, his strong warm arms enfolding her in a protective circle which, for the moment, neither Martians nor lawyers nor even death could enter.

ACKNOWLEDGMENTS

A book is a small thing—you can hold it in your hand—but it takes many, many people to bring it to fruition.

I'd like to thank the folks at Tor, my publisher: Moshe Feder, who acquired it; Christopher Morgan, who edited it; Patrick Nielsen Hayden, who provided invaluable support; and Patty Garcia and Irene Gallo, who were incredibly helpful and enthusiastic. I also must thank my agent, Paul Lucas, and the rest of the team at Janklow & Nesbit, who negotiated the deal and held my hand through the whole first-novel thing, and my excellent copyeditor (or should that be copy-editor?) Deanna Hoak.

Many people provided advice and support along the way. Sara Mueller was the first, helping me to find the core of the book in a morass of keen ideas; the librarians at Multnomah County Library were always helpful; Ian Osgood suggested the atmospheric phenomenon that I eventually named the Horn; Mary Rosenblum gave me tips on aerial navigation and publicity for authors; Dick Pilz told me about drogues; Shashi Jain checked my work on Captain Singh; and Doug Faunt provided information from his personal experience on period sailing vessels and bought (in a charity auction) the right to have his name in the book. Sorry it took so long.

I'd also like to thank everyone who critiqued the book as it went through its many revisions. Felicity Shoulders, Damian Kilby, and Dave Goldman provided early feedback; Walter Jon Williams, Michaela Roessner, Rick Wilber, Kim Zimring, Jay Lake, Diana Rowland, Daniel Abraham, James Patrick Kelly, Oz Drummond, and Carrie Vaughn at Rio Hondo provided feedback on the first nine chapters; Sherwood Smith, Tina Connolly, Eloise Drummond, MeiLin Miranda, and Amanda Clark provided comments on the first complete draft; and Grá Linnea, Jennifer Linnea, Mark Teppo, Rob Zeigler, Bradley Beaulieu, Kris Dikeman, Brenda Cooper, Adam Rakunas, Beth Wodzinski, and Chris Cevasco at Coastal Heaven provided feedback and encouragement, and helped me with my cover letter and elevator pitch.

Thanks to Kim Stanley Robinson, Patricia Rice, Madeleine Robins, Mary Jo Putney, Jim C. Hines, Marie Brennan, Tina Connolly, Kurt Busiek, Sherwood Smith, Michael J. Martinez, Pat Murphy, and Ellen Klages for early blurbs and comments.

Extra special thanks to Mary Robinette Kowal, my invaluable guide to all things Regency and navigating the dangerous shoals of publication; Patrick Swenson, who ran the Rainforest Writers Village writing retreats and (along with Jack Skillingstead) pointed me to the man who would become my agent; Shannon Page, who helped me keep writing through the most difficult days; Marc Wells, who gave up his Worldcon so I could attend; and Janna Silverstein, my greatest adviser and cheerleader.

And, first and last, my wife, Kate Yule, for everything.